T0208227

Dawn Peyote

Anthony Haas

authorHOUSE®

AuthorHouse™
1663 Liberty Drive
Bloomington, IN 47403
www.authorhouse.com
Phone: 1-800-839-8640

First published by AuthorHouse 2/08/2011

ISBN: 978-1-4567-1978-4 (e)
ISBN: 978-1-4567-1977-7 (sc)

Printed in the United States of America

Dawn Peyote it's around this time I change my name from Don to Dawn (but don't tell anybody). Haven't been able to work lately and I'm sick and dad's out of town so I'm at their duplex by the river by the park by the baseball diamond where I read Rimbaud in my teenage years. Mom has watermelon sliced in the kitchen and its bout the only thing my stomach can hold, she also rented a video Good Will Hunting and we're down in the basement watching it. It's a pretty good flick and around ten my mom goes to bed as I step out onto the deck in back to smoke a cigarette then I go back downstairs to watch the movie again, well I end up staying up all night and I watch that damn movie three times in a row and I run out of cigarettes and have no money and when morning rolls around my mom wants me to go to my day treatment but I can't, "I don't feel well, I'm gonna stay here. Will you drive me to the bank so I can get some bread to buy smokes?"

"Okay."

We drive downtown its about eight in the morning the townish city is on the brim of bustle and take out twenty from my savings and see Mickey Rourke sitting in the peace plaza. Mom takes me back home and I sit in the garage feeling really sick, fluish, foolish, looking at my Egyptian painting and my body wracked I cough violently when puffing on the damn cigarettes.

Its nice just mom and I at the house where I grew up, peaceful, by the woods, I eat some corn on the cob.

After a few days I'm back to my old self going to my part time job as a janitor at the drop in center living in my basement apartment close to downtown on a one way street. After work I ride my bike to the grocery store buy a big four dollar watermelon and ride home on the bike trail trying not to crash to get back to the crib so I can mess around with my art pictures. My psychologist left town and I haven't seen a shrink for a while, and at work I do as little as possible and in as little time, I can't seem to concentrate and I take smoke breaks every thirty minutes.

Then comes the family reunion in Missouri we pile in the car my mom and dad and brother and I and drive the seven hundred miles listening to Husker Du. Well we get to the reunion my dad's sister married a rich cat and we find ourselves in a mansion on the hills with a few familiar cousins and uncles and aunts but there's probably thirty or forty people there who I don't recognize. The only food they serve is meat so I grab a Seven Up and sit on the back porch and my brother Stick Figure is drinking a beer, I gave that shit up nearly a year ago and I tell him, "Next thing you know they'll have you drinking gasoline," and my beautiful cousin who I've been in love with since the seventies says something cryptic and I'm suddenly afraid to drink anymore of my pop.

Well we're back in the hotel room and Stick and I are rapping, "What do you think of Duchamp?"

"Well, Duchamp was an alchemist and the reason he put a mustache on the Mona Lisa was that one of the goals of alchemy is the union of male and female and androgyny is totally a way to see into the mystery. What do you think?"

Stick's lying on the bed, "I don't think that's what he was trying to do."

"I've been reading Cassady, and you know Duchamp's

idea of precision painting? Well Cassady was a precision writer."

"I know William Burroughs' assistant we could go over to his house in Lawrence? What do ya say?"

I say sure and the assistant's name is Steve something or other and he's gonna pick us up in front of the hotel around seven or so. Waiting for the ride Stick says, "I can't imagine being blind."

I should know. Steve rolls up and its off to Lawrence and the legendary Burroughs manor. Its about a half hour drive from Kansas City to our destination and we get to the house and a small gang of punks arrive too and they light up a bowl and I go into the other room and look at the music collection. There's paintings by William S. on the walls and even a Rauschenberg I dig.

We go to a backyard party and Stick's drinking keg beer and there's beautiful torches glowing in the night as I lean against the fence chain smoking Marlboros. We don't know anybody there except Steve so me and Stick talk and people watch, "They say peyote is only a hundred years old but they don't take into account the longevity of the desert, the desert is the same doesn't change and for centuries peyote has been growing there, my guess is peyote is at least five hundred thousand years old," I tell Stick eyeing enviously his beer I'm on the wagon.

After the party its back to Burroughs' joint, its about one in the morning, Steve hits the sack (he's writing a biography on William that should be out any day now), me and Stick are in the kitchen with some books on the table, I proudly open up a Kerouac book and tell him all the books I've read, twelve or so, Stick meanwhile has pulled out his stash and is doing one hitters, "Music is abstract, all music, because its invisible."

Stick can't seem to sit still he's pacing around the kitchen and he's reminding me of Cat Man's restless utopian high and probe. We go to bed around five in the morning Stick on the couch me on the floor and we listen to music as we drift off into la la land.

Morning rolls around and Steve's in the kitchen cooking breakfast, "I don't eat breakfast," I tell him but Stick wolfs down some eggs and whatnot, I drink coffee and chain smoke. Its been two days since I've had a good meal and I'm on Lithium for my mental health, I've lost about thirty pounds since I went vegan last winter spring.

In the car driving back to Minnesota I buy a bag of pretzels and orange juice and we make it back summer back to the janitor job and listening to Charlie Parker in my basement crib but a couple weeks later we are driving to Kentucky to visit my mom's side of the family we've rented a house boat its August and I've been having trouble eating.

Its my uncles Rick, Jerry, Polly, my aunts, Shannon, Lisa, and Polly's girlfriend Alicia who is videotaping the vacation its hot ninety five in the shade, my cousins Joe and Claire and Charlotte and her friend from Indiana Bev... so we're on that damn boat and Charlotte is stretching up trying to touch the ceiling of the boat and looks at me and her two eyes go in different directions one looking up the other sideways its weird and beautiful and it reminds me of Kerouin.

I recently had a conversation with Stick telling him how the color turquoise is a messenger color, some kind of message foretelling the future and synchronicity comes and Charlotte is wearing a turquoise bikini and I'm again speechless she's only nineteen or twenty and she is gorgeous and the ship is floating my dad driving looking for a spot to drop anchor, I feel queasy, drink some water, we anchor and go swimming.

Well the day unravels the uncles drinking beer under

the canopy the teenage Claire and Joe wandering around and I'm smoking wanting a beer. Dinner comes and the food tastes awful. At night me and Stick share a bed in a small room of the boat, Joe comes in, "What are you reading?" He asks me.

"This is a very intellectual book on the history of art, Pictorial Nominalism," I feel foolish saying the word intellectual. Then its sleep. Sleep. Dream. And archetypes of the night on the vast river the river of time and undulating with the murk of image and space and time, I wake up early and take a massive shit but it won't flush down and I feel stupid idiotic and the smell reaches everywhere and I am miserably responsible.

But its another day to stare at Charlotte. We drive the boat around the sun hot glaring bright. We see animals on the shore, we take pictures and Alicia is walking around with her video camera. More swimming. The water is warm. Joe says to me in the river, "I'm going to be a submarine."

"I don't wanna see your periscope," I say expecting to get a laugh but my Dad remains his ambiguous self.

At night on the boat us younger ones play cards while the adults talk their adult talk, serious, humorless, solemn, and boring. "I need to get some," says Charlotte meaning points, I laugh.

After three days the rental of the boat is finished and we're on land again but its like a bad acid trip for me the ground wavering swaying, nauseous, and I'm bummed to see Charlotte and her hippy Dad Polly who says, "He's replaced art with sympathy," I'm sad to see them go. Heartbroken really.

Brother Mom Dad and I spend another night in a cabin onshore and when I wake up in the morning I'm crying, dizzy, demented, we are going to drive all the way back to Minnesota. That's what we do and I feel like shit.

Its back to the janitor job but I can't make it I take some time off again. I'm afraid to eat. So I'm sitting in my crib trying to recover and decide to get a video and I walk out the backdoor into the alley where the cats and squirrels ramble and I walk up to the fence to say hi to the two dogs, they are barking and it sounds like they are barking out the word, "Work! Work!" Shit even the dogs know I'm a dog, a bum, a wash up, but I zigzag down to the store and rent Anywhere But Here and walk and stumble back to my joint and put the movie in the VCR that I got from my dead Grandpa. The movie touches me, love, longing, life and hope and beauty.

I stay up all night crying for the blindness of myself and First Glimmer Leatherface Harry Eastershirt at four a.m. the great Good Times J.J. Walker comes on and I watch and dig it, I'm weary beat ragged in the diamond dawn and the phone rings it's the bookstore and my Duchamp book is in, the smell of cunt on my fingers, "Where did that come from?" I ask myself then walk downtown to buy the book.

I show up at the job a couple days later and all I hear is, "You've lost a lot of weight," I know I know but that first day at the job I'm dizzy as hell and with my eyes rolling around I tell Calling that I'm not feeling well, "Its probably your lithium," so I go to the clinic nodding and they take some blood and it turns out its way out of whack, I'm relieved to find this out so I'm not some hypochondriacal freak after all. But the shrink wants me to keep taking it, I'm pissed, I want off the shit, so I stop taking it on my own, I tell people this and they don't agree so I see a different shrink and he puts me on something else, that something else makes me feel even worse.

I'm crying on the deck to my Dad, "All I want is a fair chance."

My Mom says, "Well the Indians would just walk off into the woods and you'd never see them again."

Fuck it I'm sick of these meds I go to the drop in center and crying and feeling the whole world crashing I'm fed up I've been sick for three months, "I'm not gonna take meds anymore, I want to see if I can do it without them."

"Just don't drink."

"Okay."

They want to talk some more so I have to wait a while and while I'm waiting they shoot poison air into the building and I see Nin and she gives me the telepathic signal to split before they can capture me, I'm out on the front porch and a German butt fucks me in a unconscious trance, I get up to walk home, sore weak defeated, I'm afraid to go to my folk's house they're in on it too.

So I'm off all meds. Withdrawal. Charlie Parker's death dance. I can't sleep. I can't eat. Night comes. Ruby kaleidoscope. Visions. Night. Deep night. I smoke three packs of cigs. I'm all alone out here. There's a Penthouse rag I look at the gashes, the tits, I unplug the television and turn it around, its talking to me and the messages are too much. Incest. Town of two in the morning and I'm running with the bacteria gang through waterless St. Paul, the running the endless running of no breath bandits demonically scrounging for the shit fix, I was sent there in my early twenties to find the language, to sing bash and write of the tragic war, anagram night and I look at the pornography and long to be a woman, the pills have made my dick swell up. Red white and blue. Dead rite and goo. Tread fight and shoo. Lead light and spew. Med plight and flew. Beyond peyote. The Western Lands where Set and the landing of dried up shit sucking aliens and the streets are Egyptian and the slaves ruling the Reality Theater. "And you won't know a thing till you get inside." All the circles are gone, circuits, sand intricate the living dead, dehydration, butt fuckers and a nickel means your rich. The white market. My father the ruler the outlaw the shapeshifter vibrating in the electrical technology takeover storms, we're in Europe driving evading the police (the police?) are onto him but he always escapes, Mary, Mary, there are no virgins. And morning will find us all insane

And morning, beat, deeply gone beat in the war game, I'm out of smokes, walk to the corner store, the town is waging raging and I'm right in the heart of some energy hell I cry on the street buy my smokes, the cats, the dogs, the rabbits, upright? Oh mercy. In the alley I draw in the gravel with a stick and sign it Jean. I'm in my crib and turn on The Doors and ghost dance. I eat cold corn with lots of salt. A warrior from the drop in center has come to check up on me, we talk a while, then he goes off to score. Then the landlord stops by and I confess to him my past in one raving half hour and I'm crying, he leaves and I go back into the crib. The phone rings and I answer it, the phone is some torture devise and my head feels like its splitting in two, I go out and sit on the back stoop, helicopters are whirling through the sky, the reservation is a fucking war zone. I go back inside, I take a long piss then kneel before the toilet and on my knees I scoop it out and drink it.

About an hour later I'm finally tired, feeling like maybe I can sleep for the first time in three days I lay down on the brown couch and ah its coming, sleep. There's a heavy knock on the door, oh shit, I open it up and its my case manager and a woman from the drop in center, they want me to go to the hospital. We argue about it for twenty minutes, you see the hospital is the zone of sex crimes and the head addicts are there, the case manager pulls out a cell phone to call the cops, I grab my smokes and some cigars and just in my shorts I run out of the crib. I run to the river and hide in the foliage, a police car pulls up across the other side of the river and starts looking in my direction, I take off my shorts to blend in but the cop sees me and I take off running, I see a doghouse shaped like an igloo and naked I go inside breathing heavily and hide, I'm squatting there with one leg bent and the other stretched straight, and by magic or something my dick and balls curl up and go up inside me so it looks like I've got a cunt. I stay in there for fifteen minutes then the cops finally find me, "Can you come out of there?" One fuzz asks me.

I say no I'm afraid to, they have a big cop dog with them, eventually they get sick of talking and lift the doghouse up off the ground and there I am in broad daylight butt naked, they wrap a blanket around me, cuff me, then I get into the backseat of their car.

We go to the hospital only a few blocks away.

Space age, we go in on the side, I get out of the car and see the hospital workers dressed in their hospital garb, I see one guy is balding so this eases me, they ask me my name, "Dawn, Dawn Peyote."

They strap me down to a bed in a gown, the case manager and the woman from the drop in center come into the room. At this point I'm extremely frightened and paranoid. My case manager holds my hand. My parents arrive and I say, "Those aren't my parents." They smile. The doctor talks to me, he's evil, keeps looking at me like I've done something terribly wrong and I'm gonna pay. Making eye contact with him is like looking into the cracked mirrors of the devil himself. I start drumming in hopes the Indian troops will catch on and we'll dance our way to victory over the mean fag needle priest nazis.

They put me in a ambulance there's no room here so they're transporting me to a hospital in Owatonna where there's vacancies. At the hospital I wander the halls and I hear a great gang of Indians singing in my head. To push the crystal germ ridden waterless junky square oppressor demon nazi breathless shit eating pale faces into South Dakota and they're using me as bait that's why my Dad spilled piss on me to make the enemies come to the vast Indian Edens of the Dakotas where the ghost dancing and the fire pits and the smoking swilling Liquid Gang of original America will defeat the addicts. It's a war now. How old? Five hundred years since the lie of Columbus, the lie of technology and the geometric sand kings from the other side of the universe who've conquered many but the Apaches "go where the fight is." I'm out of my head, one cigarette an hour at the hospital. I sleep in a room with a camera and the light stays on all night.

I awake the next day and there's Henry Miller in a wheelchair playing some kinda board game war game he's moving the troops telepathically. "All language is either based on sex or drugs," I tell the doctor. I draw and paint dozens of pictures write poems:

He
Egyptian
pelvis same shapes
        geometry as
        Egyptian art (?)
Defection
I wanna be so
soft even
my hardest
punch feels
like a whisper
of a kiss

Bottle rack
Bought ill (how much?)
Ra C(yes)...H...

?   (see)…
Ra   (sea)
         (average)

Ra-Sun God
         Son dog
         Nose odd

t Bo
t bow
Ba (t)ill Mac
t   Ba nill sack
t
t

ask
axe
ass

I'm a dog that likes cats a cat that likes water a fish that likes to walk a bird dreaming of snake sky feather know why white no

Pi aint pie

Sneeze not? Why? Not why, sneeze?

Cuttlebone?
Cuddle bone?   Tickle
               I mask
               Eye mass
               Kleye mass
               Climb

Max

Addiction?
Catharticism?
Prop o' shit I on?(?
Weight
Promised sweetness faked
Missing warmth
Poetry bird song (wall of
                              Silence
Doze many
Cubism
Arrow

Cum-orfusus plasma
                    Water
(A)rrrrreszzz
unfuse
defuse
subfuse
nunfuse
comfuse
cuntfuse
confuse

narrative art?
Equals: Theirs'
Good moose am
There's bad noose
Pattern
Pa turn
Pat yearn

Bleaked totems

filled within
definite geometry
white lies
why lies

Leo nod owe fart

Van?
Rud?
Run
Rudder
Utter lean
Imaginary
Science
Equals?
If we even
get outta
a hair
here
in

If Duchamp is Beuys?
If not?

Black gold
Glass of sand
Too saints

Eyes of doubt
Nose of dick
Tongue of chameleon
All the colors
All the visions
Plate of wind

Anthony Haas

Heart of water
Lips of smoke
Hands of snake
Feet of twigs
Soul of river…

Dwell
in the
of
of
of.
And the
winds
why
wise
of
butterfly
don'ts
Geometry
Of cunt
as the
earth
sighs
bleeds
spins
mo Z.'s
in seemingly
endless
true of
of truth on
darkness
like cats'
eyes in a
closet

And a
little
boy
hi
sugar
how Zen
the
wind
wind
beyond
Zen yens
And crosses
of solid
nothing
nodding
Oz he's
make sill
if the
rain
is always
fall
?
pew
Du
Heart
in the
middle

Ireland green as Jamaica
Marley=Thompson
Ireland green
Russia
Germany
Doze

Picasso
France
Spain
Italy
Cats
Separation
by water
us(S?) mote
null mouth
grind
dirge

into apellashe whirl farm eat earth ants
to get out of the chocolate grinder
same the cross and pyramids
land indigenous to the lamb
Rome Africa
Italy
Dis
Ease ease
Thanks
        Jean

Atmosphere
Still-move
Fall still
Still moon
Gravity
Relax
Dream

Fast
Yeah gal
Hey

Low
Bum bump hump day daya
Doga ho ho no sea ya see sea E.E.
Now now no oh no oh slow (ooo…
                              (um…
if they you go to twelve for foe are da no
fast haze oh oh
            roll
Gyros Greek yours

Everything's false

Dis degree
Disabelegree: ence
Personal precisionist but varied individual
Conceptual precision
Precision con actual

Ultra logic
Ultra chemistry
Ultra realism
Ultra symbolism

Du:
Straight
Perspective
Geometrical
Design
Definite
Grinding
Machine

Cubism-carnivalesque
Cubism as

Anthony Haas

the after
math of
in destructionist
Painters battered
about by technology
               away to
               illustrate
               the war that
               takes place in
               the mind of
               victims of
                    babes
                    in boyland

the inner
in
implosions
of a mechanical
phase
What may or may
nod hoping to
a potential
away to escape
technology

Gases   solids
Water   shifting

Invisible
Space
Pointillism
Oriental
Space
Smoke

Denseness
Brick
on brick
structures

Both: Naturalism of
                    the mind survival

We've to a whirl of riddles and metaphor
A train of lies with occasional Dharma Bums
Soothsayers

Hey a
Ya
Go
Go
You

A bought ill rack

Eye don't keen chin
Nuclear fallout Davis?
Wheel we'll
Stool stool

Di
men   A.D. Li, B why?
si   above Earth
ons   why?
Virgin bride   tea pea virgin
Above above   earth on above
Symbol shelter symbol shelter

Moo heart to middle peyote new home

Anthony Haas

Knee not love be a stranger's
Learn to fall in love again

Souix Cigari
"Close your eyes give me your Mayan hand can you here
my heart beating"

subjectivism Jackson
expressionism
logic, pointillism
medical technological
conditions
and how defect
defect the spirit
                    mind
                    emotions
                    senses

colored stones
for free
another cradle
or water
Naked Street
no pops.
Boston
With "H" then no is E?

Stin-small
Son-sun
Vav-vac gate open
You me
On Act Street
        Lake St.
        Fake St.

Make St.
Take St.
Snake St.
Shake St.
Blake St.
Bake St.

"She has a hot ass."
Poke and haunt us
What does she smell like?
She
He
She
He
Cloaked eternally
Ill Lee
Big foreheads
Junk?
Chief Dawn
Tea
Peyote
C
Karma burns
Chameleons
The ho Oz Q?
Le H ooze queer
Good kisser
Junky?
L.H.O.O.Q.

Under would
Caddilacs cattle axe
How to become a hooker
Fortune tellers write

Lead leed cread creed
Green black plant clover
Ma Mal Male Ma May Mayo Maya
Lies versus church
Versus pyramid
Versus star
Tech-maskusin
Maya-woman
Church? Casino?
Gesturing in the modern whirl
Pop colors green yellow
Ce hue are H?
Co Ka sin circle
Ce a sigh in O?

Love that's life
Life that's love
Joyce that life loves
Err

Dean and Neil, Cassady and Moriarty
Borders death life of Mexican cactus

India of clay
Its all money size and kick
Goo noose new front from the after check glow
Unnecessary
Where is Jura?
Was impotent
Organic orgasm
Saturn
Srgt. Pepper
Quetzalcoatl
Ma ager

Watch for arms arm arms arm
Reaches for cream
The nose the dick good for?
Eyes balls
Red white
Blue white
Three
Cross rabbits
Clear
Another shit factory?
Fill a dell fee free dumb and
Ben Franklin

Egyptian sleep trance too smooth doze a muzak
Or a
Dye to poison
Please
Please
But
But
But

And on my last night before leaving the hospital I write
this:

bracelets curtains Egyptian sand invisible angel the wind
will wind will win
All the conjugated nonsense unsense out since the spittle of
death man
gone monsters protein all back all blue all diamonds of a
fake
moon a false cloud sky in and us chicks half castrated
queers

straight and reversed where is my peach candle from HyVee
to flicker summer's Sue Tilly in a geometric hex game
Gone gone man no I'd be hopefully the about as worthless
stupid and pleasure the mind comes out turns rust hum
an on shit Ann Lucy the missing chewing Christian cuddle
in her second hand east not east Oz and everyone went to
hell and regret is the first and last real in a trapped
number blood fascisms all coins needles and I with other
eyes Hank says the artist is always sitting in a rich
man's can, hell shit man, now how they lock up the artist
and you zombie somber personality little beat greedy white
robots in clothes that would make Kurtz laugh and clowns
cry and priests cunt...the war rose sometime ancient second
and Jean's millenniums ago in planets of pure shit and geometric
and now its low how how how now its now now now
Shit man eye take a C D E over anything shit man, drum Ann
Annie lil rich Annie who knows? Most of my cornered little art
scams have vanished: parents, friends, enemies...they couldn't
care less about me (birth) but decorations hep hip in
Fuckedville is very important pop. me, someday eyes
Read red rode rite joy sea all blind wondrous green
Veined and imagination swift as a dead horse, Joyce
the only writer that makes sense love, the only artist to
jive time velocity, and space stillness and turn all the
lies into turquoise circles while beat ghosts dance with
Bill Miller in the highest school of em all every cage
cages for the cages the mind? Can it never ever return
to its original DOVENESS? Humming pirates all justice

out there in of Ireland ah fucking Ireland if eye could
let my soul separate and half and half I'd be in Ireland
and Mexico simultaneously away from the hellish mix
of Egyptian Christian Jewish sleep music the going
of reality the costumes are the dammed symbols
are for the greedy, I'll be a dumb fucking monkey awaiting
bye bi the Mississippi naked eating grass slowly slow
The water will be my knew everlasting home! If
eye make the whole crazy horse universe water
what would you say about that mutter fucker?

I met T-Bone at the art show for the mentally ill we both
being schizophrenic and attempting the old painting game.
T-Bone is a drunk, its writ all over his disillusioned face,
the sarcasm the dry humor the dark brooding flip of the
American loser. We exchange phone numbers and a couple
days later I'm in his basement crib pale shadowy T-Bone is
drinking vodka and I brought over some cheap beer. I'm
sitting on the couch and he's got books on William Blake
and that English cat Oscar Wilde and Dylan Thomas and
T-Bone's all time hero Vincent Van Gogh. Plus he's got his
canvases leaning on the walls, he pulls one out, "What do
you think? It's the Adonis myth."

"Adonis what?" I don't know mythology despite the
fact that we are both Dionysian fellows on the outskirts
of time and law. "Why don't you paint normal things in
a more complex manner rather than lofty shit in a simple
technique?"

T-Bone writes poetry too and he's got about two pages
of a novel done and its called Visions' Abyss. At the time
I've gone back into the Beats which I haven't read since
high school: Howl, On The Road, Naked Lunch. There's
something there but T-Bone wants to write like Homer big
vast complicated epics and fancy wordage. Me well this is

what happens after reading Bukowski every day for four years straight, it drops the I.Q. and well I go to the kitchen to grab another cold brew. Sit back down on the couch take a big hardy gulp then pull out my cigs and light one up I've also got cigars but I save them till around the seventh beer. T-Bone has a sculpture of the Virgin Mary, its white and holy. The clock radio is on, The Black Crowes jam. We shoot the shit for a while then I stumble the five blocks back to my joint.

Friday morning I call in sick to work then call T-Bone, "T-Bone what's up? You feel like drinking?"

"Perpetually."

"I'll be over in a half hour."

I walk the three blocks to the liquor store and buy a six of dark beer and a seven dollar jug of wine then trot another eight blocks to T-Bone's. Ring the bell, he comes up the stairs and opens the side door and says, "The apocalypse found my toothbrush and now the lions plague me with hunches."

"Let's drink brother."

"Ya ya."

Its nine thirty in the morning when I flick open a bottle with my lighter, the booze slides down into the illimitable gullet, I look through T-Bone's tapes and I put in Robert Johnson, I tell him, "First time I heard Robert Johnson was a stormy night in Minneapolis and it made me feel something I'd never felt before."

T-Bone nods. Music. T-Bone starts pacing the small room with a toy gun he's ranting about art and literature and Jim Morrison and every time he finishes a sentence he points the gun and yells, "BANG!" First time he did it it scared the shit out of me. After about an hour and a half I've consumed the beer and go for the wine, its been chilling and the fridge beckons and take the lid off and drink it straight from the bottle. "I'm gonna fuck your Virgin Mary after I'm done with this wine."

"Go ahead, its been about two thousand years."

I light a cig and use an empty for an ashtray. I look at the paintings of Blake. "What do you really think of my paintings?" T-Bone asks.

"It takes me a long time of looking at the same thing to really get any ideas good or bad of the damn stuff."

"What if I tell the world I'm a genius?"

"That's not for you to say."

"Why can't I say it? When I'm dead this shit'll be priceless. Till then I guess I'll keep at the vodka and hope for some primal revelation."

"If that's what you need look at Jackson Pollock's shit."
"Jackson Pollock? You're always talking bout that bum."

"He's the best."

"Even better than Bacon? You dig Bacon a lot don't you?"

"Jackson invented about twenty new directions in the techniques of painting at least."

"What do you think of the surrealists?"

"Dali is the last of the medieval painters."

"Van Gogh though," says T-Bone swirling the vodka and ice cubes around in his green glass, "Van Gogh did it, he went all the way."

"Damn straight he did."

"I sent some poems to a magazine haven't heard back yet. You should send your shit out."

"I'm working on my autobiography right now, Ant Man, when I send something out I want it to be the whole nine yards, and not little trinkets of despair."

But this ole T-Bone business is a backtrack, happened a couple years earlier so now I'm getting released from the hospital, the doctor asks me what I want to do with my life, "I wanna be an Indian runner." Come on lets get practical, we have planes, buses, whatnot, and here I am wanting to run barefoot through the industrial wilds of America. They send me to a foster home.

Its out in the country, beautiful really, I weigh about a hundred and forty pounds, at dinner I'm still afraid to eat, some toxic delusions, I have a bedroom, pile all my books and tapes on the floor and turn on the little lamp, I read Bukowski and Kerouac, listen to jazz, its late September, I have to smoke outside on the porch and a chill has set in. Foster home. Its two lesbians sharing a house and well they wake up at five in the morning and I've quit my job at the drop in center, I'm their entertainment, I sit cross legged on the floor and tell puns and show off, they go off to work so I go into the gravel driveway and unroll canvases and paint on the ground, big abstract pictures and I feel like its maybe Springs and I'm Jackson on the verge of creative juice contraption and utopian liberation through the fling of omnivore dance image and quaking the inspiration of thirty years old and no job but everyone needs a break now and Zen.

Well this and that happens the two women start to get on my nerves after a couple weeks and then I find spit in my oatmeal and yell and curse and throw things and I get kicked outta there, I'm back in the lush hospital, answering the same questions and so I go to a halfway house in Owatonna, I like it better than the foster fiasco cuz its right by the library downtown.

Oh black nights of schizophrenia at the library and a brother says, "Black haze," as I look at Mexican art and then I wander wander I'm always wandering without a true home, wondering in bafflement I told the doctor, "I know I'm Don Quixote," and, "This mental illness rap is nothing but a money suck." Prison camp, that old fear, war, calamity, nerves shot, eating pretzels, junkies versus Rastas, liquid versus bacteria. I need a lot of things: a woman, a stiff drink, a puff from the magic dragon. I move into the third floor bedroom and share it with a fellow named Mezzy. I buy Tropic of Cancer at the little downtown bookstore, I've started that damn book a hundred times but for some reason I've never been able to finish it, maybe in heaven, maybe in hell...

The routine is day treatment in the afternoon, there's ten other residents and we eat lunch together then hop on the bus and listen to the bearded therapist rap about how to get through the tangles of mental illness. I've got a lot of anger in me, losing my apartment, having or being forced to take pills I think I don't need. On an on.

I have a lot of free time on my hands day treatment taking up only four hours a day (including the bus ride), I buy a canvas and paint in the basement which is the only place we're allowed to smoke. So I come home and drink good black coffee and smoke and the fucking T.V. is always on and the election burlesque, Florida mishap and the Republicans win (?) but who cares? They have a great book on Marcel Duchamp at the library I check it out, it talks about alchemy and how Marcel wanted to ride his sister secretly. So at night in the basement I put on headphones listening to The Band mostly and read about Duchamp and try to modernize my old man soul, I also have a book called The Writings of Marcel Duchamp which I read and write notes in. Here are the notes:

Make a dust moo
con strup dust highways
way hi
two dah

Anthony Haas

moon
wig way waitless bridge
two be Cummings wayless

Kera
walks
??S
water
aqua   hitchhikers
hydro gin
ticket
turd

Bill Ra Ma Dain
Inn black hole

Dust/gravity/water/sun
England

Whirl:
Something of the nature of Ghost Dance
Oxygen vent
A gradation: Fish to land to bird
Dance into cosmos
Adepts dance-Miles
Look=too
Quetzalcoatl myth

Nartick mince
Sensory mergings
Simultaneous
Moon infra twitch sun
Bare ank three is historical

Endgame be: Hacsious GHHHOSED
Notes for a pregnant painting

In is la: en, wendian
Ink not "8" sideways
Three writings
The pun
Licked hair
Thy your
Flatulere
Steven

Godlty
Shitly

What were the whirl books?

Gases   objects
Liquids N=2=concepts
Skeleton spirit
Spilotin
Senses to sand to glass=time
Froze/thawed
                Spectorcles
Sighs a scream
Dye a Re of a alchemist
Steps to Spain
French buffalo forehead

Re-place:un
Place Re:in
Unfinite (or):sub
Undefinite (or):du
                then

Like # symbols are always symbols
shoe=shoe   t=t   star=star pyramid=pyramid
0=0
Symbols: every symbol is seemingly static
unless looked at with eyes of fire,
time scientifically is a relatively
unstudied phenomenon (?)

"LIX," cuz (in title of this
                            to matrix pyramid "An..."

Feline time sideways eight (or) eternity
Feeling time
Pie
Flip of 12:01 or
Pladue

Monday Valentine Tuesday guess Easter etc.
Hypo
That
Innaly
Threads
Arcane beforehand?
New calendar? Sensory calendar?

Is variable
Variable is variable
Non-exitable
Arrow a human condition
Hollow or solid?
Objects or canvas sewn on and dangling

1 is always 1 never 2 is always 2
1+1=1 unless: ?: molecular mist is perceived:

then: 1 is 8
or two ones
concept of merge (sex?)
every number a symbol of infinity

How to make time collapse how to make paint collapse?
Time merges (Hinge is possible)
Heat time cold time
Time is a snake
Illusions: whose
illusions do I believe?
Mine? Yours?
Knew form of painting? Analogous to standard stopies 3

Within painting
New shapes of #'s
New flow? New sequences
New relations historically
Place past into future

Time (instead of
alternative to
titles or signature
Latch
Anna even

Numbers are basically mist
Ruler?
Jasper's cup?
Tingley?
Cage?

Create a painting
that actually

creates or recreates
time/invent new time

Can count molecules
with a number?
Seepage? How does
a number become
another number?

Circular maybe
Time as color
Color as…
Not color but time

RWITITIGS

Turning pages rapidly somewhat
write down first
word or words (successive glimpses)
Seen
That becomes
a readymade
swift (made)
sentence, or
statements:
"…Occuring change differentiation…"
Or, "… …"
Invisible readymade
                        or,
not even "?"
no birth of the
second utterance
of a readymade
idea

horizontal procurious passage
embelic imbilec

Getting a new form of forms
Forms perspective
Perspective perspects forms the forms
Form is perspective
Color is perspective

All space is unconscious
Dreaming as it pleases
Pattern only sleeps to see
The groom eaten by cake and ring
The obtainer fabricates
the only stop
to give to suffer
Immaculately deferred
The flash is very loud

As I sip cola

I usually write for a couple hours once it gets dark I brood in that basement chain smoking, feeling imprisoned, needing some privacy. Mezzy and I play cards, rummy five hundred or gin, no one there knows how to play chess, my favorite game. The painting is coming along, its of two pregnant lesbians facing each other as the fish swims up and Marcel's Milky Way verticals its just another passage of the possessed unknown artist searching for the archetypal questions in a sea of paranoia and delusions.

My folks come to visit on a Sunday in October, we go to a oriental restaurant, it's a buffet, I grab a big pile of potatoes and start chowing down, but, there's pork melded into the potatoes, I get very pissed off because of this, I feel like its some kind of conspiracy.

We walk back to the halfway house where their car is parked and I'm cursing and raving manic. We sit in the backyard at the picnic table, then one of the workers comes out to see how we're doing, I curse and threaten him, I hate all white people, everyone's a junky, I goad the halfway house worker whose name is Gerald, I wanna fight, I wanna take on the whole needle war, I'm not making any sense, my adrenalin is sky rocketing, the war the war, and me caged, howling, frightened beyond all comprehension. I do a little dance in circles singing, my folks can't take it and they leave, I take a walk to the gas station to buy cigarettes, can't go in the halfway house cause they'll rape me. I'm walking downtown and a police car pulls up next to me, its me he's looking for, he takes me to the hospital.

I've got my Duchamp book with me in the hospital, a lot of spare time, so I continue making notes:

To have the heart in the ghetto

Exclude masculine eyes
when the feline holds you

Homeopathy "belongs to the two of us"
as the bird never purchases moon

Spangles: Small bright metal glitters decoration

Condition of crowd
Occurring often
Repeatedly
# of times an event
value, characteristic

occurs in a given
period
Ratio of #'s
# of periodic
oscillations
vibrations
waves per
unit of time
expressed in cycles
per second
GIVEN: assumed, stated
                habit, specified
                documented
                granted
                premise
Make a frequency of painting

Notes and boats what you have to realize is it's a cantankerous mystery bubbling forth and Marcel went to the other side in the bluest black of some wedding in in in, foolishly I look at art magazines in the basement the vessel the smoke and the fan, and I go down on a Friday night in the halfway house and see my book ripped torn in half lying in the garbage can, well I accuse Mezzy which he don't like and it turns out the culprit is Suzanne the talker to the self and I'm back in the hospital, wanting to cry, wanting to cry.

I tape the book back together, cracked many things as simple as glass or mirror.

District Schwitters from K-Mart platonic penny and me alias love alias Kerouin alias me and the nickels of the nether regions dance Saint Vitus to our simple hellos, the moon deserted sigh more pointed to Stephen to stop for a while delay, delay into what? From? Crimson Cummings no longer a picture or water in a fish to start back when? Copper demon ore oh? Demented child of mercury and lead, heavy mercury as the mercy waves bye if it aint a picture what is it? Snap shot grind. Copper demons crushed by the gold shadow: Dream, silver nickel cloud Jones.

Two planes-which is which? Infinite only cosmically modern Christ the opus is a strawberry one dimension three dimensional twelve in four, unthinkable. One light straight in with, with… out, on. Into liquid plain glisten star. Six moons too night the kite hears thy wind Anna an hearts wily wind dough bows wild fire oh to plastic rice is white even plants can't micro hide cunt.

Klee's plane stares at stairs I dimly fall into this romb, Latchanna, reflex, cubism to surrealism to what's next? Hex? Humanly ifinite. Hexism. Second's now second how, "According to what?" Candy cane Candy came Candy sent me to heaven tingling like an India cow or Mother Superior slashing the universe, cut deeply now and between Jack's rue and Henry's bird-like swooping the shallow river the snow the ducks a million snowflakes and I'm stranded, defying even Ophelia.

Get out of the hospital stay out of the hospital, "You're not supposed to breakdown," said the philosopher's stone.

A being be being possibilities exposed: BA. Detailed explaining. Look for what? Eyes are tits.

Shadows from the dictionary ghosts like pillars of pure map wanting time to moon perpetual eggs of angle tango tangle. Center of nothing perfectly of mostly everything almost, almost. Axis splash. A circle may determine: Axis-ratpure. Turning is (rapture) always subjective rupture (rapmuyer) how long is a second? Sour ce sigh roar and lust. Opposite of gravity? Wind that blows in like salmon into itself source exodus source love. Winter, winter, no one to play chess with. Basement trance, the self is a flower the self is like so many contingent pianos.

It's a victory song she sings, Karen Peris, I'm always in basements, it was that basement in St. Paul where she parades the sorrowful aspect of a war's demise, knowing mercy hoping mercy and a needle wall for her scary dolls and why do I have to remain here? Here is alone, alone with suicide, preying on my suffering the birds thought I was roadkill I don't know but passing through vistas of regret, the space regret continuum and her love out there in the wind in the winter of Johanna and Louise and all the masks, out there... "Its only surreal."

On weekends we go to movies or bowling, One Flew Over the Cuckoo's Nest, but no rebels, no ascetics, the days are pure frost, I take my canvas to the bedroom can't paint with Gerald and his great white ways protruding into my fragile psyche. I sit on the floor and listen to music and look at Duchamp's early pictures: the rites, the loves, the reality of possible paradise but I can't shake this paranoia, smoke. In the garden but the garden is covered by twenty colossal inches of ice and snow, walk that alley to the library. Read boy read. Alchemy and Psychology. Jung. The monkeys are wailing. The rabbits are howling in hunger the long winter. Mezzy shows me his drawings, interesting stuff. Matta, Kandinsky. Write a couple songs on the archaic guitar, that damn guitar since I sobered up I can't get too excited bout that piece of wood, my drinking days are behind me. Though I have the occasional urge for mushrooms.

I have a thousand songs in me as winter ascends the stars cold by now and light of way off, a part meant, a part meant the dying of Ophelia hold the rose to now we're alive. Sisters' deities sisters' diamonds ironized, ethereal motifs of modern clunks. Cezanne. Sure man. Into five. Prenatal echo pendulum acoustics. Delay seems to be a... rezadu. The pen moves as it pleases in Coincedinceville. Demultiply target? Imprisoned chance. The basement and now its Paul and the flat drinks of landing, the flatlands of hide, the seekers shawl in the shroud of nameless night, sober night, stupid delusion sight, beefing up the prick, are you gonna cross that anima border?

House paint blue. Cipher we get to none unborn preborn entities of the secret writing based on a track of train keys the codes brother the codes and the skeleton of such a door to seduce math to solve the key and yet there's the pyramids and Marcella cipher swirls ledgers by the entwining reflection refracted by green grins, rest rusty skin, rust dusty sin.

Hi Bloom. Birth. Up to down. Transparent ciphers of a new alpha bits one merges to too two on an on.

Flip the pages staring for revelation light another cig drinking hot apple cider no one else in the basement the T.V. off, R.E.M. on the blaster reading looking unknowing. Buddhism of Kerouin and my canvas on the wall, the bride returned, some autonomous border the brink of maleness and madness, la la la.

T-Rex, magnetic disrobing, painting trees, no symbolizations, arbor, ridge, is this (metallic) poetry? Chaos fills eight nice seven, no symbolizing by grandiose and all symbols are grandiose. A little purple for my violets in the storm, bend, recline, spread. Faller of one. Undiscovered shape, where, why? "...opticians of time..." I didn't. What about left to father left bride? "Loose obedience to a vegetable law, I will go to a vagina family," Jim, the prayers are silent now silent in winter French inhale the whistle of wind, ah a little yellow, some menaced cock implodes the midnight.

Con ascending.

If gold becomes orange, find the zodiac sign, secrets

of Atum of the bride. Pseudo chemical. Heterogeneous, composed of unlike parts.

Les the specter.

Ghost shards Q-tip warriors and orgasm raw bottle smash liquid knife, eye

> sin
> glea
> wayt
> should

> weight how flames maize and metal

elastic. Aztec to a enigma of the sacred heart. Poop. Poop. Kerouin: Pladue twelve oh one two thousand, semi colon. Knew degree adding negatives, dissolution of sieves (p.p.), cover a painting with fart spray or udder stuff, rare roll fry eyed… searching for fruit that don't exist. In coup in quest resident like bone snake tail bottle pills.

Its autumn a few months after high school graduation and I'm washing dishes while the chosen ones have all flown the coop to the expensive pasture of college. My girlfriend, Laney, from high school is going to nurse school in Iowa, I'm still deeply in love with her, I'm living at home and I lay in bed alone at night and dwell brood about her dark beauty, wanting a letter a phone call, to go back to when we first started our magic affair.

The peyote dusks, wandering walking the town walking off hangovers walking off heart sickness and the ambiguity of this rite before me: After high school. What am I supposed to do? I drink, beer, whiskey and wine with Bob DeVille who drops all the time, I can only take that shit once in while. The void. Time.

Laney comes home for a weekend, she calls me up and I'll be right over, her house is a mansion on top of the hill, her dad a doctor. I arrive, the house is dark and quiet, we kiss, long slow, hugging. "You want some of my dad's beer Dawn?"

"Sure."

Her long black hair and I love it when she's in jeans and T-shirt. We sit on the couch close, it feels like love, I could spend the rest of my life with this woman, Laney, Laney... the radio is on, In Your Eyes, Peter Gabriel, I'm getting drunk, getting to be a daily occurrence. Laney isn't drinking which is unusual, she explains that when she first left the strictness of her home and had the freedom to do what she wanted she went on a month binge, drank far too much so now she's laying off. I get up off the couch, take a beer piss, go into the kitchen crack open a cold one slam it down in about forty five seconds then swipe another one and head back to the couch and Laney's loving arms, her gypsy miracle eyes, her soft lips. "You wanna go to bed? You can stay over my folks are gone for the weekend."

"Sure."

We get naked, well she leaves her panties on, she doesn't like to go all the way, fear of pregnancy, its good enough for me just to be with her, so close, so together in the chill fall night and we kiss for a while then drift off to sleep.

Morning. "I have to go back to Iowa to perform for the music department, do you want to come with me?"

"Sure."

"Wanna take the rest of the beer with us? My dad won't care."

"Sure." There's about fourteen left. We get dressed Laney putting on a black skirt, earrings, a little make-up, beautiful morning, soul mate morning. We get in the car, a Cutlass, and take off, its about an hour and a half drive. We talk and joke around, stop at a gas station and I buy some doughnuts and chocolate milk.

We arrive at the little college in the little town and go

to her dorm room on the fourth floor, she has some of my artwork on the walls plus a cheesy picture of Jesus (she's really into the Bible). She has to play piano, give a recital so we walk to some Johnson Hall something or other and I sit with a small crowd and listen to the students perform classical music, duets, soloists, then its Laney's turn and she plays well, passionate, concise, the music floods the room. My heart comes alive in the chord progressions kites of love stream from my center.

Then came my dream: I'd rent out a little room in this little town get a job dishwashing and paint and see Laney in my spare time. I didn't tell anyone this and it never came to pass.

So after the concert we go back to her room, I pop open a beer, she wants wine so she leaves for a while to go to the liquor store and I lie in her single bed sipping beer, I put in Bob Dylan's Desire tape. All Laney's tapes are in her sock and underwear drawer. On my third beer she walks in with a giant bottle of wine. I take a slug straight from the bottle then she pours herself a glass. We are lying together sipping, snuggling, talking in subdued hushes. Dusk comes, she says I remind her of Bob Dylan, especially that song Isis. I like that. Dylan man, straight up.

We decide at nine to go hit the bars of the little town, we're only twenty years old but she says its easy to get in, we start out into the night. We meet up with a student she knows and he asks me what I'm doing with my life, "Washing dishes and going to the community college."

"Is that good enough for you?" The old competitions of the young American males.

"For now," I say and Laney beams at me.

It's a little hole in the wall dive in the basement old concrete walls smoky as hell and a big plastic cup of keg beer for fifty cents the jukebox is playing our song: In Your

Eyes. We haven't said its our song but it is because it fills me with courage and hope. There's six pool tables, some of Laney's girlfriends are there, attractive, intelligent. Drinking beer brinking dear. One of Laney's friends is hitting on me but I remain glued to Laney's side and really if it was just us two only in this crazy cosmos I couldn't be happier. We both get drunk, around midnight I whisper in Laney's ear, "Lets go to bed."

So we walk out into the shadowy streets high tingled on the booze, she squats in a alley to take a piss. Then we walk up the four flights of stairs and we're in her room again. She lies down on the bed in her clothes and spreads her legs and opens up her arms to invite me into her Mexican soul, I lean her way then climb on top of her, we kiss, French kiss. I unbutton her shirt then she sits up and takes off her bra, I take off my shirt and we kiss again breast to breast. After about ten minutes I want to hear some music, I find a Chopin tape and play it in her tape player, I grab a beer out of her little fridge, take a couple gulps then pour the rest of it on her naked except underwear body, then I lick her stomach and suck on her tits. Dry fucking. She gives me a blow job. Its about two in the morning I take a piss out the window after taking the screen off, we lie in bed her with her wine and me with the beer. We are both lushes.

I take the Sunday afternoon bus back home. But home sucks. I decide to live with Bob DeVille, that lasts a couple days and I'm back home.

I read Henry Miller's Rosy Crucifixion, obsessed with him, his way his magic, I take art classes at the community college, I'm planning on going to the art school next year in Minneapolis. But my real joy is visiting Laney on weekends once or twice a month.

I'm on the bus headed south in a snow storm with Black Spring and Hero With a Thousand Faces, reading but really dreaming of how wonderful it will be to see Laney again. I get off the bus and walk downtown, I have a few hours to kill before meeting her so I go into a pizza joint and eat and read, its cold outside. Then I see a rated G movie, damn thing almost has me in tears its so cute.

After that I walk to the college its about six in the evening, I sit down in a lobby and wait. And bam here she comes, "You thirsty?" I ask her. She says yeah so we walk down to the liquor store in the icy wind, I buy a bottle of whiskey and a six pack of beer and recently I've started smoking when drinking (disco smoker) so I purchase some Marlboros too. We hike the load back to her dorm room.

We drink for a while then she leaves to practice the piano, I'm alone in the room, sipping beer gulping whiskey, I love her so much, I feel poetry stirring inside me, I grab a pen and a sheet of paper and write her this:

Okay mouth Anna coup pal universes four eyes in a night
of violet cat glass of distilled voice her mystery
profile of a flame in a collapsing of calypso fright
The freights roll in the day and there she is! A
walking garden, a breathing phenomenon of love
One song for two flames in a sake dream, eyes
open to close to open sometimes it's the same
Awful then beyond where Faustian whiskers
and calcium clouds, now though, now, her voice is
hot water to on my grungy soul and the steam
is lovely blue in lights dim and the women of
the Golden Bough and Picasso, and Duchamp
and in my heart gently stepping, jigging with
a pink violet rads candle my lil whirl to
make ways for wondrous possibilities
to brilliant and I fear fear it's a rhapsody
of dumb fantasy and my initials spell ash

oh though I can feel something love is as real as
anything else why not believe in eternal love?
Jesus? Quetzacoatly? Big Aztec tomato pulse in
the truth chest, lil okay mouth till Tilly why?
Why? My eyes virgins to the vast rays the
love that vies the wall the love ghosts, will she
save me? Will I save me? Save to save homes.

Oh its like ancient history and what's Laney doing
these days? This baby this red this white this blue and the
descending rose. I'm in the fucking halfway house again
the light: negation of negation. Shadows are visual each
oxygen equals shadow. The White Box. Lay down nine.
Glass ground. Unsolid, sub. T or Antonin? Greenish
brownish yellowish Re's pink. Headphones on listening to
Hole, smoke, flip the page. Marcel's alchemy, Etant Donnes,
hand flesh plastic, in this basement with the mad of the
Midwest sterling around, Suzanne doing laundry talking
to herself she's Ophelia and how many Ophelias are in this
vortex nation so-called America? Not existence pre preeing
before number of eyes that see its time of actual painting
existence length of picture muy ladder the gamblers and
Pound. Apollo: omega bits macro mince sun milky way head
of lettuce bogus politicians I've almost forgotten the cross.

We'll have to forget the past as the light is the
perspective: turner. Vinny. Impossibly woman. Read The
Doll. China cow, scam, din, sky, secular, and molecular
compositions. India ink beside oil pastel. Coins or eyes?
Let me tell you about The Doll…time and Marcel with his
optics and science. Joyce with his myth, religion, relation
shits. Tip. Phantoms of life scatter imprints I know stillness
essentially the ponies of native fountains. Unborn archetypes
unborn like your future birds future wind your come and
eyes unborn archetypes spurt like sun spots waiting for
communion with the water of ye essence water magic water

water before archetypes the lonely only ache type kissing waves: native, specter, birth, undetermined, Ann, real. In incest of nature's unmolested orgasm, splash instead of Che's new year. Go upstairs make another cup of hot tea go back downstairs into the basement the vessel no windows light a cig. Tip. Form before mold sucker plunge The Doll (tip) into heavy arid status decays liberty virgin past statues with a crown of flames, quote the ghost, two dimensions, harassing badgering births a three dimensional into a four dimensional whirl…one dimensional lore doors the ajar if shut, mass, plane, elementary elements. The pie shroud the dissecting Eve Ann and brutes of inner suctions free be yawn Zen hollow like now.

The Doll calls me up out of the blue. The Doll is low junk on the totem pole. I'm Dawn Peyote. What's worse? I'm last. Like Amiri stumbling through the ghetto, we talk on the phone and make a date. I'm Dawn Peyote eating Sid in a rock-n-roll moon fall, all the Mardous are out of focus on the other side of the world. October's pumpkins metamorphosis and now its winter with the gray snake is it a cloud careening through a gutless cane sake?

Cleopatra in the basement with me as I'm painting, she asks, "What does your art mean?"

"I honestly don't know what it means, its collective its stupid its rants and rocks. The closest representation is Jung's ideas and I think that's why artists are so jaded: anyone can do it. Beuys got his wish in a negative sense: everyone is an artist but they're lousy artists, hacks. That collective haunts everyone."

"But why do you make the lines a certain way? What does it mean?"

"Its an el. El love."

We forget about the art and play some cards, she's a cokehead. Cleopatra, we play spades. Friday slowly turning into night, a movie comes on, Bringing Out The Dead, we watch it together. I'd like to climb on top of her and her full breasts and wiggle till the cows come (home).

The Doll out there in the barren night trying to score, grifting, whoring, walloping. And her victim Dawn Peyote who thinks she's just your average stupid blond. She lives a few blocks away with her ex-boyfriend, on the rebound and I walk to her place, we sit on the front porch. I tell her I'm a vegetarian. "What about protein?" Asks she.

"I don't think protein is that important."

We walk to the park there's a pickup basketball game goin on, I stand on the sidelines antsy to play, The Doll leans against a tree. I get in the game, hoof, sweat. I score once. The other guys call me Lennon cuz of my long hair. Spring. We walk back through the night, me to the halfway house and back down to the basement.

No one is down there, ah, good, I make some hot apple cider light up a chig turn on the tape player open up my Duchamp book and find a pen: Two fold into four eyed engine. Cooking la le Mary. Object empty full spatial it is and subject delay ghost the mold psychic mould chemical ghost then specter the life as if nothing is all, maze line dissipate capitulate all is veneer on specters of time the lonely mold of reversal and diagonal the bones of movie crosses and my fingers my moldy sentient conscious digits split the seem. Sun worshippers. Pale turquoise dark red. Gut rot of yesteryear. Maybe in the clit ticks native light unmucked by non sleep blue eyed man stirs being, death feed, addiction. Allah space is ghosts ignoring calendar err. Conscious lyrics eyeballs illumined lest yeast natively lambs. Fimomist

> bire why
> mo wrist
> me eye.
> God's tricksters? Fizz.

Multiple. Plane. Dimensions three is three until seeing a

four hidden within and beyond three. Space veil traversing time's shawl to four invisible planes the shift of life on this plane. Five oh. Fizz totem. Unpredictable fizz: Pulls: C pulls B, B tires to pull D, A and C shift…A is alpha.

Well life rolls on I go to day treatment and come home in the afternoon. I go up to my room and beat off. Then go back downstairs and my new roommate Roy is talking on the phone by the kitchen and I overhear him say, "Yeah smells like you got a lot of pole with that one." I'm pissed, I think he's talking to me. I go back up to the bedroom, paranoid, embarrassed, mad, Roy walks in and lays down on his bed, my blood is boiling, he says something and I ignore him, he says something else and I leap out of my bed and jump over to him and spit in his face, he spits back into my face and he's up outta bed with his fists bopping around, he's bigger than me, I laugh in his face.

The woman working finds out, both of us mad now, Roy really wants to kick my ass but I get sent to the hospital and you know who drives me there? Cat Man's mom. She tells me Cat is playing chess tournaments in the cities and is living on his grandfather's farm. She's really nice.

Back in the hospital, I've lost track of how many times its been now, they give me the green pajama clothes to slip into, one cigarette an hour, all I want to do is sleep but they won't let me until eight p.m. so I listen to the radio in the group room.

Next day I talk with the doctors, I'm a mess, crying, the doctor says, "It sounds like you've been white knuckling it with depression." So he puts me on a anti-depressant, he seems to really have empathy and understanding and I feel a trust growing between us unlike when I first went there and had a bulldog attitude.

One of the nurses says maybe I could call up Roy and

apologize, so I call him up and he's completely forgiven me and we're back to friends again. I stay at the hospital for three or four days then its back to the halfway house.

I get a job in a warehouse hanging parts. I get out of bed at seven thirty drink coffee and smoke a couple, pack a lunch and the staff wishing me good luck as off I go. Work is difficult, the clock goes too slow and I'm on my feet all day but I stare at the women running around noting their breasts and butts and legs (its been quite a while since you know what). I come home around four and the weather is showing some mercy so I sit on the front porch waiting for dinner. I love that porch with the little radio plugged in playing the latest hits and I sip coffee and read Kerouac, its great being out of that basement finally, place was like a pressure cooker, a charnel, what with that damn T.V. always croaking.

Taking that long half hour bus ride after work or day treatment at around three or four in the afternoon I get a chance to survey this little town called Owatonna. Lots of cars lots of middle class houses and they all seem to look the same and the churches the arrogance of the churches in any town or city to come to this land and make commandments about the so-called god and advertise this bullshit forcing it down the throat. It's a farming community but there's really not much wilderness left, trees here and there. It's the infusion of cars the paradox of ownership and the gypsies are extinct, riding on that bus and the bus driver plays the Christian radio station oh woe religion is so personal that I feel like my mind and spirit are being raped by lies lies lies. Animal territorialism, technological territorialism, slaves to the machine, cars cars everywhere and the last couple of wars have been fought because of cars, people innocent have been murdered so we can have cars. The bus rolling through: water towers, parks, factories, the kids getting out of school and nature and god long dead. Gasoline and math. Oil and science. Electricity shrouds the stars at night. T.V. and the hustle of the upper classes. Some days on that bus I feel like there's a war happening that my mind fragile from years of introspection is going to explode in paranoia. Try finding a white brother. Try communicating with a white sister. Gossip and lies and kicking the down. I get off the bus and hide with my cigarettes and coffee.

But I have my fantasies…the Indians…masquerading… high school the teachers create the test and the smartest are in actuality really the most obedient and stupid, scared to do it independently, they set you up the Indians, and now I see that the rich who I hated all through school are actually freaks too, and the dumb, and the dumb are (maybe?) the geniuses. Or maybe I'm looking for excuses as I live on fifty dollars a week, excuses…but here there sure are some weird things a-going on.

Androgynously The Doll, she gets pissed when someone tells her she looks like Elton John, she has entered the scene. She's fat, she's bigoted, but she's not a bad lay. I take off on a bike to meet her at her new crib on the south side of town, she's horny, she's got a big butt, we lay on the floor and I'm looking at her tape collection. I can't even remember the last time I got some its been that long…I reach over to her and kiss her, she kisses back, we're laying on the couch me on top, "Let's go in the bedroom," one of us says, and in the bedroom we get completely naked and I squirm around on top of her, she's wet, I can't get it in on my own and she reaches down there and slides my monkey in, she says, "I'm so wet," I don't come, we fuck and fuck, it feels great, The Doll man, I'm telling you, and then when I think she's come I let loose with my wad.

She doesn't let people smoke in her crib, "I suppose you want a cigarette?"

"Yeah, I'll be right back."

The orgasm has me feeling like I'm on a different planet: mellow, smooth, relaxed. I go back in and lay down next to her and I talk about Mexico, Mexico, that's all I seem to think about these days, getting there, the heat the mambo the good ganja and tequila. But I'm stuck in the north country with The Doll, which isn't half bad, I think she wants to do it again. We do it again.

Around nine in the evening I ride back to the halfway house smelling like a juicy gash, I'm happy, I smile, the other clients know what I've been up to, I feel proud. Good night Earth goodnight Harry goodnight Satan and I go up to my room and sleep the sleep of a coal miner.

Guy Anna haunts me all them cats from the art school were and are special, the nights getting high and drunk and me painting off my hangovers chewing on nails dancing on glass.

Guy Anna seems in the beginning like a hack namedropping gurus and multi-cultural wish wash, but he turns out to be a real crazy South American genius... abstract, tunnels and portals that would make Jung's mind water, and if and what and and.

Art school, what a plethora of whacked insomniatic guzzle guzzle, pictures, pullets in the Minnesota whirl, cold, snow, Halloween all the time. Paintings and drawings. Me obsessed with Francis and Marcel and Harry Eastershirt and Guy Anna says he's got a Miles bootleg and my mind goes "ah." Guy Anna put a gutter at the bottom of a stretched canvas and his heroin brown his geotrees his belly sagging from beer and whiskey and time and the suitcase of brown sugar voyaging traversing procuring in a million dimensions some lucid destination, some Ginsbergian knowing some naked hint in the overcoat dawns grilling the moon for motions of answer…

Then, several years later I meet Guy Anna in the triage, the giant of India, the elephants the eggman the gone done swilling to dementia and who returns from Henry's China? Who returns? Fled like a chasing wind to the celebrity tragedies roaming on a unsympathetic cycle, Guy Anna asks me questions in his white garb, doctor. "My dad eats his shit," that's when I got sent to the prison. To the concentration camps I harbored a heroic escape time capsule space continuums black paint Dylan shades. Fusions of Tamara. Shiva do you dance when all is lost? When the universe is entirely smog? Shiva tell me the mystery of Guy Anna as Nell goes back home. Squawk!

The Doll seems so far from Guy Anna yet they're one, this I know even in a peyoteless dawn, I've been fooled so many times my tongue cut off and sitting on the rooftop a thousand Osiris pieces someone give me a new tongue a nigger tongue a Jap tongue a resurrection Aqua Time new century old sayings and the two fold gods of narrow roads and if I'm not chasing windmills? And if I rename The Doll Poncho? You see she's in my yearbook she's at the hospital she's a Guy she's an Anima she's Anna she's the dream of migration's solace and but for the pride on my lazy brow I, Dawn Peyote, I can't rearrange my senses. The windmills are up now. I'm down now. Nay, the fool is the king of the birds the birds I tell you they were there when the counting grew strange: Lake Street. Bag and bone warriors, bloods, crypts, police, lithium. Charged with charging the charged charge.

Nights when the left leave weaving tapestries and rich with squalor and worlds so far away let me rain tonight I've got a lot of new ideas to twine into your yellow and red mystic guesses, "Let me back into your world a blink of the eye no uncertain terms," as I write Son Volt sings me into recognition and wavering with a longing unquestioned and silver, the horizon is black cars passing streetlamp spears of electricity the impasse forsaken here she comes there she goes, low low low, but good good good. I could smoke a cigarette I could drain my cup of water looking for the node the moment and visions deserted (Rimbaud) I know I know...love. Should I balance like a judge on the great maker's land in a season of tears? Could I find my way back from that forest of unknowing and clandestine elders whose hints remain unpromised? Spectacular the goodbyes. Here the hellos are almost dawning here the looks of Madonnas and seers with cloth eyes ringlet to a straight boast and faster the wind here around here my oh my.... I need covenant love songs I need a savior in cosmic velvet I need inversions, dancing, anything remote anything ghost, here the is of then the how of what the tie of end and that river runs runs, the clock eats oatmeal the buffalo fall to the ground (thud) and the matter is powerfully nothing. Ah I'll smoke.

To be dead in heaven or alive in hell?

Where to go from here? Summer. On the porch zealously reading of Egypt and listening to jazz JAZZ. The Doll and I are on and off, she gets on my nerves like for instance when we're walking to the Mexican restaurant and she sees two dogs one black the other white and she says the black one is ugly but thinks the white one is "just adorable," she's a anagram gip but the sex is pretty good. "I hope you don't expect me to stop eating meat just because you're a vegetarian." She has a lot of great and noble ideas.

I've asked the staff at the halfway house if I can spend the weekend at The Doll's crib they say okay and I pack my duffel bag and hop on a bike Friday after work and pedal on over it feels good to be out of that place, apartment living dig? I ring the buzzer and she languidly comes out of her room taking up most of the hall as she waddles forth, I kiss her and say hello. I've got Some of the Dharma with me and a pen, as usual she's got the T.V. blaring its predictable platitudes, I lie down on the floor and say, "Let's listen to some music, this Goo Goo Dolls Dizzy Up the Girl is pretty good."

"I don't know what to do when we listen to music."

I flick the tube off and put the tape in. "Just listen, meditate, come here."

We lie on the floor, its only about five thirty, I always feel obtuse when making it in broad daylight but onward Christian soldiers we get naked and I give her a mediocre ride, come too soon. And of course I gotta have that cigarette afterwards. She has instant coffee I heat it up in the microwave, we've gotten dressed and she's sitting on the couch, "Do you like the Nutcracker?" She asks.

I cringe up my shoulders she laughs she gets it. She can be funny sometimes. She says something derogatory about rap music which makes me irritated what with my history of staying up late at night high on grass listening to Public Enemy (few years back). I need some time alone so I go into her bedroom and listen to a Tracy Chapman tape and write poetry and read the Kerouac Buddhist stuff (or non-stuff whichever way the wind blows) then I step outside to smoke again its black night and there's a mound rather large next to the parking lot, I'm smoking and looking for Orion, can't find it but the stars are beautiful nonetheless, looking for Orion ever since I read about how the pyramids and really all of Egypt is based on the constellations, its really amazing stuff what with the Nile as the Milky Way and the Sphinx pointing exactly East and all the mysteries still unsolved... I think the Egyptians were or are space travelers, to know the Earth and the cosmos with that kind of mathematical precision, man, I think there are two Egypts, one here on Earth and another one beyond the galaxy and the stages are when an Egyptian died they wrapped him or her up and off they sailed you to the other Egypt where with a special chemical solution they shrink your body back down to an infant's then unwrap you and you start all over again. Spaceships man. And of course the Mexicans or Mayans or Incas had similar procedures, listen to the similarity between Egyptian music and Inca music, those half steps, the snake, the jungle, hieroglyphs with formulas for making beer.

…it was in Minneapolis at the Garage Dor that I discovered Keith Richard's Main Offender, spent ten bucks on the tape went back to my crib on Stephenwolf Ave., turned on the bathwater and with my boom box sitting on the sink I got naked and grabbed an Old Style cold and sunk my body into the hot water as 999 played and that organ came in and man this shit rocks, and Keith said in a interview, "I'm more interested in the roll than the rock."

After that I listened to Main Offender everyday for months, it just seemed like the future of music was (is) in those open tuning ideas and I went to the library and read interviews with Keith and read a biography on the installment program, that is, I'd go to the bookstore and read a few pages at a time so I wouldn't (couldn't) have to buy it. I was drinking booze all the time and going to the art school and usually around dusk everyone would go home so I'd have the studio to myself and I'd put Keith in and paint and have my booze hidden under my jacket but hell even if the security guard saw me drinking he would have said just stay inconspicuous, me and the security guard were on good terms me being a drunk and him a recovering but still dry as hell (humor).

And that night after a three day whiskey binge and I'm laying in bed and Demon comes on and I die, I die in my sleep after the consummation consecration absolution of Keith's bluesy mournful ages folding all around me and to leave…to leave…to what? What lies within lies inside lies in fate in destiny: "It's a hard game you play."

I have no foresight. When I'm homeless I go to Dylan's, his hair down past his shoulders his beard long and curly, he kneels down on the gravel driveway running his hands through his scalp, "Can I stay with you for a while? I let you stay at my place when you first came to town."

He says neither yes or no but says he's got some money to drink so we walk down to a oriental joint and he buys me beers and feeds the juke. "Johanna Floyd is reading her poetry at the bookstore uptown you want to go?" I ask him, the beer isn't sitting right, a year sober and three beers is like…you know?

Dylan stays behind and I go uptown to hear my old writing teacher spew her stuff. But I'm nodding while she reads about some kind of cunt trees all juicy and female and they're not allowed in this country. I wanna talk to her when she's finished but a crowd gathers around her plus the booze is wearing off.

This country music has me swaying, Gone Again, listen again… ah that's it. The journey the roads the illimitable disasters the construction sites the playgrounds the sand boxes the jungle jims all this flashes before my dawn peyote eyes and singing a lazy blues she's "got all this inbetween," maybe I'll see her in the metropolis maybe I'll see her in the staggered garden maybe I'll see her like Dante as the last circles have passed and the fires have left my psyche and Howard and Harry will give the great ticket to Heaven, maybe… my heart my heart and all the fools congratulate me for my trip around the world with the language branded on my iron sleeve with a no way with a little train that should with the company of three hundred flaming dandelions, maybe… distortions and Alice should be a mushroom by now. If I don't make it just remember me to the blue girls of Hickville or Artaud's witches or whistle in a sphere with dirt and grass magic grass, give you the smile the stranger's smile of love making, my eyes dance black and brown there are several phantasms by now out there in the farmers' terrain, the corn the banjo she doesn't wear bras wow. Who's standing behind you Earth woman? Who's that stalk ripe and Mona Lisa perplexing surrounding you all green and the echoes and the point is that I love here I love here with her and I'm jigging to an unbearable song. Ah relax, I was drunk and stoned everyday and all she could do was sigh and in all this mortality just to know again and again and kick the dirt to know, what to do with a bum cake? What to share before a pitch black five thirty? This dog will have its day? Georgia.

Courting the phantom drinking ginger ale the travail of the Beats the flutes the guitars the past and all its leveling. Now I glimmer the shimmer and shiver the do, a lucky lack of indifference and what's it matter the cats have a shaky heart the winter, the winter, the wine cheap the cigarettes rolled the stone thinking and instrumental bar rooms oh the melancholy dogs and throw it away. I know your body. I could hold you for a dozen winters, thanksgivings and new year's and Eve and Ann and letting the night be longing alone for a silver junky coin to half dollar a box of chocolate, give you the heart and bleeding all over the place, give you the heart on Aztec steps and reincarnations and all that jazz, (trouble with you is you expect too much) the point is going round and the sleek snake is night a night of republics and poison. Allies of the vestige the watch on the girl the chips and greasy star hide. Form and hurries to Paris, elegantly crude.

Some inexorable initiation. Some devilish knowing and the initiate trembling the leaf the flower the rainbow. Into the thief. Into the oblivion. Out of the ghetto. Sonic it is as the country music bellows forth and maladies of uncertainty blush explode fish come and hearing the anthems now I a stranger thinly veiled the glass is black zodiac central the point the here they go and the storm the storm… republics of secrecy the gaze ineffably threshold, life is black bocks the chips on Saturn the sense leaves of leaving or a post ghost dance the other side did we slip into a moon or sun or faraway orbit? Did you castigate the lone drummer? Bone now how. Skull and sunglasses. Stories from the warehouse sisters and brothers thinking is like wind sway stir through the tracks and a single red light way on down the line. Bones know glow. Calcium for the children and studying the blanket between the pistol and the Bible, what's that on the dangerous path? You said, "Trust," the headlights visual Doppler and a train in the sand and a plain in the hand and a flame in the sham… brought here by truth deposit the coins into a lawless zoo.

Secret no more…the means of the ghosts on a crazy ship on a screaming punk bop subliminal Jura child and the drums like canons the father like fodder will you tune the waves to a chilly beat? Orbit. Only poets belong in this sphere where the feather hangs where the frame is filled with cats the Ank is my wine the yin yang is in my soul. Guardians man whisper it into my banana ear. Shrink the magic slope the forehead lower the stomach, you are there archaic don't you know? She is androgynous and that's why I love him (hawk nose show me your spirit) that's why the town is my home. I don't need philosophy I don't need a new land. Rivers keep time as the mask is alive as the gorillas as the eyes shine in all this electricity new age space age specter age. Sing the rebellion sting the fellaheen show me your feedback and flowers and I left that world years ago lives ago dreams a hundred million ago I left to smoke my legal and drink my icewater.

The music jams the night is darkening winter in Minnesota Mingusota and I went to the abstract I went to the abstruse I went to nowhere and back and words are all I have words for a thankless whirled shouldn't be shan't be to be lone on yonder milkless and a new sunrise the night so long you can see it uncurl like a snake before foolish eyes of masquerade eyes and clowns recoil in the wan waves of justice, Jack said, "See the picture," so my picture is Pollock and my answer is stars and fish leafless trees vortexes and windows of a pale suicide boy fetish motif of dick and the flask of the side of the road the plant the tobacco smoke ah electric millennium Dante's curse Beatrice and will I find a fresh love in all this dizzy solitude?

I feel the age unravel I see the time slurping the dirty dishrag sundown and I know this is to be this is simply is and I is are the tap tap tap of Joyce when I go down in that ragamuffin day to read, read dig? I find the skeletons of instrumental the slow down in the ravaged punk drinking coffee and ice water dripping the snow in the parking lot winter is here friend…I'll take the train I'll wish for a new snake like prayers of truth prayers of justice the progressions and the signs standing in a foggy spiritual awaiting the deaths of machine, I don't know who at last will contemplate the frozen Zen of carnival gone glucose of self and on the now the bets the basements the games towards a blazing zero don't look when the song is raging these reflections my skullcap on the table and crying dry for a rendered applause.

Summer nice hot summer on that cozy wonderful porch of the halfway house reading Jack's stuff: Subterraneans, Big Sur, On the Road for the sixth time, plus books on Egypt. Them books on Egypt blow my mind, how ancient, sublime, sophisticated. Makes me wanna be Indiana Jones digging just to dig digging. Drinking coffee and smoking as the intersection rumbles I watch the stoplights change and I go to the library, Joseph Campbell books, Jung, art books. Occasional chess game.

The day comes late July when I am fit to live on my own, get my own crib, but I'm pissed at my folks for throwing away a lot of my old canvases and my social security check for seven grand which I thought they saved they spent on a prior treatment. When I find this out I tell my dad, "You're a piece of shit I hope you fucking die."

I'm really flipped out, mad one moment crying the next. The woman working at the house says I'm just nervous about moving out. Well after a few days I get back on good terms with the folks, my mom helps me move we go to the Salvation Army and get a nice easy chair and a ashtray. I've got bus tickets and the windows face west, Set, Set, where in the Egyptian Book of the Dead am I now? My last night at the halfway house I pack all my stuff: clothes, paintings and drawings, books, radio…

Then bam! I'm on my own. Southside. Liquor store a ten minute walk away, but no I stay on the straight and narrow with my pop coffee ice water and hot tea. My mom waves me off and I'm truly alone for the first time in nearly a year, it feels good I walk around the crib in bare feet, I watch the blazing August sun scorch to down down. The hundred dollar trumpet sits waiting in its case.

I start a journal (which I'm tempted to use here but no that will stay a book in itself). The Doll lives across the street from me. We fuck in the heat, she sweats really easily, slide grease slide and suck. But I like being alone with my paintings. Although I've decided not to paint in here, too messy too many possible accidents, so I buy a box of colored pencils and draw on white cloths. I buy my own food, its nice to be away from meat eaters, that shit grossed me out watching them clowns devour dead animal while preaching the Christian shate all the while it even says in the Bible not to eat meat though I don't wish to get into any arguments so I keep it to myself.

After all this time I want you still. The Doll the transmigrations and on the downpour I've opened the red letter to let you loose as I go bald with my two stomachs the time the time and the half is still all is emotion too, to say the brightness is eternal in this night of singing golden songs writing a foggy standstill of German decline all that once was and now its future time on a galloping message the sudden drop, to grope and drop its been years, the constant peyote of me, shaman conjured the storm and in disguise the junk junked junky I know there's a war going down and my hands are all scraped up, wailing that Inian justice who goes forth to the bacteria the cancer the flagrant sword don't leave me behind I'm still a child I know the train of Kerouin she is my true sister a Artuad silence descending like a spaceship while the way can't be reached merely, nearly, the word, the words…

Peyote peyote visionary visionary out in the laughter the mathematicians the come the haze the rolling tomb the rap of insanity in a wheel in a star to burn to burn with the devil go down go down the race is on and I light myself on fire without an ounce of belief the mansions of hell Babylon

Hades when once inside the guns the engines you went too far parentless nights the feminine feline voice of tomorrow the road the well some home in this whirling in this whirling The Doll midnight and terminuses of tragedies riot man riot the lizards fellaheen falling go come go down river of the labyrinth you know its like when the crooner holds the moon this kingdom this crown and my plant has ears all over and the charity of The Doll as she's young again on a millennium of dancing and those windmills it's a hell of a show and the clowns open a door like milk and the referees open a door like gold out there in a zebra acid tramp…here it comes…ah another smoke won't kill me.

Like that time I bought that Bukowski CD and a gigantic bottle of wine trotting Dinkytown in a cold cold and I get home and my two roommates are out so me and the cats listen to Charles on the stereo. I just swill that wine and the poems are incredible, "I'm one of those uneducated minnows," truth and truth in drunkenness. That bottle on the porch and I open the window to pour myself a tall one. No woman, no responsibilities, I drink in solitude and maybe that's the best way.

I could go for a bottle of wine a six pack of beer a little whiskey a potent batch of mushroom and a couple of joints to round it off right now how I yearn to trip stumble into a new dawn revelation colors and the solar system to see to freak to surmise freewheeling and all this music, drugs make music heavenly Nirvana hellish beauty esoteric and I need the altered the profound the radiant blues the city jazz, "Hey pass a New York," the jokers' slyest meekest probable euphoria America birth place of the brothers' toil and Lennon anonymous Indian, time out, dance man, boogie child, love child all and I see the night in all her charms I could dime the eyes I could set the village on fire with poly love ah right Buddhist blood on the frayed flags.

Previous, incarnated by the walls and Egyptian rolling the babe the solutions, take a chance, the addiction is calibrated the chess game is too much, who out there will take of the fall, the old needle fall? Who out there will take on get it on? Columbus isn't the culprit. Spheres orbits and apogees, in a room alone with my charts in another lifetime, the maps the legends the longitude of escape… cadence of what? "Do you think I'm smart?" She just turns away. And what if night is all smog? What if there's a justice so brutal and impossible that to even exist is to drink metal with your Oz eyes? Maze. Television. Change all the names Baraka Amiri, Antholee, space age I tell ya, but where was I? insurmountable…and yet…go and…WAR. WAr.

That was a lifetime ago and now I'm just Dawn Peyote. Dawn Peyote. Funeral trip. Full moon. Coming down. Alone with my fantasies.

Dirge to the calf offer up thou's wine Ibex is hungry, today we flutter to the space of the Earth today we capture the polluted, straighten out the winding roads of Hades swill like fish the coffee and smoke and smoke, the corners are here, seek the bearer of ancient love, that's what Eji is: LOVE.

Come through the vortex still blind but a million words like bullets swarming around, horny flies, my odious skull my broken wheel my fractured arrow head my breast feathers. Looking for his child in the ruins and night winter night upon us some bird felt the crying and flew south. Curled up in the catacomb, witness of the poke, sting stung, I walked that park suicide raveling Serpico blues ten feet of songs on the corners.

A little sleepy.

Its time to take off the mask. Its time. I'm not Dawn Peyote, I'm Stewart Coates, a wanderer of rain a fiddler of night injunctions of moon and star gazing. And The Doll is gone and I won't reveal her true name, her true essence, her apocalyptic change. How the city gets high on my skidmarks, Stewart Coates man. But wait…now I'm Dawn Peyote again, I can see this is my destiny to be in a constant state of fooledness to be tripping to be high when sober to wonder over Bury My Heart at Wounded Knee. Daybreak comes with the fungus with the cactus Samsara windmills, Siberia, ocean heating up, I have come far to still the bishops' hope, to see a universe completely willed by anonymous fuck ups, its time to put on my mask again, flowers for Renaldo folk music for Clara my father singing wailing and the tooth of Jesus the breast of Joan the head of John all goes by the wayside in a bopping shroud. Hear the train, strum the waist for a new belly, ah its intense its linear lies, we go round and round the chips are piling up for Ann Glow and what's green is the hairshirt of Michael… rapid thigh movement.

So where was eye? Oh yeah new apartment new sobriety new chance however tenuous the it all of is, I buy mushrooms and raisons and have my drawing on the wall, its August and hot, writing short poems the folks come to visit on weekends. The Doll living across the street and we mingle our dales we drive to the store we talk but something about it just doesn't click maybe I need a claque maybe? I have my books and cigarettes and coffee to keep me juiced, its living, that's about all I can say. Nothing overt. Life of going to work and going to day treatment. The best thing is they wouldn't let us walk around the halfway house in bare feet so now in this situation I come home kick off my shoes and throw my socks in the corner and let what's left of my hair down. Scratch my balls pick my nose turn the tunes up, even dance occasionally (I'm a good dancer I have carpenter's legs). Delving again into alchemy, Jung, spangles and circles and dicks and Stick calls my new drawing Lizard Guy. Some of the Dharma on my coffee table. Library books on Kandinsky, Miro, Klee.

Oh I just wanna let go with my baseball cap on backwards and find the voices hiding in a viney heart, green vines crimson soul machine spiritual pump of chest chess, let go remembering the wind the tide the low pulse of sober joyful void, the empty is alive, I think of telepathizing with a garden of stones I remember how the stone of monkey liberty and the petrified bread the lukewarm beer when I crash I crash hard and even hints from God or Lucifer can't shake me as I spiral as I need the song the song Hairshirt or Isis or Like a Rolling Stone, say one word to me Doll: Desire. Let the waves of your eyes envelop me into a love madness…bury my hate finally…I can't see her as she is, I can't find the state of mind to curl and coil my ghost prayer, I can't live the lie, complicated lie oh now now what's truth when the animals are afraid of us?

Then comes the inexplicable vast bizarre Indian question. Who shall walk in this land awaiting a second religiousness who will hear the Howl who will pray in the face of any demon to outlaw the lie? Ah but the liar lies too to the too lied and back again, see the face molten ancient pagan in the park three Inians some wars don't make the front page but no less the victor go the noise. And me in a silent bubble. Prick the moon streets wandering Jews the lost tribe of Israel the Zep Tipi go on gentle your mind to the tune of a soft ground soft with rain soft even sophisms of grass and tobacco soft song, you must come down, you must find a mantra to quell the fascist industrial television nine to five suicide find oh find the old truths but where to look wear the book we're on the verge of some puppets' fringe, I can taste the whiskey, ah Don from Spain your story if only the other Spanish sold yours could have seen the witch as their sister. Burned the books boy. How and greeting and land and been too much, intellectual Inian with a white past bleached snowed coked in the melting pot of unblessed over blessed stew the slaves homes the slaves.

So I drink coffee and yearn for The Doll. Is she tying up? Is she cynical jaded riding that stool wave? I have no love to give I have stones I have words but nothing can bring me back to the holy origin, I've come too far and now the medicine lodge I have nothing to give because everything she believes in seems false to me. Turn off that god damn T.V. turn off the lights, lay on the floor dream of grapes.

Summer in the new joint becomes winter and The Doll and I are just friends. Ah but I can't resist maybe I am in love with her? She's on top of me and I can feel the heat through her jeans, the one time I didn't come I think she did. Water flowing from her, splash, the mystery of the female the Eve of horny Adam the snake of diamond delight the garden: Africa. Pale as winter we kiss and roll around, pale as winter we get dressed when its over and she does her hobby painting by numbers and I'm doing a drawing, a derivation of Pollock's Man and Woman In Search of a Symbol. Where the diamonds fall there in lies the circle and where the circles fall there in lies the diamond. Realm blue Never Mind the Bullocks. Surreal the sent like obtuse mail, we chat, we joke, we laugh, and then…

Down comes America. Pentagon and New York City. Another hoax. Bit. The snake cane revival. Jean tagging. I watch the news and stay home from work. Moslems aren't Egyptians. Don't go there. I'm not playing this game. Go where? What game? Double talk faster than a casino dealer. "Throwing sand on the floor." Read the Koran someday and let Mecca be real, just the name Mecca releases heavenly ghosts from my shimmering rust beaten heart, I saw the Spike Lee flick and I believe. Malcolm vision. Rimbaud vision. Dawn Peyote vision. The Doll vision. Babylon of American squandered wind, they say the answers blowing there they say every road leads to Maya and how.

Go to work sleep on the bus having nervous breakdowns on the job talk it over at day treatment.

She comes over we take off our clothes.

Keeping track of the moon vigil of locution and swept wept September.

I go over to her place across the street we make love on the floor.

Fallen in love with the women at work especially Shasha.

Together with the clovers the trains the voyage of atonement.

Purify Talmud's freedom with… stay up late watching T.V. and The Doll's reveilles as I fear the knife in the kitchen.

Walk to the gas station to buy cigarettes. The field by the funeral home.

Clean distillation of thought on the love song's truth, I come alive reading his singing mind, the wall is too high yet not to climb is to sin to sin the decades of possible forgiveness and now we're strangely strange and visitors exit the violet I can't see Orion I can't see myself falling but love sighs with looking jests with difference monumental forever man forever is here is now and how can I changling of the future how can I find you again?

Face to face she doesn't appreciate my music, she doesn't shutter upon my terrified gaze as I go into the abstract the seasons of schizophrenia.

"Sing my praises make me an admirable character," June and listening practical like rock the world makes pawns of messages the universe frayed.

Barefoot as I meditate on Shiva and read Ginsberg my walls covered with the soul of my drawing.

Waiting for weekends when I can stay as awake as the moon trying to decipher Joyce and living vicariously through the Beats

I found a feather in the leaves of fall.

I found a heart in the pulse of dawn.

Gray winter on us now, sundog sundown on the dale of my being.

Shaving and bathing glimpsing sobriety the fight is with myself.

The Indians to the top unless the voice, Henry's voice, is no more.

Tired in the chill the androgynous scarf and the gaze ambiguous tumult of sorrow.

Erica Campbell. Of course I'd like to be with her but its her choice. She brings back all sorts of memories, she taught me in math class when we ignored the egg head teacher drawing and cartoons and puns and the general absurdity of life, I laughed often and back then she was only known as Eric and she was a he, ah life what and where, how and when??? They threw away my reality theater painting and I'm back up against it, the wall or the swastika? With time and insight brings trainloads of fear, Erica will you teach me of Judaism? Will we smoke bombers and blast away the platitudes again? Will we be naked in the nest of crime? Lanky, you went down hard growing up and so did I, other side and knowing pain struggle sweat blood, what goes blood? Did you know the Aztec tomato? How it beats strangely in obtuse (you used that word a lot back when) mandolins of the scarred diner jalopy American bean faced cat like jump of Jim's wilderness night, how it succumbs to oval eyes and peanut heads and telepathy and Alice and Dorothy and The Doll, the past is a monstrous mountain big, big I say, me and Mardou flipping pages in the crimson electricity the myths boy…the word failed me and now I'm on the search even the trembling crucifix can't banish the fire I harbor within.

Burn love. Love burn. Indigo Girls know the crash. To be the Earth new in a fresh hazel morning mourning morning and where to come away long the away way is it the profile of Rrose haunting us now or just history forgetting it's saints? Quiet inbetweens who will be the next to kiss your holy breast? Erica I'd love to. Mystically. Celtic computers and songs so snake-like and the echo of proceed.

And maybe I'm the only one who'll ever read this.

To paint this situation.

Why why why?

How many Soft Machines will it take to unveil the chaos the fugitive the unghostly? I just turn away nostalgia and grieving. Callings like wildfire lakes of Mars after Hi School I read Joseph Campbell and knew not any tomorrow, drinking smoking drinking smoking dropping waking in the veins of sentient not know. You must understand? For we're both artists in a cooperate nightmare in a confined dementia in a rubber check institution, have empathy for my crude male phallic leer learning lusting for your tits hypnotized by your ass wordless in the plasm of potential fucking.

The moon laying down weekday nights of fish mystique, black cosmos and I'm holding the rust with the unbled hand of desire, holding the high while traversing utopian piano rapid swim in the sea of money flights, holding that Jack of diamonds while the jokers slip away under the table. How long this life is, how much longer? The fork in the road jars me from turpentine sleep from serpentine ladders all the while fuel and vernacular pow wowing in the stones of my face. Coming down again, hey but this time its legal with the shrink eyeing my bandana moments America you're either red or white or blue, I happen to be all three tonight but breaking china the bull the centaur the churches' mundane dust, all this and I'm not even married. Ah blah. Catcher of the wry. Jester once I was. Now its cold soup from wormy apple lodged in the receptors of a hooked brain my mind Jesus the night where He wandered sin desert circle to escape the plagues of Man. Who's out there? Who's roaming where once mammoths sang? Revealing longitude Bacon Pollock Stipe exit tent yall looking into the song's mirror, climbing out of reach sometimes and diving.

I go blurry.

Reckon.

We were once all blind, that's what the war did to us. Vibrations in a chemical temptress. Bait as we inch to the Dakotas, showdown man, dangle dangle, nodders' requiem in a cat's hood as the drumming takes us to a hellish source, one is many, entity of the carnival breakdown revivals funhouse skulls quake the cream of twelve inch dicks tricking twisting midnight and take a load off, we in the region of nectar and milk beer elixirs clowns fighting welcome to the scary coincidence the ban Che riddles the rosy injection the contact high of Set these western freak shows all flowery shit all rollicking on the stage of white paint and in his hat the mighty vagina.

Fast Dylan. A few words and then the abstract harmonica the train of sob the journey to a faraway protest. When we were kids we got excited by the idea of the band, rock-n-roll man that's the way to go blood, rolling from a poor slum building steam from the outlaw's valley to hold the no flag of truth, TRUTH, Bukowski in the back seat and all this time washing rapping over us, Dylan, I could go on but… listen for yourself.

I look hard at his picture on that morning that dawn that now of city warfare (war fair?) the homelessness creeping all around me, the militaries all fucking about, no sleep for days no food no booze, yet I awake to a further awake shrill hot mighty sun coming up and an umbrella for a head the crown long ago gone and the rulers (or is there one?) put the insect put the image into my veins into my boy lamb toy land. I know nothing.

Then there's Polly who doesn't look at other people's art claims then his chances of being more original are greater. And it works. Memory fog but his canvases are still alive in me and but I need another look, to multiply truth to rest on the rock and simply dig.

I could go back to all sorts of madnesses.

I could go back.

Now its Isis and his great love veiled by obscurity and insanity, I'll find her too, the town the horse the junkies the crowns the birds the wily spiked petals of sleep. In her out her of her because of her with her say her. Chaos. Oh brother I aint no blue blood, my tint comes from the sun not the bum and moonlight cascades half stoned on remembrance. Proust man. Henry and June. Layton with his Latin, fucking clown of the absolute. Cats crawl mystical. Jump that god damn bridge the fish just swim in bliss as I piss amiss you get the gist?

I see her sitting at the bar more lonely and drunk lonely than a orphaned dove, lovely and sad, should I talk to her? I stay at my end drinking a Jack and coke my eyes entranced by her red wine breakdown. I should get up on the bar and sing her blue songs back to her. Nursing these stars heart sleeve the bartender is fat and indifferent, I could see if she has any green chronic, its been a while since I've made Rasta love. She pulls her bangs out of hers and in this solitude I think of Visions of Cody spying into her ancient Indian soul, her cheekbone spirit, her back slumped as the smoke makes a Van Gogh pattern in the dive the hole the joint. The T.V. is on with sound off and jukebox is playing white trash music. Its closing time, she goes recedes into her violet nowhere as I stub out a choke and go home to my five remaining beers and a bottle of cheap wine, weekend, she just ghosts out the portal alone, ah and I'll twist the fate too someday.

I see her sitting under the tree her red long hair smoking a menthol. What have I done to see beauty in hell? Tempting the rebels with melancholy. I'm at a distant remove only my eyes only my essence only my world. She stares at the clouds and takes healthy drags, I can't get the nerve to go up and talk to her so I pull out a cig and light it up and wonder what her name is wonder what her true meaning is what her thoughts possess all the days all the premonitions her Buddha tree where is the inverted sin the friendly impossible snake? These love songs these sisters mad with lush voluptuous bodies and pennies and trains the park the city the town the birds wake me up and I realize what comes comes.

I see her I see her I see her! Erica the wheel belongs to us to us naked in the life of a dizzy garden in the blues of a hearty storm the rain man let the love fall like rain let the why prod us into the shinning heavens. Another song for us another battle cry of the pacifists from the sea of potential Utopia breathing heaving all the waves in other words time pouring into eternity stumbling yeah underneath you. When you hum, when you cover the stranger with Madame George flowers, when you see my heathen knees exploding like stars of One Verse City, when your voice holds the dimming horizon and my ears burning with want, when you breathe life into ashes, when you meekly turn your Eve gaze in my lost direction, all of this, when it happens it happens and it happens that I, peyote of the funeral dawn, peyote of weddings demon and angel, dawn of rising understanding, I am a sun chaser, I the veiled waiting in edifices, once more desire pointing into the heart of survival: Love.

What do I do in these winter wasteland moments? The Doll has found a new lay a new victim a new fly. So I'm alone after work or day treatment. Read a lot: Kerouac mostly. His Dharma his voyages his jazz his alcoholic bopping compassionate blues. Training the gypsies with the bowl and the cloth. I need an adventure, yearnings to go to Mexico City or San Fran. My tongue is ready. My crib. Oh solitude. I've been sober for quite a while now and I like it that way worming my way through books, head clear, drinking coffee at dusk with the lamp as my best friend.

Hold the flame tight dissolve into a million doors, mama, Johanna dances for all of us tonight, looking at the stones for solace, climbing the mountain to see a jazz new ocean. Rolling dice, distantly I can see them the wailers the howlers and what's left? What's left of America?

Siberia Minnesota and the great coat independence, Rubin as my godfather. Vaudeville, sit on the stool with your myths snaking around my pigeon skull, ice fire, unpromised. We have been far and we see with sparks with shadows the success of Rimbaud, his visions my god my gods, crumbs of a past century illumined by the wise assassin of time then veiled by the hawk nosed gypsy crooning beyond moon for a love true, a love essence a love of headlines untangling my pale blues.

In the hearth away from the streets, Coincidenceville not so bad now not so good now. Camels and the flags I tore it up. Leroy systems of quick. Dante man, let on, the hangover. In the hearth lip reading the sisters' Bible, I have had visions I have been fooled by love and hate. The bitter was sweet nothings on a table of numbers my snout revealing the Sphinx's nature. Malcolm. You will bleed till the tambourines scarve out the sculptures of India, you will hide in haste till the jazz discovers the closets all and the past like a house of cards, the Indians outlawed, just a dance?

"Your daddy is an outlaw."

Lowell and you reading Mexico City Blues. Best damn book I've ever read and with each new reading it gets more complex, obscure, diamond-like. Discourses with Allen and my bookshelf talks to the plant. The Doll Sara is our song,

Fusions of Tamara and now that I'm mildly sane the rope the pail the vessel. Fowl and electricity. Oh Doll tramp of nowhere speaking that rags and bones gospel come and open my heart with time on our side to the bells in an ominous neighborhood. The bike away for the winter.

Midwest where the ore is a memory, Midwest where the snow buries everything. I came out of the crib and to wait for the bus, smoking and shivering and sulking, ah but to see her face now…light years travel and thirty three years, fate to fate, vis-à-vis, séance for the babes of cheap beer, rituals for Black Elk. No god no gold, coins or eyes? Wind and my thoughts bend like leafless trees wonder who will mind find me in this town of farmers, grocery clerks, various folk, the bus arrives and the bus driver asks, "Are you Mexican?"

"I don't know."

Cassandra and the fourth dimension.

Cassandra and the fourth balloon.

Cassandra and the fourth beat.

Ophelia with a fifth.

Visions man, I can see us dancing together I can see us close close as flower and wind. I'm in love now. I don't know how to make it happen as the heart on my sleeve beats beats beats like a shiny moon amongst the madam stars. Hermes and all the hermaphrodites. The streets of revolutions. All this falls from me bitter in hope the mystery of wondering of fate of all the oblivious colors and we're sailing to an iced equator, we're building pyramids we're thinking of a million ghosts while dreaming of the gray subterraneans. I can see it now, I can open like a can of corn, I can stretch my arms clear to nowhere, I can sing for the cats an opera of grotesque desire, I can count the looks the glimpses the Chinese Henry the future I can look at the road and see my specter "piling up the death masks," if I say I love will you run away to a dangerous forest? If the sand of camels' mirage shows you the absolute will you forgive your father? Can I hear the sound of coming long distances ambivalent jesters and Salome and a headless priest? Can I come to you when my soul embraces the whole crazy universe and your nest as black as Egypt? The moon doesn't reflect our madness. The poets say nothing. Who will sing a soft ballad in this hard herded world? I will sail through every tomorrow to catch up to your ageless yen. City blocks and sidewalks, ways and rivers, this and that, today we propel an ancient creed to the followers of poly, to the hermetic roustabouts to the humming maids to the he of she and the she of he, flipping all the rules in a quest of truth. Bitten kicked down wailing by truth but still in love with truth. Truth will cast us aside and yet, yet it will lead to the dreaming dimensions of intention. If my spirit is true? Make it out to the platonic soul dance, pow wows stripping history of its primal lies, brother at the breakdown café, "You can't defeat the lion," he and we, soulmate and when will the return return? Lets shoot our soul load to the crimson redemptions.

To go against the priests in the calico night. My visions? Where was I? knocking down junkies with Egyptian dancing? Karma man you'd better believe, mama is tap dancing again and Johanna is hiding like Anne Frank. This war upon the land is like brutal farms of injustice. What do the Mayan codices say? The end? Would heaven devise all this treachery? And William S. sneaking around on yage knowing the word the image and I've become an old woman. Systems, calypsos, ravagements, the upswing, The Breakdown Café, the door between heaven and hell, baby blue ringing, some marriage, sexist to call her The Doll.

I'm a scientist. I planned like Marcel the crack in the

mirror the karma the telepathy the beat tambourine men long time long odds. In the hospital is where I told Peanut Head, "It has nothing to do with luck." He knows. Serpico in a hungry world.

I thumb my ass to The Breakdown Café to play with laws like toys, to be sure the epiphanies happen sometimes outside the temples, to take out the politicians, with one wisp of smoke to invert the signs saying No Stop, ah lazy Indian finds the nations boiling in technology, descending like a falling star into the young Jung anarchy, scholars in the storm pull up a seat The Breakdown Café home of denizens of The Dead Lecturer… "Your daddy he's an outlaw a loner by trade." It's a dump, they haven't washed the garbage cans since some peyote B.C., they haven't erased the swastika drawn in dust (the yins the yangs don't seem to notice). Its in the valley of a thousand oceans the valley of cats who keep time by stealing diamonds the valley of strong coffee cheap for the nickel and dime prophets of chance. I sit in the back and read Leroy Jones and Pousette Dart. The squares come in to get high off the shit stains in the can, I've spent fifty dollars in two days just to keep my carnival rolling just to appease my namesake. Then The Doll appears, blond to red but I discover and read her through the fog of illusion, homeopathy, sympathetic magic wagons we discuss, well she offers me her camel, "I don't like Camels, the cigarettes not the animals." Camels are the junky smoke. But she's gotta go off to score, she says she's on booze but I know what she really wants and its not me.

But what if there's no war and all my paranoia's for nothing?

Taking classes at The Breakdown Café, Irwin is the chief he's got an aura around him, not really electric more like a soft blanket of fire glowing through and his big thick Malcolm X glasses, entranced I let the sparks of Irwin's knowledge fall on me on my soul confusion. All over painting is the subject, The Breakdown Café is open to all and sundry, there's witches there's punks weightlifters hodge podge and Irwin is talking rapping singing and the history of art sparkles comes alive. "Pollock's early work is thought by some to be his most important."

The drugs are everywhere though I deal mostly in booze. Crazy daze. The floor is covered by gems by Anks by hands visionary, Rimbaud's thoughts on parade as the spell of realistic Sheila, her pictures, her long gypsy hair and rugged boots, the spell is time and how to transcend it how to plunge into the spirit sea how to forget the mind's eye before the jangling moon Creole of the clown and splattering on the floor dancing out a mama baby sugar tangerine trance the music is the redhead babe in her short dress (The Doll even then) like neon she opens my wine bottle she winds up my watch with an acrobat's slur.

I got more than I bargained for. I got a handful of temptations on that mound of brown. I got lost in One Verse City clinging to the night with a mouthful of prayers with Whitman and Ginsberg and Blake unable to assist my falling star cataclysmic running from shadows thirst as the outlaw in the inlaw on the strangers' repose, requiem, all the Black Jacks roasting that tar I stumbled through unnamable alleys and the coffee cosmos just rained down curses unfathomable on me, or was it Coincedinceville? One Verse City and Coincedinceville are kissing cousins and the moon protests all the lies in this witch hunt of obscurity.

So after the flood I make my second home The Breakdown Café.

Okay, okay.

Trances of the seers in an expensive suit the clovers the spades the hearts the diamonds, pulled from a snaky top hat. I could tell you about Jean who died in the Café on a morning when the military finally busted the four headed saints of ganja. But he, Jean, left behind a wealth of cosmology, notes from a silver underworld. And Jack with his Golden Eternity. The Breakdown Café man. They've all been patrons sooner or later.

So I take another sip of tea. Rotating Sirius, Dog Star. The Buddha letting his sensuality roam free. Twenty five thousand years and we're half way back. First fist time of jalopies and Grand Canyons and champions of the calypso abstract. You have to pass through the belly of One Verse City into a puppet of The Doll then snap the damn mother fucking strings to demented landscapes so as to land on your pawnshop belly. The saints making pacts with wolves, demented America, Joseph tied up and now the liberty just echoes from a post Columbus dream, hell even the rats go blue.

Its big. I haven't escaped. I've lost. I'm tingling like a plastic flower. I need wine. Its big. What's big? The poppy. The poppy has infiltrated the very core of Jung's collective, we can't go back, we can't drop the ball. I hunger for boyishness for a yonder truth plane I need to land. After the Ghost Dance we still run from the pale minions I want to run all the way to Africa. Or Dublin. Amiri took the cure but the slums blew him clear to Hades, crack pipes, whores, toxic potions by the crossroads.

The rose opus is our last chance last stand in the house of lint and armies, he wears it on his hat Serpico with war paint. Aretha and the truth. The possibilities the parlance the ragged hopes of dawn's peyote...I can't see it.

The young ones who sing love songs in the daggers of oblivion and chasing the sun, I bought the cigs, I guzzled the beer, ah but who said I'm young? Sometimes the years coil together in a unfixed zone of barely understandable crooning, wiping away the tears changing the cards. Egyptian tears made the nation thinking in the heart. Pig tails for Alice now. Rock painting and sun dancing can the road art the glance? Desert snake. Who wants the rattle who wants the way of lust? The dale is where I've landed, my my, fitting the pieces, rocking the descriptions on a June of witchcraft she releases demons within (me) she loves in the coliseum despite heckles despite the fence that says "die." Sisters now sisters now.

How bout a brief history of the now modern Lame Deer? Lame Deer's my shrink. Lame Deer is Erica. Lame Deer is Guy Anna. Lame Deer is The Doll's platonic main man. Lame Deer came to me by the Tubman railroad tracks that night I exploded into monkey consciousness, he didn't say much but he listened as I spiraled toward death in a deadly plane of D.T. in a deathly rapture where the white birds thought it was my funeral there on Shake Street, oh exodus, oh Christ moon of the violet shakedown I knew the score yet obliterating the multifarious multilateral Philosopher's Stone. But who said Jack is an eighteenth century love drunk poet? What matters? Lame Deer how old are you? Centuries, that's my uneducated guess, Lame Deer I've seen you dance and know you know Egypt your hands your frail thin body as I stood there drinking whiskey the great Indian curse whiskey and Lame Deer who will you baptize with the desert flower? As I stay up on all nighters blind shrinking in between breasts coming to I see you with your elixir coffee chanting down time chanting down the illusions, but, like Shiva, you create illusion as you remain in the old, Escher confused by you even, dance to the modern rock-n-roll in a ganja ecstasy the fumes flooding The Breakdown Café…bread under the bridge, beer by the factory, hookers lunging for the crack pipe, Indians deformed dehydrated in a cow's oasis, Amiri Baraka and you on the vast side far conjuring keys to invisible doors of heroin of cocaine, Dante's wondrous escape kins of Moses, any Valerio, any Malcolm, any disguise or lie now in Graffiti Land, take the subterranean desperations and fold the flag burn off the veils for they the lace of the Golden Bough will Will To Power till the dwindled corners of politics are no more. Lame Deer caricature of the white man, sliding thoroughly through the dimensions of this age, Long Journey to the End of the Night, Slow Train Coming, Shot of Love, Tropic of Cancer, The Brotherhood of the Grape, do you know my visions my colors my closet my problematical need for the dark naked stranger?

The Candyman digs Lame Deer we were watching T.V. and old Jim Lame Beer twisted to the waves to the vibes and the Candyman that Marvin Gaye addict of the smooth of the sensual nodded to me in the anarchy of poetry the rye rum subtle brotherhood of ethnic cadences and a complex plexus we dug, we dug, mutual, the Lame Seer crosses every border in these nights of head shop fry, these nights of boiling snakes. "Tomorrow we enter the town of my birth, I want to be ready."

Invisible emperors empty the chalice hissing in the bloody myopic destitute waiting waiting waiting for the raw naked sun to traverse a personal underworld and we greet each other as veterans of that Season In Hell fire man the lotus licks the cunt of Nut, the yellow gypsies of a lost Babylon dance for Geb, and I just turn down the light and write…

I lived for a year at the folks' house after hi school, I slept in a big double bed and lamp beside me, well I only snoozed on half the bed with books on the other half. I had a dictionary to help me through Sexus…the voyage of learning the orgasm of the written word the intellect of secret natives, ah I read and read, I also had Bukowski's War All The Time which you don't need a dictionary to read. I was going to community college failing a math class and through a succession of flops I wound up an art student. I remember my brother Stick coming into my bedroom in the basement and me making pyramids out of plato, oh and at the school I looked intently at Van Gogh, imitating, derivating, and with the discovery of Jackson Pollock I was in the ocean, I was the initiate of time and space and ritual and mystery. But that double bed, I'd ebb out poems with the folks watching T.V. in a room next to mine. I remember being fascinated by the word ebb. I remember the Chagall book Lame Deer shoplifted for me.

If she comes back I'll eat her, the only one to ever call me a soulmate. She is the goddess of meth the contradicting cheating humorous beautiful love fuck of all time. Calling from Ant Man. I can see her returning with our child. I want her to return. Badly. You just can't write off a soulmate so easily. She's in my blood she's in my questioning heart of hearts, together we lit the candle and stripped and our eyes piercing into our eyes we fucked and fucked and when I went down on her she swallowed me up into her womb, in her womb I've been living all these years as the police chase us to unknown perimeters, I play chess in her womb, I say clandestine prees in the shroud of her water and come to the gods of chastity. I think I slipped out when I jumped off that bridge, hell she was rolling a joint, I should have stayed with her and got high but Leatherface had the morphine waiting in the castle of sad sack. Since Zen I've been looking in every corner and all I find is my forlorn reflection.

The lips of Judas now no more, echoes of the child's moon, the crucifixions in the ballad of believing, and a thousand monks marching to the song's end. I have come to say love, love, its possible knowing the telephone doesn't ring, The Doll went to a new carnival on the outskirts of One Horse, and me well I have forgotten nearly The Ghost City where I jangled the curses in a black box in a mystical come…so why is it that the war is still waging?

The ribs of Moses now no more, reverberations of the child's horoscope, the crucifixions in the fallout of denial, and a thousand monks swaying into the death see.

Where the roses bloom.

And synchronized by the flight of the crow who gave Egypt its first taste of divinity I fall into fall, winter beckoning in the Indians' angel like exile, fall into fall into winter, deep winter of unfold: innocence, words on the edge of mind, schizophrenia. You want to hide in that clamor? You want to fight the silver desert in a rim of seasons unfathomable? I can't fade like I used to I just see that long night journey to its end, to its criminal untouchable laws in the land of Breakdown. The Don is hooked up into the electricity spastically chanting a Jewish homeless mantra, I saw him after staying up all night and walking the streets early morn by the gas station thin as a pencil and I shuddered at the hushed fates of poverty.

So I've been dizzy lately and I ask The Doll to drive me to the hospital. We wait a while then the doc sees me they take blood pressure and blood and ask me questions. "Dizziness is a black box," he says then gives me some pills, suppose a dories, "These go in the rectum."

Back in the car I'm rather frightened by the idea of

shoving that shit up my ass, "They're trying to turn me into a queer!" I half yell to The Doll.

"Its weird I know," she replies.

"I can't do it I'd rather be dizzy than raping my opus, fuck it man," and I throw the pills out the window and light up a cigarette.

We go into her pad, she turns on the television of course and plops her fat ass down on the anonymous couch. I'm pacing the room. "Sit down," she says to me. So I sit down next to her, nothing else to do but start kissing. I turn off the television and take her by the hand into her dark bedroom. I let myself fall back on the bed, but, she's rearranged her bedroom and the bed now goes north south where previously it went east west so as I fall there's nothing to catch me and the back of my head lands on her hamster cage, I really land into it hard and I'm laying on the floor laughing hysterically half crying. I get up and lay next to her on the bed, "I can't go all the way," she tells me but by this point I'm just happy to be alive.

Within the rooftop of my mind, beyond the heart's sight, over the above and under the below you and I we'll retreat to a soft bed to a clover to a now so now the future will burst stars Sitting Bulls and Paris there for us. The drums start the glances and love long roads trying to predict a flowery arrival, so many in the forest running (no religion) so much now that waiting for time the eternal Jack and early from a point's departure I have seen you. I have seen. You. Bisexual and leaning on a totem, radiantly young leaning on the streets' jive, before the finger in the mouth singing for the birds of exploding morning, I have seen all this and know the Kaddish (just one) and how things can waver like neon like peons and I have my hot tea. Unknown. I can wishful think she's migrating to my confused cell my everlasting doubts my catapult bloodenings my father's white mask, she will strip me of all, she will help me leave behind phantoms broken mirrors novas of my vein's despair collapsing in shuddering with out baking the brain with soft breasts…ah now, now, now that the Book of the Dead has played itself out my journey the scar of spirit the sole of soul and the dreaming, one dream ends another begins, one seam bends another chagrins. Subterranean. Mardou. Listen closely to the wind of four seasons and notice my billowing sadness then take heed and dance down the festival of sobriety, oh young one with your tongue speaking in plums…

Sad Halloween tonight, all the costumes just bring tears, all the lies befall and that damn train fathered the sorrow, whistle whistle, and Whitman waits in his grass for me to sing his words however magic, or, Blake mystically evoking the weeping chants of tomorrow, sad Halloween tonight, and coming again to the wild wild mask of shapeshifter chameleon denizen Corso witch fourth dimensional personal apocalypse, canyon inside, knife inside, fork in the road, "run to meet the world," levitating frown, where down doth lead the foreign want. Sister sister. Connecting here with there and my moon room tomb and drum roll Roach Watts, connections of the untamed no weddings no rings no white lies, just desire alive like an archetype like a hieroglyphic soul patch, thousands upon thousands weep for the destinations of crime of injustice of clattering flags in the heat in the wine of Jesus, but who wants to remain without love? A world of baggy baffling illusions. Give me a glimpse, give me sight and hearing on that blue bus on that ship that sails where no storm occurs only Tarantula only Allen only Simone. "I shall be released." Hop on the wagon and stay there. She sings and her voice trembling the weight of growing up growing old then at last simply growing like Grant prophesized.

Filled to the brim with words new woe new words from Allen's chest. Open. Open to the shaky snaky flaky Gnostic conflagrations of desire of new generation of ancient generation of X and 0, the opus of seeing through the Vast Trap…liberation man. It comes with frightening scar-like omens to the Shaman of Judio Buddhio traversing like a thunder dandelion coming to me through the dissolving walls of eternity. I read and read, its there all all Allen, and once Bukowski was it, once Bacon was it, but sooner or later you have to explode like a fish truck you have to refuel with the vernacular of the demon's last round and the skull tastes of water now where before the whiskey killed the angel within. So now I recollect and cook noodles. So now I smoke only tobacco. And I'm waiting for my senses to catch up to the wisdom of Grub Street.

Fate deals a lethal hand, on courage with fire darling honey sweetie take me to India or Africa to play the Joker on a anarchist's gamble, flush, straight, three of a kind, all this, and some folks don't slow down lazy what a way to play. Fate deals a bizarre hand, drowning like a cat wily in the dirge the mystic drone of the Irish universe, fate deals and Sinead croons raps struggles sweats "don't let it die just hold back the night…" Destined in the suffering inevitable drops the dales the terrain the very Earth and that Breakdown blues can you hear it? I'm out here now on a wheel of prayers searching perplexing the pit of deep turn around, turn around the despair turn around the voids of disbelief and I don't do and don't don't. What did Marcel say? "Living is believing." I can't take that philosophers' competition, not Marcel's, but namedropping into oblivion historical ghost. The mighty dealer at the mystery table the score is different for the clowns and the kings, night and day, year and moment, peyote and booze. Fate deals a feminine possibility. Fate deals a white nigger preaching a dead lie. Fate deals love in the folds of Shiva's belly. Fate deals compassion beyond the shit of factory warlock American society. To go through, to go through that feline door, Egypt, or Dakota, and the brother asking a revolutionary question like Coltrane and Sun Ra, like the invisible future where the seer asks the mirror the looking glass asks Alice and Joyce to fold, fold for the secret, fold for Dublin, fold for Israel, fold all the wars into real love into real Russian landscapes of lineage and the rage diminishes, the rage it dissolves and what's left is eyes in hands, minds in hands, hearts in hands, fish in oceans, Christ uncrucified, hand of lamb, hands that touch the sister planet with news of a esoteric reality, completely waiting completely patient for the human waste (race) to come around, to not be jealous of the system's still born money, to not be ramming home the misguided prick of monopoly, and finally to be reborn into a shining heart thought, so there.

What's to be found? Here? I can only live on songs for so long songing longing I press my lips to the reflection stellar the nova pessimisms the blood's choice. That moon full blooded circle of origin and the orgy of the Milky Way and the believing freedom fighters of last stand trenched in One Verse City drinking beer smoking spleefs and the laughing comes from afar to daughter the man, to father the valley, to own the spirit of timelessness and clutch the hellish flowers of truth, of this it can be said.

I have a new muse. Priest Bi on the wee small Pete. I take the Blue Bus to the dumps of Eden, I sail on the U.S. Splintered to the ruins of Washington, I fall into the plastic false liberty of slave owners, I breathe the rancid atmosphere of cancer Henry predicting the execution of timelessness, I have gone to the violet fungus nights and been fooled by clowns of the university, I take the sacrament as they put my grandfather into the planet's cunt, I've seen my cat on

a morning bursting with dream. I have a new muse: Priest
Guy in the steal away. Hide that disorder, bluster that damn
dawn, fill the chalice with dust. My father eating a sandwich
at the Breakdown Café as the sweep swept the sweeper into
out of and how the hell to survive Babylonian coincidences
crash crash ha its going to be a starry newspaper to tell us the
war will never end, the war will forever crush our hearts in
astral decay. My schizophrenia my ties to a alcoholic world,
high time to fasten onto nothing, even the snake respects
nothing for Buddha took the storm by the rain and smiled
from the nineteenth dimension.

We never said a word to each other all those years of
school high and junior and yet I dream about her love her
wait for her in fate's wildfire, this sleeping I go back to the
time coming down on acid where the houses on the hill
pill hill looked like a cheap prison a sad television ghetto a
morbid carnival, this is where she lived this is where she'll die
this is where my spectral mind visits shut eye phenomena,
I won't name her but she comes to me in my rosy sleep like
Sad Eyed Lady and me farming the Lowlands the sickles
the cotton the flesh of fire the candle the sandal who are
you to haunt me my bachelor nights three blankets thirty
three years old and living in the nation of No Chance?
"You only live once," she wrote. I hope that's not true. Love
goes down like Atlantis. Memory Babe they expect you
to marry a doctor. And what or who am I to kiss your
wealthy strait? "No man cunts," as I paint in the garage,
my god the universe thundered nightmares wakan wakan
if only I could've reached your dancing bed your child's
pillow and the possible romb of love making. As I said we
never said a word. The school system is segregated, the rich
are "advanced." The rest of us roustabouts just dread the
employing thiefing hours in a ghost fix, storming the time
clock with the come of money. Ah you have soul but no guts,

you should have grabbed me by the heart and kissed my everlasting silence my harmonica mouth my sailor chin my Greek histories my slouching indifference, you should have just said hi instead of all that turmoil in your ducking eye. I could go on like Rimbaud but my folks threw out most of my romantic shit. But if you ever read this: I love you: I dream about you and I don't know why?

Some bridge man. Pushers of coincidence Tarot of coffee shop running Corso of surreal streets New York City who blasted reality with a hit of acid, now the history comes time, now the man comes water and who will rag the ragged Dawn? Calling the brothers so many accidents so many bridges so many premonitions I go crazy like a black dog listening to Prince, crazy the things conspired to blue ball Antonious, I'm alone. Writing the scene to purge all this voodoo. The Breakdown Café I flipped the chief the bird I wanted to sleep under the bridge and sell my plasma for twelve packs of monkey piss. Manifestos, verbage, brand new suits, beautiful Negress, alchemizing the constellations with grapes of soul juice "the blood of the gods," sitting high the bridge the flung body in space out of time land Jack land run westy run glow Paris glow, but I survived even if the shell shocks me into falling flashbacks…

We're all slaves to time.

Michelangelo at the A.A. meeting.

Some miraculous time rite. Visions. Speed. India. How hollow far the descriptions honey I can't tell anymore? What's an act and what isn't? Lightly I tread ethnic churning the flower wheel of reality, I'm happy for the Yin I'm happy for the Yang. Time Rite Boy his skull abstracted his soul in a storm his spirit thirsty for some answers. Who are you? If he's for real he's a piece of shit. Love goes down like Hamlet. And Dawn Peyote is swimming in a replaced vortex, a shallow web engulfs the light the probable litanies just don't matter anymore, Christ doesn't matter no more. The time rites are far too hellish for the commercial ready made shit on a stick failed revolutionary savior. Jesus failed man just look around.

Criminals man, "they outlawed the Ghost Dance," and we take the secrets with us everywhere like Allen saying we know everything or Jung plunging through the ages searching for one more vision one more crazed heavenly demonic saint of the great Maybe. Sacraments of delusional Satori which way to the Breakdown Café? Which way to grim beauty? The mystique of the bare gazing weary into a Scorpio mirror. The loss of Isis your partner in crime dead Poncho Virgil can't even tell the difference now. Nexus of reckless again. The journals oh they tell of things language can't hide, the language oh they tell of things life and lust strife and trust can't bye. There in the river the fish gods dwell any East of chance and Mallarme says yeah yea soothsayer oblivion smithereens and bait. Murderous possibility. Suicidal plause the protest the jump the Jack. Diamond sic in the falling circles the copping of extemporizing gargoyles. "Love is a dog from hell." Love is a cat from Egypt. Part the seas, trace out the dusty relics of Cassady, precision and a meter diminished, I gave Kerouin my Last Tango In Paris pictures, tomb, tomb, tomb.

I've seen the parade for a wile now I know the masks I've untold myself several times various ways its nature and the mothers are bald and the breasts include the respect of animals lemurs and the more mysterious it gets the more truth mixed like alchemy's revenge (ah revenge is the wrong word) like alchemy's shivering clandestine scopes of unwittingly serving the free coffee at the Fakedown Café the truth mixed to the tune of Robbie Robertson swallow the tooth and nail don't hide in the cross come out come out today to play once ye have stepped off that Drunken

Boat the sky is ours and stirring ghosts on a train out of One Verse City, ye must leave One Verse, the laws are too old and don't measure up to now Buddha now tulip now New Orleans now…

Long night long night coming to an end. Ecological studies in the harmony of despair, "Try whistling this," and the long Egyptian night how I've traveled through warring dimensions wrestled the snake swallowed Sirius lived in a dark dark how I've sailed for the truths of I Ching or the sense of some female female incarnation the she of Jesus hiding in a howling mountain from the coins of bacchanal politics…twice. So in this long night I search for my mouth for my finger to place it in like a trumpet Book of the Dead and these stick figures of saints prophets Francis and birds understanding the propinquity of moon. Seasons of strangers. Impossible tongues. Ceremonies of light await us on that mound of ancestor in that river of time. Long night and Egypt echoes in the trains Egypt reverberates in the retrievable church of space of time of lion of elephant. I can hear the singing the ballad settles me. Guesswork. Tired but knowing it's a new beginning. I can see the chance dangling in the dream catchers of fate I can feel the gamble in the streetlamps' gloom. Winter. The Doll gone. My horse invisible. Down. Sing a rueful tune my ears are in my belly my heart on a dramatic arc we love each other we emptied the room with naked fire. What poisons the rites offer up, what implacable desire it takes to shake off Babylon, what new incantations the clown will have to prepare in his laboratory of tears to somehow the never. Seems like silence sapphire keys the believing gesture of Indian finish and out there in the long night hailing an encroaching Ra believe it's the beginning relying on a drunkard's Hunger we all have passed through. Its an Indian experiment what with the booze of Main Offender delirium tremors, dying on the ground, sighing conscious, safe for a nearly morning, rise sun rise.

The Child Proceeds. Come out of the sea. Black moon black star on the farm of alchemy. Clown dog trots and resurrections occur. The holy pyramid, the corn, and Lame Deer slopes his brow in quick agile sight. Wheels and flowers, chessboards and the yellow woman of no self. Did they want me to be an artist? Setup? The Child Proceeds as Jackson said. All this abstract all this fated to all this and the coyote night hails me in its reflection, social values and bunk stereotypes, ah this is all in Ant Man but I keep training the closet bewilderment to a desert flower sunrise the windmills mentioned and the Ovarian Trolley skips to the dance of Ruby Read. I call on you to show me the habit of hares in a nationalistic funk, fallout, dribbling the ball looking for a burning soulmate to scorch my spirit. Glancing into the future, I'm happy here, "an intense calm," so the gold is gone, flushed. Some difference for the homeopathic chiefs. Now the angels sing of falling to never land to never orgasm the moon. Angel angel. Craving kisses and mammoths. Through the mystery The Child Proceeds what fracture what locomotive of near what Drunken Boat hath shed its enigma skins?

I woke up in Coincidenceville and I had Jesus in my eyes, weird eyes of despair and frenzy and I caught the bus to One Verse City, when I arrived there were protesters protesting medical people experimenting on animals and I thought of my dad who does that for a living. I wouldn't like to be experimented on so I accepted a pamphlet by Hitler's network of ugly modern buildings. Not to be locked up again. I go to group and Kerouin has on a short skirt with striped panty hose. "I thought we were gonna talk about what our favorite color is," she says with a gesture of jester and a wave of violet swarms over me.

And I'm in my hometown eighteen or nineteen reading Tropic of Capricorn carrying that book with me everywhere reading wondering exhilarated by the language of New York nobody Henry. I take the book to Chicago and in the traffic jams I read, "Sleep on father, sleep on, while we boil in terror." The abstractness of it like walking through a thick jungle of coins buildings foliage women clowns visionaries workmen and my dad glancing at me occasionally and I've entered a new world the world of intellectual spirits and the questions more important than the answers. Eyes bleeding with joy, mind menstruating with roustabout gold, the read fix…it really started with S.E. Hinton's Outsiders then Salinger then Vonnegut then Bukowski but I always go back to Miller, sermon on the mount Henry preaching that soul juice on a allowed dime of neglect.

Vision seekers in the plight of America peyote trance trembling realities naked lamb of justice the lunar the land is "an Indian thing" and we roll and remember the tragedies Charlie Parker ah but he's alive in my boom box the Beats alive in my eyes as I read and the liberations the expansions of compassion, its all a breathing sensual history and me existing and able to dig appreciate wonder fume and still my heart of atomic fear beats flows dances and somewhere out there in Time Rite Bardo the masks the acts the confusion it will all resolve itself in a cosmic conclusion…where the stomach begins. The only lonely one writing in a Valentine haze for a love to whistle true. I went down hard but I don't want to repeat the past. Hey light bulb nose, hey long hair optimist, hey holy woman, hey jester of the heal, lets all feel the Earth, respect the sun, adore the moon, make angels of the desolation, sing an honest ditty, let the plants be free, just wander to a new heart revelation in this flower of empathy in this flower that touches the stars. My plant sways to the ballads of Nina of Dizzy of Eastershirt, to go back pain sweat struggle regrets inner blindnesses inner cries for freedom. What's inside you now? Prayers? Justice? All the colors conjured by the Pablos of uncertainty? When you take a new name when you crouch from the police when you taste the ambivalent Eden chance, you'll know it's a long road to heaven, keep walking thumbing trudging dancing reading. (sip of water) Corner man, get out of the corner and see the brutal truths man, they'll kill you in that malnutrition corner, they'll let the D.T.'s slam you into silver oblivion. The truth isn't given silver spoon you have to set yourself on fire with reason with hope with balloons of insight. You might make it, you might not. I'm here and alive for now, which is the hand I've been dealt. I can't take all the wisdom of the world and throw my dreams down a sullen vain, drain. I want a low heaven, a lovely garden, I want to be like the stone cat of Africa who knows when the morning will break who knows Malcolm's vision even a prison can't delude. I tell you its gonna be okay. The violence of actuality, the impotence of half seeing cloud gray wastelands and fossils, replaced with a shaky love hope a "belly sweet" union of halves, half female half male, integrate and meditate, the world is okay.

Oh peyote child, my god, nervous with visions past, hoping it's a mirage, hoping cops aren't cops, hoping Grant is a Rasta priest. Fire and vision Rimbaud's confession all the fish Jones sin, I entered Job's curse with amnesia curled about my legal sight and shoveling snow and Paradise Lost the jail horny for me and my criminal thoughts. Peyote man it can take you down to the smallest dimension of thumbnail obscurity, it will lead you to a red Buddhism in a white land in a white romb, it shall arrive Black Elk and all on the doorstep of money starched ravaged untimed unforgiven merciless till the autobiography spurts needles and camels, one puff, one night, shudder for the love lost.

Out on the prairie the silence is deafening. Effigies elegies on that Motherwell moon, fantastic female cosmos on that Season beyond death, when will she open up the heart tomb of my heartstring cobweb rambling impervious odious claptrap void soul soul? When? And the harmonica Ka's the pyramids the pictures the tangled hairshirt of linear pain, sage of the songs sage of the eternal rain sage of the billowing fall. Finnegan done gone down in a hurricane of words, what does it mean? Whitman blew Whitman blown. The answer guesses she crazy she laugh she reveal she love. Just like the time in the autumn and the peyote confused me till I hid in a taciturn removal of silent love, silent love, love silent. I could introduce you to the genius of telepathy African by the bar where Marvin Gaye is getting it on. Some priest of the high water ballads the this of catacomb night and I'm alone chasing zodiacs chasing a dim reflection in the glass. I could crack up forever. I could stand underwater. Why that ship in the desert? I take another sip of hot tea as Feb. valentines anonymously "if tonight belongs to you then tomorrow's mine," pick the heart from spring's heavenly tree, the tree of life, the flower of justice, the hell of ignorance. So old the Earth is. Cast off cast out, we move zoo-like in the brazen laws seers and drunks, my demon masquerading as a saint, my angel drown in the cantankerous tongue of bitter destiny. Hold fast to the orphan mulatto's final word. The drum is blazing and foreseeing a Black Spring, this sky, this map, this legend, Lee back from a newspaper dead, Allen sucking the spider in a cosmic bed of experiment, and Jack waiting for me to write a romance novel. Its just the prescription talking now.

Clarity. The flower of justice, just us, find the bouquet, hide till you can talk straight. To care for a lonely moment like Celtic songs in a cold valentine, in a punk love song, to care for the lost souls oh Babylon takes it's toll the lost souls of ubiquitous torment falling that booze spell the nights like rancid hope, I've come out Drunken Angel Lucinda to the other side charity, hope, perseverance, building the soul thought to a farm town of friendliness. Smoking straight drinking straight missing The Doll's exploding cunt and me languid in my love attempts. Neither respecting her or…what? Being fooled in the chronic motley Breakdown bells and sand? Being fooled like a dog's cane? Oh its either here or there but now expunging my beer whiskey spleef past to a new cane I gather up the spirits of Innocence on that yellow train to Somewhere, the bird boats cutting through and beyond Marcel's Milky Way. I need poetry, revolutions, trances, I need to stare into the fish's mind and find a brotherly repose. Don't get in the car with Time Rite Boy, Bardo Thodol can wait. And Kerouin said she never wants to die.

The Time Rite Boys, you can go mad in that liar's season, you can trip and fall all night long to the bandana chiefs' ragged sly humorous deadly grunting reactionary maze of Food Rite of Drug Rite of Homelessness Rite of Jack Daniels Rite of Rap Rite of Upsidedown Flag Rite of etc. rite on and on. I am Dawn, I can remember my nights now. The Time Rite Boys are starting to hate me but I'm safe here cooking spaghetti. Time Rite Boys go fuck yourselves. Drown forever. Forever possible. I have returned to a flower of justice out there behind The Breakdown Café, you gotta dig, dig this bud, dig the Queen of Primacy in her blue Z. representatives of the motion to speak. I can't even hear my own voice. Baby I need to know schizophrenia will it follow me like a devil's deal? Exulted tired beat ready ragged sober high trigger of orders compromising cheater damn shate shat shine swell but the swill lives in a concentration camp, lock up your ass, question till the high goes lower than a happy worm. Exiled I don't care.

Get the funk, get into the rap's insides and shake the golden Earth. Ah religion at The Breakdown Café. If only Buddha could whisper sweet Nothings into the ear of apocalypse, The Artist raving get out of esoteric wars and find a sensual justice, respect of Aretha, the world hymning jiving rejoicing to the drums of Egypt and Spain all the wile this Indian Prince Adam the gods have given us the Poly let us spangle the beliefs, one or two? India created sex, Africa created the heart, Indians created the wrists of mystery, and I have created sobriety. My delusions...what if they're true? Does it even matter anymore? I have spurted with morning, I have shrunk like a modern day alchemist into a scruffy hermaphrodite, I will arrive into this day and love myself, surrendering to the thought: Emptiness is my name. Let the yin yin and the yang yang. My tongue spake in primal lips of, of, of, lets create a new religion. Eastershirt has his language. We need to water the cities we need to water the cities.

Something beautiful is happening. I can feel my heart swelling in fish bird desires human androgynous soulful desires. Write a love song for dreams' mysteries where I chat with her intelligent beauty. Ah she stood close to me this afternoon. Ah she has a child within her or a wine belly bread and hiding Malcolm X specs. Something wondrous is happening, I hold the lone flower of justice hard life redeemed and the hearing crowds in on the powers of story, folly, heavy love, a flowing redemption, a rising sight of rising truth. Keep the rolling days in your cat arms as I stumble clumsy the trusting schools of swim.

Sue renders and I haven't eaten animal for a while. Something miraculous is happening like the moon reading my mind in a month's cycles. Climbing the only freaky wine dance naked bangers flesh on soul and soul on spirit, a strange life, a strange fire, a strange within, ah I'm turning inside out and finding a thousand lilies riding the violet night's gleaming streaming oceans of every incipient desire, every incipient longing. I could sing for your gypsy dance I could croon for your tangerine chance my muses encircling entrancing enfolding and a different existence awaits to sag and go soft: emotionally spiritually…so far on a cosmic train.

Surrender. Surrender to the female universe swirling in the very heart of justice. Choices line up and look with the autumn eyes of locomotion look with the joker's indulgences and the stars will wait till the rebirth regenerates in this Eden in this Utopia in this Indian land of consequence.

Something unintelligible something frost the wind whipping the streetlamps the highway the parking lot and me inside lazy writing for time's lay zombie zooids and future galloping with a water horse on the strains of man. Should I love you? Too late. I love you in all your beautiful dementia, I'll smile through the carbon tears I'll run till Christ reveals his true dark face I'll strut in the cities like a cool priest of voodoo and the witchdoctors and the lawyers and the doctors will bop and sway to the ganja sweet breath of baby baby baby.

Recipient of sisters' obstacle, I paint the sky blue everyday, receive me sister…for I know not what I am but this erotic skeleton this crazy brain blitten smitten all the rain all the planets all the moons all the stars tonight revealing dancing justice. The sections fall, Blake sees angels, Allen rhymes man love, I on the quick star see anew. The new the now the node. Sister take me as I am with a marijuana crown. With television wine traversing the cold country sister brother sister sister. New words, "absolutely modern," glimpses of the horizon through eyes of water the city where I ran wildfire paranoia drumming on the bus all this and just a simple taste will do.

Yeah man me an Lou would paint in the basement, south Minneapolis, with our beer and weed Lou's stretched canvas leaning against the concrete wall, my shit on the floor ah la the great Jackson. High and drunk listening to tunes, the spiders and their webs, yeah man those were the daze. Lou was heavy into the figurative, clarity with slight fantasy, his theme the boyhood of Avalon the boyhoods of sad heavens. Me? I was into the idea of movement, Marcel's simultaneous concoctions, it was around that time that I tried heroin accidentally. It was around that time also I read Stephenwolf and the I Ching and what else? But painting was all we had really, that and playing cards on the wagon wheel table and consuming vast bottles of wine. What were the paintings about? What were we about? Artists? Community? It's a waste of time to try and explain a painting, but we were both autobiographical painters, our life was our subject: the streets, the isolation, the existentialisms, the beauty of religions various, and finally towards the end madness. My madness and Lou getting sucked into it too. "I started to feel like I was going insane," Lou said later. He painted a brilliant picture of a young man sitting on the wagon wheel table with a incongruent shadow haunted bewildered fraying the edge the egg of sanity. I invented around that time the realization and conception of Coincidenceville, there was just so many coincidences happening in the carnival of a strange opaque translucent city town village and to go down and to go up...the booze starting to wrinkle and set in the craziness the loss of jobs, no food in the kitchen, spending your last cent on booze instead, riding Mr. D.'s train to nowhere, oblivion, Hades, Tingle Town.

Well this is the end the end of part one. We have seen the dawn, the new day upon us rankled by thoughts, this bone night long, but here is the sun and the crows of early afternoon with messages of the ancient language. We have been fooled and followed the moon to highways of feedback and catscan. The lotus of tomorrow shrouded in white now the snow and the train that knifes through the town day. There are no horses to ride blindly to the windmills of mummers' last act just cars and smog. Dawn Peyote with the pills for sanity with the apartment home and working part time smoking a thousand cigarettes and the occasional yen for wine or beer. We'll have to go back and study the past again, read Bury My Heart At Wounded Knee, Black Elk Speaks, Lame Deer Seeker of Visions, we'll have to probe into the heart of vision and weed out the truth we'll have to write the consecutive divides in divine safety. "Everybody's been burning in a free land."

The media paid off like a sullen car salesman the president drinking the milk of Sunday brother bought you off hyper war mantra and the rich behind him the claque the façade the uselessness of believing in Jesus in this land of oil addiction "and the poor carry the living on their backs and the poor grow more poor." Its only the wealthy who hold the strings and me on the sidelines barely caring barely Buddhist to let it go if they're stupid enough to believe in red white blue let fall, let 'em fall, a soldier fate, a dure sole bringing together a community of lies and I won't die for you pale face, I have painted your flag brown, brown for the bloods that live on the street brown for the red that hold the secret revolution…the booze obstacle and how the president's addicted to cocaine hell he can't even cross his legs his prick so big his brain so small. We need ego breath and mind breath and why do you hide female where are you female to append some truth to this dirty vulgar obscene machine of war? Why not change everything?

Cat Man said, "If John Lennon would've lived society would be different for the better." And I agreed yearning for Lennon, Marley, Malcolm, and all the unknown Indian saviors. Society? Money is the windmill we all chase and its illusion is just as ridiculous, sad, tragic. Society? Society?

The end of part one which tapestries back to the beginning and the artist's quarters riverrun and pirate patch. I was. I was.

...END OF PART ONE...

DAWN TWO.

Wagon wheel falls off and the traffic that blind child running with the wind through the woods across the playground. It starts off in the morning, bright sun and childhood it all comes back and after a few years in One Verse City I move back to... where The Breakdown Café is just beginning to roll. Put on Charlie Parker and open up Old Angel Midnight or Finnegan's Wake, I fail to understand as the witness trees come alive in that hydrogen ball of Feb. weary, show me a sign out here, show me to the Mama's pearl: visions, delectable cunt, loneliness quelled. I should call her. Tip. And crawling beyond the hot water of days past I hold my cat true love, I come home after suicide to eat gallons of cheese and lithium and in the fall I move outta my folks' house into my own crib.

Stick is with me and it starts off with a simple beer and I'm up and running and four shots of whiskey in fifteen minutes, first night of independence, I'm roaring with the tide, that whiskey bam! Boom! Two in the morning I throw up on a canvas. I tell Stick I think he's my dad.

Basement. Get a job at a grocery store. Three bars, two liquor stores nearby, I go back to Lushville drinking, spending my S.S.I. money on expensive beer and whiskey and wine. Smoking too, Stick.

Stick comes home and has some good green we smoke

up and I'm as high as a Jack of Diamonds delusion, oh I hide in the basement and all the loser thoughts come crashing, what do the neighbors think? I listen to music on green chronic and its quite beautiful but I'm relieved to finally come down.

Stick goes back to One Verse City and the war the heroin war the crack war and I shattered by showdown damn shadowy time I drink I drink I drink. Fallen angels and choosing one, one savior one Gabriel one someday, casting the spell of failure on these fiery shoulders raw crawling in the Silver Village rum dispatch to the Ka's of mantra. Dodo bird blues and the rum silence inside my neo plastic skull. Paint and drink, write Ant Man and drink. Do anything and drink.

Ecstatic night: Mallarme and wine two in the morn, reading and reading, T-Bone just a few blocks away. Then the wine is finished and I go for the beer, ah cold golden liquid of the gods, dark basement and Mallarme Mallarme or around that time I get hold a Artaud book too and I'm receiving like a gong the fluid madness of comprehensible floppity flippity gypsies knees offerings and the rain summer Shelly Tom Waits bulldozer of the coliseum and take them sacraments take them snake cigars, ye will hold the be in fathoms of gold, scriptures of space deeply lavender she has been gone for a while now but the geniuses of not in the jazz of holy fortunate the greater be see the rhyme I live by a Aztec building I ride my bike to King's Crossing, Mugzees, but the bars and the town have closed solitude French and my seasons are transmigrating to a blurry chorus...ecstatic night...the candle the coffee table the book open delight mystery wants revealed and the roads scarred with the fourth dimension what how wine why who and where the great moon abides to a circular destiny stin'd in the flux all the signs pointing to Mexico. Fibure of colossus, when of leaning, hell of food, flood of expect, sea night of revelatory remembrance. All this.

Thinking about my life, ah oh om, how Buddhist how, Babylon wine devoured the potential saint, thinking about my life, ah oh om, no wise in here clown naked but the echo of diamonds Queen Mary of bridle brick brittle rack Grant of pure gospel in a crimson remembrance we all sing like birds like fish like the ocean like the come the absolute come of way word truthness. Thinking about my life and how I let slide Marta that red haired midnight soul gasp why didn't I stay with her? Too much man, too much peyote, can make a man into a science fiction like Lake Street man and the lander of bandana crunch crunch, they made it out, pyramid, cat, Sirius, connect the dots Orion, dance with a sister to Small Planes she asks so many questions in the songs' incubate trigulate investigate oh the Tao the shaky snakes of koan the twenty five thousand miles of Zen retract, can I sit by you on the Blue Bus? Hold my hand child I'm still a child. Love counts up.

The campus, One Verse City, University Pladue, Jack the Daniels, Southern Comfort, ze walls of ze mart, gullible and poison headaches turn out strange, female Mondrian punk and MacShitters, I hang Barfly on the wall my hero, blood, strange blood, Jesus falls blood, Soul Asylum veins, Rastafarians, madnesses beginnings river flies sours soars, everything turns out a certain Creeley way, shooting pool and bachelors on that green boy riot, All Shook Down, aboriginal T-shirt, long walk with Cassandra, carnival, dog gypsy and the moon and Meg Tilly, magazines of underwear and lesbians kissing, Ophelia lifting up her shirt great wondrous teats as I swallow swollaw, getting laid in the shadows as the eight turns sideways, painting Buddha three eyes gentle glowing flower, welding a sex dance with Starko Michelangelo swilling fish of Time and Bible knowledge, eating three thousand pizzas, guitar boy, roommates went to Jamaica after smoking hash oil and drinking gas station milk, discovering Bacon and Marcel and buying from the used bin Electric Warrior which Sen really digs as I dig her in blue jeans and few hours later naked together together, Bob DeVille has no home so my couch becomes his jack off, abortion, drinking beer and digging the pink sundown drinking beer and hanging with speed freak Joker Elvira Candyman done can did does, D.T.'s, reading Hamsun in my little bedroom then writing Banality and Healing Water.

Its all slave language out there the president brick brain and all us tulips oh to be trampled down beat by slave lingo rhetoric throwback obscure history, this war won't matter till the daisies sing in mourning, I don't own any white (shirts). I'm out here the crossroads the room of Joyce gazing the haze with transparent maize, amazing the tulip of drown amazing what might be and yet shell shocked hem knock on timetable of rite to rite, Shelly beat, that train, embalmed like that time in the park Saint Paul I felt the tombs ring jingle jangle to historical resurrections the placement of a warrior dribbling a basketball autumn dizzy cardinal alone…what's impossible is what's going down this very moment. The dirge will find you Time Rite Boy and Mr. Jones will collect. Hypocrisy of scholars all the kings were never born I'm leaving leaf to Mingusota to conjure a new dance some 999 of the quicksilver and the Inian soothsayer on speed with the delicate drumming we talk chat commune, oh the days just filter down to pinpoint regret, to the Snow Chick young innocent chaste I won't chased her. Now that I'm thinking of her…Erica…Angie… and my dust and my revivals, "The Indian uprising known as the Beat Generation," wow I dig that, thanks from the top of my heart Jack from the bottom of my soul where I harmonize with Lucifer thanks.

Gone to the bars of Fuck It.

Spirits from a dream form the hollow hello, spirits dispirited from a bare night of water and rice sadly solitary offering the rain the chorus the ring fling and summer almost near here rear of the winter's come, if I fold my hope? Take what you need woman I'm existing for the new world wake. Still the refrain given silently celebrates the used to be like a wan pawl the masks the ladders the rain the snap. Snow Chick, ah that's not the rite name, what is? How bout…Careful Prudent Moon Child? Too long. I don't know what to call her. Now I remember, Erica, Erica with a new role on a spangled stage, with a current in her eyes she's rivering this streaming and I'm a hornfish starfish horsefish smokefish. The song ends.

Na I'll call her Prudent Moon and is she really a child? Softly turning flowerly looking up sideways eyes almond mouth of letters sent but unread. Do you need a portrait? Vaguely I am. Stars and electricity, Prudent Moon tides the Blue Bus to The Breakdown Café and cold and empathetic and broken arrows and down the road just before the clouds Yeats just before the birds yap then she arrives. Bee's wing blood. The flutes. Promenade witch. Beside the sill where I write my Rembrandt reflection, torn deflated obtuse, I think we're Irish. Classical Ire reversed. Suddenly I feel old. Prudent Moon reads self help books, I think her eyesight is blurry, she's not dumb, a little slow in a young breeze of dispossession. The night sky. "Only the young can say."

Jingle the Dawn.

Ego fix.

Karma junkies Emily and Dindy's, so long ago.

Now is meek which is fine by me.

Now is meek and griever runs by the wheel fire in a haze

of farttle the kissing of night and morning this day, and you who give gave the Howl to a dozen denizens madness sought through letters of the eighteenth century systematic calamities you who fouled the junk of heroin and methadone to a Beat all nighter in the throws of hold tight and I sigh.

Ah before I moved here I went through two months of alcohol withdrawal crawling to a flaming fate singe, that first morning in sike warred convinced that heroin is shit and my father Kurtz Tom Pickle I write my own version to gang the troops of water and I call it: Fusions of Tamara: aint it just like the blind to play tricks when you're trying be so riot/ Your shit there is branded doing your worst to defy it/ And Fifi folds a handful of pain tempting you to define it/ Fright flickers from the apostle wall/ In lint rooms the fleet fight the crawl/ Sputtering tall stalk so small/ File through Apache Mall/ The geese are all wrong there just fear/ They seem to defecate in the clear/ But just make it too concise and veneer/ That tomorrow is not here/ How can I expand its too large to get off/ But these fusions of Tamara kept me so cold and soft…In the heavy lot scare the lady stains high man's fluff with the tea train/ And the fall is gay with pearls while I escape to the see frame/ And you can steer the small sight whirl flick his light flash and mask himself too that its true that he is insane/ But my momma she will not unfold/ Be this heavy age now untold/ On the front of the dish fuck that blows while my tie implodes/ The spirit of the trees bowels and coal to the lame/ And these fusions of Tamara are cows in the rain…Yeah little toys cost he plays with himself so imperiously/ We rag on his ceremony she likes to give in dangerously/ And when ringing the raindrop she peaks with a farewell bliss blissfully/ She sure gone a long haul/ To be so fuseless and tall/ Muttering tall talk in the fall while I'm a orange leaf in the hall/ How can I change jingle jangle it's a tambourine gone gone wrong/ And fusions of Tamara are mushrooms in the twilight dawn…(just me and my knees needs deeds so entwined) Hide and seek with Moslems sensitivity grows up at least a mile/ Cherubs spectrum what is this starvation without style/ But Kamona and Liza a Rasta man musta had a chocolate cigar you can tell by the they smile/ Be an isolated wallflower in the trees/ When the honeysuckle fags in the freeze/ And the pun is milk mustache praying tease/ I can't lie with sleaze/ Fools and rhinos dangle from the bed of my dark nephew/ Fusions of Tamara makeshift and spaceship through the Louvre…

Marlon's women know me, the white pow wow, shaking trembling in a whiskey froit, on then on.

Believend in all things ancient, "Satan will fool ya," running smokers this rain and the age of numbers Willy won't? The green leads to the brown? Oh I've been to many white pow wows and know I'm out on my known…so there. The autumn rider the sad snow of Miss Spelling and I wonder. Prudent Moon she can dance, she can thumb all the way to arc and saw. Oily tips the yonder opiums of disordering night. Ah Dawn too.

Anyways I'm alive and festering to get back to the mare a tiv in Rotten Chester and I'm eating mushrooms and drinking all sorts of fun stuff and my god I'm thinning like a atheist onto the girl world. What do I do? Sue? I tribe the tonight and television and whatnot. I write letters to my brother Stick Figure:

Ah I'll go into that shit later rite now I'm shot through with love. Is it junk love? Been while The Doll and I bet she was talking sex. I'd like to make it platonic with Prudent Moon Womb Ann Erica, she's a regular at The Breakdown. I wanna talk I wanna holy glance in the post of biblical places and rest easy I say platonic brother sister meeting in the temple of girl and boy toys and rainbows wails and Whales and water tongue leap maybe if the trust is genuine if the trust safely sagely unrusts the lonesome wheel of time. We meet in the dimension of Cala la ka and helio me hello low heaven laughing angel at the choices now made: Sobriety, honesty, Re and Ra discuss the destination of Stinny Huge But. And now "asking me lies" I answer my love with a billion moonbeams swelled to the allies of drip. Oh cock.

Ratfig flipped young Jung to un anknown going on, all these people think Ratfig, swapping piss at The Breakdown Café talking trash to the velvet moons of Rasputin or Alex, Alex wined to Columbia where any in hey Zeus was be born making it with the coup pawns, that's all it is, flip the bird, flop the words for worlds are writ in Prudent Moon's lips of kiss cat, I could pay up like vomiting hearts special sleeves on sale due the rest on rent of be…couch she whispered an immortal to me I love you as the golden lamb just in justice worn out rings of fingers might and been to the children Rex and tea and landing baked on a parched at the job downtown the water how many years sing sense since? He girl now. Plop. Go to the justice Job in between lick heaven with an eye of say, séance, say aunts say ants say humanity city love you love you arms hold memories and on that quaint sacrifice hotter than a gypsy oven as long as there's the birds the birds they call 'em but angels dream and cotton on the couch and Ratfig smiling invisible Ratfig God Dog the gods backwards stars if you can just find a mind the parasites paradise rise oh yonder experience! I know? Little gold shushed the sold slaves and houses to be moved, prove me a Mardou Fox in this frozen beetle, she could be my mummy forever. Tipsy. Tip sea. And round that irony is the cattle kid Mick who goes eggshell soft Genet female and notes of a cranky, iceman runneth, mummy forever. We floated on the a while but the Reality Theater oh man lay down and pretend you're dead the bells the mess the bicycle carrot ride, beer and oil, Reality Theater, needle of the desert mile of the come on in your rock-n-roll romb you take out my eyes and for dessert a hand or tow up to your under your shirt to feel to congeal come on. Iggy Pop. Guided By Voices. Young Fresh Fellows. Oh kiss my cuddle, plan the fan scene and yearning and yearning and yearning, I can't bear to sleep all winter…sparkly my nor lets just kibble and kick looking for a ball Dandy was Sandy drunk Dawn Peyote and take it off. Like a minute plane. If this? Otay.

It was on a night dusk like this, Lou, Lou, my pay pound saint, lending me chigs cookies fish noodles, roommate bologna, visits from Egypt, I watched the sun dip skip away and Calling is pink too, she dangled her love and I under naked stooding storked the valley the outlaw handing over bound and Lou my coffee is the elixir if you're listening she was glistening, time deals, crime of love, saved by the aristocratic telephone gal. Call and past. Here comes now.

Dionysus man, who sobered up in the calico nights any nay the blues blood, I got the happy blue untangled like a freight of fright, wrong and snap, fact is I got a flower in my mind, fact is I got a shriveling nova belongs to Lame Deer, we're gonna dance with the Greeks, we're gonna stay young for a holy forever eternity jealous infinity bowing nova sunburst son thirst its water now brother sister, me veins are jigging, me heart is glowing through to some eventful knock a knock. Dionysus, what's he doing tonight? With ideas and silver with Eden wine with right about now, out of the wilderness superstitions and buoyant clouds for eyes, Jesus knew how to party, Last Temptation man, shoes gonna go for it? Now that the fray is afraid and truthfully tooth. High time. Sober for the duration and sliding Mexico. Know its kinda cold but we have ridden the ride and ride about now writing the summer's wish in a blanket of stereo. Who do ya love? Coincidenceville keeps coming, coming, coming, and upon that bard's first with Latin fist and Ron Wood the jubilee done begat begun and we are here, now, here, and how…the secret is in the how?

The cheap deathly burlesque subsides. Clearing. Like water man I'm coming to coming outta and Prudent Moon blind moon it's a rock no it's a bird. "Time will show the wiser." Rising "the Inian uprising known as the Beat Generation," I'm musing on that all the live dong night and relishing the possibilities coming out coming out: Closets of whiskey. Gal just swings and I bight my lip and sway. Jim was rite. Amazing the debts, a scary karma a laughing madman a calcium cane, anyone anyone, rivers of replies reverberate Reality Theater versus The Breakdown Café and me betwixt smoking endlessly pissing up a stormy tempt… island eyes, vigilant ear, corn of dance, ride that number dream. Aside. Witch. Doesn't. Flee.

On the edge of a demon night. Come slow the craziness seems, seems to last for a ever, seems seems oh this river I need a transfusion fluid ghost tears the ground come slow land slow land mantras and worlds, the passed is treacherous precariously shading my violet boned blade of retraction and soul. Sorcery and spirit. Jung delving into Robbie Robertson's Shadowland, sing for the loss of baby and slavishly retuned traces to not return. To not go back. To hither forward spiders' all. Originate in the demons' backtalk a fiery recognition, clouds are for the blind, burn mask burn, let the demons continue and I'll take that ride to source.

Simple fact.

Simple fact is the times gone done I think of Bob DeVille, his bedroom, slicing up acid, his dad a lawyer who doesn't give a shit, we drop in the winter night, seasons of stripping the mask have begun. Seasons of nothingness. Pre Zen day shun, into the night the mist the forlorn streetlamps the curve of the bony moon skull, trip, amazed by the dancing pens where have them drawings gone?

But to dwell on the past…those returning from the long chat chat night, crossing over like Patti prophesized into the lake by the valley ingesting ice water now. What hath time done to me? I sit here like a violet sphinx. Anywhere small homes. Towards the freewheeling dreams hypocrisy boy who shall take the beyond into his all and delve the sources, monetary, spiritual, classes, naked clowns, glass politicians, about the dirge, by the painted river, to take an illegal sacrament, to go to the deep streets, the seasons of stripping the mask have begun, but what does that mean?

Ever since she called me an hermaphrodite, ever since… what? Silence. Angels of faces embracing the wind and the witch. This land sold, sold again, this crucifix bought, bought again. And eye just toys. Ann, she little be fate my and interrogating the crystal palefaces. Heaven's blueness turns India ink the séance riddled with was. Maria Maria. Folk songs outer crest of cusp one thing's when. The story? What happened to the story? Where is Dawn Peyote tonight? Like a broken down Cherokee straddled Tao to find the rings of Saturn to moan for the Laz of history blinked. Old Angel Midnight man, and I'm going to the land of eternal jest, wait! I'm already there! Here! Now!

Eternal tricks on the warriors' flame lick, wheely, kin, man, heart, kidney, pissing into the bleak fleet, that dance will save us…oh ghosts everywhere spirits and streams of offering now that come on come on cannibal Kabala Allah the snakes don't care. Or do they? I threw up in sike war, my hands shaking, my shaking hands. Delirium man, where am I going? Nowhere. Aggressive intellectual, I'm just then now, abstractly wow, now then, rite about now. There's no one here. Tibetan moans go far in the Ophelia crack glass, I don't wander like I used to, shit man I've walked the Twin

Cities upsidedown. Where for the job the hustle the flower of justice? Disgust. If you seem to if you seem to?

Grant's a poet.

You want Orion magic? There in the farm every halo done shy, empires old, all the waves, all the fire, all the magic. Reading Season In Hell, some visions hold, Howl too, picture on the wall, writ in the sand, what's the chain gang doing now? Lamb of crutch clutch the silver before eyes are coins, dollar bills, receipts, commerce, come to the down, come to the mountain, come to the true, strange the seasons, strange the Fall and how I'm barely sane…barely rain, barely bare, barely nearly the land man, once you land the days grow tricks crucial fix dreams hairshirts and Buddy Buddha Holly Holy, who can sit through all this muck? Rats man the need to survive, the need for something more, amour, shine Maria and my love is silent, my eyes my threads of compassion, can you hold me naked in the naked cosmos? Eden. Dangling sorrow, grief encompassed, Henry and Arthur and Jack and Watts and Joyce on my coffee table. Here comes Miss Spelling conquered by the voluble. Rhyme Grant, Orion, North Star, wise men three, Orients of telepathic original karma shuddering like slaves, exploding markets, fish left in peace, all the all alling omni and Tathagata and despair and blues and punk. Heaven? Come down, Earth ravaged, the songs the prayers the illimitable the door the glass, all taken away in a oily refrain. You want Orion magic space traveler? Hitchhiker? Denizen of the gold beat? Take the be and Hamlet the rest.

Anew character emerges through the shroudy rite: Pale Black Witch. Anew and the story goes away and I'm left with reveries of breast ass cunt and long black curly hair. This rite, this protest, this season. All of this in a thin haze of white winter rolling and rolling along the path running through the woods the trains half stopped if I cry on top of the mountain if I write E.E. about the moon Doctor Sax and all will she chase that dream of pale mix, black and white primary, witchcraft, Moors, boys, warnings, and the revolt of a landscape in disguise. Pale Black Witch I want you, I've said swung elsewhere inside platonic, inside a woman, mentally spiritually physically. And the gods…guesswork, sophisms, sad sacks, pearls and faking, worlds and the dates are invisible, I'm invisible thirsting longing thrusting at your Ophelia ghost as the night rattles on, as the beliefs line up on a fiery trial. Hunger for mysteries rising in the East like that mighty ball of fire where the underworld creams, where the nipples are hard and the thighs soft soft, what lasts in all this vagabond? Orphans and sunworshippers gather to the blue to the white to all the yin yangs of fucking, a slither and fold me into your enigma I want the blood the sea the armies of shadows and headband, I'll take my clothes off I'll put my glass eye on the mythological table I'll talk to the Witness Tree like Robbie. Oh start anew, Pale Black Witch, Dawn Peyote, The Doll, Prudent Moon Erica Lame Deer, Stick Figure, Tom Pickle, lets Zen the very heart of justice and flower forth like a sonnet of sisters' rebellion.

But now I see you're Irwin Garden Pale Black Witch and James Joyce at The Breakdown Café doesn't say much, verily. Just like the sphinx is a woman and Ladies of D' Avignon is really just Picasso. To discover the anima in the smoky twilights. Tom Pickle's songs out of the Bible come to the Egypt of sacrifice, beauty, rebirth, liberation.

That trip to Mustard country with Mexico City Blues, my dad's eyes turned into olives, I read in the kitchen as the southern slave train ghosted the midnight bleary. Ah read a cow's moo like a Buddhist dream. Now I see you bearded Pale Black Witch bald, by my, his, grave, grave bereavement? No, just words timeless. Pickle and Irwin, America and Lucifer, Grant and Bob, Hamlet and everyman. Revolution.

Revolution. The days train around the bend bent benders now almost wisply forgotten, sobriety, knowledge, Greece, sing for the unborn day, dream for the buffalo spawn, dance for the burning leaves, speak for the elders draped in ambiguousness. Its all a vast wow.

Skull read on this night, what a flower Buddha. Ann the and the an the Ann. Tipped topple funk. All ya need.

What winter breeds the soul shift?

A gentle day of reading, a train of thought linking Rimbaud to Kerouac to the history of Buddhism, cut to the Zen, long fuckin winter. Kite reaches the cities, ever ever, and I joy unbate to hear her voice on the phone. Ah I'm just writing, waiting, hoping, knowing within unknowing, fear within love. Don't try said Buk, but Blake's visions and Allen's receptacles Harlem Columbia boomerang, encircle, come back come back, and here I am on this dark winter path jingling jangling to fly to her...a new hope.

Erased the end, void, valley, mist, gems of unspeakable lesions, Old Angel Desolation Midnight the madams say little to this boy of sapphire, the madness of choirs rotating on the colored vowels of promise, the fault of around and here to speak the plaintive urchin's begin. Again with the flower of justice I take hold of books out here in the country patiently weeping sighing praying and just one one. To wake like rice in a field of quartz knowledge wrapped the lion and needing running intent without intrepidition to now and transcending any mission.

My computer facing the window facing the west I can see the moon tonight. Hopes slivered like the moon itself, but feeling pretty good. The night envelops all this desolation all this purged desire and not even knowing. The Breakdown Café was wild with heartbreak this afternoon, falling comets of destiny, crashing fates like angry dishes of divorcing thoughts. You got to take this sobriety thing seriously. No hinging. Cut through the glass of time like Fydor (who I haven't read). The none is all. No illusions, no trajectories, no horse, no wine. The rose wise of simpleton project collapses no innocent by degrees she he them we us no now no past no future. Dissolving, vibrating, forsaking that rigid Jesus curse for the Zen, Zen of see alley sneeze in a surreal truth tooth. The moon is a piece of then, when you look into the moon you are looking at something very old, very wise, very prudent. Erica hasn't been seen in a while, but last night I had a dream of Mala girl I never talked to in hi school, she was in the garage as I was painting, her eyes man, her eyes were dancing oval Spain love gasp...dreams deemed seem...love cat, art dog, star fate, meow bets alleys and sleeping sleeping. I don't need a self anymore I have the dissolution burning the candle on the coffee table and tales of Baraka and Rimbaud's tragic mysteries. Unpeel the diamond and the arbitrary numbers will all be forgotten, don't protest a mineral, the chemistry lessons have led us to a shining Utopian Oz and we'll dangle for ions in the flux of night's dollish refrains, forever fooled, yeah, and wanting the demur the demise of Shitville, deep dancing in the water of now...

Sister moon will you take me to some Biblical reprise? Some foreign flip? I know not who I am but a brother to the brothers, a Mexican in the white, a diminishing mist entrenching the moon seems to cradle my hesitance. Knock on that ole moon she just kisses my ocean eyes tonight in the tomorrowing plaintive-ness in the tangled web of laws' fatal decrees. Some go down. Some stay down. "Don't try." Zen err man I hear your long song life rosy drifting in the crux of alone, close to the past Sen and where is she now? Sidelong. Withdraw ye bird of blue and go back to the allusion to the scales of ruinous rap wrap to the Ginsberg of truth. The Breakdown Café pirates of the mull sort. To trick the stir. I'm going home to summer my knees don't wanna know.

"There's a new star on the modern jazz horizon," I say to myself thinking of her, her, her, her and slyly comeback shyly come down wisely cheating come on baby ah the moon has, is growing into half, and my heart noticing the want, my heart gate opens to her potential song in this thronging silence, I want to see you meadows politicians, "Saviors who are fast asleep, they wake for you." I wake for you all Finnegan in a churchly flowerly spade, in a wail all blue with in this black night resurrection complication if you show me your calico love I will come out of the inexplicable forest, no right no wrong, looking into the eyes of your esoteric truths, and mine shrouded by false dignity, to face to flinch to apologize to the gods. Let me show you I'm real with my careful running parades carnivals taking touching feeling revolving and cat-like. This new star, what's her name? Cleo? Justine? Call her Three Years Fast. And I go back to my dreams to see her commune with my unholy reason, unquenchable lust, tireless sorrow. Three Years Fast.

Three Years Fast lived in the biggest house in town, slim and vigorous, telepathic and sensual, I've got a way with rich chicks. At the time Laney was all I could see but now I know there's others I could love equally. I look through my yearbook and dream of incarnations love trust respect. Mutually. Three Years Fast in the past out of the future, oh if she'd look me up I'd explode like a thousand eternity belly bitter heart sweet organisms and like Erica in chemistry class said orgasms, orgasms, (I got to read The Function of the Orgasm by Reich) so unchained by the mind's Zen I read ponder musicate I'll find heaven knock knock if you find me. I could be the King of Pure Land, I could rap like a crack head, I could commit adultery with the president's wife (witch I've already done done), I could set you free like an exotic bird, show you worlds of poetry and remain unborn.

Oh sonnet, psalm, litany, hymn, mantra, all the unspeakable satoris, all the unrecognized saints in America's vertiginous vacuum (didn't know how to spell it, vacuum, vacuum). The reservation's on fire, thunderbirds thundersticks, grew up in the sack religious town city afraid, like Cat Man I had no desire, no desire to work, like Cat Man I listen to Joe Cocker sing me through this. Regrettable no speak, the history unlived unwritten, ghosts of white paper I believe, gospels and bells and home deeply blessed by the magic wonder of Oz of You of Three Years Fast. Oh prima Donna.

My god the moon is big.

And Sen loved to listen to T-Rex when we made it.

The Liquid Gang, Grant looked twice, drinking coffee and smoking American Spirits. Outta sight man. It's a long road, sip and sit and sip, it's a gigolo artist copping the watery in the war of bacteria. One Verse City is crawling with needles. The only one flipped flapped on Smelling Ave. and refractions of conspiracy blanked the booze fallout. The elides were of course invisible, and that Egyptian dog just trotted the parking lot of the big grocery store and waggled the horns in a Bolan plexus. Jiving with the winds of silver and dust, Dindy's and I walked the streets reincarnation the sun THE SUN was setting raked rapped parlance and I thought R.E.M. was Hitler's creation. One more time, but I'm safe tonight now the prayer wheel swings to, "Interstellar Zone," and I'm just dancing out the clowns' wishes. Handclap and mad zap.

Hot tea in the black night, prairie of contemplation, town of preacher man stuttering, folk of farm, kin of laughter. Reunion of the diameter in this circle beautiful. The characters have dolled and I'm running out of word stuff I'm telling the story like those days stoned on the couch going behind the words with Bukowski, ah and the man throwing up into the garbage can on Nicollet later as I walked to the liquor store to beef up on what? Beer was it? Or wine? One of the two. And Sam tripping in the metropolis. Where are the pharaohs now? Now that I'm gold? My dreams connect, I saw Marta again, ole redhead unbelievable beatitude French in the dawn's flower Marta, she went from one artist to the next, I don't think she dug my drinking, she found a sane gent to fuck and fly with (I wish she'd come back in the flesh in the mind in the soul) (I'm ready). Digressing with the stream of reality I used to sing Never Say Lonely but now I feel it churn, lonely, all the bleeping time. The Zen of it being. Irony. Crusader of the memoirs stalling falling came a long way on a train of hairpins, some mud pie of the spirit roaming in the sad rain, standing before the classical strains of Utopia. I just want one kiss from the night's delicate murmur.

Papa is a Rolling Stone.

And another character emerges through the phosphorous glow of the old day, and me dreaming of cleavage singing the blues, but I walk home alone as usual. For the key is in the bluesmen of slice and sway and the lock is released, I sing and sing and no one hears, my raps my sonnets my tears are real (to me) (if nobody else?). Subterraneans find me, I'm out here in the love find regrets welling up upon the darkest beauties of yesterday and tomorrow but what time is now? Heart and hand, tame the lovelorn, Tom Waits croons for all my broken arrows sways for all my gone rituals, "I'll kiss you then I'll be..." this new character, her name Sun Baby, she knows time, she collects my rusty glances like a mysterious gypsy, and I always fall for small creatures, petite, like my ma maybe? I just can't say farewell to hope's communions the wine bitter flaying Ling and last night I red the Tao Te Ching and saw some light, saw some gentle practical irony. Oh Sun Baby the thoughts, crying onto this keyboard, eyes that almost see, blues that almost jazz, anachronistic folk singer of the chill season my youth almost moon, that is old, old, old I tell ya, and drops of ears and ears of corn will save us. The season's about to collapse, bookends, endgames, tally up the rain the snake the apple, and age is coming in the midnight calypso of Pure Land dreams, like babies in the crib, like nursery rhymes, like fairy tales, like Leroy rediscovering the windows to revelation. The spree is love, the rosy refrains of persuasion silent, Sun Baby let me love you deep with my mind on fire, with my heart a rice paddy, with my very soul wavering in the never know. Let us love. Le why of fathers' fountains and please. Peace, cats, Africa born for fire, and us stuck in the north country of sad terrains. The windmills haunt ye Maya outlook like eyes of decision, I can be a periphery I can remain ghost I can reason the void till the witches grow honest, I can I can...

Now I'm out here, alone, as the sinking pink orange sun slowly dips descends, and wanting that girl who lives a few doors down. I'll leave a note on her door, "If you're horny go to 207." I slept to till two o' clock, still drowsy yet restless, its been about a year since I fucked. I need it bad. Damn some juice, love juice, sixtynine, love kiss, thighs of love, and eyes burning for a naked communion, a fleshy union in the desolation absolute. That girl in my building is fucking beautiful, she smiled at me but I just stared barely awake taking out the trash. I need some. Man.

A new season now. The sun oh man the sun is finally waking upon us as a pickup truck rumbles in the parking lot, and that damn moon hiding from me tonight, hell I even opened a couple windows this afternoon thinking the plant would dig the fresh air. I've had three or four cups of good black coffee, I'm gently buzzing and the chigs bop me into a sober life high, I'm listening to Latin music, I'm jigging, my hands tap out words and I'm not quite as lovesick as I was earlier, I've accepted this solitude even rejoicing in it.

In the sacramental hours, in the streetlamp of Apache soul destiny, in the criminal origins, in the reading of Henry, in the yubyam of my own, all this and I wait, I wait like an Indian lady for the devil to reveal my fates for the drums to lead me to the fellaheen wonder. Tonight, tonight the western lands are quiet, ephemeral, and the diamond of desire glows like Karen angel Karen baby honey darling Karen Peris…I've got a chime in my heart for her and no longer waste my waves on gray.

Hot cup of tea. I've read the Tao Te Ching, poetry man, haven't been that moved since Mexico City Blues. And Alan Watts too. The Colossus of Maroussi has been sending me to heaven recently. This new season, spring, Easter, Saint Patrick's Day, I am alive to the hilt, reading, digging, absorbing, music and paintings, writings and drawings. Filling up the Zen playground with all sorts a shit. Grilling myself in this sobriety, revelation of being, just being, breathing, blinking, smoking. They say remove desire but that's what I'm swimming in these violet nights: DESIRE. Old Angel Midnight fries potatoes, has his dictionary on the table, chessboard, six dollar Buddha, candle and ashtray. All I need now is a woman to discuss the cosmos with, that's all I need, naked discussions in the calico Scorpio night, Sara, Sara, where and whence have you gone? The Doll done gone into the hoary past. The genius of nights passing through. My silver cross, my Indian picture taped to the bookshelf, Picasso's final self portrait laying on the floor. You have to let the thoughts domino, the prayer wheel roll, I think of Lennon, I think of Sexus where I swam twenty years old into the Paradise of words. Can I do the same? Henry writing about writing, writing and writing, his words imprinted secular horizons, enigmatic cataclysms, fleshy speculations, and the radio playing Bach who Jack said is the greatest… ah passing through.

War is brewing, where are the Aztecs? Where are the Indians? Where is sense? Why not a female president? Some Isis of the modern whirl to worship the sun and moon. The dollar signs boil in the oily water of lie, the blood worthless, the just poor invisible. Where are the women of truth to change this rotten affair? The honkies man…I have visions, my dream of war and America actually the slowest, weakest, stupidest, greediest. Who will bring me down? Who will let the pink horizons be? Ah fire in the sky crew cuts racists Christian obedient crock o' shit it is, shit is George Bush that mechanical monkey evangelist of the shit lie eater of shit speaker of shit thinker of shit, George Bush came out of my ass this afternoon and stunk, I had to wipe several times and send him off to the sewer. America will fall, its only a matter of about fifty years and it will be no more…

Some bizarre synchronicity, that heroin jungle, that cocaine skyline, the tarot, the falling falling falling. What can I do? Alice, I'm Alice. Don Quixote, I'm Don Quixote. Schizophrenic impossibilities, one guy alone by the cornfields by the racked night time sky pondering war. My blood as confused as a million ants in autumn. Passion play Hamlet Ophelia chaos. Celine just rides that scorpion current. I just hold my…speaking in tongues screaming in insolence, police report, newspapers, television. It's a desperate song to take this away.

These visions these visions come back to hunt ya, haunted by the like, each ghost comes clean with revelations of beasts and that snake in the abstract. I don't know? Zen Him memory, Zen you His little big lie. The clock vomits the hub tortured. Eyes shifting hollow to the hollow cost. Its been a while said The Doll to The Dawn. I've forgotten god and gold and zebras, all I remember is hidden within.

Breakdown Café, bad weather, bad water, sick vibes, sick sad hysterical wasichus. I come home my stomach in knots my mind spiraling then I drink some black medicine and then ice water and half a dozen chigs and read Howl and Illuminations and start to feel better. Another nameless rite before me another cloudy reverie another gloomy destination. Conservative aint even the right word for it. Fascism. The Breakdown Café man, I won't say hi to the dying anymore, I won't involve myself in the slave tics of repressed static anymore. I am mortally documenting my sad life in the throes of an insane society. I have no books to recommend no nationalistic convictions though the English get on my nerves. Artaud and Rimbaud chroniclers of the lost the damned squeezing out an iota of justice to my ragged eye. Ring the bells like the slum of St. Paul where I lost it all delirium tremens paranoia I was the ancient spider of time strumming my guitar to the vacant dimensions of loser. I was wild. Tombs and embalming thundered through my winter to spring to summer to autumn arrow broken mind, come back to life in the galaxy bringing the wine to a desert carnival tasting horse as the mean clowns staged my fall…

Coming off booze, head on collision, trains, the spirit sags splintered, "Somewhere down that crazy river," rolling to the proletariats' last hope I guzzled fire and swallowed a thousand swords I rapped in the bleed of a starving civilization I walked a tightrope made of lice I burned beyond hell itself and read and read, Bukowski guiding me if I knew what he knows? In this last night? Wail now blues now half steps funk rap the mighty drum heals me. This and yonder the deceiving plane, tests of mirror, jests of crack, lest moons congeal in the frog's gleaming. The fucking Twin Cities, I'm headed back there tomorrow, my blood still echoes in the streets the birds still sing my name on Jake Street the plasma bank thinks I'm suicidal the forty of history enfolds threefold fourfold Jeffers Blake who I have not red. Speak for time now speak for now time. Jack went to Golden, I weep in the child's shrill coyote fathomless enigmas, nights and rifles and knifes and lions, it rained today…

There are people out there.

Roads and wind out here the drums the crows, back from the never tiring cities back from temptations to my little world safety and prudence. Back from conversations of shit fetishes and brain eatings, repulsed and turned on, dazzled and spooked, educated and blissed out and like Bob in the rings my afternoon hands empty and beat, empty and beat. Writing on this computer my folks bought me, still owe em five hundred or so for it, writing to see my own mind unfolding and wanting to read Blake again, really dig in, I've seen his pictures some, I need the mystic the angel possibilities this experiment. My cleavage is hairy, my dick small, my skull balding. The blasphemies, "Cracky Crackerson," skateboard, the anarchy of the law abiding in the afternoon of sun and warehouses and coffee shops and music oh lore the music is everywhere. I feel for DeQuincy trapped in a shadow. Now I have to smoke.

Day later: the night is rain still chill and I'm thinking of sex, thinking with that lower region bone bone flesh flesh flower flower and Picasso just stares primitive man jive cleaving me to the subterranean and the totem lying down lying, maybe I'll water the plant…wind, my sentient self blooms woman, my butt getting bigger (Calling said she liked my butt) (I liked loved everything about her cept the needle), my eyes and I haven't seen a hawk for a while. Orbit, go out there, see the truth, mo lot toe me, cusp of rights for animals, the flag oh the flag? Which one? Real? Really? And the landing is okay the landing and I think of India, go back, go out there, Old Angel seven thirty, Lucien morning, Neil mourning, Charles the sifter Charles with his word Charles the angry cat of moccasin, me? Me? Well I'm sober tonight after a close call with temptation's ridge, Twin Bloom Cities had me on the mental run that cold turkey waiting joking mocking. Am I real? My back hurts, my dizziness for the future, will the roast roost? Naw, gaw, see saw and see see and E.E. and B.B. who said wait till forty who plucks as I want to fucks my lust scares me, my lust carries me to dementia, my lust wine and marijuana scares me. Chaos is just a word…

After the chaos after the flood my eyes raining again drumming that mystery book of black fire, the magic of Ricki the liar of square the commerce of the ages falling through and Sitting Bull ah what a chance what a radical decree to dance to justice for the ancient flowers flowering forth a periel truth. Demonized in the haze schizophrenic walls and health just a fart in the wind. The horns man the horns. Cradles of gas and the spirit sags the rhymes Z and X so it goes Kurt curtly the city just a expensive playground for the lunatics of self destruction. The sadness the sadness of it all united like clouds: the future. So little time so much for the stroke so be it the It and my blood waxing they're a gonna eat my brain the treasure of the insane, Artaud wanted the red earth to open and Miller wanted the flour moon to open. Oh compassion babe, the philosophy boy and the French were around for the Zep Tipi and the walls were painted the fire and peace pipes, modern me I just roll up chigs and Buddy Buddy this fix. I want some. Millions and the fish just show up talking gibberish Irish fish-fish ish ish any know. Sounds sober. Sounds crooked. Sounds circular. Well tell the dam story Jack (there's nothing to tell). Anias could be lurking sexed hexed Mexed and my I love her shoulders, strong, the comma of indifference, the information of missing sham makes me mad. Ah the omissions nova in the kangaroo courts, bells and pointy boots for Dawn. Sitting Bull? Lil list for the stagger. Piss.

"Who are you a disciple of?"

"Homeopathy."

"Who are you?"

"If I knew?"

"Night comes in."

"Yes it does and the moon's light sheds like a pale snake."

"Do you know much about Sitting Bull?"

"The Sitting part I don't understand though I used to drink Red Bull."

"You like malt liquor?"

"It was my dance."

"What happened to Layton?"

"Drew gave him up for adoption and now."

"Now?"

"Now is how."

"Like some cool river?"

"How can there be be another day?"

Accordion of wine the lovers the dance lost the mind walking on water and turning the few pitfalls and apples and ballads, this newspaper is just blowing smoke, I don't have a pooper scooper for One Verse City. Kerouin got her hair cut she gets cuter by the second. Bukowski thin? Abstract? A protester? It'll be bird. We'll see the word. Pulp. Women. Mockingbird Wish Me Luck. No other protest just dance and the boxers' feet hovering home some hearts play.

On the revolutionary edges playing that chameleon beat, loser of the cross, despite the many despite the night's protest…bacteria, business, drugs, Stipe recall ealizing the drops. Tell me does the border shriek? Do the thanks equal anything? "…first we take Manhattan then we take Berlin…" I can rise and burn any flag, I can see the storms and inhale the pubic love, and and and. The ache crazy come on everyday. Coming to war em on a dance beyond Nietzsche and Leonard and the tropics and the lines the trains the boxers and the karate kiss. Ways of pree whose descent was a sister's pledge. Trance. War trance, revolution trance, Henry Miller trance, Zen trance, all bouncing all monkey and silver in a forest ripe then the pale the monarchs the music bring me in bring me away. Electric typewriter in the closet. Whose stratagems now in these arrangements of gold? Delicacies man, flush, "plush safe he think." My birds are barely bisible on that flower flame on that palace of voodoo and bald, just drink the water.

I saw Duchamp in the alley, time travel, the fourth dimension (did I mention? Did I die?). Ah science fiction, Thirteen Monkeys, Body Snatchers, Star Wars, and Duchamp witch dimensions witch angel red cataclysmic dream stepping stepping in halves your hair long the mystery of you all the libraries all the lights all the organs and dimensions have the fantasies come true? Come to pass? Where are we? Where are we? Touch this simple plan with the ancients' magic, always new, always neo, no blessings cured, no mountain tombed, no gun loaded. The French? Something, something. Where the sidelong bends. Waves of Buddhahood in a soldier's refrain, pain man, and darkness oil all the colors which predict is true? Some prophets, some wastelands, some Kurtz, some showdown lowdown on the mounds of wonder. Bells and Dawns. The guitars waver to the save dales deals crossroads the ghost of Neil how Beat Atman can the paradox grow?

Just ring and I'll frown.

So it's the weekend and I can still remember how to type, drinking coffee ice water and now peach tea. Thinking ruminating Beats Buk Zen my own shit, that sun out nice hot alive glowing glaring. Smoked two cigars what the hell? Came twice last night and itching urging to get laid, to go down on a woman, to have her kiss my breasts like The Doll Sara and it felt great, rite here on this floor. I'm always looking back at hidden love. I'm always regretting my indifference towards the gals of Lee. But off the sauce which is fine infra fine in fact, my little boring life but boredom mixed with peace and serenity, mixed in all this the magic is alright (ite) the white sun and Cat Man on the farm. Peace cometh to those who accept (accept what? The immaculate mystery of life itself). I could leave myself and purchase a bottle but those days are over they didn't add up to anything but migraine despair and body hellish odes of wrong. I'm getting closer to South Dakota, Wounded Knee, I told The Doll in the park I wanted to live on an Indian reservation and she said don't you have to be Indian? I looked at her through the ages and my eyes wrangled out I am an Indian, full blooded honey, Apache is my best guess. Apache in the Western Lands living out a book of the dead the souls' stripped return.

She liked, The Doll, to sit on the floor, she liked to fuck on the floor. Oh I wish I could go back and try it with her again. I thought she didn't understand me when I was the one who didn't understand her. Fucking hindsight man! I love her. I love her now, or, maybe I'm just in love with her memory, memories. "She cut through to my blood," Richard sings as I write this. Various thoughts at the time: she's a junky, she's a gold digger, she's too white. And when her and Gary didn't get along I said goodbye, got my Kerouac book back and she was crying, crying, and me thinking she doesn't even really know me how can she cry for that? I told her I wasn't in love with her. She said she loved me. Now she doesn't love me and I love her. Amazing.

My lover sings sings of my coat my grandpa hand-me-down and Fin seems to know too. On this evening of cookies and tea I will rest in the Zen I will find the mystique of my shrouded lover. Perdition maybe but the quails aren't as intense as they used to be. And Miles blows in my romb. Herby too. That I've read the story of Alice and Quixote in fragments is, well, okay. Someday someday I will opus the loose ends I could shake the horns of Jerry co. and ride that diamond to solace. My lover my lover...bent, forsaken, tremulous, eccentric, echoing. Soldier of fortune, mammoth of math, evangelist of lies, religious quacking. Oh to look into her abstract face homeopathy and magic and rites its all nature, No Nature, Dharma Bumming, Jung Angel Afternoon, and off in the distance the thoughts wait like smoke from a peaceful pipe as the runners machine gun the neighborhood and I never thought I could run that much? Decoy blues man. And sometimes I'm invisible and sometimes I'm holy and sometimes I'm nothing and with heroin ya git all three at once. Some ghost, my love, the death charades forming lined all the way from here to Hades to Pitsberg. Cassidy with the precision takes me in, who'll remember the Beats in the total X of dehydration and sleeplessness? Who'll rite the chickens? Travel to Henry's China and realize the revealed of sacraments' end? Eye with my I in the vortex of possible truth casting spells hooks geometric glances at the cows of India. And the beginning has just begun.

How many other lives do I live? Babies and singing? I smoke the nights away. I yearn to get laid almost constantly.

Simple confessions. What about the mushroom of past and Doctor Sax? Or Mardou Fox? All this wailing in nights, nocturnes, eves, churning and yearning and burning with a desire untold (cept here), a desire in the secret. My body changing. "Wazzz up?" Tell me the stories, tell me the fantasies, tell me about the flood and windmills. My illusions…my illusions. I have nothing to confess anymore the kids fooled me under the bridges of time and rolling hide smoldering hide dig the blues dig the bad. Indian drum, dry, dry, Midwestern collusions now, mumble mumble, and Corso with his surreal eye lop effervescing in the rabbits of tomorrow. God I love boots. Sneak. Sneak a look, red haired librarian and France in my pants. The red specter catches my spirit in her soft eyes of intensity. Wild.

And so what if we are nothing? Nothing, nothing. Neither existence nor non-existence. That's fine by me. Dwindling ego in the night of the fiery consciousness. "Everybody been burning in a free land." I love to burn, I love to let my desire go. I have a single rose blooming smoldering in the diamond of my lion belly ready to conjugate with the trains of forever. Let go let go, nothing's alright all left and everything in between, pulse of a pink sun my memory beating out the outlaw's curses in a mineral of love. Golden the way, gray the way, Cummings the way. I have read the sloping mountain and these morning Moors river to the cousins' delights, I and I, in a perplex of diminishing un. Un my un. Let the ocean return to river and the birds and fish let the gods remain eternally vague, obscure, bordering on disbelief, bordering on winking dreams of the spirits' final spell, the road, the tracks, the bridges, all this. I have not seen to be. Be to seem or see to beam. Seem and seem. Onion boy. And unraveling like a distance the distant idols of a park long forgotten glow in the wax, the wane, the Zen. You, I see you Kerouin, still but vibrating, lucid yet simple.

I know we're together in this never born in this impossible moment, impossible, impossible to exist. Any explosion will do, back of the truck dance, womb burst, dick slave, and all the eggs just sigh, what asking what, never mind the wan discharge of politics in a stranger's hand the land is full blooded by the shaman of tomorrow in a Mississippi wave the regrets Coltrane the wants the yearnings the desires the loves the hates come from the pinpoint hub of never. Never have I left even before birth, never have I succumbed to the movement of kings to the travesties of queens. Debauching the white with my India ink eyes, the roost, the wars, the inexplicable. Where did it began? Nowhere. Blue whore and Van Ghost sun dance immaculate. I stare into the void.

Angels without wings. Some are deeply religious. Yet silent, yet silent like, as if, or, or they meld, they become the void, becoming a void. Within? Within. Yet yin yang is only part of the story, the ank too is one. Seven souls, nine lives. The cat on the rooftop. The systems of Amiri in succinct clarities of confusion of ecstasy of heaven of hell rolling to the great one witch is without end, without borders, without preconception. Each now is a possible wow. The will can't conceive the sadness looming in the cities of Rimbaud traversed and terrains and books and creeds toppling echoing climaxing, the will is just a cracked mirror amnesia sand. Wet the sky, defy, look, and returning return. The forest where I saw the King of the Wood illusion flame, animal demon human fates, angels without voices, tilt, listen closely. Far from miles of early today. This writing hurts, but my scan is young. When will I feel your mystery? Shiva? Sphinx? Eli? The history of art man, and I smell rice and soy sauce. Some scriptures some arrivals and the prophet machines giggle. I can feel her out there waiting but not waiting. Her wings a choir of leaves of leaving like autumn like Atum like Dylan. Never and the hard rain, why the long face? Irish? Fathers and mothers. Hear me, my lost hopes replaced with a plant-like pree, peyote, dawn. The country where I corn the response waking to coming hearing again like a orphan the calypso of virgins. My nothing full of nothing.

Listening a night later to Buffalo Tom my veins seething with fire, with passion, with desire, with dizzy trust in the Now. This season, its new, its new like drizzle and wet streets and mind would mind could. I press these buttons and hope for the best. The blond in the hall with the fine ass. The chick with crazy love eyes at The Breakdown Café. Seasons man…and I change the cards, deuces wild, very wild. Period and ball. Dourly my past and The Doll we were once naked, together naked climbing into each other, our souls, our spirits and the pride of new lovers in the autumn of transubstantiation. We were once once. Buffalo Tom sings, "Could I have been mislead, could I have misread? Please don't punish me for things I have not said." Rock-n-roll homes, saves my ass everytime. Its nine oh five and dark as ink the streets reflecting electric light my eyes in the glass as dark as phantoms.

Maybe the crow has the message? I was and was and now I'm Dawn Satori. I saw The Doll today, first time in a year, barely recognized her. Dawn Satori.

Silent ruse take me to the other side, salient word show me peace, metaphysics, the unnatural laws of you and I. The Doll…Sara…I can wait, maybe its time to move on, carry on, find a new mind out here in the sticks, find a new body. Clank goes the radiator in my crib. The tea steaming, Alan Watts' Supreme Identity laying on the coffee table, the sun radiant on this April, two years since I've been in that hospital, two years since I painted the black bird of eternity, two years since me and Sara got it on. Time appears but to move invisibly, incoherently, mystically. Red eternity. Red infinity. Red underworld. Red ghost. On Go Street back when the feeling was knees and silver I ran to the image to the future to the nowhere out, now way out, no way out, and the scene, yeah, and the alone. This no for the castles in the sand: yes to love. The past man and I have no present for the future. Geo logical splatter the great divide, don't cross my line. And The Doll hath vision'd the wish.

Dawn Satori goes to One Verse City: Stick Figure my brother picks me up on a Thursday afternoon we go to the bank where I try not to salivate when seeing the gorgeous bank tellers, their slim bods and juicy tits, ah horny Dawn horny afternoon horny blue night all the time fucking. I cash my check then hop back in the car with Stick who navigates us back out onto the highway driving seventy and Stick finds the jazz radio station, we bop along, little conversations and smoking with the window rolled down. "Can we stop at the bookstore by Jode's there's a Johanna Floyd poetry book they had a year ago and I wanna see if its still there?"

So we stop in Saint Paul, Six Dangers is the name of the joint but the book aint there no more so I buy for three dollars Living Zen and they got Charlie Parker playing and the woman behind the register is beyond beautiful Charlotte-like my cousin and I wonder: when will the next Flesh Communion occur? We get back in the car and drive to Stick's artist's warehouse pad downtown, climb up four flights of steps and bam we're home.

I throw my bag on the floor and roll a chig and sit on the couch and Stick puts on some jazz. Then I call my old friend from art school Bra Tea, she lives in the next building over across the desolate alley of manhole and streams rivers its been raining. She says come over so we do, Stick and I, and she greets us warmly happily at the door. Her crib is fantastic, artwork everywhere, books, music playing. We talk rap about the old days, what all our old chums are doing now-a-days. She asks us if we're hungry and throws in some manicotti. I tell her I'm vegan but would gladly accept coffee, coffee, black medicine, "the blood of the gods," (Only Hank was talking bout wine, I've made the switch) and I roll another choke and sip and we continue to chat. Bra Tea, her real name is Amy, but I like making up things. She shows us her shop, dusty, filled with art. In the last half hour I've seen more art than in the last two years, its fun.

We go back to the manicotti, Stick and Bra eat it down and I wonder if Bra Tea is secretly a vegetarian? All women vegetarian? Well she has an operation on the morrow so me and Stick split and go back to his pad after saying bye and see ya again.

So we're back at Stick Figure's, high ceilings and all and he calls Grant to join us at the jazz club downtown, The Artist's Quarter. Stick's friend Geb arrives at the crib, they smoke up as I sit on the couch and listen to tunes from the great turntable. Well they're high and I'm sober we go out into the nine thirty night and drive a couple few blocks to the jazz joint.

Its in the basement, pay the cover, Stick and Geb buy beers and I buy a Seven Up and we find a table in the corner by the drummer. It's a big band, bout thirteen players. The music doesn't really hit me. I roll smokes and sip the pop, we chat a little. Geb's writing a book on Dutch Schultz. We talk about The Church and how Steve Kilby got busted for H. I smell haven't had a shower for a couple days and Geb's mister clean cut so I'm self conscious. After the second set Grant moseys in, belly free Buddha, I feel a thrill to see him.

Grant's starts complaining about rock stars, his head and eyes never still bopping around, his voice melodious with a lunar twang. The war is going and Grant hums some

Wagner. He razzes the musicians. "Its like he's trying to smuggle walnuts into the forest."

"Why would you wanna smuggle walnuts into a forest?" I ask laughing.

He rolls his eyes and turns away, his middle finger bandaged. "George Bush and his father call each other 41 and 43."

"I've never been too patriotic."

"You're a different kind of patriot Dawn."

The war has me kinda frazzled and paranoid, "A veteran called me up and wanted donations and I hung up on him then I thought they were gonna harass me, a brick through the window."

The jazz kicks back in and I wonder if its because Grant's here but the musicians seem more intense and loose, the drummer doin some amazing shit. Jazz. I buy another soda, chain smoke. The music rolls and weaves, its great.

The show ends around one, "Well, what do you wanna do now?" Stick asks.

"I got one rolled up," and Grant pats his pocket.

We hop into the cars and drive back to Stick's. We're walking up the stairs single file and Stick unlocks the door we trot in and Grant's way in the back but before he can get to the door it slams shut and relocks, he knocks, I turn around and open the door for him as he rolls his eyes and laughs again.

So its Stick and Geb and Grant and me. I take off my shoes and socks and sit lotus position on the couch with Stick who reclines back. They get the chronic activated and a wave of panic seizes me, it only lasts for a couple moments, the desire to get high, I've been straight and clean for three and a half years a lot of people expect me to stay that way and I expect myself for my schizophrenia's sake to stay sober, but I roll myself another chig and its no big deal. Life's pretty good without it, at least the paranoia is under control.

Then the rap session begins with Grant walking over to one of my paintings, "Your colors seem to be coming through now. This blurry one, its ugly. You're influenced by Basquiat."

He's the first one to mention Basquiat in relation to my stuff, it makes me feel good, the last time I had an exhibit they thought it looked like Clemente which didn't make me feel so hot, that cat's pretentious. "The blurry one's all water. People want illusions, like the fact that oil painting looks wet but physically they're devoid of any water. My shit looks dry, the illusion is gone, water man."

"Do you go back and revise? I've never seen one of your paintings in progress."

"A little bit, a line or a dot a new pencil here and there."

Stick's just taking it all in leaned back cool on the couch. Geb paces the room. Grant is swinging from a thick rope which hangs from the ceiling. I'm still sitting Indian style on the couch sipping water and smoking, smoking, smoking...

A little break from One Verse Metropolis: I see you hiding I see you hiding. And the Che of a thousand nights on the boys' before when the doors are all visions when the love is all comedy when the voyage becomes irreverent that's when you'll see the hiding and everyone I know knows me and they know I know and we are all actors here. The silver cross and the plant and the opuses and the grass of Walt and the Rimbauds of now and the swinging eyes of melancholy and the vast land of song. All of this all of this, and with the beds of cardinal we could swim to the foreign shores of bet, all of this all of this, what's written in that gypsy moon?

Now that the empress is low will I prophesy any drum any drunks any gates? Open that gate sister brother. The kings, the kings, and the Canto Queen I'm in love with. Rug blues Antonin as the cowboys sway in nonexistence as the sayings of come wilt before multifarious lies. Farming that sun in the rain of truth. Blaming the feet for Hamlet's demise and Corso a house of cards a Arabian woman a waiting bloom.

Its too late for The Doll and me, the candle went out. But maybe someone new? "I want to be in love forever like a memory that never dies the moment of truth will it be now or ever? But if now is to be our last night." I smoke and wonder Hunter S. and the ballad shroks me to the bones, this night this night, Dr. Sax, passion, justness, eternal longing, dark sister with her colorful scarves and dresses and so young so young and ancient. Whisper to the night, "Drown the sea flight in a city of seraph." Wanting, wanting, what does she want? Really? Really the really? Laws of the last night sings singes flares heart dig must be. Then slowly softly fades. Hamlet's father ghost, go down on that ghost plane train strain pain jurisdictions of the deathly echoes in burning of the questioning drowners like a flower that never. Time and sense on and on and yet the colloquial the infinite the dance the sun the…Let It Be. Celtic. Celtic. Whales. Ireland. My dream of animals, my dream of Blackfoot who said, "Ticotta." You want the flame to make sense? Love? Love. Many bids adieu. Stirring and my eyes glazed blind drown me in your love little flower, take me to the old Dawn to perceive the way of magicians witchdoctors Morrisons. Some Lord to the spangled town piping in the creatures. New, so new. I can feel the tears in my heart, my nipples eyes, a crown of leaf, a zillion cats, the fire brewing just, and our simple vow to the invisible spirits: Sitting Bull, Wovoka, Buddha. But not Jesus. Not Jesus. Tangles. Promise to love you in this red perplex in this untruthful zone of forever, promise to love you in this fish cloud in this Wounded Knee memory ancestral and Jung. The flutes play and relax me.

These songs, what if its me? Miracles man. Every woman miracle.

So they get to be talking about homosexuality witch makes me nervous. Then came the revelation from Grant that Kennedy's brain was eaten, all night I can't stop thinking bout it, it turns me on, to eat a brain, wow, how much more wicked does it get than that? But that's One Verse for ya, all sorts a surprises.

Then I'm standing by a Breakdown Café and Jack and Grant walk up (day later) and Grant's skateboarding and flips and rolls right out in front of a car, "Look what fell out of my pocket," and he holds up a little glass vile with a little white lump of crack in it.

"Cracky Crackerson," says Jack.

Grant skates off but he aint really Grant this time. Me and Jack Vilmer sit on the stoop and smoke our American Spirits and talk rap sing as St. Paul clacks all around us. "I like that feeling of being a stranger, ya know, weird cities different dissident cats. I've been living here a while, too comfortable."

I say, "Yeah this place kinda freaks me out, the drugs the booze the whores."

Jack says, "Joseph Campbell praised Buddhism."

I dig that, praise is one thing but to put into practice… like Bukowski took Buddhism farther than Kerouac without all the preaching. "There's a lot of homeopathy goin on, a lot of tricksters."

Jack nods, he looks like a cross, a cross between James Dean and Sitting Bull.

We make the town me and Stick Figure, weekend of jamming weekend of looking at art. I stay up all night

Saturday and into Sunday morn mourn, Stick's in bed and I dip into his vast collection of records tapes CD's and Ghost Dance to Dylan, Apogee, Sun Ra. The immense sun dawns between the warehouses, I brew a pot of java and roll endless cigarettes. Peanut Head and Bagel Buns (parents) are meeting us in the afternoon. I drink down that Black Medicine and put on another record R.E.M. bootleg. Around eight Stick awakens, "Ya wanna go to The Breakdown?" I axe.

"Yeah okay why not?" Stick rubs the sand from his brown Indian eyes.

We're in the coffee shop Stick does his usual routine and finds a newspaper and reads, I vegetate on the wondrous jazz coming from the speakers and girl watch, oh girl watching, ogling, tight jeans tight T-shirts dyed hair funky boots short skirts nose and ears and lips pierced and esoteric tattoos short tall thin fat black white French African Oriental it's a veritable parade of beauty. Then blue bam Charles B. walks in, he doesn't look so tough I could take him, ah but he's an old warrior an ancient rainbow his big Polish nose his Buddha eyes his Larry Bird legs his slumped boxer shoulders, la la lie.

"Sometimes I feel trapped."

I see Peanut Head in the window, we go out and greet the folks. "You look like you've just come back from the Seven Seas," says Peanut Pickle.

"Yeah Alice In Wonderland," I haven't bathed for a few days, my hair wild and longish.

Stick and Peanut are running a race at the college. They get their numbers and off they go to gallop six miles. Me and Bagel Buns drive o'er to Grand Ave. she wants to look through a bead shop. I go in with her and find a little Yin Yang, I stare at it but something about it disturbs me so I put it back, I then find an Ank and gaze and wonder at that too, but religious symbols are for the dying (or the living) (I aint neither).

It's a warm chill spring night and I go to sleep in my single bed and I dream: I'm in Chicago with ma and I fall down some steep steps and deeply cut my ankles and wrists, I wander around the town bleeding asking for food or change and am ignored, finally I go back to the bus terminal and fall on the escalator and anonymous people or tramping walking scurrying over on top of me, I find ma, "Why didn't you tell me the those steps were so steep?" She vanishes, I'm still bleeding. Then a unknown man tells me to go to the yellow house on the corner of the street where I grew up, I go there limping and knock on the door, Blake answers and looks at me with compassionate eyes then his old lady comes to the door and we sit on the front step. Blake goes off to do some errand. The high school basketball team I played with when I was a teenager arrives dressed like hipsters. They bring out some food and start eating on the floor, I join them eating the vegetarian stuff. I wake up and know the woman living below me with all the brother friends is holy. I go into the living room with the windows open and the moon the moon is gigantic beautiful setting in the west, never seen it so big and white and lush, I close the windows and go back to sleep.

Some ancient gypsy in the saloon of desire, some vines from a hollow beggar on the horse to nowhere, the drunkard shows up at my door totally changed dancing with Mr. D. and I can't help thinking that is me five nay four years ago demon, demon, demon of the stone bed never sleeping in that gasoline frenzy. All my letters burning in a gone cabaret poor ethnic and writing to the tunes of Tom Waits, writing to find me…

It's a wan slow gray today getting over the flu and resting up future battle future parts on the Shakespeare stages of engine of Mary praying of bartender solace. Will you find the flowers in the plethora of emigrant tears? Many names for the sis bone and wish dog. Put the memory in the ever my mind instead all, just mixing the melancholy in a song of age of vestige of circles. I have painted the words and the blankness of how recoils to the river called morrow. Noise from below, birds above, trees swaying, cars eating the earth, highway Doppler and hands red stomach red eyes brown. The green coming to. Singing questions of regret, oh time oh remembrance oh kiss oh goodbye, and out there their holding the hearts for a feast of plaintive desires and pensive skin. Close my eyes the room and her playing naked…her playing with crayons and India ink as I dress to find my whiskey.

With a demon's hand a whale's nail with a what on the cusp of your wine red lips your wine white mask begging shrieking. The Book of the Dead I'm trying to transcribe this. To descend to detox, counting the gates…nowhere… counting the tunes. Throw it to the wind and step into the eerie or? Or? Or? Dance to the dirge my eyes brown diamonds my eyes blind bats concealed in the cave of pain. The questions haunt me haunt me like the rolling bone like the lips dying of Hamlet's…I can't think…the deal what's the matter? Did I partake? In the hellish rituals of addiction? Did I purge my sinning skeleton till the doves wept? These songs of Hell. To be human, simply, and the halls of sad clowning toteming the mourn. Iconoclasts of the Hades carnival. Oh shit, ma I'm writing writhing. And its weird but for the ghostly trees of time I'm sitting still and scared. The rite. Whose lie is it now?

We could stay up all night painting with the Halloween

Woman and listen to Talk Is Cheap and Big Star and Main Offender and Born To Lose (Too Loose)…them was de daze… reading rock magazines at the record stores the library the uptown bookstores, ah fuck, what a trip.

Halloween Woman, you got to understand she could be a junky I mean I tried that ole brown flower once and I can see why one would wanna live in that zone the trick being not to come down the vicious never come down and you got to admit it's a biology world, it's a saintly deception, it's a political Apache nose ring of impossible. But on the other hand Halloween Woman like The Doll and the whole fucking Orient could be the way the answer the riddle being THINK FOR YOURSELF! Cuz cuz one's mind is one's mind own mind itself, could be a kite?

Esoteric, the way to find a way a personal way a independent way a succinct niche of Beat histories wailing in the gray gray dusk and Babylon is just a commercial no more no less. Ah Motown you saved my sorry ass. The graffiti of lambs inside the wall-less lawless pa-less sha-less quakes of forever (I use the word "of" a lot) (so what?).

Think for myself? Who am I?

Oday okay so I'm listening to The Beatles staying up late, nothing to say, just the think thinking looking look.

How'd he do it? Raise a blind painter a deaf musician? Ah coming off booze is the hardest thing I've ever done, art a pittance an ease compared. How'd he (howdy) reinvent music with such gusto? The poet supreme. I'm gonna cry just, just thinking bout it…the years pass like gullets of time waving into the slipstream of consciousness. My coffee almost done I can hear it boiling.

Dad, dad, and its still mothers' day, raining a lot lately, got the window open to let in a nice chill strong breeze, my plant thriving despite the chronic smoke, I got a Dylan New Orleans bootleg on the box. But I feel sad, I feel at least I feel something? Had a dream of Charlotte last night she got on top of me in her bikini and she felt magnificent, I think I think she's my soulmate, and later I look at our family pictures, beauty, beauty everlasting. I'm crying. Too alone tonight, too much now. The illimitable absence of am in the fellaheen village as I blues the conjunctions imaginative and stir the spirits with useless word, as I electrify the foreign spaces of why in a drumming release, oh victory oh rite oh time. The history man and crawling upon any star's final flame, I need loveglance, I got it the other day and it scared the shit outta me: Halloween Woman is back. I'd recognize dem voluptuous knockers anywhere. I'm not old enough to partake in the charade The Reality Theater, I'm still Hamlet Peyote brooding horsely the run of wine and pomegranate.

("Twas in another lifetime one of toil and blood when blackness was a virtue and the road was full of mud I came in from the wilderness a creature void of form come in she said I'll give ya shelter from the storm.")

And I whisper to myself after listening digging hearing absorbing this, "God, that's so beautiful."

On a silent black. On a silent black night the witness trees jigging cuz of da wind, pastoral glimpses and sober recollecting the was of am, crying and sighing and my whole body wan in the electric cross white of streetlamps and gloomfunk. Waiting for her, not as simple as waiting on my sacred coffee. Waiting for her. I'll take off my mask and my eyes still to see clouds but I will search through the fringe gray dreams yesteryears and silly wets to counterpart the visage of smile.

Ah time I remember Sad Eyed Lady and the apocalyptic prophesies and when she heaved her chest and her breast lunged forward I thought, "Never, never, no chance, Jesus help me." Everything had conspired against me. Delirium Rimbaud on outskirts chasing amongst the flames of consumption to a distant revolve. I am out of it now but I remember. Remember as I was painting my Blood Ghost picture, "No man cunts," and I collided with Nazi collided with the clashing deceptions of a blameless war. How? But now the rolling winds of I Ching have brought me through, saved, not by some mirage honeymoon Christ but by the simple blessed ancient Buddha-original mind, original man, divisional man, that is, a flower's divisions. So sing for the ancients of future. The arcane in the phallic sing for the infallible angel of stoned that stone of mercury of Jung, and when the tide is high let the moon frown, let the moon frown...

and as these words sing out in the night I let the night night as fools of gold caught and fold I think of my father, do I even have a father? Some Tarot some crazy beauty of the want-to-cry Ann the returning god do I feel it, the ancient dream of some pink dawn, the future harmonies of yellow Jesus peyote, the gripping cunt of childbirth random and actor, the changing of the guardians as the gates blind but for the moon of Indian grace, the harps of illegal diamond sacraments in the sacrificial found, the disappearing fog of a long night in beer wine whiskey to dance under the seas of circus, ah shit all of this I feel in my heart's heart beating mysterious retreating like Richard to the back-to-you, go on, don't hold back, way of the transpersonal transparent funk of tribe half stepping to golden. Sip of water, my love my love, with the silence of doves your out there in the Liquid Night baying to a dime of situational rock, some distant throb of amour a séance a Café la Breakdown, to match the light of myth in a flickering swirling strike, to hold the very essence of love with hands made of vulva or rambling to the twin of spirit ah man the night just ravens to the between of wings cast unremitting the glow of history. I'll call her Melanie...

Ten twenty tonight, listening again to a New Orleans Dylan boot, just trying to ant the quall of going crow disillusionment though infra in the fine, I'm waiting feline shelter in the midst of transitory ghost past and beyond any electric eagle the wane for veins' justice to train of funny stride the rill em rhymed rewind request ashamed as I am bugged into a junk of prescription and wondering where Alex is? To take the peyote little pill little ragman...little ragman in the flux on that Mexico morning the specter trumpet and the damn dog knowing fooling it's a Tricksters' Paradise and yea only sahant the fibs with a bellyful of gel. Ah your plasma money's no good here go back go back and git greener.

Golden the Bough of this dawn this Dawn this peyote this Peyote, in ecstasy, in Luciferean pursuit of some future symbol, shit what about Goethe? Jung and his lover Pickle the magick bluesman swirled and jazzbeat of the glimpsed existential junctions, oh pursuit, these Oedipus possible tangibles integers and roses planted fresh in the flour of her mask caught fish in the hour of my ask. To quartz the body in a El Greco sundown to listen to the dogs' legends in the make of so-so with diamonds for eyes and limbs of vegetable, hey that song beyond sleep bubbles through the vortex into peyote evenings of Mailer and the nude disembodied King shades of Jester pladues of Queenfall jangling down the stairs of Blake to the Alice Chief at Ze Breakdown Café and candle burning strongly purple purple and Picasso's rue coup final eyes chained to deathhands musketeering the last doors of sensation in a exile of fog of the last third. Crazy Jung dreaming coin to the fate to the today to the tree and all's well. Mythic orgasms flowering into some Halloween some rezzed pale cloak shadowing the silver crosses and old time traveler in the empress crescent numbers the alpha bits my love my love and iced of Kurt gray grow glad ah fucking dusk underwater drawing inclusion to telepathic homeopathic at all dangling wrangling ceremony The Doll crumbles we draw the circle inside our microscopic tent. Where did Dawn Peyote last claims and chalk tremble feather seeking expecting howling? The usual us Allah and Dixie murder to beg fakir and she is absolute dark eyes scarves whatnot. Then a man mammal'd like a drink on fire to evolving shrouds in the threads of a overture fugue once the green poly ticked and we cruised the alleys beers joints acid. Peyote.

Sacred dance sacred song sacred street. The laced child moves forth proceeds like a tulip of insight into the magick of come. The cross and all the yin the yang the rivers of holy. And within this dance this gig jig is the radiant flow of err in a wavy wave borning the new is regrets of limbinal poor beat be. The in of Indian in a inverse inverted in clux the crux to sway in the in of out outer and experiments showed the Hermetic a Hamlet of now of nowhere that now blues and nowhere gray, madness flips and Mardou the hip Ophelia of the West as Jack and Jackson paint the words of East and coming so down, the lowing lowering of some anonymous Christ and Buddha there with a silent blessing. Oh the granite grave oh the Sartre confusion oh the holy glances of Allen Babylon Lotus Child in the ghetto another another and my hands companions of real, companions of real, silver surreal the crash the empire the wine the lovers, and forever tired in that Ghost Dance and losing all minds BLOP and turning turning turning to the gravitational ecstasies of bees debris sure choose that or this and the asylum uptown has concocted a ocean so vast even the peripheries have specter'd. Will you show me? Oh Melanie where were you today? Eveing the apple Adaming the peach clinging to a bird like profusion wax of spiral. I had something, what was it?

Melanie Melanie I grow my hair long for you I see a million flowers flying in the illimitable skies of Earth and Heaven, Melanie I read Shelley (or want to) I want to sea you again and again. I'm in love I really am. The distances now voids of desire honest and the ocean that is now my heart a flaming ocean a sun ocean a ocean that sees, and in my imagination I see your face and body perfectly perfect perfectly woman perfectly brightly and my eyes growing stronger more romantic and the tomorrow of yesterday prudencing the rose tulip swear of vow's remembrance and I and I want to just be with you, no more no less, just to hear your childlike green voice of emerald distractions your tight loose clothing your everchanging shoulders and the yoga within. I have heard and dug your music Melanie, "And it was my shadow growing smaller…" someday maybe when our prayers are immaculate we will be together, belonging belonged belong, and the changes without grasp of blood's mortality will pass through the eyes of many needles and kiss the camel. Melanie I'll teach you my insides and all my blue wishes and all my invisible trains which yearn for moon and I'll let you take me to any city any farm and communing before the wildflower I'll look you in the eye in the mind in the heart and say communicate beseech my deepest truth, my age, my name, my mask, my soul and spirit, always and always, I will show you, I will show you my past I will sing you now I could hope for a future extending like a highway into a happy mystery. Jesus went before us to talk of the underdog, Buddha came before Him to speak of the sentience and rippling currents of a how existence, me, Dawn, Dawn Peyote, I have come to simply love you, "I was not born to lose you," my father Tom Pickle sang but they're my words too my sentiment. Returning from a thousand visions: Nazi visions, bacteria visions, buttfucking visions, cannibal visions, going to sleep in a whiskey deathbed wile sliding on Keith Richard's mind: Demon, and in between in some abstruse space in the colliding forces of raying street hustle I am now growing, growing LOVE VISION. And you're the season of this reason.

Meager, its meager and the gods and dogs and goddesses of Hades have no sympathy for the suicide childs the landing the landing, when all's left is a…shit and I can take a hint. Sometimes I can't wait for death. Sometimes. Like now, knowing the total control the witches and Halloween, infra facts slide I'll go soft anyways, ah hell the story sieves out anyway, not much to tell to yell to hell with it. Till some lighthouse of obscurity beams into this shipwreck. I won't go back, go back to the booze no. I used to be green now it's a nice shit brown even the flag mocks mocks the tingle.

I'm in a trance tonight Dionysus and The Rolling Stones no Breakdown Café tomorrow just wailing all night long with my hot tea and summer turning hot, sweat, see. See the plant growing see the cipher of winds' gentle see the yeah of Mick and Keith and intense dancing Peyoteville man got ya where ya wanna go wanna be. Doesn't it just drag the Pharaohs of electricity the androgynous brotherhood Whitmanic, we need we need. And priceless the stars of cat love and priceless the stars of songstress in the flux of birthing a ride. Watch you vanish watch you show me to the golden exit of death, ah we'll never die, the gates open forever, the apple untouched, the snake god, the window Vishnu, the web not a restive trick, the faith unbroken, the profile Pickle's me, and Sticky Fingers. Dawn Peyote, Midnight Peyote, writer Peyote, angel Peyote, horse Peyote tingle tingle. The grail of bop and succinctly I grace the planes with a desert glance of suspicion into a market of un unconscious and deeply green greeeeeeeeen man and the riffs of raffs the jangles of jingles the spangles of little dangle and the horny horn horning in on a blanket of respect, I just don't know anymore, (tell a story) (okay) so I go to One Verse with Bagel Buns…naw it's a night of blowing not narrative bowl sheet. Got to read Genet man, got to digest Sartre. Sip of tea.

Wild Horses man, and I imagine Jesus and Mary would dig this, this night of hope, hope for Melanie and the potential: I can feel love. August is my month when my heart conspires with my mind and my body flows loose in the heat of Africaesque close to the sun. Melanie, so sweet and soft and soft spoken. My faith fluttering Phoenix like in the come back. The life of gray yesterdays is turning pink yellow orange red and I in a happy ecstatic hub. That Ant Man hub of terror is now slower and more lovish and I'm glad I didn't hit the liquor store today I'm glad I called her. Maybe I'll have a story to write instead a this automatic crap. Wild Horses I sang to Calling and she said, "Beautiful," that sums her up too, sums Melanie up as well. Sums up all the women I've been with: forest first time to cars and basements and dormitories and apartments and schools and random lovemaking of the bestial amour wild true just, The Flesh Communion. She said she'd see me at The Breakdown, I'll be there with my eyes flowering before her and her young lie (I know I know). "Young girls make shadows shorter than the shadow of death in this town," I'm not sure what that means but any shadow shadowing me from her blanket smile in the godsun will do, she's too much, too much beauty. My heart I want to be heart to heart with her, mind to mind, hands gentle and voice bread in the wine of time. She is the angel come. And me in my crib dreaming dreaming dreaming of the body sanctifying any sovereign resolution to send my thoughts into the wilderness and rock the roll of and show her my genius of compassion all Buddha-like like a streetlamp winking at the moon like a tree making secret vows to the wind with her roots singing a modern blues like a stranger's plea to the world and finally it will never make sense but hell we sing anyways in the hearing universe microbing yinning yanging total pop in a candle sandal I see her feet bare and the last words of some prophet goes bang against all the ghosts and we see the bop the horns the calypso of violets tulips roses all and the all just a wavering reincarnation to traverse the cosmos alone Egyptian Book and all for a thousand nay a million years a million trillion years of them unknowing clouds and to come back to the nightingale's reward of respect like the time and how not to fight time but to acknowledge any Dionysian riff and then hide or hike spy or shy flow but go shimmy but gimmie and just that fact simple that she knows my names after all my destinies after all my wrong turns and this ending this beginning what song to bring to the banquet what child am I to wonder beyond my own milkless bones my karma free of The Quivering Meat Conception moving now to a new plane hoping someday I'll be able to say to her without scaring, "I love you." I want to make her eyes sigh.

Maya to Mayo. "I'm Mayo I'm mayo I'm dago I'm Mayo…" crown of thorns, the suffering, the murder… begin, begins again and again. Sacrament. Drums for wine. Amiri. Life inside. Asexual. Raising up, forever spiked to wood. Spears of government. Gabriel. Accept what? Cross? Before the moon speaks? Blood time. Turtle ghost. Decipher the language, partly Tibetan partly African partly Indian. However angelic. Naked death. I'm pagan. Smoke and light, the straight and the ethereal. Tribes vast roaming desert speaking a infinite truth. Classes fall. Revolution. Demons of the lake train. Mixing…we. Nervous trembling on the shafts of Hades. Bring me back. An act of behavior said Bacon. Wail Wail Wail Wail. Then come the angels. I still don't believe. But I see. I see why. Off. Off and dead. Off. Off and alive. Outlaw father fucking outlaw. Who is he? Judaistic. Mohammed. Did you get boo'd on? Uni. Unless…spiked two three. Guess what. Bouts. Doubts. Rise into and not up. Lettuce. Lazarus. So easy to spell. The math of history. Serpents' reprise. Wail at the walls all walls. Supplicating any accomplishment. Lords. The final not even last but modernly ancient bring the daaaaaaaaay. Cave shadow. Promised no lamb. Om may co. may go. May is June with Henry. Wait. Sleeve. Oh this crown. Pictures of the pawn gill. Allen's science. Journal. Went befoe. No R. The wake finishes the wake. Tempting every grain of sand every hair every snail of destiny. You was hey ya hey ya. On Mayo. On Nayo. On Mayo. In between the beat is a flower. With the choir electric. Dante. A film. Beatrice. Two Marys. Ong. We a la oh. Chanting up secular and storm of empathy, compassion. Let it fade. Hold. Hold hell. Hold me. Popular opinion. Stands alone wolf taming what? Wolf taming man. A different high on high. Almost over. Over…

Cast that demon out boy rejoice in the wail recoil like a snake to the dancing Jesuses and bulls and buffalos and ants let go of the train and walk walk simply to any Tibet to any hell for within isn't always doesn't always half to be winter within cuz its summer boy and the healing done begun, tears in my eyes and my heart taking over the rest of my body in the chill plant-like drone of the cattle tomorrow so I rewind my mind and step up to the fate to the will to the ghost's arcane revolt and know the mysteries will deepen. The drop, to drop farther than an ocean's longing and see all the fish to talk and fall in love with a bird, I tell ya man I looked out the window other day and I swear I fell in love with a bird and know she is in love with a me, "Have you ever been experienced?" have you ever fallin for a simple beautiful bird? Any spell the genetics replaced with honesty, oh booze of Bach oh Peter Gabriel helping me through. In a dream I heard the word "resurrection" could mean something? But they Ba now and cowbells for Alice the table set like a opium specter in the drums of NOW and the thunder rolls and the abstract folds three four beat beats beating and how now I is alive. Oh question. Through a haze of strangled self I get off the omega boat ah land. Through a daze of hatred I dance to everlasting love on a Melanie glance. Run for Thomas thumb of poetry, sleep writing ghost writing moon quirk of telepathic trancedom in the frilly belly of liver damage and a gargoyle leading me to the lions to the tongues speaking in eyes to the foreverhood of black to the season of water to the male to Whitman's song to the heavenly fire of always. The living man.

The monkey happy this, this monkey happy, I've come out and synthesizing Gotama and J. on the chocolate of Marcel and talking to the French spirits the African spirits the all of one one within all and and and in in in and without is alright too. This monkey sees. I am monkey. I am snake. I am spirit. I am am. And neither two and either too and seether few and camels chew. Neither too for Bodhisattvas of the diamond sung funky apples spunky eyes of the now requesting sanity. Bliss of sobriety ecstasy of pure of Pure Land of fellaheen of still of know. The scent of vegetables bespeaks an ocean of birth. The feeling the climbing word the uncovered the hide the revealed the howl the bestial forecast casting unions even unions of Lucifer and me in me and of me and I the devil believing in any sprouting child vortex and virtue and crimson and sapphire and the jewels of Nazism brake crushed and all I see is shit and the fools of Nazism make…what am I saying? The moon isn't really white. Go back to your source India Africa

Ireland and tortured by America diagnosed. I could write a book called Nazi Fear. Why don't I fear Russia too? Or Rome? Why Hitler? Most recent I suppose. Ah shit let it go if they're gonna eat my brain…you see there's no escape, no escape through drugs through alcohol through sex through politics through religion and it seems some methmatical scientific fix, woe to the biology of the number, woe for the imposition of the dead symbols, woe to the man who thinks with his schlong (me), woe to the angels for hiding in heaven, woe to the politicians' mold of suit and tie and short hair in a generic nightmare of normalcy, woe woe woe woe woe to Lame Deer for holding on to the past. Ah preach me a rotten asshole…

Its too much, within within within, and Jesus and Isis, all of the masks, all of the asks, basking before me as I find resolution in desolation in conflagration, go back all the way they're still alive and Robbie singing now to now ear to mouth breast rosy and the dale sinking up, its too much (acid mantra), the fifth day of May this is June and "the law of the sun will protect us." The underworld was it worth the visit? My bathtub Mexican my walls poly my love India this Sindian living in Zen living in the yen of poems replete and outside the birds with blue heads black bodies peck away in deception. Takes so little…and something has landed something has taken off. Egypt? Israel? Where to wail when the walls fascist blame the lion? "Our relatives from the sky." Zen and the outskirts of thought when the moon lights up my bedromb in holiness rock light stone glow androgynous universe and Shiva has a nice ass, he he, the telepathic the hug thought the history the anthropomorphical the mill the…the blind one, feminism cures blindness, I saw a Becky.

I was within him on the cross.

Or is it just another archetype? The cross…waves from the valley timetable of curse and dust and privately running to the forever summer in the matter of some E and out there in the brother alone the drums get in the blood get in the blood and every symbol alive every subtle shape breathing nature and form from the living emptinest of traversing. Into the mythic we shall go and it was terrifying now I burn with a translucent wonder hot hot and even in sleep I'm thinking thinking and even awake I'm dreaming dreaming and gathering up the close the first of moon thank moon Ra descending can't find the senses I burn in wonder. Baptized in Hell, finding my way, studying the flames and I Chings of despair ascend in the spirit winds of old of primeval of ancient of dice and Tarot, some gold passenger, some ordinary ride, some diplomatic scourge.

Whence the summer high of lasses gold in the way of find, Tracy, is she waiting for me like her songs say? Should I cross another bridge another bridge to lesbian? Hold the space of the heart in the possible stigmata of your knowing hand your knowing song your knowing eye of mind of America of Africa. Wake me wake me. Wanna go to you I hear you where are you? The Doll Sara, was that you? Some Buddha of the deceive? Is my baby suckling on your sacred breast? Our, our. To take the sacrament in the divine afternoon and come alive to the going saviors of East and that dance where the skeleton wears bells pointy boots Finnegan man I tell ya, so you sing of readiness as I read Millett and Osiris and Isis and Lame Deer and The Lost Years Of Jesus…I read so I'll know, so I'll know when I'm ready to see you through the shroud of diamonds and hearts and Jacks and clovers, I read so I'll see the esoteric meanings of your vast madrigals in the shinning wait as the winds and the witness trees and the poems of Rimbaud totter then grow, grow to the reading of Oriental secrets, Atman, coyote, Gotama, Jesus, Henry, all the secrets glow like a heart of heaven on some purging fire to nowhere, nothing, desperate, hallow, hollow, one, One, and the abstract angel of modern witch brew throws out the staid curse of male into the blind nation of red rain of crystal ghost of drunken prophets of towns made of silk of howls in the goldmine of highways dominated by some Seth of the underworld man and how the snake knows knows knows and finally one has to become a bird. Some eventual crown of feathers to replace the square. I went from Tracy to Jim so now we go from hope to madness, Greek replacements, Apollo and Rome, Bush and oil, and any moment the One could return. Dionysus.

So friends stop by.

Go high with the voice cry in the walrus, rapping the visions I close my eyes and it matches night nig night the black egg of thought. Joker of the universe in a tower of climb to the Hare Krishna of bop, Lennon. No smokes burning, no coffee brewing, no desire of the geometric idolatry, I'm a fool a clown a upside-down man. The wind is a piano the grippled streetlamps and the sun hath gone down, Buddha Christ, this answer to the centuries this Beat scat of the injunctions this Ginsberg of modernity feeling like an idiot. Some real heartbreak despair at The Breakdown Café today some chick and mouthful of pills and her laughter wants agreement, really though it's a wail of tears…oh fate twill slide to a justified end for all. One must purge. On the own. At The Breakdown I said I was afraid of the world. Buddha blessed Buddha. And the eyes in my head see a cripple in every corner.

Lass of the dark who sees me for what I am. Islam. When shall I study this? I live in ignorance. My love in fragments like pennies scattered on the floor. My love poisoned like the intolerable addictions of America. Lass of Africa who sees my crooked eye my demented vision my lackluster insides. Islam. When will I wake up? Love need not be a compromise, but equally sharing and equally departing to other lovers, other rivers, Egyptian, Hindus, any sacred onion of the dialects' seam seeming to glean the readiness of song. Ah my scarf, on this table, I was wondering where it twas. So many thoughts in my heart which one to believe? So many thoughts of her heart and I wait, I let her make the first, if she wants me, I'm waiting, I'm waiting.

Thin the cross, vanquish the crown, "When will I see you coming so many miles?" I wanna hear her music, her CD player wasn't working today at The Breakdown Café, I glance at her beautiful brown skin, her cosmic Earth round eyes intelligent, her funky shoes and colorful garb…I'm simply the stranger, I do not know, I've come to hear and receive any question and settle into more questions astral limbo clear. African women you are the origin, the heart of a plethora of mysteries shinning acoustic as these trees sway on the farm town of sobriety. Amiri and Jean, Sun Ra and Malcolm, familiar distance and gray fog of knowledge the piano quoits of galaxy leader shrine falling to my. Storm of the heart. She could hear my music? What would she think? My favorite The Innocence Mission, my Irish birth birthing to the planes of equality, circle, circle, and the birds yearn, the men yearn, we could trade places for a lifetime, birdman, manbird, scarlet of the ghost gypsy in the very center of oblivious sin. She speaks another language and I should be speaking Lakota I can feel the obtuse math of English shrouding our possible way, words, words, and if we come to love? If we come to understanding? Mahila is her name. Room of nations at The Breakdown ruminating should I call her? I wish she'd call me, my no-self my abstract haunted running to solitude like a hermit of thrope missing Ann. Who knows? She left when I started to roll a cigarette. I can feel her spirit within me.

Maybe a little history of The Breakdown Café is in order, a Breakdown Café is anywhere the outcasts gather, the misfits, the righteous, the meek, the addicts, the schizophrenics, and it can be a coffee shop a hospital a crib where brothers and sisters congregate, ah hell fuck man America is a Breakdown Café, everywhere the show's the same, homeopathy, needles, smoke, booze, madness, aftermaths of losers and freaks and if you're lucky you graduate into a clown. The pree and pre of shapeshifters' futures, and like a hill a mound a pillow or as Patti Smith urges "cross over boy cross over." The Breakdown is full of temptations and ironies and deluge and tears and forever the game (is it a game?) changes like the I Ching the chance just flows and flows. After spending years and years in Boozeville I withdrawaled into Coincidenceville where I saw all sortsa unspeakable things, miraculous stuff, crazy to the core, and now it's The Breakdown Café where the other-side-ones seek a reprise from Grant's Main, you can find the first traces in Walt Whitman and then onto Henry Miller witch transmuted and blossomed into the Beats. It's a poly whirled whirling like "four seasons in one day" and the pale the dark the rainbows all search for the fucking flower of justice.

But before all this I was reared, I wanna talk bout my religious upbringing. I think the first taste of the ole religo I got was on television watching that seventies flick about ole J.C. and when it came to the part where the Roman king has all the newborns slaughtered my dad said, "That doesn't mean anything." Then it was on to Sunday school and church and there I saw the true ugliness of the Wasichus so ever since I've had a bittersweet feeling concerning Christianity, but now all things considered, Christ wasn't a paleface so now I dig and love that rebel outlaw saint prophet while throwing out the bathwater, Rome can go fuck itself. So I musta learnt some things some shit though at the time I couldn't have cared less all I wanted to do was play basketball rather than be locked up in some tacky building. I didn't take it very seriously, still don't.

Then in Hi School I met Bob DeVille and big Bob was into Buddhism, mythology, acid, cheap wine. The best was just the two of us in his rambly bedroom tripping sipping smoking discussing. Bob had Joseph Campbell books and his fave was one called The Tao of Pooh. This is and was my true education, DeVille's bedroom. Bob would talk about enlightenment and I would do acid induced drawings and his typewriter, I didn't understand his writings at the time and I would give anything to see them now. So just a hint of Buddha carried me through the nightmare.

My chick at the time was a Bible thumper, a Jesus junky. But my Bible was the discovery of Henry Miller's Sexus, I've probably read that book two hundred times and that's no Harvard lie. I was in love with her body and some of her soul and mind but this praying this asking and begging imploring to the white man's concepts I just couldn't and can't accept. Look what Christianity has done to Indian America, to Mexico. Within the last five hundred years the whole way of Indian life and many lives have been obliterated in the name of so-called god. No flower of justice there brother.

When I moved to Minneapolis I took a class called Chinese Philosophy, I was also reading Bukowski and Duchamp probably the best white exponents of Tao for my generation. They didn't preach which always turns me off, but their language was stripped bare, concise, relaxed. I also started reading Oriental poetry and listening to Miles Davis, and Miles is probably my real introduction into Egyptian ideas, Bitches' Brew. And all this time I tried consciously and unconsciously to move away from any and all Christianity, consuming vast amounts of booze and marijuana.

Minneapolis is secular, cosmopolitan. And I was pretty much basically a bum. There is a fog of years there, I don't know what I was really thinking if it all, smoking and drinking. I didn't give a shit about any religion, I fell asleep during the Malcolm X movie. I hated A.A. cuz of the bullshit of "higher power." Simply put, who cares?

It was after my suicide attempt and moving back to the folks' house and staying there a few months then getting my own pad that I began to read again. The Egyptian Book of The Dead. The pictures too are miraculous though I don't pretend to understand it logically, I was procuring my way through my own underworld, dead really, but searching. Then I bought Desolation Angels for ten bones at the local bookstore downtown. Then I read Mexico City Blues. Quetzacoatly. Artaud's Peyote Dance. Black Elk Speaks, American Genesis. And a discovery of Jean Basquiat. But it was really Kerouac who opened my mind and with the purchase of Some of the Dharma which my mom bought me and took me three years to read I started to feel the purity of the East.

Now I can sit down and read with jubilance any religion, they're all fantastic, sort of, more or less, but I am a Buddha, in my heart of hearts the Buddha speaks rings echoes the truest, so put that in your pipe. Though Islam awaits, or I await Islam, my curiosity growing, I know nothing of Mohammed.

Africa in childhood I saw an old friend at The Breakdown today, amazed to see a face I hadn't seen for twenty years, them shapeshifters man I tell ya, beautiful. And is he Tracy singing to me now? In this simple room? Africa. Africa. And I was pretty sure she was Bob Kaufman who I read last winter, brings the toddler days full circle, these African spirits watching me grow, not over me, but with me in some angelic periphery. The other African kid I grew up with is adopting a Chinese child, oh how I love this poly mix because, well, I'm sick of whites who think they're all gonna go to heaven. I don't mind deception but righteousness I can live without. Africa is pure. Brothers sisters sentient purity. Not afraid of the true light the true fire the Sun. That sun is the soul of god. Rimbaud knew this. Nakedness.

Ah go off to Joyce Land Pure Land, Lennon, John Lennon. Message of love. I wish I was Roualt to paint his portrait, or Redon. The amazing thing is I think he's my father. I could be wrong I've been wrong a lot in my life so ya know? But I was sixteen when I heard this beat beautiful music. Now I see Yoko as Buddha and Lennon as Christ, my folks, could it be? Why not? Of course I'm clinically insane anyways so what if I like to dream on this typewriter? Let the miracles occur, they'll happen whether you see em or not.

To a feast of fools in the peaceful vale I go and the homeopathic cats get under my skin at times, and scratch that back man tork that Peter because the only word is silence and the only silence is music. Let ye snout Sun the Ra. Old Angel Midnight is dead and gone safe and happy nirvana of common heav to the glimpsing searching crowd of nothing and strangely my cup isn't glass, I drink the ancient water nights of recovery sobering up dancing chanting my to reality way waywardly caught in the salt of old money Jeaning all that is, cuz once there was something and that something was FOUR, ah but the Forever Boys and Girls loused it all up by crucifying the cow the turkey the pig and even their master and now call it justice. Dig this man, the initials of an X in the surreal cumdish of any wind now their white now, oh to see beyond the veil of last, Neil and that hard crash to heaven precision man dig the eyes that note almost nearly everything I don't need Benzedrine I got my smokes and coffee and the rest you damn well…Dawn Peyote tonight, Dawn Peyote night and the nonsleepers injuncted by the pleaseable kackle memories crumbling to a blind sphere. "Do you have a girlfriend?" she'll never know. Hum and wail, Picasso has some strange treats and Duchamp tricks any.

To see truth through the haze of impossibilities, Irish Jesus, Indian Buddha, all the rites all the candles all the Allahs, and the days longing of Sinead or for or now I'm faced with forever will I find love in another? In all? Will I see the search for what it is? In the curves of snaky truth I sense the life the history in every leaf like Whitman singing of grass like Celtic songstresses of the vine growing reality, if now is to be, the star they came from vast faraways and the reciprocal teaching began and begat a zillion wars countless havens forever thoughts and ineffable heavens. Crying begins in my Irish papa my mother of the yard and store my brother of music, crying now, crying to sea, see the love and love within sight and sight because of love, it must be. Tremble my being my soul with these songs and they are ours, our first night, our second night, the flesh communion the reality theater, and the tales are staggering. Anyone can see I'm in ecstasy, this song better than heroin better than grass better than wine, this song is my spirit finding my body, my soul stripped bare to the even, the fingers the eyes, only a rolling orb, and the peyote nocturne is blazing in revelation for realization. Daystar daystar they and the red moon, the moment of must now overlaps and she Persian rugs Oriental tears of nowhere and this wasteland this copper demise this unholy string of the puppets final release, all of this speaking in shoestring tongues shiver you and the giver mischievous runchild in the spangled live us. Here comes the drums here comes the flutes, can I decipher the cipher? Choose for her the Lucifer? Date of the forseen upless doors in the gap in the drone: BEAUTY…more and stay, bishop gay, away from, be lay, Ricki Lee long face, oh shit I lost it. Celibate cigarette in the sheltered night.

I've been changed, changed by merely a presence, who? Some angel of the schizophrenia. We walked to the drugstore I had to mail a letter to Stick Figure and Grant, and now I'm in love. I can't describe it. I feel different. I feel different and at home with this soul. I can be myself. Previously phantoms of beauty of passed through these pages but this time its more tangible. She said she'd been reading a book about angels visiting real people, true stories. Ah chivalry, just be, be myself: a crooked man. And those lost in the breakdowns at the cafés of serious. Those forsaken those broken those who yearn for the spirits revealed, and what will be revealed? In this world of bay ought plays and traps snags and mazes what is to come? Cast out the preconceptions and replace em with a heavenly demonic clown, insight, thin to the vegetable of truth the moon rice of speculation and let the mornings Aretha. The Celtic prophecies now days seem ecstatic with the static of rumbird of kneefull or cross legged potential zap oh don't you know I've been in Doubt Town all my life, come out to love, its there, its waiting, that blue bus and all the snakes all the tomorrows all the counting its here waiting wait for her in the black eyed jester. All these times I just wish and wish, pree and pree, idolatrating any women for the moist slide and the hard nipple of cum, all this time wanting and wanting, and here she is, Jill? Halloween Shapeshifter Woman? The Doll? How many myths away from now will it take to believe in now? Make or mac? Shawl of eye in the ideas in the one, I'm not gonna fall anymore, I'll just stand, stand and let the sun know my name.

"She heard rumors she heard talk about the trail I left of broken hearts," ah but its my heart that's suffered too, suffered like gray my reason shrouding the haiku sundown, my heart pangs for fusion, my heart is bluer than bone, my blueblood crown rust, dust, my charkas little glimmers in the vast possibility. At last Dharma, karma, charma, in this rented romb I seek thy face, thy heart, thy spirit, thy whispered choice and hope its me you see in the dim spectacle of shroud in the sinned valley of coffee, we could steal away to the red dawn the pink sun the pale trust the eyebow of dreams…look, my fraud is the "always pondering my fate too late," for I know now I'll love you then and now so confused that I hide hide like sad train in winter the snow falling all over the torment of fishes who don't need light. My skull is talking, doubt of a conclusion, Earth of eye to eye, breast to breast, and the beat gods just stalk like corn growing us to be hopefully wild and free.

This book is the book of my thoughts, inspired to write tonight cuz a the sliver in the indigo sky, that little curve that little white almost S and how bout that? Reading at dusk Kate Millett and starting to see to see my chivalrous lust, I dreaming of the female body a lot, just the cunt the breasts that's all I seem to want. That moon is there, thorium of the night's justice, to see, to hear. "Careful what you go and wish for." And the witness trees fellaheen in the post-suicide attempt of me. I go from extremes, she just stared at me without any expression today and I want some sign, I don't know what I want anymore? Who knows just don't cut it no more. I go from extremes the old love hate male lust and no middle, charkas shock Ra's and staying up at nights wondering, wondering about all this the fear which seldom departs the old locked up forever fear. A life it is and alas the sins are but signs are but sighs. Abandoning the phallus for a independent mound of seahorse in the white banana moon night of actual possible possible actual. The omens are within.

Ah but the omens are…reading Kate Millett's Sexual

Politics today, frightening, the parallels of Nazi Germany and now America: Fatherland, Homeland, blind patriotism, propaganda...I'm afraid. Afraid of this nation, afraid of the elders who set up these seemingly impossible rites, afraid of raping a woman, afraid of being raped by a man, afraid of the mysteries: Schizophrenia, histories Indian, Zen Arcade has come upon me again though this time I'm a little more awake, a little more responsible, responsible for my very shivering own life and where I'll go from here? Afraid I've been brainwashed by a Nazi Bukowski who eye read nearly everyday for about four years, how I succumbed to the booze reinforcement man of the bum man of the fuck man of the fuck you. Or Henry Miller who namelessly characterlessly portrays women the way in which. I'm afraid I should be in jail, or am gonna end up there. I am me, someone who is attempting to be a writer and painter. I can live in solitude. I can live with myself though others frighten me. That's all for now, the dawning of Dawn, Quixote of Quixote, my name my name and that closet that unconscious that mound that dick...

The Sara formally known as The Doll, "Duped him good," she said as I sit on the grass smoking. Why do I call her Doll? Or fifties housewife? Or junky? Her name, why am I afraid to write her name? We have a past together and individually and now I'm alone to ruminate on this. I don't understand women, their truths are abstruse, and me the nothing simple leaning on Buddhism the Beats. To repent is a excuse to do wrong again to know the repentance will coddle you further and its endless. No, I would like to try again with Sara, to see through, to see through the deliberate confusions. No male gods this afternoon as I listen to The Black Crowes and wonder wonder what the future will fold?

Next day crying to The Innocence Mission...mystic

woman of song and me wishing preeing glad just (glad?) to
be alive. Nothing is clear, clearly nothing, clear as nothing,
cleared of nothing. Surreal, "Fumbling in the darkness
the darkness is only surreal," tis surreal and much more.
Visionary blues from whence ye get the bargain of more
than. Rattling off the visions, peyote brain funeral, slow
long days and Rick's mandala and now I the emotions
overtake me…some justice for the blind some tears created
by the sublime some plant-like satisfactions in the only of
a famished mercy turning turning to feminine possibilities
to the vast potential of unfilement, dede, and the fires I
welcome and the art shows of what? Art shows what? I have
no know now. I'm stripped bare by the Halloween even,
the orgasm of solitude the writing of beatitude and peace
for me now.

My sister so many, her violins her hills of the body truth
her colorful third eye her city of coincidence which swallowed
me up, over sacramentaltized in my blind jubilance in the
pavement of no crack Mr. Tambourine Man justly invisibly
and she smiled at me today my sister smiled at me and my
first thought of commerce then I looked later how young
are the old how young are the old and how old the young
(?). Sisters? I'm forever quiet in the out of maybe in outskirts
of memories displayed on this page where I write to recover.
No way is the know way any way anyway way knows the
waves there are no red carpets there is now but no cheese at
the end of the maze there is no crown waiting for the man of
nowhere now here to unchain me self, still I wish Sara would
show, I wish I wish and the leaf baby of crimson growth
yonder the moon then that cipher dream, Dawn Peyote the
cipher dream, and the sphinx and the Buddha seem to make
nebulous predictions, snout and eye, some things grow in
and the proportions of Africa unmask the distance of us of
us stars in the lion of Leo of August twenty five thousand

years is one season Zep Tipi. Hunch and guess Run Again Finnegan to the River to the circle to the very existence of essence a droning lullaby of a proletariat of a loving liar of a wicked candy bar, I am and was scared to the scarred scorched bone calcium electric and white death white debt white for some other womb green red green red and my computer is getting bored? Right black eyes? Chrissie.

Sad tonight.

I've been taken out of the game. Schizophrenia where the revolutionaries are contained. Forced to live in a "Christian" "America" in a state of forever bowing forever compliance. To live in the hypocritical nation, the whites who prosper the most pathetic the biggest slaves of em all, the sickest of that which is "normal." Schizophrenics have no options not even death but the sap of forked tongued Mr. Rogers in a conquering doubt. Where have I been? Where am I going? From one nowhere to another nowhere, and like Buddhism's truest sense it's all nothing, nothing passing into nothing. I don't forgive I can't forget I simply know it's a self complicated nothing, and wow man it just is and the actors of a Halloween old I'll never bring a child into this awful place this "world" so-called. I will pass into the most nothing nothingness and I will be forgotten even my own memory will dissipate and the fish and cats will rain once more. This is no supplication no prayer simply facts from a defeated individual, a half man who wants sex without the delusions of some balsa American dream, why can't we just exist noting the vast passing away of it all, the transitory of the all the imploding futures moons blood battering the consciousness? I'm naked now, naked in a country of masks.

Ah I'll show em all and live forever…

People folks come by my crib, there's really not much to

tell about my life these days. Mondays I wake up at eleven and drink a little coffee and smoke a couple legal joints then go to The Breakdown Café (day treatment) and listen and wonder if it's all an act? The old Halloween Chick and Time Rite Boy blues. Three hours I spend there and it does help, learning and communicating. I get home and eat and then brew instant coffee and put some tunes on and read: Beats, Millett, The Lost Years of Jesus, Hettie Jones, Jung, Buddhist shit and so on. After reading a couple hours I write this or poetry or journal or piddle about on drawings. Tuesdays I work part-time at a warehouse doing menial labor, not much news there either, lets me buy a book once a week or two, and there's some beautiful women to gaze at too. Wednesdays I'm back at The Breakdown so it goes with Thursdays and Fridays. Drinking coffee and smoking cigarettes, writing and drawing. Every other weekend or so I visit my folks in Rochester where I paint in the garage which is a blast I get the boom box activated and do my best Jackson Pollock impressions. On weekends where I stay here I read a few hours then draw and write. I am a pathetic aspiring artist going nowhere fast, my crazy days almost four years behind me. I don't have a girlfriend don't know even if I want one, I'm not well ecstatic about my life but I'm not lowdown bummed either.

I have a few friends if you can call them that one I think is Bob DeVille in drag. She's the most free and interesting, digs music, used to do a lot of acid, we get together and smoke and laugh, she goes out with a Jesus junky and I wonder, wonder sometime if I should ask her out? For instance, "If you and plastic Jesus ever break up would you wanna go out?" I think she'd say yes. Its been over a year and a half since I've "made love." So I'm a little on the desperate side when it comes to women, I wake up in the morning with a unhealthy hardon wanting to plunge once again into some moist oasis.

Another friend is my former preacher masquerading as I hip twenty something, my old roommate from the bughouse Mezzy. My first impression of Mezzy was he was pretty stupid, or like everybody else I come in contact with "pretending" to be dumb, patriotic, idiotic (the three are inseparable). Well the more I get to know Mezzy the more I find out he's fairly smart, funky, he's also afflicted with mental illness. We play chess, smoke, listen to the beautiful Sinead O' Connor, "She's yummy," I tell him, she is that album cover where she's in the garden wearing a bright red dress kinda bent over, plus she's the best damn musician since Aretha Franklin. (I'm starting to feel like Salinger)

In the ninth grade I heard Dylan and now I listen to Hard Rain's A Gonna Fall, its in my blood, my core is symbolist, my senses are mystic, my dad is a magician, a joker, a stern old ironist, oh don't scratch your head fool I know who you are like no other…we are both poet pests of the modern whirl searching for that flower of justice, Thurber too, and Brazil, why did we go to Germany? I know why you have hid your identity for the offspring of the famous are cursed pathetic, I dig you Dad, I love you.

But I could be wrong, maybe you aren't him and I'm only dreamin and all my Halloween vision is for naught, maybe the revolution is only D.T. fear, maybe I haven't glimpsed the future the now the aftermath? The war? Why do I feel like Ginsberg's my brother? Kerouac my sister? Why is Rimbaud greater than any Christ to me? Why am I possibly Indian? Halloween and leap years and anywhere's beat justice, I'm alone, alone I tell ya man and the shapeshifters of India of Africa why do I fall so in love with her? Characters straight out of Tarot mischief and that fucking Golden Dawn on my bookshelf, I wanna read everything. Especially Genet someday, he she sounds like a for real, queen of the revolution, dragster of the reign, and my hoping for a great change in America a womanly change a androgynous zone of possible Utopian freedom equality and brother all. Sister all. The show the show. Together in the immortal universe.

"Lost my life in cheap wine now its quiet time and the stars dig Jesus Christ could not help my faith but I'm underneath the cup," trying to get it straight, Buffalo Tommy sings tonight as these words hum in my heart. The story goes on and on and should I go to some gone savior? Should I drink the words of a heart torn by controversy? By hypocrisy? Can I see through to the truth of truths? To come out of a thousand storms and be alone in the why, to stretch beyond the reach of stars and see a million wise questions? Blue tonight, August almost here, my birth day. The lion of yellow. Left behind in the staggering seasons half heat and planes of innocence. Lean on look on and I remember Leon I remember Calling I remember Sara The Halloween Doll. I'm out here alone oh July oh sun oh high ways oh un-united states. To reconcile the months and the thoughts Catcher In The Rye now that I'm beyond, what happens after? After the ghost dance? After the eternal night dawns? For I am in a eternal night, blindness, deafness, muteness. And like The Don the dollish refrains of male of man just smoke and ashes to another delusion on that train of wombs' discoveries miles and miles, she travels distances and so far so far and yet the worlds she hath found she retains love and shines yellow red, bod blood and gold, and I in the desire seeking forth another round of peyote light.

I'm just fucking sad tonight that's all there is to it.

Put on Tracy Chapman to taxi this melancholy, and I swear she's singing to me, about me, and Ant Man was the ravings of a drunkard, this? This is the aftermath, the total gloom sadness tears and no wine, this, the baby baby I need you blues as she sings, "I've got a red hot heart," I hear you Tracy to my diminishing bone. "Your heart's as blue as the blood in your veins…" Darling One when will the time come? Darling One where are you tonight like Dylan's Street Legal opus? My plant is growing happy on this table, the dictionary sitting there, various CD's and my pen and my A.A. medallions. This dream of you through the speakers where reciprocity is African where you she knows my gray heart my shriveled clover my shaky hands writing for hope, hoping for hope in this journey to the infinite, everlasting is the life of our arms entwined. "I vow to come for you if you'll wait for me." I'm ticking I'm tocking in the wait under the weight like Joey sings of and I don't know if I'm ready? Wake me Africa. Wake me before the sunrise pales the stars' lament of unconditional love. These songs Tracy go straight like an arrow of justice into my trembling soul into my windy spirit into my heavy eyes. Where will you go to see me there crucifix in hand diamond in my joint on that day where red and black meet forever in love? By the river of Jon The Baptist? To unfold fate and decree a final trust.

Ah oh to call her to connect ghostly heavenly in this Too Far Down, too far Dawn, there's a good chance she's as lonely as me. Melanie was back at The Breakdown Café today, writing in her journal, within herself. I painted with watercolors, I tried to read. I caught sight of her breasts. Now I'm here alone, crying, crying for no reason, crying for rock bottom loneliness. I've been alone for too long. I could cash my check and buy a bottle of cheap wine? As Paul sings, as Paul sings…crying, I have no one, no one to share my brilliant tears with…but Melanie her tears where lead to? Any ocean, ashamed in the solitude, drowning, despairing.

Coming out of it and like Bob Mould dreaming of standing on some edge again, any edge to look down instead of up. All the rivers, all the dams, all the seas, all the hands holding the bleeding hearts of nowhere. I smoke too much but its my little legal relief in a world of junk conformities and bewildered clowns. The pool table of thought and the cue ball always lands in the hole. That Breakdown Café man, that heartsick blind Dawn just lurching through the nameless day and what's that woman thinking? Writing? Now that the Earth just keeps on a-rollin?

Halloween Melanie old young. Can I comprehend her lives? Her thoughts? I want to lie naked in her arms. Timeless silk of the any other day. Irrelevant prick that I am. Laying waste to calendars in the two fisted party talk, those years are far behind me, I'm ready to love, to love for the first time almost lesbian. My tongue between her thighs, my tongue and lips on her sacred breast, forever kissing, forever loving, coming and coming. Ah fantasy, the thoughts used to be trains linear now I'm moon-like in my glow one little speck in the vast black blanket of space of memory of time of Jesus…so it goes homes. Melanie could you be my friend in all this? Just to listen to music together, trade books looks, hold hands in a darkened movie theater and I can almost hear you sigh laugh cry, my call I thought went unheard, I am struggling. Caught on a Dante myth, the hell of rites discovered uncovering the temptations like a million lies from a president's wish, wilderness, forest, town, part-time job, buying used books (Flying), then onward to some destination unknown to all and sundry. The yellow of my future is beckoning in the black eyed dawn for to give you my truth, some honest jester of the bleak fate now. And how I hold back the night formulating eyes at half mast, black, black. Out there in the summer carnival the monkey is chief and the Aztecs have the arcane strum of countless months, and where? Where? Where we will we become?

She said, "This music's weird." We lay there after making love and I had Tom Waits' Black Rider on. Now it's a couple years later and I'm listening digging these tunes again only alone this time. Only dreaming of breast, only wondering where the moon is tonight, only speculating on the possibility of becoming a snake. The Black Rider man, cabarets of anything possible, that night ride long night homes, and the howling the wailing will land ye in some form of prison. Period. My red hands peck out the mystery, peyote high tonight fifth cigar, there's heroin in this town, there's waterless demons runnin ze show tonight but I'm sage safe here in my cocoon of ice water and tobacco, and the façade is it good is it evil? That façade of white. Belly bowl and Dawn three hours away tonight, I nod through any every dream. What else did The Doll say? We were certainly close there for a wile...close and wet, hot and pale. Come on man remember. Ah nothing doin just the foolish importunities of lassless me on the train of past midnight.

Crash smack rattle.

Toot.

Train whistle.

Stars.

Weasel guess.

What about talking bout art school? Could write about that? I'll just puff puff.

Now its Tracy singing Tracy Tracy singing singing. A beautiful dose of reality, revolution, "runrunrunrunrun," this gets me tinkin, thinkin about hi school and the lesbians' first voice, you could tell something was happening, something spiritual, social, and yet it was the wealthy who prognotized this intelligent proletariat, this scarred African angel of the ghetto supreme singing about caste but beyond too. Incorporated into the Greatfull Dead scene, no that's not it, the Dead were exclusively dead, it was the return the return of Robert Johnson's art after the fifties and sixties and seventies rape of the folk form: James Taylor, Eric Clapton, artificial. It's a pretty safe bet that all lasting great music originates with the "minorities," Tracy will shine on long after the plastic of ready-made radio crap (which is forgotten halfway through) is shelved and never dusted. Ah but I should be dreaming not analyzing. The love of her voice is enough.

Tired of smoking I think I'll go to sleep, goodnight invisibles.

Sometimes it surges up in me: I'm a genius.

Sometimes...

I could write about the Beats? How they've liberated my mind. Existentialists I don't understand, I've tried a few times but I'm not ready, Bra Tea has Being and Nothingness on her bookshelf, she's read it, she goes deep, sculptress, worker. What philosophy do I need? Beyond Good and Evil? Pompous. First reading though. Intellectual...I'm just a abstract expressionist, reading Jung and The Golden Bough and Joyce, their influences, Jackson, Willem, Dart, Gottlieb. Coming out of the depression to jazz, to abstraction and the great Mondrian, Picasso, Miro. But the American boy drunks took it further, myth modern yet primeval, primordial, and John Graham waving that blood flag onward lost damned to the other side. Modern art has its roots in Africa, Pablo gleaning the hellish ritual of survival, of eyes that actually soulfully see, fused with Cezanne's cosmic Eastern vision, the great return to imaginative primitive expression. The Beats too went to the East, Vincent for the image, sparse, and Jack and Snyder to the haiku, Basho. To express the inexpressible, the secrets, the gardens, the oracles, the guardians, to delve and prove Jung's great intuition, mandala, labyrinth, dream, Shiva, Buddha, Christ, Monet, all the visual revolutions exploding the unconscious conspired for a vast love of truth and daring. Beats mean beats, dancing, singing, rhyming, and this twentieth century will live on and on for the magic these artists created: E.E. Cummings so modern he will live at least two three four thousand infinite number of years. Endlessness expressed. Modigliani. Hashing howling consuming then on canvas the sacred stories of people in the throes of honest gesture, the greatest portrait painter the world has ever seen. And Klee spewing out a masterpiece now and Zen. Kandinsky bringing music to two dimensionality. The cauldron bubbling with ideas, the New York school swung like no other, taking chances, risks, to be ineffably now so as to stay now. What's next? I carve out my little theories in this solitary farm town the jig of pictures unborn galloping through my Buddhist mind my Jesus heart my Sitting Bull ears of corn, the swans of Proust and too much, long time ago? The evolution will be documented by the swaying Tambourine Men on that fate beach diamond pistols and bibles the opus the captain the peasant the androgyny the feast…all will be redeemed in this crazy play.

Ah let me think…who will be the next? I can see now alcohol is the reason for all this strife. Sen I was numb, I could not feel emotionally, psychically, I was a cardboard clown in a city of steel. Come back to me? This mend, this recovery, I'm coming to, scared and ravaged, bewildered and small. My eyes feel like a half working Salvation Army lamp, they flicker on and off in between the dimness. My heart too is a boil of lust. I only work one day a week when I can make that. Sen? Can you find me again? Old Angel knows the score. The downward sheepish glance of Tracy, the King Brother in a ordinary chair, and me typing alone listening to Buffalo Thomas remembering my one trick tricked tricking heroin and "you're so green you're so great" as I flew beyond any Kate. Soft fear now tonight, don't look away, the monstrosity the revue the index, and evil is done to the one without within, ah that vast void devoid created in Sunday's poison: wine. Okay I'll write till the tears get in the way I can feel em churning inside my half spirit being, maybe I'll go to work tomorrow and laugh with the saints of menial labor?

Richard and Linda singing now, on the street the only shadow was my mind, I think I saw you there Sen, now this song Dark End of the Street is my regret, my hollow redemption, maybe its us singing? This is our song our story, lived out in the nocturnal travesties of Time, drunkenness, crying for the waste…crying.

I bring out my silver cross from the kitchen drawer to look at simply to ponder, simple enough. And as I do this the Calvary of Thompson kicks in and I want to know, I went into the mystery. Kerouac's vision at the end, at the so many ends. Threshold of seeing, border of straining to be, transit center, black cat, "why don't you follow?" Lowlands and the poetics' come.

Out here with the mouth of water and smoky prees the prophet sad, I am riting, brutal Jones homes man, Indian boy Indian man Indian girl Indian woman. Then what?

To rest. If you read Ant Man you'll know I'm due for a mend. But its boring sometimes out here in Owatonna, no woman, no art friends. To rest in the restive trick of sobriety. Be honest with my self, drink the good stuff: ice water, coffee, hot tea and honey. And the occasional splurge on pop and chips. What does the rest imply? Mean? One Verse City, Coincidenceville, ah its all in the past and now I'm nominally satisfied with a Breakdown Café. People come-n-go, Melanie hath gone from my lusty eye. The hoyden who lives in my building is quite cute but she's got someone already, so I have to dream. Thinking of buying a porno? Oh rest and be happy Dawn Peyote the game has just begun and Artaud will present the Zen at The Breakdown and the Halloween is tamed, I'm safe here.

As I write the orange Sun blazes in the west my western window, my second floor refuge. I came home today and brewed coffee and read Kerouac's book of letters then got excited again with Mondrian, gazing at my own art and really in love sometimes with the plight of being a artist, the plight of money but the freedom of mind and soul. Solace is the imagination. I want to draw and paint my life away like a two dimensional Duluoz Legend or a Book of the Dead, both really merged now.

Since we're on the subject of art I'll go into a little personal history of my own trains and trials with the wonder of drawing and painting: it started by seeing Van Gogh and I began painting landscapes, I've always loved painting landscapes, just recently after years, well no, I've always painted that diamond horizon in some form, one of my first landscapes was called Malice In Blunderland and was inspired by ganja and hangovers. But before that I liked to draw mazes, cars, cartoons, animals. But it wasn't till high school that I picked up a paint brush, I picked up that damn brush and let the paint paint itself, just blow just flow boy. I then started painting characters out of my imagination, usually old men in the sun, I don't know why? My grades were so pitiful in school that my only option for college was art school and my folks really wanted me to keep going. I probably woulda been just as happy washing dishes but oh well.

So I go to art school in One Verse City, I remember

drawing then doing a painting of a three-eyed Buddha while listening to Van Morrison, I also welded a few sculptures in the shop. (I forgot about the summer before art school and the year at community college where I took up oils: I painted with oils la de da and my stuff started to grow more autobiographical.) So anyways I took an abstract painting class run by an Irwin Kent who was this energetic great little man who knew the whole fucking history of art like the pope knows deceit. Started with painting shapes, I got T and with various materials abstracted this T and whatnot. Then Irwin wanted us to choose an artist that really inspired us, someone to model ourselves on, I chose Francis Bacon and did triptychs, rooms, figures, lamps, couches. We also had an assignment to paint in one color so I experimented with blue, very abstract stuff and playing around with collage, fun as hell.

School let out for the summer and I went back home to work and save up moola for the upcoming semesters and I crafted out some more stuff in the garage still inspired by Bacon, reading the book of interviews he did with David Sylvester.

Then blam summer's end and I'm back in One Verse. There in my own crib I buy a stretched canvas and oils spending about a hundred bucks and do a distorted self portrait Allah Francis, it took two or three months to finish the thing and when I showed it to Irwin he said, "When are going to stop resting on your laurels? You need to paint all-over, cut loose."

"It's the Wandering Jew," I said pointing to the picture.

"Oh I don't care, you have to go all-over."

So I buy a big plank of wood and having discovered Marcel recently I did a picture called Fall With The Apple, I was fascinated by the idea of painting something falling and in this case it was me that was doing most of the falling, in all kinds of senses. It was more abstract, loose, moving away from naturalism. The underlying theme of the pix was an abortion a girlfriend had, it came from my unconscious, it was very Duchampian. My first conceptual art! When I showed it to Irwin all he said was, "Ahhhhhhh." My art during that second year of school was a mixture of Duchamp, Bacon, abstract expressionism, Picasso, surrealism, and I was listening to old Big Star tapes.

That summer I stayed in One Verse City, read The Brotherhood Of The Grape, painted nearly everyday my shit getting better.

When school kicked in again Tom Waits' Bone Machine came out so I did a canvas that was like the paint equivalent of that great album, bones and fucking, glowing spoons and canes and Duchamp leaving out the cosmic door to an ethereal orange. My pictures became erotic, maybe it was Marcel's influence, but I did another one titled 101 depicting the sexual scenes with Sen. (Is this getting boring? I'm gonna have a chig)

Then a buncha shit happened (literally) and now I'm in Owatonna drawing and on the weekends when I visit my folks I paint in their garage.

Resting, resting.

Its Monday almost August and I got them no-chance blues. Sitting here so gone depressed but my eyes constipate as I shudder as I shake in the no-chance. Trying to review my life? It seems like an endless inexplicable long odds cycle of the no-chance. I'm blind, I'm deaf, I'm still a child, I'm Dawn Peyote all prescription and fear. Where is the future? I know it has a lot to do with the recovery from booze and drugs and lifestyle too reckless, but how much longer can this sadness prevail? I come out of it at times, shinning and reading Li Po and that soul sigh relief, but other times (like now) I sink and sink. I'm schizophrenic, I have to accept it. Black black and white white. I feel oppressed by all the systems of America: money, sex, religion, medicine. I see no justice in my life.

Indian woman where are you to hold me? As the sun orange pure brilliant Halloween fire of eternity glows grows goes down where is she? My Indian woman, to heal the rings of despair in these mandolin daze of remembering subtle few in the hearing heat of lift, my Indian woman, to tooth the nail worth more than any side however Morrison, my Indian woman, will she save me from inevitable ground? I dream of lots of women but the Indian woman…how vague it all is…how stunning the black hair of ancient remembrance and the bones dance whistling small songs in the back of the universe while the war…I know there's a war. Portrait of a sister, ya may as well paint Neptune that's how far she is now in this forever seemingly. Indian woman her majestic veneer of ghost in the covering of Earth's flowers by the demonic gets, oh money oh commerce, she'll flow like a river to any Eden to any astral domain, one day? Then the dream dice roll and all our numbers will burn like judgment. Or will it be the paleface charade everlasting? I just don't know my fingers thinking tinkering la brain, I will wait here like a disgruntled Buddha. Now the orange unblinking sun is making it with the trees, blossom forth, take apart my puzzle Indian woman and we'll be truer than a thousand Rimbaldian seasons, bluer too perhaps but quenching the spirits with a underworld play.

A day later I sit with my peach curtains and feeling the hints: war hints, mind hints, heart hints. The heart hint comes in the Mexican joint where I eat and the beautiful lass smiles, she smiles, she even smiles at me and shocked by her splendor I mustered a smile back. The war hints come from my various visions and listening to Paul Harvey, a hard V indeed. The heart hints are seeing the butes from the bus or at The Breakdown or around town. Hints. The clouds are emeralds soft and the summer sun bangs down on us Goo Goo Dolls us Dharma Bums us Halloween kinder and elder alike, summer and I'm alive alive I tell ya and weather the hints are true (love, war, revolution, miracles) or not they glow like embers in the furnace of this mind. My brother coming by tonight, bother Stick Figure, I could write a book on him: elusive, vague, brilliant. Go back and read Visions of Gerard again to glean the gone-ness of growing up with a fellow saint, Memory Babe right? Rite? Write.

We live in the Space Age man I'm tellinya. They took out Lennon they'll take out anyone different. There is no room in this country for eccentricity. I'm just a normal guy I take the bus I'll I buy is rice and books, I have no real ambitions other than just to be left alone. I would like to get laid now and then but what the hell? I'm broke so therefore I'm ignored, I fart therefore I am, right? Ah fuck space age, read the modern visions of Burroughs, who is masking sense who is unmaking since. In this world of blue eyed demons who will far sake the cross? Its much more complex than a newspaper and the television "people" are bought off sure as shit. I'm schizophrenic, I'm unemployed, but I'm an artist? Ah to hell with it all, I'll go up like a flood.

Just write whatever comes into my head like now seeing...don't force it.

Couple weeks later now the rest of the rest resting wrestling no. Calm. Slight. The window reflecting a yin yang the box Sad Eyed Lady and within my skull two wet eyes. The white cross of night out there in the star-like night of card mask, but in this romb is the silver of youth. The drums start up cobble waddle cowboy. And with the voice comes the oceans two in the clay of original at last to play in the mesh of face, la low lazy, I see ah your black eyes your white and black hair, I look in the shaved mirror in this August fair all mechanical in a haze of guesses in a yellow prime mumbler of vowels incandescent sing to me Shelley in this nocturne of as. Should we midnight? Secularly? In the iris of mur and dock the papers all flew away. And me demented sad enchanted wan convoluted wax in the spirals of a farming dexterous decision (derision) and accepting the game for the fire that it is in a arm of. The no man, noman. Flop goes the canvas in the bedroom. Go I'll go. Show the soy to the goy in lew of a elephant jewel in these cubist wandering finger finks and the crescendose peyote pie O.T. and that plant just beckons the screen with green. Drew on Drew.

Morning Aretha she sings. Were we? Where will we meet? Some shadowy street?

We're all brothers and sisters in this.

There's a snake in the crib the crib is it a prison? It changes back and forth. The snake too changes it becomes a sphinx then back to a snake then holy shit it's a boar, finally standing up and walking to me to say he's three thousand years old. Then he changes back into a little red snake. I walk into a large room and lay down on the floor and pull a blanket over but a old boyhood friend climbs on top of my back wanting sex then he vanishes and I somehow sense the snake is in the room, a bit of fear in me. Okay then animals start running around in circles in the room protecting me while I feel the snake bite me in the ankle, on the terrace a Egyptian statue has somehow come alive and is playing the flute. As if that's not enough one of the animals is now making a speech to which the janitor on the side shakes his head. Then the animal patrol appear and think they're all out of control the animals still running in circles but I know they are very intelligent.

I wake up, wow, I feel Egyptian, its five a.m. and I take a piss, then go out to my chair and roll and smoke a cigarette.

On this Egyptian Satori night the sundown Tanguy and my influences of the half step.

To dance with Jesus. Sad poor happy dance. Wineless. Fellow clowns in the void. Into outta the portals of despair. Cuttin the rugs in eternity. Librarian savior on her knees in this very room, me biting my nails wondering about her cunt.

Out here in the fallen where the oasis gleams in that roundabout moon thank, the blinking the electric jubilee of Robertson, I can hear and see you brother father. Any bird flying toward the someday sun hath landed in the bleeding shadow to find the spirit within. Count the beads on that shrine, pick up the angel cast out, find a tear in the blue eye of a brown prophet…and the out there gleans like a flower like a descending Gabriel all the choices, choices made or make, for the candle is silent red on a shelf made of timelessness. Pickle's bro can burn, cook. I see the hall fold and churn predicting a tomb believer of crimson cross archetype, in the dream the past comes to future. Like a village of bell of corn of wind the abstract waves splinter the heart with mind beauty, funk, roast, (beer?) give us a holy ring like a circus song to dance around in infinity.

Ah a new song a old song a groan of beatific justice: Broken Arrow. Robbie making it real, the miracles, the prophecies, the very trembling emotion of a man on the edge of desire. And this time I'll bring you my shinning eyes across the desert. It's a magick whirled babe. Crawling that heart line to shores to daisies and who else will mend history? Who can reconcile scarred dominions and domains of heresy? The mood of beckon on that light light light, say every little everything, the mood of reckon on that night night night, say nothing to nothing. Let the Indians wail (anyways they will) and lie to the fire, lie to the child, oh holy love the mysteries the gods the rivers all mix in my demon thought angelic comey cognizant little sail snailing to milky days of alone to drum to chandelier to Picasso to low cross in the salvation ghost of a million sweet somethings. I can't get out anymore.

The Beats my family?

Sixth grade was the best: reading The Outsiders in two days feet up tranced.

Ninth grade was pretty good too: Catcher in the Rye.

Tenth grade read On The Road, didn't quite understand it, it seemed abstract but when they got to Mexico I was blissing.

Those days too dipped into Rimbaud and Blake and Ginsberg.

The year after hi school living at home in the fall discovered Henry's Sexus and Tropics, those the all-time mind blow.

After seeing Barfly spent seventy bucks on Bukowski books, read, digested.

In my twenties anything on Duchamp.

Late twenties back into the Beats. Mallarme big fun discovery.

Lately Surrealism, Breton, trying to get to the source of that, Dada, wanna buy The Egyptian Book of the Dead sonly. Read and read. Motherwell probably currently my favorite art/paint writer, touched by his memorial to Rothko, the painter of the void, hated objects which diverged me cuz too into Picasso and old strong Pic was an object junky. In the arts the convergences are as strong as the divergences, and the only way to art is research, so many opinions floating in the skull discriminations that one has to delve dig deify on own. So most of my time, between dreaming about tits and ass, I investigate the arts the literatures I WANT TO KNOW EVERYTHING!

Pink orange sun setting sitting in the Buddha tree, Pure Land meditation rite. The jewels are here, now, and the vegetables know and I don't know and you don't know but Buddha don't know neither so don't take the sidewalks for granite.

Listening digging loving my lover's response: Glow. Brave..? my mind transparent, the fleetingness, and I understand..? The abstract season enfolds me, I could be? Be and beat and bewildered and bedraggled. Witch country is this? She was fine, around, I let her slip through my frozen whiskey hand like cards old, like then and now I know knock cowl cowtow the yeah, her sad alive yeah, kicking in with the vast compassion question: "are you alright?" Scent of a cigar in my apartment scratch my old nigger skull like Arthur predicted. Small, small planes of my mind, not glass not elemental jests, but a feeling dimension of gratuitous markless rye wanderlest sundering the yellow hap that is me just lie just listening to her...ah cry again middle saged, a zend one, shiva'd and all. And Harry this book report will it find its way back to earth? From my afterlife scowl? Its time, send us off to four.

Damn and I thought e.e. cummings was the best, but reading Lorca holy high wow tangerine bang brow! I'm home I'm abstract and bloody and my mind fire fires the heart valve to so to soul to Saul and back and beyond. Poet In New York I read, amazing, after reading four poems I can't sit down I pace the room finally sighing towards a brotherly communion. I'm not alone anymore. I have found a kin in abstruseness in the wilderness in the very holy eyes that wander this insane world. Lorca. Lore Ka, "inevitable

Africa," border the brother with invisible strings which only Jesus and the outlaws can see, sing. You have brought my mind a new focus, thank you martyr. I'm with you now on this Earth where you once raved in song's deep to the half and half spirit flesh, the world you saw is still here some parts sheer horror most in fact but the expression of the one to the delusion of civilization you cast will last a pharaoh's gold forever, you Lorca hath added my seventh soul where once I traversed with a crying umbrella and eyes that were dead on dead and ears that could only hear thoughts, I am alive and you are the proof of this, the reciprocal the fundamental the rebop of re-turn relook retrieve the forgotten now. Ah shit fuck bam.

Honesty is the way to love. Loves' ways through the clearing, ah I feel, I see…there is hope.

Reading Lorca wondering where the September moon is?

It musta started when I was sixteen and hearing R.E.M. for the first time, Murmur. That's mixed with an exposure to Kerouac and I remember hip high school students wearing concert T-shirts and pretty button-up sweaters. The now and Zen of it the perception however unconscious is still samely true. Close my eyes and think about it. What a thrill it was to buy a new R.E.M. record the first day it came out. Then rush home to the basement and the stereo and lay it down (man). I don't know what it is? Listening nowadays to R.E.M. Ann they seem (unseemly) as great as when I was a lad. Nowadays…nowadays. And the East now I can see in it. I just shut my diamond arbitrary eye and bounce my skull, "Green grow the rushes grow," and I have tread through any and every wasteland to discover the ecstasy of water and tea, legal child. To be sober and sway. To be swirl and not have to worry about the fuzz. Music is my drug. Poetry is my gateway to the extreme of thoughts' engine all moonlike in a Indian drum of obscure reasoning twilight and much. Infra mumble Stipe. And Peter Buck (cow ski?) wow what invention, pluck, wash. Put your travels away and listen with me. The days have come to this, this music, this zoo, this alchemy of mystery in the form of sound, like how Jack speaks of music in terms of "ideas" "forms" and the breath as important as the gist is the gist is the outblow. Oh ballad oh of oh Indian, hidden away in your tent of dream tune and trilling observes. I just let you guys pluck my heart in the night of come down…

Now its Chronic Town.

Wish I could say more about the experience with eighties music. It moves me still. I can feel my insides alive. And the friends I met too back then. Like Skull or DeVille or Iceberg, each different each brilliant. Musicians. Poets. Philosophers. I got Skull drinking. DeVille got me trippin. Iceberg got me the blues. We learnt a lot from each other smoking Camels and pot staying up late listening to Jimi Hendrix swilling cheap wine, that cheap wine five dollars a bottle was Bob DeVille's fave. I remember being drunk every weekend and pot high during school, hell I even loaded up a couple few times before sport's practices. But I don't wanna go on a drug dirge again, either writing about or glorifying it. But through it all the music is still true, time hasn't diminished this return, return to my creative roots and be alive. That's the bottom line, alive.

But I don't wanna go to bed.

Well its Friday night and I'm listening to Robbie "after a hard day of nothing much at all." Maybe I'll angel maybe I'll what? I called but Melanie melony was gone. Gosh I hope sense perhaps she's in love with me or maybe its just her natural nature her beauty in the shinning autumn as I tune my heart to her soft little dropping words few. Melanie one of the many wondrous creatures at The Breakdown

Café, once I get my mind back I'll make it clear in every sense. But for now I'll just have to settle for The Dream... ah naked body dream, kiss kiss dream, bird and cat unions. Ann the bang she bonged my gong like twilight my cig in the gig of past. My pa Head Scratch goes yellow when I git specific. Witch isn't too off ten. Its coming, Broken Arrow, broke end me begins now. Big night, rereading Sexus for the umpteenth dime time Henry you stand Henry The Human Song underdogged yolked celestial urban bizzarely real. Let this be injested in purgatories' changeable liver: I love Henry Miller! I love Melanie! I love Reality! I love water! I love tea! I love love...! and Chris? Lou? Too? Yass. The very world seeing memorying behind a collective grow yet as I crawl I know the mountain is and aint. "A bottle a rain." Ah it's a reigning buts still there are loophills slideholes and gutterflowers to eschew from a spectrum of receive, like yin, like Sen, like the lanes of nowhere. Punch us back to it black to the beginning: ISIS and Christ. What flower lay hold of me tonight? Like a spore of shore I swim away and to. In the dark. Red candle and a circle lover's refrain, "We've got a little genius nut on our hands," said Pickle to his daughter son Dawn Dotter sun and spirit, lets talk about spirit lie to my eye and blink wind wink spy falling with the apple man, Handy got the hands, but mine were tremors, "All the tears all the rage all the blues in the night," Shadowland return, all animal, pure as farmland, ready as Tracy.

Okay Melanie I'll show you my insides, I don't know what's in there, here it goes...ah I don't know who I am who am I who I am. I'm growing the walk on water seeing with believing. Waterdrunk. Fall thump. Quilt the news un you in yin be before you flee, trill the magick and under the stands puffed sixteen year olds. Then on the couch...

But this song's for me, I know it, prophetess androgynous, very little very little penis, alright. Summers conclude cool,

I'll knee some one two holdy. Slow my insides. Lets pretend not to pretend, lets pree Zen not to, lets partake of love. That golden arcade. What four hither two?

Summer stood pyramid naked on arms and mind and sun up bright spangling jangling. Cack a due!

Ah narrative? Orange sun and soon the leaves too all veiny and fallen. I sit here feeling good, three cups of strong java in me and reading my new book Jack's letters early manhood true. Turtling through reality, maybe I'll see Melanie on the morrow? That would be great. But for now I'm happy. With my western windows the curtains don't care and the sky, the sky, the sky goes lil patches of blue then waves of gray and Zen a shuddering orange as the witness trees dance cool, bending and beckoning beauty. I reckon I'm alive so as to perceive nature, Snyder, one tree has bright green leaves another dark green. My plant inside is healthy, sits beside the computer on this desk, just watered it.

Put in R.E.M.'s Reveal after listening to Thelonius Monk. This story this story. And Christ at The Breakdown. Bunch of em. Me too? No, me Buddha non-god, a simple man of complex escapes.

I've never been to confessional. Who am I? Oh I'm just a short little prick with dark eyes and hair who loves and listens to music constantly. I lust after seventy percent of the women out there. I love my folks, my relatives and especially Stick Figure. I've got a few friends here. I lent my book to one of em, haven't heard back about it yet. I miss The Doll sometimes. I have tomatoes in my icebox. There's not much to say not much madness action like the old days in the Hood in Minneapolis but I'm recovering, a recovering alcoholic and that's a wonderful wondrous thing…how the mind clears up and to listen to the heart's true beat, those Egyptians used to believe we think with our hearts, and me Buddha-Egyptian and Indian-Irish and Mexican-French and I'm all mixed up in my deluded origins because my pa was an orphan I never met my real grandparents, a real mystery and regret.

That making the mind formless is the trickiest thing, the mind formlessly unforming: Thank you Buddha Motherwell.

I've been drawing in this crib for a little over two years now. I'm not like Jack, I don't feel the need to traverse the globe, I think a lot a painters like to stay in one place. Paul said he could travel farther with four walls around him, and I think that's the case with me too. The Heart Needs a Home. All that. To be a visual artist? I don't know? Nonetheless that's what I've become. I've been drawing since the age of four and right from the start it's felt like magic. Drawing man, drawing not man, drawing Atman. I'm gonna go to the library and find some books on calligraphy, Oriental landscape Zen painting, to actually read the word of Buddha, to actually see that a non-discriminating state is best is the best because then you can look at everything, everything's nothing and nothing's where I'm headed: Chief Nowhere. Formlessness. After years of chemical nothingness its now a watery tobacco somethingness but no need for words (why am I writing then?) no need to talk my self into a philosophy corner. In my own life I've seen the death of my mind, I've drifted that whiskey river bloodshot beyond the destination's core, but now I've landed and by crashing hard I've learnt that its best to be prudent on the outside and wild inside, that is, art is where a crazy guy like me can go crazy without destroying one's self or others, pictures don't hurt anyone. I don't have to be high and drunk to create these days. The sober mind is just as dynamic as the junky mind. Look at Burroughs hooked on the most ecstatic drugs in the world and his creations were nightmares, granted the world is a nightmare (at times for me now, eases), and fads come-n-go, I don't know if my pictures are gonna mean anything to anyone else? They mean (me an) a lot to me-doing em then looking at what I've done, a real great thrill.

So that's where I'm at, some days I just read all night and not create, I wait for desire, a kind of soul spirit desire to express the mysteries that lie within me and also the enigma of the world refracted back onto the canvas while reflecting on the whole history of art as I know it. Just as blessed as it seems.

Its sad this world. Listening to Monster, R.E.M. and remembering my little drunken spangled nights and mares of the past, the passed. How shitty I treated Sen...tears are starting to remind. Remind the tears to tear at the tear of remind. Ah I don't need reminders? But this...I tried suicide. I tried to end my own life. It was hellish, whiskey desert, it was more than I could fathom and fathomless still. Oh don't let my emotions stilt tonight, I want to cry and remember and in this remembrance some sort of supplication to comprehension. My life is no angel play, a demon amongst ye, a gargoyle in the stone of Nefercity, a drop so heavy the gods wait, wait with no remonstration for the call of the wise may tip the fall of the cries. Crouching metaphors versus gray reality? Its almost fourteen years since I fist first moved to Minneapolis the city of only one verse and that verse: addiction. The art school buffed my spiral for a wile but once out there in the abstract hunt in the fields of cement I fell and landed flat mind "hysterical naked" it seemed like there was drugs everywhere and there was: needles in the jon, crack smokers in the streets, crackheads and hare on and me thinking the whole fuckin time I'm smarter than all that sticking to my booze and ganja and the sporadic trip or speed use. Its weird, the very drug that destroyed Indian culture is the only legal social drug easily available to us. And hell is coming off a ten year drunk: sleeplessness, delusions, massive inexplicable paranoia who is killing me? Who is killing me? Me. Poison Land man.

A golden fleece ah but a golden return, grifting incalculables and the death of the grid, gold and gold and gold and gold, its blurry its letting in the elegiac pattern of no pattern, read the Buddha Prince word and fine you'll be. That Poison Land lingers as implicit as anything else, oh but the Pure Land rains too just like a Dolphin like a rolling room like the union of female Ann male oh. The words of heart beauty escape me, fluttering start, and the come back, reincarnate to the Re that mighty Re brother. The electric lines the anthropoids the asymmetrical seraph this country this democracy this very swimming into the old girl, ah sag vale. The words the words and was Burroughs a bona fide skitzo? Its scary but he was onto something: virus, the proliferation money power mind. Mend these ins swaggering drunk stoned lie to come up to truth and wail, to come up to a vexing be. And I don't have to kill myself anymore. When the day Motherwell's onto any mind a few precious a couple and all leads to some vague ONE, wrapped tight in the flags of nowhere Mara Mona June, wrapped in the skin of synchronicity Mardou Fox, we will all flip in some myriad notion, its just a matter of when and where? Mars.

Rereading this book it gives a kick, even though I have no narrative I'm currently interested in explicating, I'll just write with Monk-e tunes coming out of the sound box. Am I a-gonna go to work tomorrow? Ah I don't feel like it right now, but maybe in the morning I'll get it together?

All those years of reading Bukowski. Usually hung and womanless, I would lay on the couch in the Minneapolis afternoons after a night of Southern Comfort and read his poems (if you can call em that) and I had the experience of the third dimension in his writing. I was going to art school so I had a lot of free time on my hand and Charles made me laugh and think simultaneously. I would read the day away. I could finish one of his books in five hours and understand everything. Then once that book (War All the Time, Love is a Dog From Hell, Hollywood, etc.) was ingested I would put on my sneakers and jacket and make the half hour walk uptown to the bookstores and for ten dollars buy, say, The Roominghouse Madrigals and not feel like a phony intellectual, but feel like a man and there were several bars in uptown and a few liquor stores on the streets back towards my home so I might have a quick whiskey coke for two dollars in some dive then tread the age old sidewalks and stop off to pick up a big eight dollar jug of wine for the night. That would just about finish me off for dough for the week, my earnings going for books and booze and paint and canvas. I remember reading Roominghouse on Cold Facts Ave., tucked into my single bed and the wine in the fridge and my roommates working. Drinking cheap wine and reading the drunk's easy going word. I'm reminded of this tonight because I got the new one from the library last Friday, Sifting Through the Madness…and I recall all the booze that ran through our gullets Hank, ah but to break on through? Self destruction so you might as well learn along the way, "that road of excess leading to the palace of wisdom," its not a straight shot, that road, but the words, I don't know, its paradoxical cuz you taught me so much yet I used you. I emulated you. I lost my fucking mind. "The madhouses are the only place where you KNOW you're in Hell." I lived that. You were just a drunk, booze brought you to life, but I have schizophrenia now, I am almost afraid to read you again it brings back the past so much. I hope I'm not blaming Bukowski? We are both demons understand? And like Miller you wrote for madmen and angels, I can see this literally. But the tea is getting cold and I've run out of rant.

Oh seasons…listening to The Replacements, I can't tell ya how much they mean to me. Oh seasons of reasons revolving and revolving and revolving. I see the silver cross on this desk and the Picasso self portrait and my recovery medallions and my gosh the karma of it all. Someone's here, me. I'm alive and I can't believe it. Opportunity grant me salvations, its almost winter again, its almost, well, my eyes are welling up, I feel that crazy mixture of light sadness and heavy wonder, err, err, and I feel like a thousand happy guitars of Lorca swallowing the consequence, oh tea oh hot tea. Paul sings and Bob jams through the speakers Chris bops and Tommy plubs, music, Dionysuses man. "Its too late to turn back here we gooooooo!" Everything sad everything eye everything immaculate once you see the karma come back in, in coincidence in synchronicity in everlasting love.

The light in this place (my crib) is amazing.

Indian Jesus Paul and his sad songs.

Ah pink and lavender ripple clouds kiss the nearing night towards an unshakable dawn.

Now its Crowded House as I try to write.

I need some electricity man: Keef.

Maybe memory lane? Memory Laney remembering her, wow, she is beauty.

Omni joker on the box, perk up your son is ablaze.

Slint of orange sphere almost descended the trees lonely the birds getting ready zig-zagging the insects crawling on the screen, warm October. I sit here with the flu. Sold a painting so that makes me feel good and I'm listening to a Stones' boot and I think I'm up to winter's wrath all cold all windy. With a trip planned to One Verse in the works for the St. Paul art crawl, Stick's gonna do some jazz in his marijuana scene, cool, or raw, I'll be sober nonetheless and Mezzy is comin along, got to give him some gas money. Ah jiving life its great, what can I say? I'm hap and knee Dawn Peyote any glory to monkey of easy on that lively James Joyce livery. Raw cool in the rolling fates.

Remember the time in the bar, "Keith Richards is the greatest guitar player man."

"No way Jerry Garcia."

"Garcia plays in about three scales if you really listen."

"Bullshit, Jerry's the best."

Then I didn't see the dude for a long time but the next time we met twas in a bar again and he admitted Keith was pretty good. Ah the white boys will realize someday. Keith and Africa wedded alchemized in the ancient modern. Swing dig? Primal. All this shit comes back to me as I absorb The Mighty Rolling Stones on this beautiful twilight of Monday. Jack jumpin flashin gashin.

It's a perfect dusk as I look at the window while writing, pink orange mix with streams of pale glorious blue and its all moving, in motion, ocean, slightly as the trees tremble wind and the streetlamps like eyes just waking, am I starting to sound like Gary Snyder? Ah its nature and it's a bute and I've got the Innocence Mission on after crying and rewinding Sinead's Franklin song over and over, and I started think dreaming of gay ole Ireland and the amazing songs of that bright green lamb land lamp on now the sky a gray blue conjunction the likes of which I aint never seen before like Henry in Paris and all that spanning gray, oh yeah Ireland, I have an incredible urge to know everything suddenly about Dylan Thomas, I've read a little few years back, but now I'm reddy. So the next best thing Bob Dylan's acoustic stuff again with the sailors and the sea, that lapsed into Lee

Jones and her Stewart's coat which is me incidentally. Oh now there is a spear of crimson orange jutting up outta the horizon, I don't see any birds but I know they is out there naked, naked. Some a the trees bare, nude too for the seasons' magic change, Chang.

So just the other day, last weekend in fact: Mezzy picks me up at the Breakdown and we roll o'er to the bank where I cash my S.S.I. check and off we go glowing to The Twin Cities to visit Stick Figure and the wan great fabulous art crawl. So we're chugging down that highway doin a solid eighty and Mezzy's gots some tunes on that box and we puff chigs and talk rap and in forty five minutes we've made it from Owatonna to St. Paul, driving through downtown the brothers out in their jerseys and baggy jeans and Mickey's is still in business (all night diner) and we spot a parking space and Mezzy parallels us on in.

Ringing the brother's buzzer, "Its Dawn and Mezzy we're here man."

Through the intercom, "C'mon up," Stick intones.

Four flights with my backpack full of one change of clothes shorts to sleep in a toothbrush and toothpaste, and a Mozart CD and a book called The First Third to trade with Stick (we're always trading shit, he's got my Charlie Parker and I got one a his Dylan boots, Dylan in New Orleans if you want to know where its at, ole Bob goes all the way in that moon shiny town of towns). I borrow Huesker's Warehouse Songs and Stories the album that pulled me through ambivalent hazy Hi School so we is square, plus I find some older things like Paz's Appearance Stripped Bare about my all time here oh Marcel and a picture book I bought for twenty bones five years ago of Roberto. ANYWAYS…

Stick has a job working for geezers that he's got to skadaddle to so me and Mez go back outside and then Mez got a wireless so I call Bra Tea, she not home, probably later.

Its only about three or three thirty in the afternoon and the art crawl don't start till sex, six I mean, fraudian slip. About a block away lies a coffeeshop entitled The Black Dog, that's where we head.

Nothing like big city turbo juice black medicine java. We sit at a wood table and play chess, three games and in between I'm checking out minus the library card the squaws, one in a dress that stops at her beautiful knees and oh oh oh boots. I got a thing for that, a little skin a little dress and BIG BOOTS! Wow.

(Oh yeah Jack before we go to the coffee house we went to a plaza and there I feasted on a vegetable burrito)

So hombre we're back in Stick's artist warehouse crib, I put on R.E.M. on the ancient turntable and we smoke and brew more Joe and talk and pace and sit on the couch, I take off my shoes and socks but then put em back on cuz Mezzy wants to scout out the art in the various buildings, WE HAVE A MAP EVEN. So down a flight a stairs and walk in on some fresh stoners, "Try 103," they say.

Up and down stairs in and out of apartments, art everywhere, eyes wondering eyes placating eyes dogging the infra searching for a Charlie Parker of the art whirl: nothing. Then Bra Tea comes huffing down a hall twelve of beer in hand, "I'll talk to you guys later I just got done a twelve hour shift." It sound pretty shifty to me but we agree to meet later. Me and the Mezzer continue. After the third building and seeing a guy wearing an Ank proceed to home base, Stick's and the stereo plus I got about fifteen new canvases up on his giant walls.

Stick's been there, or, here, (where are we?) while the curios have passed through inspecting, so now me and Mezzerious play host, hold down the fort, while Stick and a chick named Lucy his friend go off into the night. People aren't too interested in my paintings they walk out quicker than they walk in, which is pretty quick.

Betwixt the comings goings of folk sundry I rummage through Stick's vast array of collected junk: books records guitars flutes letters bongs bills, and I find a hardback of Sexus, oh this all this time he's we've been communing through brilliant Henry, and right now I thought of calling Stick and asking him what he thinks of my Bible? The Rosy Crucifixion is the greatest American literature ever written (what about Jack and Allen and William?). No one none has Henry's clarity, dream and fuck and reality and guts. So me and Stick are connected, blessed, by this common man's poor high scribbling and Mara Mona June the portrait beyond Modigliani…

I don't sell any art and come ten o'clock the art crawl concludes but tomorrow, Saturday, it starts again at noon till six, early brisk October. Stick's gotta gig playing jazz guitar at a party a bash around the corner in the same building as The Black Dog. So Stick and Mez and Lucy and me carrying the music gear and big bop writ music binder we find the party. They got food laid out it's a typical rich white kid's crib, swanky. It's a congregation nonetheless though and Stick plugs in his get tar and a androgynous chick thumps at the bass and there are couches and chairs and as usual nobody pays attention to the music: white people busy gossiping. Stick starts doin one hitters of ganja and I get a cup of water, Mezzy is having a good time he's more of a people person than I. The drummer sets up and there playing a snaky blues, really sounds good low down. I stay for two hours but when the crack pipes come out I split, don't want no part of that scene, that bean, that queen.

Walk home through the night the "sweet Minnesota breezes safe cool and warm," I got Stick's keys and walk up the four flights, fumble with his crib door, then I'm safe inside, sober. I take off my jean jacket and pants put on shorts and walk over to the stereo. Ah what did I listen to? I'm trying to remember. Anyways I listen to something and brew some decaf tea and roll a smoke and look at my canvases. I lay down on the couch and try and sleep, I can never get shut eye when spending these weekends in St. Paul, too much music to blast and plus I get to see all my new pictures hung altogether which is a kick.

Amy buzzes she walks in in in dress and nice boobies and she says, "You're still up." I nod and hope she gets naked with me but she smiles anyways and goes next store next door. I'm alone again, alone to look gaze at my creations, ah I get a thrill from my painted stuffs and that yin yang coming to after my years in a Book of the Dead, I'm emerging more alive than ever then Mezzy and Stick come in, Stick stoned as usual that's not to judge him or nothing but I have to admit I Jones for it once in a while. "I had a glass of red wine," says Mez, Mezzy and his wine that's what you get for reading The Bible, alcoholism.

So Stick lays in his manger with the T.V. on surfing and me and Mez are pacing jabbering Mez has this look in his eye: I call him Malcolm In The Middle sometimes cuz he reminds me of X. "Ya want the couch?"

"It doesn't matter I know I'm gonna be up all night," I say and I am back at the stereo and put on a Three Songs tape for old time's sake, real rock-n-roll brother.

I lay down on the floor and Mez reclines on the couch and we start conversing about religion. (I don't know if I can remember what we said? I'll take a stab at it)

"So wudya think of that book?" asks Mez, referring to Jesus in Tibet.

"Religion is wild."

"Who's more cracker? You are me?"

"Well you own Phil Collins records, I think that answers that one."

We talk and talk and suddenly its about five in the morn and I say, "Lets go outside and watch the sunrise, see that ole fire god wake up," he says okay and I grab Stick's keys and out the door we go.

Its really gray misting lil we walk to a giant parking lot where semi-trucks are parked, its too gray to see the actual sun come up so we trot back to The Black Dog Breakdown Café and Mez buys me an apple juice, I sit in a booth parched red eyed, Mez is talking to the dude at the register joking and whatnot and I like I said earlier he's a real people person. Then he comes and sits across from me and we sip, I then start talking after Mez explains megalomania, which we're both afflicted with, "Yeah I've been through some weird shit, I thought the whole world was Nazi junkies and they were toying with me, torturing me in the sike warred and really now I see it was alcohol withdrawal."

We finish our drinks, "Lets go outside, they got tables out there, we can smoke," says Mez. I order a strong coffee and follow him out there and catch a glimpse of myself in the mirror: birds' nest hair and Rasta eyes.

"I'm afraid of Christianity," I tell Mez.

Mez says, "The Old Testament is what I'm into."

"Its just that in this world there's so many hoaxes, plus the fact that Christians have desecrated Indian land for so long 'with god on their side.'"

We roll smoke and light up and take healthy drags. Sip at the hot medicine.

"But I do dig Jesus, obviously he was a prophet, he prophesized his own life. Do you think Jesus was omnipotent Mezzy?"

"Yeah."

"What about Buddha? Or Malcolm X? They had visions

like Indians, you can't be a real Indian if you don't have visions. Sometimes I think I'm Indian," I say sheepishly.

"I think you're Indian Dawn."

Mezzy is the first one to say that, it makes me feel good, I am Indian you know, I'm an Indian Jesus, I'm a Red Buddha too.

And Mez is an old mutt chief high priest of the big city warehouse morning. We go back to Stick's.

I remember being in the studio looking at my painting and Rich Mo said it looked religious. Minneapolis early nineties.

The journey takes its toll. Some lost in god, some just lost. I fall into the latter, a secularist, but I'm coming to, slowly, soberly, with Buddhas gazing at me level, equal. There is no god looking "down" on me because in this universe there is no "down." Space is without judgment. The Earth is a woman who cares for me if I care for her, everything equal, and the justness in my heart is the empirical thoughts stretched beyond infinity to hell and back and here, in this innocence regained, my mission now? "I've got to be a boy again," sang Paul. My mission? My mission? To keep learning, to strive for "rigorous honesty" in a baffling world. I will read everything. Everything? Well I'll open up, stop being so damn hermetic, become a feeling creature, polymorph, hopeful pagan, Zen Hart.

So I smoke and drink water and clarity is coming gradually to me. Ah bless the secret Jesus spoke of. It is secret and all that follow some may not enter, "but this means little to those who have not lifted the veil." I feel for the Beats, but poverty made them what they are. "The land of poverty bliss." Infidels. Beatitudes eternal shake wake and revolve. I am here, I am writing. It is life within life that I now feel and almost see. My mind a garden, first times all the time, growing and growing. Karen Peris sings me these revelations and I think I'm barely ready, contemplating Red Power, barely ready to share my heart with some again. Still a clown but not a completely ignorant one. Cloud-like, flower-like. The valley as sacred as heaven, the valley is heaven, for the whiskey of the valley brought me to the books of the holy vales, temptations' ridges and trances just. Monkeys and lions and fish and humans and ants all blood brothered by the majestic One. Ache tongue babies. The lifting, oh ah know. Saul Mez called me. As I bellow the raceless. For the raceless I have come. Pure as yellow.

Deeply we spiral.

Will you sing for me tonight Dad?

Thank you.

Feeling that Inian blood stirring in me, buffalo man, I'm a buffalo bird cat and the lions know.

Oh story song and how thank give thanks to the spirits the lions the Jesuses all anonymous and vibrating and lunar smooth. This is my story for whatever its worth and the one day is the one day. Its like a cello of hello to write in this hush moon. And I watch you watch me from the blessed distance and removing the poison hathed redeemed me to wake...ah the fine wake, the simple. Finnegan's influenced you too I see. And a sick rose in the dry white, bend that bass thumper and ignoble ease I just crane my neck for all the flowers all that justice coming in.

Never...I don't know, suicide. Life itself is just too miraculous for that early ending, think, think of the chapters unread both past and future and most importantly Now. The tribe knows. I think I see, and that road that road its alive, Midwestern boy just rock-n-rolling all the plausible possible probable populated paradigms of anywhere.

Natalie Portman's movies. Weep baby, the endless is just the beginning.

So I sit in my gold cloth easy chair and smoke my legal, look at Hart's paintings Mezzy's drawings and know we're all saints all jokermen all all and all nothing. My CD's on the floor the television unused the plant trapped happy in here and From Jesus to Christ sits on this desk. I think one of my lamps is burnt out. Here Comes a Regular just started up sound bleeds truth bleeds allover me, I know my past better and better, the traps The Irish Curse the madman forgotten and Jill…my special love, unfucked in those teenage mystifying daze. Once the pain lessons lessens once the compassion felt, I don't know, I just feel better than I used to. Piano. And Moon Ra hangs on the wall, my dry drawings and de Kooning's woman and the lamp oh the Buddha lamp holy. My coffee table with the little brother buffalo and the Rothko book opened and my diary and my Mexico City Blues breast pocket notebook called Wave From the Valley-Valley From the Wave. Been reading Lame Deer. Been reading Kerouac as usual. Even read Jesus' Beatitudes last Sunday and felt calm. There's an Indian picture taped to my fifteen dollar bookshelf. Mez came by today and smoked me in chess. Allah's well on the rez.

Its like a patchwork my beginning faith.

Here I am Thursday night buzzing on tea listening to an R.E.M. bootleg, just talked to my dad on the phone and we're all looking forward to the weekend.

Through the fire John Fire I go, after three days of illness dizzed and frayed and worried about my medication the storm hath passed. I read Lame Deer, I am his successor I know Eric Erica who played the androgynous clown of morrow. The Great Spirit who shouldered the wheels beyond time into the small, I'm alive. Heal thyself. My blindness for to sip hot tea. No wine, no beer, no whiskey. And out a the linear I quest upon the a-tangle of a Christ of Medicine Men of Ginsbergs and Kerouacs and prophecies like saints circle round me in this deep winter autumn night black. I think I'll put Jack on the box.

The piano tinkles and Jack knew the macro was is the micro, provender of the journals to Nowhere. Where are you now Jack? I thought I saw you at the bookstore coffee shop sipping java after having purchased your Golden Scripture your Eternity of spare square circle and X and any ole thing-a-ma-jig. I feel so good rite right good goo now and longly the carnations of time and how and wow we know it. Musta been seventeen when I saw that orange book then onto the flowers of Subterraneans my thumbs smelled like pussy all the time in High School, poor Laney I don't think she knew or held back but I'm getting off the track...

Seven oh seven late October it snowed a little the other day. Fuck I need a story but alls eyes gots is me sitting here typing tie king pie ling.

Its been a heavy sojourn. But I'm here writing my story journey told and tolled. Its holy and terrifying the life and death plays throughout. And I have fifty bucks and my songs and some tea and potatoes, that's enough for now. When ye is hungry the cup will suffice and the bread is true, rue. Black night harmonic. The miracle is that anything's occurred at all, anything, any morsel any giant step any descended messenger of X in the folly of Dawn's peyote in the PRN that I just swallowed Ativan man. Recovering alcoholic for real. Even though I long for sex I can stand alone for how for now for four. This crazy unfathomable treacherous wild wicked cosmos, oh mother forgive my consumptions for I repast on the plants piss away like Genet the gifts of Wakan. And Amy she knows as we grow, Bra Tea and Halloween just a few nights ago.

Reading Enid Starkie its painful to go back into alchemy.

Its two forty three a.m. and my eyes hev, I saw Time Rite Boy and Cassandra arguing today at The Breakdown Café and it recently occurs to me: they're playing me. Stripping the sole search and out here where the cars equal death the hey ya of backwards. I just don't feel like goin to sleep so I'm coughing up vowels and phlegm and misty vision of the want to get laid.

I feel like writing so I'm writing though I have no story, I could talk about Mezzy and how he's turned me on, on to a new world, Qabala, Tibet, religious ideas and the future spangled in oil shimmers glimmers glitters. And now my confession a real Dawn Peyote confession: I am Jesus. "See the face behind the face," sings Peter as I soar in megalomania. Ah shit I'm Nobody Dead Man Depp too, green tea not Jack's kind kind that's what we cats used to call weed The Kind Bud but the liquid that ole Buddha juice and Li Po with his wine and revolutions. Now its bagpipes and deep songs of a deep Sunday night songs of desert the desert creature Palestine and jackals and us blinds whirl in the non-sleep of truly awake, or Lame Deer Wakan, the famines of times passed the thefts of Dylan Irish my hieroglyphs of paint I was crazed with Egypt and Mexico and Jasper and Jean Michel. A simple tooth and a simple eye the vortex is healing me, this vortex of Atman Ant Man Brahman Maya may I tangle with the dog star tonight as I come to the speaking hands. I feel joy, gay, Satori of Judaism Satori of Howl Satori of my dad blinking the screen to a paper heart to a diamond midnight to a taxi of nowhere holy. And I think the thing to remember is that now my wrestles are silent whereas I once punctured the air with a whiskey pair of serpent fear fists so now grateful of the tongue speak the tongue spark battered I have been and yes I have asked the dust John I then diabetic defected from that grape brotherhood and yes its an immaculate escape drop man drop. Further of the road friend fried thirty five highway after a poison demon dance the Eucharists of heroin of again and again straying straying swaying to the dirges of Pluto further than a apple's apogee crash! I can read my stare.

Hallow journknee. The hollow and the real, oh coming out coming in, I sing hold me holy hole me in my regular mantras of dissed belief. What am I coming upon? Some loose change vegetable-nesslessly discordant in the wilds of know. I green and al the all forsaking and it's the unconscious speaking? Jung? The Christ? The Buddha? I don't know what's happening to me something's changing changling and out here where Jean hears the words I hear em too but I don't know what they lead to? Just wanna heal myself my empty self my blood my spirit and to dream of the ages to dream of the Phoenix in reverent orbits of the mind. The mind? The heart? There is a chasm in me bigger than dream, flesh and sound Mohammed and Abram and it just a learning leaning experience to mystique the chaos. Ah oh confessions. The tears I can feel in my brow the unfollied ways of tea and water I'm coming to. This song of the pawn, this brink of the nocturne in a High Moon November as I write. The yellow bright thoughts, this at the moment is my only story as the scarlet runs pure through a pure valley and bound to see the stars and some are miss. Like that time when the silence was a giant teardrop in the codes of oceans born and water oh water is it eternity the azair of time and space falling like Einstein falling like a fruit as the wetness trees hide from me any wisdom in the unreachable drugs of dawn. And the prescription has calmed me down. I'm fine but a new sadness is being churned within me, opening, opening, any shape will do and no two the same, all my wishes insane, and here in this Owatonna quiet I flower forth into a esoteric justice.

"You're open minded I like that about you," said Mezzy today after I tolled hymn about the fact or idea that I'm searching searching young and not wanton to put my chips in one conception. You know, there's endlessness in nothing, there's finite-ness in everything, pick and choose the reign off your blue shoes I used to sing in Minneapolis. But now I'm here in Owatonna South Dakota not too far and the alchemy fading to believe like blood to believe like heart to blood, these are my questions. Carried to the extremes by booze and weed and acid and mushrooms, a Nellish beginning now in the past's hellish fallout. I can't believe I'm alive.

Tonight I'm really digging this gift from the library Neil Young's Sleeps With Angels, I've always loved stripped down rock-n-roll, but for a while I thought Neil was just a Dylan wanna-be, but now I can hear the real he's really singing about real as real.

Shaman.

Magic.

Healer.

Neil Young.

Another dawn beckons.

GHOST FOUR

And the three entered…

    to a horn of question
    in the fish of dawn every moment
    to a thorn of redemption
    in the hole of night's starry starry sagacity like chains
of
    And the three entered
    And the fourth
    And the fourth
        where whence is the fourth?
    Like Lame Deer
    Like Lame Deer

of
        famed to a shore of contention
        in the wish of Donna's every splurge
        named to a wasteland's
        in the hole of
of
      …
      …
    and the three entered
    and the three sheltered in the clouds of blood
    and the three remember

        and from three the thinking four
of
        Like Tom
        Like Waits
        or weights and potential

and of

        hiding the
and of
        hiding the

          The Stripped Moon will
          The striped moon will one us
          Onus
          Plato
      and of the harbor
          the sinking will begin again
                    EARTH
Ghost five alive six sex you know
              the rest

ghost four'd the oh quasi

DAWN THREE

Dawn, yo Dawn can't you see? Can't you believe? No faith?

Beat in this early winter night I wonder chantlessly reading reading and now bursting with the new old I write for the mystery for the history is real is veiled is a shaky reveal. Thought it was this thought it was that but now and now it is one, One. Healing somewhere plays fire bands find the way slur and out of the young. Listening to The Innocence Mission to glean the small prayer, the secret, personal Jesus. I'm sane how? The wanting the feeling I have been missing the soul scarlet and someday its run far to the time and she oh she messenger we walked the campus, I drew pictures at Ginkos and now I'm in reverent solitude glad I understand. Of hey and the songs. Pianos and umbrellas and wine and dictionaries my eyes ready for a new vision, I opened the cupboard and saw in my mind the word "Passover" and my dreams conceal. Its sad. It's a weary journey this, but the obvious is a thing of the past, Buddha I pass through too and to the Middle East now and Augustus and all that nastiness. A magic certainty, here to stay, to learn, to believe what I want to believe, the hand that finds a ticket on the rainy porch leaving you poor on other hours to a fleeting feel she Karen with her vision her prophesy beyond all the Halloweens into a swaying love and she dug the drone of angels gentle.

I'm cold in this apartment. I feel like all my art is for naught. The arrow of pen's poems and to hold the door traveling into the swing of nick and hours of early cold mornings where I dream unfathomably. Its holy sobriety I finally realize. Growing how could we Maya? I don't care. Where her music is bizarre like a hush where and what is she? To sing these worries from far face to see again Maya

Maya lie to hearts beating something when something still weather something....every utterance meaning. And the Greeks? The layers and cloud of her heart she is within me, two thousand, and Sunday any. Home from the question doing a far fetched hope in the art say, "No chance," beard and failing and suffering. "The poor in spirit." Butterflies. I will wear a dress someday. I will bear a caress someday. I know I.

I know no I.

I don't know Robbie always gives me the urge surge spirit write. I'm out here alone offering up these self portraits in the midst of a confusing sobriety so it goes as Kurt says. I can hear your voice beckoning my ignorant tears to cum to fall to cast to yeast. The sufferer heals the suffering, pathos and survival, Indian survival in your blackfoot voice. Messages...decipher...codes...ah the great red moon harvesting the horizon's godlike spin. Choosing a single blue sapphire tear to let you know in this silver spoon war that I'm still here, here, I hear you Sen after all the nights of juice transfigurations whirling like the gnats of Nowhere. And Maria in the bookstore, Halloween almost revealed. The soldiers all turned into fish and the fish all turned into sky. The hooks are flowers, the evil is the geometry of the nice. I don't mind contradictions. I don't mind miracles. What do the Indians think? Think of Jesus? They know the desert they eat the desert they grow small in the twilight's weapons and telepathy ghost big Jones almost home so I'm drinking water strength in the free in the cheap, bread and water and rice. Light a fire tonight to eye the cat that plants love in my crazy heart. There are animals in my apartment that's alright cause who else will save ye but the diminutive? Flux and world. Opening the arrow of your arms' justice in a simple song in a November whisper you showed me that the trees are witnesses and for that a everlasting vegetarian thanksgiving. And Eve you know Eve they put her in a zoo. Call to the animals some license for tooth in the mystery question but some deceiver willing up the charade 1995 man was the year the world said FUCK YOU to me and fucked I was by a dangerous karma. No bread could save me, no amount of wine could quench me, don't dwell on the passed cuz now I've caught hold of the canoe to paradise and fearing only my thoughts. My thoughts…

I wish Crystal was here to hear with me Prince's Holy Riverrrrrr.

So I'm listening to Crowded House and Crystal was writ previous as Sun Baby, she is for real beautiful and I'm content just to see her once in a while and admire her figure and radiant face at the weird Breakdown Café.

I went into her romb and hung up my Jesus and the Buddhas drawing then when I looked again Jesus had a white beard then we got close with our clothes on rubbing against each other and I felt a warm wet spot and she said, "I've come." I felt (and feel) deep love for her, Calling, Kolleen, and then I went downstairs and there was a lobby with a refrigerator and three truck drivers came in, Kolleen opened the fridge and took out the drugs and needles, one man paid her while the other two decided to pay with sex so they went up the stairway and I left to go to Ginkos coffee shop and it had changed since the last time I was there, and I noticed Cat Man's younger brother sitting there and I said, "You're Cat Man's bro, I know you." He denied he was the brother and suddenly the coffee shop was in an uproar at the mention of Cat Man's name for he had written and published a book about the joint which no one liked, hated even and I remembered seeing Cat Man writing his book in the backroom of a roominghouse and then a small group went into a secret room to discuss the great Cat Man. After that I left to go back to Kolleen's to get my drawing and to see her again but when I entered through the window in back I found her in bed with two men and then another man entered with a pistol, Kolleen held up her arms in the air and the man shot a hole in each hand.

I wake up, worried as hell for Kolleen and remembering with stark detail our love our past together and also haunted by the black pimp who said on the bus on the day of the birds that he set the whole thing up, "How'd you like that girl I setup for you?" he asked and my whole being shuddered, the love of my life a prostitute? How can that be?

Soul and heart of the moon Kolleen, I miss her to my core now. I walked the streets of Saint Paul wounded to the gills my heart flooding with remorse and yearning just to see her again, just to see you my love again, even now, its been at least a few years and my fondness, nay, my sisterly ecstasies of you have not died out. Come and find me again Kolleen, read this, read my telepathies through the wildernesses of black nights and silent rueful days. Shelter me from the storm, laurel and grief entwined you are my heaven. Voodoo on this night of pale reflections I'll go beyond Blake in my prayers to flee to glean to reason a one day found once more. It hurts being real.

Love is knife. Love is a knife that cuts through the mirages of normality and nationality. Love is knife man and like Picasso the flesh bends the mind to the outer limits of soul recognition, to the periphery of sanity the knife makes the wind weep and the migrations of cultures of the air and underwater and deserts, this love knife churning and rupturing the clamor of my actual heart. And remembrance…

But what's left? In a deep red world in your blue spirit clothes with arms outstretched. There is so much left unloved. The stones and birds, the thoughts and the make-believe, everything received in twos collisions of hiding. Let my hands rest a moment on the keyboard not knowing what else to say but my insides a-whirl, like a Jackal I see all the misery and mystery of a thousand desert seasons. We were once one, I dwelt in her womb the old baby, licking kissing sucking to get in, and lo, garden she is, garden within her and wastelands transformed by her mere glance.

I'm glad though to have been pierced like a Messiah by her holy random existence in this Hades-like dimension.

Eve is the Fruit unquenchable.

Eve is God untranslatable.

Out of Eve God came, cummed.

Eve is singing to me now in the form of Joan Osborne.

Eve likes to drop acid and sit on the couch without a shirt on.

She dug me eyeing her tits.

Eve tonight in the jealous thunder.

"I'm gonna love you anyways."

Heaven schizophrenic heaven nonetheless and like Blake the delights of genius look like murder to the normal. I could rail against the normal but they'd still stay normal. Bukowski's journey poverty, slipping moments, and in the end ravaged by the number. But me I have music to pacify my insides, don't need that gutrot don't want that Egyptian chocolate. I have my ears in these ears I hear what ifs and why's and I shiver in the mysteriums. Back to the corn and rice, maybe the pope is a good guy? I see all these people believing in what they are doing and what they're doing appears meaningless and needless to me, me content to drink water and eat dollar meals. The donkey appeared and Mary's father murdered, for me the data overwhelmed dehydration and a Man's World. Ah but I escaped both self torture and the torture of America. And Eve she wonders.

Now we're descending again to the tune of World.

Demon Keith savior confessions that saved my whiskey ass.

Standing on sumac standing on childhood the blood of caffeine hithers me on to winter to witnesses and anything's confessions. He wrote a song about it, Pondering, and that was long ago in the Watercolor Sky. Murmur plays in this romb and Bill Miller the same? I don't know? Question oh question sing thy sequestered questions to the infinite night. And I'll find that bootleg. His sister knowing the deaf, our world of lips and minds read. "I can hear you." Sacred stops along the sin, rally round the guys and sit still in the ballasts of nocturnally sagacious crazinesses and that bass of pennies and nickels, a fable man.

Hey this song brings me back to shapeshifter Franny's those hungover morning mournings. Loving the rosaries of frank admittedness, throes of sinking ships and snakes speaking English. Lets folly over to the windmills and ingest the quiet Indian's sacred plant, knowing not I rove my mind for unfathomable answers and sometimes the tears are the only compliant treaty in this lawless land of Feel. Rewind.

Dawn Peyote I am, sanadhi samadhi. The warp, the ripple, the telling. Let your tongue waver in my soul like a tune of truth the we of us and to the core I tell you now I miss all my soulmates all my flesh to flesh adventures and they vastly equal a blinding love. Woman, women, come and teach me. Tell me what's the solace of heavenly biddings in a purgatory of man-made wars? This is how this is what? And across a cross bridge into the empire of Rimbaud red in a Eucharist of African moments, this mouth on the bridge and the pyramids turned into snakes the sun imploded and the fish dangled upward between my being. Turned out in the Beginning, turns in in eternity.

Go through the history of paintings and drawings, where the word is concealed and the omni-ness of color but now I'm in my November house and I can't paint so I write and my drawings. My folks' garage is the only place where I can paint. My last painter was the androgynous naked reaching for the mighty sun perched atop the pyramid of Giza. Then I had that animal dream. I dream of animals, mostly cats, a lot lately. I think I'm a cat. Leo ya know? August child.

So I go out to Mezzy's in Waseca Halloween night and feel the warmth of his home, his books: The Golden Ass, Notes From Underground and so on. We turn on the soft lamp and just like the days of Cat Man we open the chessboard and put the tunes on and Mez brews some tea (legal). Well we stay up till four in the morning and I awake around nine while Mezzy still sleeps, I go for that first mesmerizing cigarette and put on Tom Waits and read Jack's letters in the easy chair. Then Mez wakes with yowl and we go down the street to the corner coffee shop and I down three large cups of wondrous Joe, after that we walk the bike trails around the lake, Waseca is really a beautiful quiet place, I feel at ease.

We go to the library Saturday late morning and Mezzy is excited to checkout the Cabala, he's getting me interested in all sorts a new worlds. Then its to the video store and we rent Dead Man the great Johnny Depp.

Back in Mezzy's crib I recommend we brew more coffee so Mez does that and it's nice to get away from Owatonna for a bit. With a hot cup of java Mezzy puts in the movie, we watch and I've seen it before but I'm astounded by it now again and me and Mez make our quasi profound remarks about this Indian lore, at the end I'm holding back tears.

Gentle lovesong guide me gentle.

Zen ze Ghost Dance of Richard Thompson Night Comes In.

Jesus come to the Indians.

Not the imposters.

I'm in ecstasy tonight I don't know if it's the liquid tea or the meeting I setup with a preacher tomorrow but I feel good good as good and the music, well, I'm listening to Robbie again, Robertson ya know and out of the turquoise comes a slash of swaying red and I know in my bones I'm Indian, so I'm not Jesus tonight I'm Dawn Teoyote riding the codes "with a wounded heart and a sober mind." Robbie your teachings, preecepts, sues, go straight to my forever formless fates the gods the people all the peoples tribes conditions and ghost bird on ghost street on ghost planet, ah my prayers are prayed as I live each trembling moment breathing that holy ghost and mountain and shapes and tonalities and underworlds and I forgot what eyes getting at? Oh yeah, the chameleons. The chameleons of knightly colors and like the Zoo unloaded we is all tamed by the untamed anything goes and lost admit lost admit it.

The bus driver was Shiva today, my pale neighbor a beautiful Negress, Grant a dumb blond, Stipe a goofy fuck, chieftess winer with the white and the frown, and me on that Celtic bus route reading The Scripture of the Golden Eternity and really understanding the book and accepting the disguises. I'm ready Africa.

Urge to smoke so I will.

He wanted to keep it a secret.

I think I met Tracy today, I met someone beautiful that's for sure for real. It started with my mom picking me up here and driving to Rochester for the weekend, she got me my money, fifty bucks a week, I dropped her off at her house then I returned a load of art books to the library, books on Rothko, Motherwell, Frankenthaler. And I was sad to depart with the Peter Gabriel CD's. I parked downtown plugged the meter for an hour and a half and sauntered down to the used bookstore, first looking for my eternal heroes Kerouac and Miller and consequently just browsing and mostly in the religious section wanting to know wondering if there are books on Jesus after the resurrection, what he did the mountains the quiet place the heaven? But they didn't have any books that shook my onions so I walked into the Peace Plaza walked by Macs and there in the joint is the cook I used to dishwash with, his name is...shit I'll give his real name because I can't think of one, George, well George is smiling and we greet and we pass through the kitchen and dishwashing area which brings back a million memories then go out back where we can smoke, we smoke and talk and somehow get on the subject of art, he wants to see my stuff so he gives me his phone numerals and off I go to the Calvary Church where I've setup an appointment to chat with my High School preacher, Father Nick.

Father Nick tells me a little about his past his family, and I confide in him all the crap that's done gone down in the last several years, "I became addicted to alcohol when I was nineteen and experimented with drugs. After ten or twelve years of use I was downright nuts only I thought it was the world that had gone mad, not me, I didn't know anything about mental illness, I was psychotic and suicidal so my dad came and I went to a hospital, after that..." and on and on about my life which is really in the story of my poems and Ant Man and my paintings and drawings and music, its all there, here. Documented. But lately I've enjoyed talking, rap kicks, opening up flesh to flesh eye to eye and I feel the Father's empathy as I rattle off how my life spiraled.

"What about your art, has it gone abstract?"

I like it that he's interested in that for art is my purpose my existence, "Lately I'm trying to formulate a way to be abstract and tell a story at the same time," I say a little hesitantly.

"Wow."

"In ninety seven I became interested in Egyptian art and culture, my paintings actually looked Egyptian. Afterwards it became intermixed with an interest in the East," I look at him to see if he approves, the East, nonchristianity. I go on, "And now I've been reading about Jesus, The New Testament. I've changed and I'm entering new territory and I'm looking for truths and fresh ways to live."

We conclude and hug and I'm back out on the streets feeling naturally high.

So George comes by later that night, we go into the garage where've got a lotta old art stored. I pull out the paintings on wood, a sphinx, a fish, abstractions, totems, he's interested, wants to buy one, dig. "What's with all the crowns?"

I reply, "I don't know the shit just comes out, I paint and paint but I don't know what they mean, I guess my stuff is hopefully an extension of Jean Michael Basquiat's art, Haitian art, voodoo, national Kaddishes, personal rebellions."

"Huh, never heard of him."

"They got a book on Jean at the bookstore, check him out."

But George leaves that night not purchasing a picture but promising to come back, only with his girlfriend who's gonna help him decide.

Sunday. I wake and go for that first immortal smoke of the day, my folks going to church, I'm recently wanting to go back just to learn and hear the biblical stories, more to learn than worship, but George and Tracy might be coming by. I'm on the deck in back and smoking again and their car pulls up the driveway, I greet them, shake Tracy's hand and we proceed to the garage where my pictures are waiting to be looked at. I wanna stare at Tracy but I resist and take quick glances and form in my mind that she is extremely intelligent, also I feel self-conscious, I feel like my pictures are sheet. I don't say much, they look and don't say much. So eyes surprised when they agree to buy two of em, money wow. Its started off to be a good day and I've met howling beauty of Tracy now forever lodged in my circus brain.

White robe in the corner of this room by the four stigmatas and the innumerable Buddhas.

His music plays and I feel inspired, good, spirited. Good ole Harry Eastershirt.

I cried when I heard Dark End of The Street and now Meet Me Down The Alley has got my brow curdling, these songs of loss of youth of risk, its to a lonesome love we go, solitary in sweat pants and flannels and Picasso and Lorca know the dull intensity sad. Come on its only five twenty eight but its pitch black with silken clouds safely folded away into my oblivion and yes Paul I'll meet you anywhere I Will Dare I will love you for the sister that you are however foolish the game the androgyny. You got me wet in the eyes and I hope ya aint drinkin again.

I don't want to write about war I want to write about individual peace, the peace Krishnamurti may or wants to expose. There is so much to live for, there's so much beauty in this world, wow, Paul you and I are alive for now for together now tonight. We've been through so much, it was worth it for the prophecies of Jesus do come to pass like "he who loses his life finds it" I'm finding this one true and beating my unzipped heart. And Bob walked those alleys like a priest of nowhere. I hear the echo of your love for him in your violet voice sing songy its when the clown gets tired and confesses that counts the most. Streets, trails, winding lies, complex routes of love tolled. And maybe its me who conceived the world like Jack's always saying if that's so find me in this fantasy let the parades boil let the greetings tear and we are already in love so what's the rush? I've got your acoustic electric blue tunes, that's enough.

God its Sunday and wish Sara was here to hear and dance with me.

Almost five p.m. and the sun was a pumpkin a perfect circle and now the trees sway in the chill wind. Again like last night I'm digging Harry Paul and the spirit of it and the broken tambourines of Jesus' blessings reading Robert Graves hallow the hole hallow the holy of Now. Goin to meet the Hairdresser goin to see Lame Deer Chris Robinson tomorrow, but for now eyes got the green tea cigarette joy and music music music like boxcars boxcars boxcars or jacket jacket. The wind is the sacred songs to witch the naked trees dance to and I'm dancing too safe in my crib.

When spirits are released from his dove heart "I just feel right."

That half moon out there daring it looks like she could fall and if she The Moon doth fall I shall catch her in my guitar hands.

He sings yeah you're makin it, I know I know, Sunday's spent and now I'm just writing for the heck of it, end of the dusk night blues black, space and no finish. The dictionary sits there dumb my CD's on the floor my back felt fine today and I read thirty pages of King Jesus and thinking about maybe the casting out of the mighty demon of…what? "Standing on the water casting your bread while the eyes of the idol head are glowing…" Thinking of that vast mystery: Jesus. The Middle East, the turmoil. But I'm listening to Indian Paul who sings about the ordinary you know ordinary Minnesota, all of us who really feel the seasons warp and waggle and the deepest winters these days.

My beard is getting long and there's a few white hairs, I

clipped my nails, I showered and on the Sabbath I wash my balding hair. The lamp is leaning a little maybe cause of all the tobacco and I haven't looked at my yearbook for a while. I bought the Dead Sea Scrolls for five and some change up in the cities, Midway Books. I talked to a gallery cat I might exhibit my shit in the city that'd be a thrill a kick.

Stick Figure smoking the ganja, hiding in that, he smoked up in the car on the way back to Owatonna and it smelled like Hotel Sickness. They don't call it a drug for nothing. Hiding from the shattered self for the fate is scary. Stones more alive. I used to really miss drugs, I was a pothead I was a acid eater I was a mushroom man, hell Ant Man was writ on tons of booze and mushrooms, it has its own sense but I wish not to return to that territory whiskey wine beer. Now I'll look you straight in the eye now I'll look with my heart. Not with some quasi mystical crutch.

I can tell Paul, Harry, Martha, we have liberated each other and like that time mortally walking the streets Snelling Ave. and the pure sun gold bless I looked up and we were reborn like now listening to your trembling joy on the boom box bless this blessed life even the gods even the devils dance they we can't help it its too much joy you have cross the thresholds of unholy Indian water and we see the clear clay of clearly near. We live on high like Van Morrison prophesied. Astral meek.

Soldiers playpens fakirs.

This life of song hath saved me, I know its ours, I know I'm your daydream, I know the will owes, I know the baby babies and all over a want expressed. Ya I know Bukowski lingering like a stinky debt but I just write whatever pops into my pigeon head my Starry Night and I saw the moon at four in the afternoon as that fleecy sundown downed the down of this down up. We have a new dance and we're not even ghosts this time but flesh actual. And morning am a.m. am is. Finding a fish in every gown even us "men" will squirm multiple new comes the Dawn and no need for peyote no need. Joyce set all this up and Jack took ole James to drear America and unfolded the too, Pully Pauley and Alene that's her reel name foxy foxy we all rose to the occasion by believing in humor. And so it ghosts.

Maybe its that book I'm reading the continuing knowledge seeking the sought in thin desert Jesus. Did He take me to that alcohol cliff? Only I stepped off splat. He sits under the Tree of Love, He gave his sexy untouched lover choice. He read thoughts He was raised in Africa He waits for the valley to all. Never once waved to my wave but like the banner burnt the mission forsook the windows cracked the Hood dragging I see You eating potato chips on Lake Street and I see you in my subsidized mirror. My father's shoulders echo with sacrifice. The crucifixions…everyday the crucifixions and He left the lamp in everyman's heart and he shook the lambs to refraction madhouses of narrow. Entrance without door, needle without cloud, pillow camel jigsaw vomiting water I lay down for the last time.

I'm not Mohammed but I've met her she left when I started to roll.

Snow a-fallin on the ground on the Earth, today I woke at noon and did some errands then came back here and drank my green great tea, got hyped on that and talked on the phone to various folk and in between all that I was reading Enid's biography of Arthur Rimbaud. I took a bath and then now just now I read Illuminations which is a thousand years ahead of its time. I feel like that one, Genie, is about me. Megalomania they call it, it happens a lot to me.

Genie? Moslem? Was he predicting his future? Predicting the future for all us clowns and freaks who take to the rites of wildfire like wildfire and end up like wildfire? It is the supernatural this supposed derangement, it'll lead you to places you never guessed you'd end up. It'll lead to Allen's Holy it'll lead to reading of Jesus and after years of submersion you'll come up to some sort a High. I don't know? It's a crazy set o' roads. Jean Michal went down it, I'm beginning to think this is a Bait Generation, Bayt, or you know all the temptations some modern some old but the rites…these rites open up, survive them, see them, transcend them. And the mystifying thing of it is you'll see there is no death. Omni sentience, some things go small very small womanly small insect small while the mind Surangama shutters shimmers and its all natural.

IMMENSE.

La de da.

Candle lit tonight valley dark and dark, Breakdown Café then the grocery store then the bus back home to my green tea and Rimbaud books. Rolling Thunder on the box, buzzing buzzard of the legal last caffeine and I used to paint kings jesters Christs and now lately its Buddhas but Dylan Pickle staring white paint at me from a photograph, and my last lover was called Sara, Sarah, "calico sphinx in a Scorpio bow," and love passed is love real is love. Pickle sings with the Passion, in his bedroom I looked at him and tried to glean his secret, sacrifices, is my true father two thousand years old? Did he reinvent the calendar with fish and bread? Did he spawn the geniuses of France? Did he create these rites of self bondage? Self slavery? Because there is a way out. D.H. said he coupled with Isis, Father Nick said he went to the mountains, I say he's the ultimate outlaw who the Indians took in, wounded beside God, healed by Lame Deer's vast and various ceremonies. And now we see and sing together in ethnic America whistling down the sacred night diffusing the wordless, the worldless.

He crossed, He crossed, he crossed the ocean to

commune with the oldest: Indian. And here now ignorant of his rule she passes she is fecund with nobody's child, gold bastard, beads of time fall apart dollar stores and cheap cloth. Cane, I never used the cane. But there she is again and he's walking in the blindman's trance and I sit with my avocados and bread and mustard and video the chance and like medicinal echoes there he is again but she does not seem to remember for "the water is wide" and I'm a lonely old Whitman in the throes of a not-so-bad nothingness. Kristin and the everyday angels you gotta read these little signs of the boisterous times, they will call it coincidence they will call it delusion they will definitely lie but the angels they are here now on this very soulful planet and I find myself in a massively light realm of Providence. Providence as the blues pound and Pound pounds the purple.

At The Breakdown Café a new Lou and I talked of Hunter S. Thompson, we're a-gonna meet tomorrow for immaculate coffee and the deer hunters will shiver.

There is healing in Enid Starkie's book. Understanding. Dare I say charity.

For a few days I'll read Jesus, then I go to Rimbaud, those two are in my mind these days. Both are poets like my father like me like all of America and especially The Bread Down Café. Miller's book made me want to get back together with The Doll but it was too late, she had found her hometown diamond. Me left with what I cherish and hate: solitude.

I'll just sit and listen. Stories of redemption, songs of struggle, maybe someday we'll live together like Jesus and Mary and Mary.

High on green tea and Celtic music I'm in India with the Ginsberg book, Barry Miles. I feel great like green tea is the best drug out there and man its legal. I met Lou earlier today and he gave me a Jello Biafra and Noam Chomsky

CD. We sat in the cafeteria and drank the black medicine, he'd broken up with his chick, six months sober and in A.A. they say to wait for a year of sobriety before entering into any kinda relationship. I told him about my experiences a lil.

Mist on the window which opens out to black which reflects my uncombed mop which dimly reflects my mythological drawings through which I see streetlamps and snow and the parking lot. I live beside a highway and the cars roll by in visual Doppler. A home for the handicapped with some of its lights on and I see a person in a wheelchair. I just read Allen's The Change and realize I've got to let my visions my delusions go, go. I'm listening to Miles' On The Corner and I feel logical in this winter mellow. The cats are inside and the ladybugs live with me.

So what would happen if I dissolved my fears? To ring to bring room for new fears? Or replace the fears with hope? Hope of what? Hope for what? I think as I age and the terror fades I will see again like youth or see with a pleasantness a vague future. Karen she's Hiding Away from me, I look at her picture and say Mother Sister Lover? Which one? She taught me how to sing and not be afraid of speaking in tongues in tongues that will ever come together? She is the one. She is the nation I have defected to. Her songs are my hopes as a unitary thing that is not a thing, "The guy who aint a guy," now that I've asked this fear question in the vast quiet of a specter'd night what will the answer, where will the answers bubble forth? I have just lived. I will continue to live.

To no longer seek ecstasy? To no longer quest for derangement of the senses? Self destruction? Should I quit even my lonely tobacco habit? Should I fall on my knees and worship deities who killed and destroyed my Indian ancestors? Ah but Jesus himself is not to be blamed for Cortez and Columbus and all the diluted truth of the self righteous Simpletons. To have that "private revolution" and not hate my mirror my eyes my fates. Come up its alright to slur my words for my days are Red Clouds of Unknowing but at least they're red, read as red like Tracy's true heartbeat in a life of song. What is my story tonight? As I sit on this chair as I listen to The Innocence Mission as I feel calm from my prescription Ativan what is this story or stories I cannot write nor see? "I failed, I failed, I am always beginning the world beginning the world..." "I had hopes for my music..." dove Karen did you see or notice or partake of the Day of the Birds on Lake Street? Ah don't go back, lets just say I came awfully close to death back in 1996. I can almost remember revolutions.

Surreal.

Now I know the Cross.

Technically I think Subterraneans is the most superb, but twas Desolation Angels that expanded and healed my fractured alcohol pot lifted life mess mind. Walking by the Catholic school and knowing, "I'm going back into The Beats, I'm going to Mexico, I'm going to dance on the Sabbath in a scarlet clearing." Downtown Rochester where I lived for three years and found a bone in a bag of potato chips and found myself thoroughly insane, drinking and drinking, writing poor Ant Man and letters to my bro Stick Figure. But to get back to Jack K. and his floppy harlequin sentences who Jones gleaned inspiration from and now... and now.

How influenced were The Beats by Jung? Pollock claimed to be a Jungian, it was certainly in the air. Back around the time I was re-examining Jack I bought Psychology and Alchemy at the downtown bookshop. I didn't know that I was an alchemist in the form of a painter, that is like Marcel said, "Unwittingly." Well I read half the book and it inspired many of my sloppy paintings, but wordlessly, it came to me in colors mostly. Tonight I opened the book again after a bout a two and half year lapse between readings and bam wow the journey Carl describes, both ancient and modern, both Gnostic and Agnostic, has come to pass. I have been baptized by fire, I have drowned in the elements, I have been as silent as stone. Through the journey I went and go and now I can see the magnanimity of life itself, forever a light as the universe waits to be born.

Feel awfully sad tonight, inexplicably.

Overwhelmed by world, by names, by histories and poems, by my own fallout of megalomania. I'm just a guy sitting in his room glooming ruminating into a wan nothingness. Hollow Men promenade in the dreadful cities, I'm out here in the country without a lover. I slept to an early dusk Monday while the toil of the town waged on I had incontrovertible dreams. Witch I don't remember.

I was first diagnosed Bipolar, I think I have some of that because last night I was the happiest man on the planet and now tonight I'm a sad sack. Called up ma to tell her I was sad she said, "Hang in there honey." We shot the breeze in this heartless winter of oversleeping of over smoking of just plain glum.

So I put on my Kerouac CD and I start to come out of it. I don't want to end up like Vincent or Arthur dead before forty. My grandpa is still alive and when I asked my ma how old he was she had I look in her eyes which said: ageless, hundreds. Old Irish Indian Harry Paul Grandpa Boy and the apostles too live poor and have seen the centuries alchemize. Heaven is at hand, oh old haven of heaven, pop, esoteric, who will enter the invisible Pure Land of Earth in eternities' azure gazes? History man, I read Jung a little bit today and want to get a hold of some Hermes. I'm gonna write the history of everything someday.

My old friend buddy Skull out in California, talked

to his brother, wrote him a letter hoping he'll write back, maybe I'll see him this Christmas?

Oh time, oh angel, oh hallowed season, when will I cross another mental bridge to a shinier state. I have been given the gift of unemployment, I don't have to work if I don't want to. My schizophrenia both a curse and a blessing, I have time to write and draw and read. Lou ole Robbie Lou on the sound bleeder again. His songs brother me to some distance heavenly and descendings and eyes choosing me. I write a story of thought.

I wish I could create like Leroy Amiri, concision. Takes time and growth, just let it spill out, willy-nilly.

Evidence scarce but I think maybe the Indians love Jesus.

I know they dig Buddha, who doesn't?

"I was standing on a wave when I made the drop, I was lying in a cave in the solid rock, I was feeling pretty brave till the lights went off, sleep by no means comes too soon in a valley lit by the moon."

The parking lot white with snow as tea brews and reading Allen.

Okay so we're both in the belljar off in fantasy, me and Mez.

I've listened to Coltrane three times afternoon dusk night.

I don't know what to believe in but I feel that African blood in me as I blow with The Jackson Five. I don't know what to believe in as I look through these western window to infinite space and recall Buddha's words, "Space is permanent." I like this feeling of not knowing what to believe in, man means I'm open to anything. I accept and will espouse the songs of the Jackson family cuz I FEEL it, bones and soul, spirit and heart. Maybe I need Wu We? Ah tonight I mean this afternoon read Allen then Jack then Buddha then talked to Stick Figure on the phone then talked to Peanut Head too. After a heavy night and to be honest a protracted season in Christianity which Mezzy has bestowed upon my fates I feel the weight release reading of Tathagatas and the melodies of Africa. Desire and control released in creativity.

"How can you keep it all inside?" sang The Raindogs. It's a good question.

So now I put my father (?) on the box. Who is he this time? Oh delusion. Working Class Hero? Real Love? Man who knows the blues that's for sure. Imagine my father singing Imagine? Wow.

Irish and Black and deep.

A little dizzy I put on Rod Stewart's Maggie to recapitulate my times with Franny, that crazy demented beautiful song brings her back. Its what I feel. Its good but it breaks my fucking heart. I was a wretched beast for real.

Witch brings me back to Layton and swilling the cheapest and truly bluely digging Harry's favorite The Faces. Stick's still got the record A Wink is as Good as a Nod to a Blind Horse or something like that. Oh Maggie…first time I heard Ronnie Lane's voice singing Debris I was shooked hooked in. Such ordinary-ness, down and way out of it, as good drunk as hungover and now December something I listen and my heart creaks out like grandma's stairs. Layton loved seventies music, we used to go to Cheapo's coming off acid and ramble an hour away looking at all that sound and for a few bucks we'd come home to our shack in the hood with three or four new platters, stuff like George Thoroughgood or Booker T. or T-Rex or…I don't know anything cock-n-roll. Layton bought a drum set and jammed a few times his brown hair down to his shoulders.

Franny was more into painting, wanted to "talk" about it, art. It was weird, for the life of me and to this day still

I can't or don't know how to talk about art but once you get me started on rock-n-roll you can't shut me up. I'm a music know-it-all. I can remember the first time I've heard practically everything, Sex Pistols Dylan Stones Miles. Its all filed away in my shaky noggin.

Glimmer of a mental Dawn: oh let go of the passed oh let it dissolve, my mind underneath the turmoil of the "world" shall be discovered by me alone. Sentient guesses and trembling departures to a non-discriminative state which shall be innumerable in its causeless reflects. Twenty five hundred years ago the flower of justice spoke and tonight I read his retractable words and the games the wheels the lilies all beyond beginning. Dharma of discovery in a silent veil, behind which is the briefest brightest holiest face innumerating eternity as is what is in a tangible see-able everlasting ocean sparked by the great face of mystery: SPACE.

Eyeless in a read eternity.

After several days of flu, since Monday night and now its Thursday afternoon I've been bedridden, but now I sit here in my gold cloth chair and the tea is goin down good and the cigarettes feel fine and reading Jack's roller coaster letters I feel back to normal. I feel good well it's always a little itty bitty miracle to come back to life again, now I can write and read and draw. My plant happy getting some sunshine after a week of gray, Christmas in a week, done all my shopping, hopefully get some new books, that's all I want is books and books and more books. My CD player hasn't been working so I've been listening to tapes, right now Miles. I'm back, lookout!

Mortality defined, defied, Chinaman omnipotence and flashing with Mezzy and the three crosses forever spiked archetype on the skull, Hebrew anthem Kaddish

I'm listening to now. Accumulated by the karma of booze and drugs, kicked or dropped out of universities and now madness kick out shun dick in son. And below Mezzy is me with a Mexican pyramid on the torch of my mind.

Mez gives me a ride home from The Breakdown Café and we're talking easily about women, our mutual frustrations, our pasts and me with two abortions really weary of everything. Then we rap about our college lives, Mezzy kicked out of one of the best schools in the country for his private study of alchemy getting high all the time and me I dropped out with three credits to go, maybe we'll go back? He asks me if I wanna go out to Waseca for the night so in the eight o' clock dark winter we climb into his car and drive the fifteen minute route straight west and listen to Keith Richards. He has to do laundry and I'm hungry so I go across the street to a grocery store with deli and gobble down some grub. Mezzy turns up at the store with his humorous face and dig the cashier women buy some shit then we're back in Mezzy's crib warm.

I brew up coffee makin it strong and black and Mez gets the chessboard out. He's got tall ceilings and art on the wall and a big sketchpad on the floor. I put Noam Chomsky and Jello Biafra CD into the machine and roll a chig. I've lent Mezzy my Golden Bough book which I bought used for six bucks about the same time which this book starts, my war vision my Lithium fallout. We play chess but its not like it used to be it feels like its grinding up my mind, chess is for the scientist not the artist. The coffee done and I pour some into a nice poor sill Lynn cup. Then Mezzy says, "Its show and tell time," and brings out all his old notebooks and I sit on the floor looking at his drawings. By now we've put in a new CD, Peter Gabriel.

I get tired of chess so we shoot the breeze Mezzy showing me his drawings and writings. Then he pulls out a Cool

Ridge (don't know how to spell his name) and I read it out loud, its about a dream or a vision of a icy dome, me only understanding the fact that's its pure fantasy, a opium heaven lust. We talk about the poem for a while then I'm back on the ground going through his drawings and I realize me and Mez come from two different traditions: Mezzy the scholastic fantasizer which he's broaden out to include Christianity, his key big word when we talk about religion is "believe," he's out for eternal life through Jesus. My tradition is simply reality itself, neither belief nor nonbelief, but Chinese Philosophy and The Beats, I'm not looking for eternal life I know now is eternity enough.

"I have felt the presence of Jesus," says Mezzy.

Half believing hymn, "Huh."

"I know you say to want eternal life is selfish but I believe Christ is the only way to reach that."

Now I feel pity for that statement, and say, "I think Egypt is still running the show and Rome Rome hasn't changed. I think Rome is hunting down Jesus who's still alive and hiding with the Indians here in America. Rome is the ultimate puppet."

"Yeah they say it's the eternal city."

We talk on and on like that through the night and after the conversation peters out Mezzy's doing a drawing while I read my poetry, Valley From The Wave. Eventually around two we hit the sack and I have wild dreams then come morning its off to The Breakdown Café.

One goes into the garden the other goes into the valley as the sun shines on both.

Painting pictures with songs Van Morrison man and the eternal veil of peace on a war drenched terrain. Got to rewind, Philosopher's Stone. Yonder write about the valley the zoo the ocean the reflection the…and a wave comes over me, like a ghostly promenade like a soulful before like a beginningless merchant like a first tipi like a garden of Zen Christ. When He was in that garden…begging mercy…mission…deaf father me to the witches' windy zoom. I'm like your pace, "Stepping out Queen, just a whisper away…" Charlotte read of the valley at Leatherface's funereal as I stepping in to the violins to smoke ah oh to smoke. And the time just crawls over me D.T. boy, salvation man, bright woman. I can see Allen typing his opuses in the drear light of few, and like Allen the madhouse has haunted me, I have burned out a billion suns I have lived like a cat in the vacuum of unborn. The terrible truth the lovers departed the dictionary a lie. A simple once again for now is all I have.

It gets unreal at times this sobering up. The ecstasies entwine with the wrathful sorrows and I'm listening to Black Beauty and wonder…wonder at this technological whirled? We're here in America, I know that much. And Finnegan tries to explain it to me but I'm not yet ready though I dig the puns. Now I'm reading Peter Farb, I'm either a shaman or an anthropologist? I don't feel like an artist man you know? Just recording what ghosts down. I don't even know what nationality I am? Sometimes I know I'm Indian, sometimes I think my father is Henry Miller? I just don't know but I like his beginning to Tropic of Capricorn where he just plunges rite in and lays it out bare: this is me. Ant Man structurally is based on that wild book. This book was supposed to be a derivation of Cervantes, a parallel, in the modern whirl only. But its just turned out to be one sloppy confession after another. I know though that I am a modern Don Quixote for I exist in what I now deem The Bait Generation. Me and Mez talked about it, just the drugs alone are enough bate to bait the abated. Not to mention that golden carrot money, moo la, bones, bucks, bread, dough. Through the network of American prostitutions one does not escape without a few unlucky scars, physical or mental or spiritual. So we go…and like I said sobering up is both real and surreal and plus the dangerous unreal. But what's real anyways? My confessions? Your paycheck? The Holden Ka Fields will inherit the Earth? Ah shit.

On this wonderful morning with Melanie's Christmas gift a new coffee maker I feel great and can conceive us two sharing music together, just sitting around in our sweat pants and T-shirts listening digging contemplating Dylan and The Pretenders and whatnot. Ah beautiful life, how I feel so good right now with my sober friends and Mr. Bojangles is dancing in my heart and Buddha leans on my mind and I'm smoking and reading of the Eskimos.

Next day listening to Pickle high on brewed java Joe and wondering about the Indians again. And how I've had anything but a normal life. America the abuse of the sacred wheel. Shamans are needed now more than ever, more then never.

Tracy sings I'm wired lucid genius stupid but she sings man and she lets keeps letting me know that love real love true blue honest love is possible in this impossibled world. Her heart in her voice her heart and she she bringing Africa close, close to me, humbling my wild tangential mind, soothing and smoothing yet like a delicate blood flame we are alive, she is anyways in the form of my tape player and I listen listen listen. I am the river that could wash over you Tracy, you the very Earth itself consciousness. One more song, one more wrong revealed to me. My fractured heart thanks her on this keyboard computer. She's making promises. Africa. Africa.

Christmas sliver moon, "Where are you goin? To a ghost

dance in the snow." Not much to say tonight, feeling good feeling like John Coltrane sounds.

My past, did I have em worried? Or did they know? I sure as hell didn't know what was happening. If I had ten bucks in my rusty pocket for a case of Old Swill that was all I needed to know. Did they set up the Nazi visions? And that one morning when I tasted lead in the water? And the insect who said go ahead boy murder me but I let him it her just stride across my canvas in Midway that suicidal week, is it all pre pree rite? But tonight I actually feel normal, not ravaged confused lonesome mad, a calm envelops me and the future not so bad after all. Still the mystery lingers not painfully tonight so I give thanks to the musicians who sung and sang and sing me through: U2 has been there all along and that's who I listen to now in the genie now that Arthur R. so elegantly prepared.

Out there in the demon fall.

A night of music, my own my friends and The Others.

She's some angel of nowhere.

When will she say, "Come in I'll give ya shelter from the storm?" I can feel tears again tonight and tomorrow's New Years. Or New Year's Eve.

The Indian Uprising known as Jackson Pollock.

The Indian Uprising known as Dawn Peyote.

The Indian Uprising known as Bob Haze.

The Indian Uprising known as Hairshirt.

The Indian Uprising known as mental illness.

Now it's a couple days later Friday night and I'm pacing the romb wondering if I should call and invite Vicky over? Sure would be fun to spend some more time with her.

It's a new Dawn it's a New Year with Vee who I got mixed up with Melanie but her name is Vee and she's lovely, we went for an hour long walk yesterday then we sat in her crib and smoked talked and she brewed coffee and she doesn't hold back in conversation she's had a rough life she's been raped she's been in the state hospital she's tried suicide but despite all this tragedy she's come through and she still knows how to laugh and be goofy. I'm falling for her. We've even kissed a few times not like The Doll who I rushed in too fast with Vee wants to take it slow coming off a divorce and going slow is fine by me after all my reckless years and heartbreaks. So I listen sitting here to The Jackson 5 and gleaning the small chance of a fate change in love with falling and its dreamlike crazy true I'm in love with you Vee.

Tom Waits is fallin down again and his tunes his will his wail is my octopus destiny. Where do I stand when all I do is fall? With Vee even…just remember, and take it slow. "Fallin down fallin down…" and then I'll flip the tape over to Astral Weeks. Ah I rewinded it again that accordion comes in with the melancholy hillbilly strum of an ole git tar then ole Tom lays it out, a little Dylan a little Coleman Hawkins, and these songs, what is it about these songs? "Go on put your heals to the ground you'll be hearing that sound fallin down…" And two buildings have burnt down in Owatonna this last year and me I'm burning down tonight with a mix of friendship love lust. Like some a this other writings I have tears welling up again, but they're love tears alive I am alive tears. Would Vee, would you understand my love for music Vee in all this? I can't separate my music from my flesh, I can't displace melodious confession for soul. "I made a supplication in this prayer," saith Jack, and the only prayers I've ever know have been music and flesh entwined. Ah this descending to reality this reality ascending to love, what and where and when? "Someone's fallin down…"

Well I'm back at the typer still listening to Saint Petersburg Tom and the sadness, the dadness, gladness, and e.e. off in the fours and don't ask God for nothin. I dirge my tears to a mythical real woman: Vee. Every song brings my feelings to her image.

And me and Wheat Thompson used to listen to Astral Weeks on those long benders binges and Wheat put his hands on his heart and the vibes passed between us and it was the first time I saw a MAN'S eyes well up well up well up like mine now ten fifteen years later except I'm alone with my sacred tears in the immutable flux of love.

Vee you make the songs real. Thanks love.

Tonight proud as a Blackhair.

Strum and glum and garden and valley, seems like something.

The thing a haunted hint like jazz.

In a deep black January night wondering when I should call Vee?

Eye call Vee and happily she uses or proclaims the words "relationship" "euphoria" and I tell her the songs I've been listening and digging remind me of her and it's a true blue beginning. Friendship, partners in time. What else was I gonna say? I had something? She's a fragile one though and I don't want to hurt her.

So I put Sophie B. on the box to tilt me a little further into this brewing love.

I'll dream for both of us.

I'll dance on the perimeters of any Hades for both of us.

On a new vein use got to understand blues and jazz are the roots of the great twentieth century painting.

How I know dat? Junior Wells.

It's a journey and a half.

Its good to listen to some piano music tonight comin down sad glad.

Not a spectacular sundown nonetheless I feel righteous and fine what with Vee giving me her old CD player mine hasn't been working and we talk easily goofily on the phone and she's a shiny apple of my heart's tamed desires. Oh yeah too she gave me a funky cap like the kind Jackson used to wear, I'm sporting it right now just for the hell of it and I see an airplane flying through my light blue window sky.

So much has happened lately with Mezzy and Tommy and Vee I don't know where to begin, lets just say a new story is a-brewing.

This new story? I feel like a new man (man?). It starts on New Years Eve, no, a few days before Christmas when me and Mez have long talk, cover a lot a ground, talking our respective histories in the early night, both of us college dropouts and wondering what our next move'll be? But we talk intensely about politics then religion then back to politics and when he leaves my head is a-swim with ideas, the talented Mr. Mezzy and is he a Halloween Boy? Like Halloween Chicks? I just with it, Coincidenceville no longer scares the B-Jesus outta me, I just roll like a cigarette.

But New Years Eve, that's good a good night first Tommy and Mez pick me up and we go to the store to buy groceries for the night then we get back to my crib, turn on the tunes and brew coffee and rap, I lend Tommy The Golden Dawn which I've barely started though the start has me intrigued I'm into other stuff like The Horn, Kerouac said, "Good book," but I say great book, also Salvation Army has paperbacks for a quarter and I bought the Amiri Baraka reader the other day when walking with magical Vee. Anyways its night and around seven Vee calls then comes over and what do you know it's a party, Vee sitting in the cloth throne and I got a foldout chair and a couple plastic lawn ones and we sit around the coffee table with the radio on. After a little while we play rummy five hundred. The talk is easy, good, fun. Then about eleven Mez and

Tommy split and say, "We'll leave you two lovebirds alone." Ah this love stuff excites.

So its Vee and mee and we watch David Letterman the first time I've been alone with a woman since The Doll Sara, I try not to stare but Vee has some nice knockers and I imagine how soft my soft lips and hands would feel on em in this late soft night, I get a boner, I'm really turned on. But we just talk and then watch Friends and its about one thirty in the morning and Vee brews up another batch of coffee. Vee is really forthright freely rapping about her difficult past and I tell her, "You've had a hard life." And she has but I want to help, I let her leave around three without makin a move, I don't want to brake or shake her tender heart…

She comes over a night or two later again sitting in the easy chair and this time I can't resist, "Would you mind if I kiss you?" I ask.

She looks a little confused but not angry, "Well I guess," so our first magical kiss in the night immaculate, lips touching lips, communion, beyond wine and blues. When she leaves a couple hours later she leans down and gives me another one then I standup and hug her and give her another kiss. Kiss. This book has turned into a Vee love kiss. I am in love, in love with her.

Saturday we go for an hour walk through our neighborhood then she invites me into her pad, she's got a cool unpretentious place, homey, and she brews coffee and we talk and we smoke. (God writing about this just makes me wanna be with her right now) She tells me about being raped, geeze she's had it rough, I fall silent, then she had an abortion and I tell her about some of my experiences. The radio is on. I sip my java. At times we look each other straight in the eye, her rare green eyes and my melancholy brown ones, what color do you get when you mix green and brown? Love colors many. So when I leave delightfully we kiss a couple times and I go home to cook some dinner and I'm in ecstasy.

I'm in ecstasy tonight just thinking and writing about this little history, the start…

Be a good night to go into some Allen Ginsberg.

So here I am Sunday night almost Monday morning listening to Dylan and just read the Metro chapter of The Horn and I thought I'd do a little type-thinking ya know just let the mind go like music in the streetlamp'd windowed jestered little stars of a calm nocturne forever, and have the directions done gone homeward to some prairie mist in the frowning blackity clackity of good? Cats done farmed the farm and I told Vee bout the great Cat Man who taught me the tautology of chess and marijuana I taught him drink that whiskey straight straight from the bottle man and now we are a-here in the singsong night bleeding bleeding I say from fortuitous blindness and I say don't look the other way cuz soon as this alchemy stone rolling song's finished I'll put on Alice and really understand. Or will I?

Alice Peyote man.

And Tom waited.

And we both sobered up dreaming like seas now in the meadow of reason. Baby math, don't need it. Maybe I'll smoke maybe I'll good my will? And Time thinking of Space. Fyodor man, Jack and Henry's fountainhead like some misnomer of greatness into the jazz of absolute, a Russian Dance, will take the peyote again and my skating vision was Moloch too. There's a chance the surrealism will get stranger. But I can only imagine steam whistles now out there all Midwest all lost like vents like skeletons like Westy running from the deep heart. "Make it weird."

Oh so Tuesday night and I keep thinking that early star's a plane but it must be a star cuz its always there in my window there and now listening to Van's night in San

Fran and talking on the phone to my various friends and drinkin a pot o' coffee I'm feeling like a could dance with Charlie Parker or get in the ring with Ali…just to dance you know? But I here that horn and that electric masterbox and it's a Victoria Fellaheen night for us under the dogs where the ladder don't matter where the visionary bars turn into luminous stars like that early plane star that reminds me this is eternity, it is man and the new Lou was blowin on the phone about all the great ones of the brush of paint and now my being being real is really being real! So put that in your pipe…

I'm listening to Ricki Lee now pacing the romb practicing my imaginary piano, "We belong together," and finally decide to type down my nebulas feeling, grasping beat in the late twilight at visionary feathers of romance, thinking of Vee and we just get a little love-goofier everyday witch is witch which is fine by me, the pleasant peasant on the Ville of any joker's bets placing my invisible chips of lust on compassion, sympathy, felicity, any trumped glance forgiven like light in the nocturne of a Chopin past of a beer past but now eyes got the tea steaming all apple and cinnamon on my transient coffee table, Lee she in Coolsville and its disturbing you know a ambiguous woman's point of view, I'm waiting like Rimbaud for to go for to sing of the Desert, quiet knees, Eucharist of back way back Jack, and the somnolent fingers fingering this for a brand new start. Ah that ole guitar kicks in ascending then descending then back then forth, I'll create new rivers with my trumpet for her: MOTHER. And how did we get here? Mystic, it has to be mystic as I sneeze, and she says we'll, wow, does that mean us? Her and me? As I listen dig this tune…

I don't have a story now now I just gonna rock-n-roll my mind. Like an electric piano I go blue and red, like a Indian enunciating a sad love song I let my being sway listening to Bad Company's Straight Shooter. And today I was Monk boggled glad, Sunday, and the jazz, the jazz, I tell you the jazz is starting to lift me to a new sense anew (even though I got to get my rock dose). Calling on Vee today it was a good conversation even if she dwells on her past a little too much, but that's okay, we're getting to know each other and this love song playin right now lurches me forward to future's fires all aglow in the swan of disposition of satisfied.

Good night what with the phone raps with Lou and Vee and Stick and Mom and I've got a decent start on a new drawing and I'm studying the modern shaman Monk but now I got Grant and Bob and Greg on with Songs and Stories. I'm just rolling and waiting for the new moon like Garcia like Plath like anyone in the Lapis Christ Parallel that Jung reveals and The Breakdown Café they know, they know the pitfalls the lifting the redemptions. But me I'm feeling good, slightly wired but as lucid as any Ireland.

I don't think its gonna work out with Vee, I don't feel like going into why.

I'm down tonight sad where is my passionate singer woman? Where are they hiding? Where is Barbara S. except on my jukebox, Woman In Love? I yearn for passion and not another T.V. slave like The Doll and Vee, I yearn for soul singers punks anything anyone just a hair different than the rest. But I'm alone tonight and its one of them nights where I feel I'll be alone forever, ya know what I'm saying? But Barbara sings I listen and want an expressionist gal an artist of some kind. Why is it I'm thirty four and I've never had a deep intellectual relationship with a woman? Henry had June, where is my June? Something like that I need I need deep deeply, I don't care what Kate wrote Henry and June had something special and I've never had that and tonight its what I want most, more than anything else: money, power, fuck em all, I want a crazy passionate lover who will wail with me and understand my blues. Am I blind? Deaf? Do I not see what's obvious? Why has no crimson harlot found my fiery trail? Maybe it's a Zen test? A Christian jest? I don't know.

So now a few minutes later I got Bette Midler on The Rose and it sure does seem like the truth, you know, some say this some say that, the tape is old and warped, I've probably listened to it umpteen times, but I dig her, I dig her passion (my word if not world for the night). "Get someone."

My eyes watery with fate and regret and potential uncast.

The sun is a mix of yellow and orange and the trees raw bare in the mercy wind: sundown. I got Tom Waits on the box and Vee had a bad day yesterday, today she was her old goofy self and I'm back in love with her.

Pacing a lil wandering the room with my Pollock book open wondering what to do with this mostly blank canvas, I'm Lionel man, and I smoke and I listen to Gabriel. Next step blues but I'm not as down as last night, almost February, Eden of unknowing.

It hasn't been all for nothing. At this end of the day I look at my pictures, I listen to Tom Waits and now Peter Gabriel and feel it: Victoria.

Just the variety of tears man...

I can't seem to draw it I can't seem to write it. Whiter Shade of Fail. Pale in the night's dark hue, the organ roars out a wave of ghost in the Blue Poles and the King and Queen and the Swift Nudes and we talked of the wandering of the playing cards. Mezzy said he...well...he opened up, feminine and said something tender, sweet. It scared me at the moment but now I can see or feel it: mind communions in impossible America.

I rewind the song the song that I first heard in high

school something procol something harem and its still a mystery. Old Inian wail blind drunkenness and sharp contrast of space's time or time's space. The truth ah the truth, let her be let her find a new coast as I ponder my drawings Friday night eleven thirty and its ten degrees out there.

Oh tender us Ireland Sinead, I put her stories in my private jukebox in the private night of these private thoughts trying to love the whatever may be. She makes my water heavy in the ambiguous aura of eye. I can feel myself opening up as she sings. And when Franklin left the scene there was born an eternal song, all these turns and tunes of loss, love loss and the lost lass searching through hints of saints and history. Oh tears, oh tears of the real. I was born to reach or make that mental pilgrimage to great Ireland but I heard on the bus the other day, "He's not Irish," ah but I am, I is, I will be. Just ask Marcel Joyce chameleon and voodoo and queen con and canto veneer, just ask. Shit I need a smoke, for Franklin the specter is coming up and I want to sail.

Shit I think I'll change my name to Franklin Finnegan Fan Again. Shit.

Shit I think I try Joyce again and again, lord.

Okay it's a few days later and I got my favorite U2 on, Achtung Babe, and it brings back a lotta memories yet it propels me in the nowness of now and even a slight glimmer of futurity. The cards were dealt and the hand and the chips but I lost, I shot myself in both feet, I galloped on a frozen horse, and when the game was over and the lights went back on I was locked up in a hospital and everything junk everything Nazi "every everything." And as far as the avant guard was concerned I might as well been a Bowery bum. Things change though for now eyes a Dharma Bum the Dharma which makes the mind bright even in the blackest of black nocturnes, eves, dusks, grays. And the garden is full a brown eyed wonders Indian and the forest shall become forest again. Unpaint this desert and take off thy mask the escape is upon us, upon us Genies and gypsies and vagabonds and that baby no longer blue to have gone to the ultra violet the orange the cracked reflections the baked refractions to have gone through and come out pure regret turned to undiluted consciousness.

So I'm just sittin round and listening to tunes. The secret of ecstasy is in the drum and turn that damn treble all the way up Paul.

Its too much man its too much beauty this January Friday afternoon listening to Charlie Parker's All Stars and my pictures on the walls and the Pollock funked open book and reading Go and eating oatmeal and its just too much and may be the coffee talking but I feel good. Mezzy's gonna come by hopefully for a trip to the local art center to rap with the funky Vinny who runs the joint and I'm gonna show him my Diamond Sutra opus, biggest picture I've ever attempted, roll it out on the ground and let the ideas purr. It's a pure white desert cold out there but I'm cozy safe inside writing this and the only way to way is to way the wayless.

Putting on Live In Seattle in the caffeine night looking at Jackson and wondering, wondering when the half moon will arrive in my hairy window? Ann was Coltrane influenced by Pollock? There are some affinities in their infinities. Last night the moon appeared and I almost felt impelled to write, but tonight I'm gonna call Vee and piddle around maybe read Blake. Vee called me her boyfriend which is a nice kick. She likes to be alone at night so that's why I'm here alone typing away into nothingness. No story to tell, no great dramas protruding like a drunkard's belly, I just listen and look and my pa is coming over on Sunday to break secular bread.

God I feel like painting.

So what do I do instead? I talk on the phone I pace I smoke I drink water I ponder…

So there is the moon.

So the old moon is in my demented window, Fresh Widow night, and admitting its beauty through the flourly glow of winter cloud mist I see like a piano the perfect tilt of moon strainless in the expression. Lorca, "Where is my moon?" and I ask, "Where is my Lorca?" in female form hopefully. And I've spent the night looking at Leonardo, Picasso, Jackson, and my own pitiful stuff which I dig just out of the simple fact that man I did it I did it with my own two devising hands. My dance. Recorded in line and color and form and emptiness too. I'm listening to Kerouac sing to me alone and I picture him alone in the booth trilling to the mike and laying it all out on the wavering line, laying it down for real man. Been reading Go and been going read. Like Paul sings, "Makin me go oh!" But to get back back to the moon, what mystery, what Doctor Sax out there tonight riding the ancient waves, the arcane waves of justice. And me cooped up, twenty below zero out on the merciless terrain white white now just simple dimensions of shadow. The season. Man.

Next day and I got that coffee happy surge listening to Dylan's Rolling Thunder, rolling thunder being Indian for Truth, and truth it is. Damn man I just feel good and its almost February and I've even got a Valentine in the form of the beautiful Vee. And I slept till two but that's alright because now I can stay up late and work on this book or my two drawing nearly finished. The Jackson book is open again and I've reread some a this book, Dawn Peyote, and it gives me a kick, it really has nothing to do with the original Don the madman but its me the madman in the process of a happy recovery. Tangled Up Anew.

Its really gray so I think I'll turn on the lamp.

What does it really matter what I believe in? I'm just a spec in the universe.

Listening to Six Pence None The Richer and looking at Van Gogh. Van Gogh Van Gogh how you move me, especially the self portraits, I see a tough motherfucker, a intelligent passionate outsider who went up against all the odds and proved the political hypocrisy of this world hath no justice. I just send a little prayer up or down to you wherever you are Vincent of thanks, I will go further and try and read your letters again, I tried when I was nineteen but couldn't grasp you in word form but I think I'm ready now to really try and understand your life. Your life, how you gleaned the geniuses of the East like so many other great artists, how you painted the within through the without and caught both worlds inexplicably on the flow of your canvas. Vincent Van Gogh a god in the godless nations and ghosty histories.

Town down depressed slept the day away now with coffee and Coltrane I try to get goin again. Uninspired, just waking up really and its quarter after six. Bum.

Talking on the phone to all my sober friends bringin me outta my gloomfunk.

Where am I at now? Motherwell, Jazz, and Buddha.

Tonight I'm Lionel Dolby pacing wineless in the absolute Indian night with my canvas just begun I don't know what I'm doing, I've got Leonardo and Vincent and Marcel and Jackson and me all opened up on the wondrous coffee table and Procol Harem on the Juke and I think I think I thinking maybe I'm a genius? I look at my shit: damn that's pretty good. But then I look at the Great Ones and I wonder for instance the technique of Da Vinci man, flesh so soft makes ya wanna kiss the canvas, so then I look back at others and myself and everyone's a genius tonight. I just want to let you the reader in on that.

Flying.

I think I'm on acid, everything's so intensely beautiful tonight.

I'd rather listen to Bad Company than go to the Louvre. (however its spelled)

Indian in the European mirrors.

Good night for reflecting, shaved and rolling.

Robbie Robertson.

Robert Rauschenberg to Da Vinci and Pablo to all of Africa and Pollock to the greatest mother: Earth.

Mezzy telling me about Durer, how do you spell the spell?

Leo opened up Up on the shelf and World Party asking the deep question.

The square was invented by a square.

Nearly a week since I've wrote, now its coming to the middle of February and its morning and I'm reading Vincent's letters and listening to The Trane, smoking and coffee too.

Went out for a walk with Vee to the bank then the coffee shop then the Salvation Army where I bought a book for twenty five cents and Bach's Greatest Hits which I'm listening to now.

Two paragraphs later and its pitch black night and wow I'm blue. Things just aint goin anywhere with Vee, tempted to label or call her a simpleton like The Doll and say all small town chicks are the same but maybe its me? I'm just deep down blue alone and sad, nothing to say saying nothing.

Just finished a drawing. Think I'll buy another canvas this Sunday at the white trash store. I'm just sitting here after turning off all the lights and lamps except one, my great Salvation Army lamp that leans east a lil, and Desolation Row is almost over, what should I put in next? I've had enough of Vee, simply she lives in the past, dwells, and I called Stick last night and told him it was a-going nowhere but he said, "You're pretty different, can't expect her to change overnight." Yeah man but its been a month and a half and she hardly ever even comes outta her crib, I've stopped inviting her over because I know she'll say no, so what's the point? Like The Doll she's content with the lifeless T.V. and no thoughts of her own.

Well its Friday and the sky is pale with the gone sun and I'm buzzing on Columbian Supreme Oh java and listening again to Highway 61 Revisited and everything's pale the blue housing apartments and the streetlamps just freshly turned on and I've got my lamp on and even that's pale. Valentine's Day tomorrow and I think Vee is mad at me but I don't care I'm just feeling coffee good and I'm gonna reread some a my poems after ole Bob's done singing.

(seems like I had a dream last night, something to do with a harmonica)

On this night I remember recall the Ones, the Ones who end too soon listening to Harry's Crackle and Drag and my library book of Vincent open to genius and the night just hair away from forever. And the night of me being one of the Ones only I will survive. Only I'll Ann the and an begat all the way back beguns of begin. Turning into a hairy Finnegan Harry and poetesses sing boys ball in this immaculate nocturne. I called Irene hoping maybe that black haired bute will give me a love chance, a love Chan, a love of no wan. Irene from Ant Man who was dating my beast friend Polly but I remember that time in the Dark Helmet in Minneapolis when we played footsy at the bar both of us drinking beyond any zenith's end. So I'm forgetting Vee fat bitch that she is and maybe Irene will be my naked savior?

Got the Stones on the box and man Charlie Watts is for real.

I've got my Indian Crazy afro Horse back tonight as I dance in the window's reflection.

I think it's a Bodago night. Shiny.

Dylan's masterpiece a Burroughs set to music?

I am a genius you know ha ha ha ha…

T.V. uses sex to con fascist.

Good phone conversation just now with Vee I feel bad about what I wrote last night, she's alright. I'm moody.

Just reread Loading Up The Now Zoo, its fun to go back into the past and pass that word bottle to my thirsty eyes and lips forgoing the expensive piss.

Just took a shower, just call me Soapy Soaperson.

Listening to Syd Straw and cooking spaghetti and just being a little good ole home maker man.

Bellyful of rice and it wasn't too cold today waiting for the bus to go to the Breakdown Café to discuss and learn and lean.

Looking, Pollock as a prophet? He seemed to explore all the rhythms of modernity.

War dances and all the rest.

Tried to call Irene her phone battery goin out I asked her what planet she was on and she said I don't know.

Raining in Redville. What's more important? Structure or chaos?

World aint word aint aint aint.

Got Miro and Parliament. Wilting in the ballad and the personages are vastly tolled. Totemic Queen all my friends are troubled. Ice water my saving grace. Listening to The Mats but I got Junior Wells Chicago Blues rewinding. Thinking of the correlations of the blues and Picasso and African art. Get back man. Thinking now Miro is more important than Matisse. But even in this war they find time to sing of love: Santana. It's a beautiful season. Plus knowing how Prince digs ole Carlos as I sway in.

Waking up coffee brewing first cigarette wow and U2 on the box.

What are my rhythms? As I stare at Jackson's Mural I wonder. What are my thoughts tonight and that fish moon will probably Lorca and return soon end of the month and what and where is all this leading to? The descending of roses the motion of this planet the very heaviness of impossible heaven and am I just typing nothingness? I don't want to be just a intellectual artist, its got to swing, its got to take wing and Miller the water. But I'm just sitting here, alone, and the night is so close and Mexico so afar.

Pondering, pondering the new art. Pollock. But is he new?

Looking at old books, the ideas just grow and grow. Its cosmic man I tell you. And then the dream entered: Monet. The dream of man into the reality of paint. I guess I'm in a artsy fartsy mood this evening. Got my books open and the whirly world of paint is something. This tomb this tomb got smaller. Well its nine thirty six what time is it? Okay so its been an art night and now I'll bolster my nonself with the Mission of Innocence. Still no story on the horizon but I'm looking. Smoke? Smoke.

Here we are and I'm reading some far out shit Edgar Cayce man and its wondrous but am I spiraling again into megalomania? Thinking I'm some kind of Jesus genius of the sad eyed? The gates are open tonight and my mind of midnight and the cards and the basement of sixteenth street but here I am on the second floor of western window and the ghost gypsy of my empressed shadow and the horse of shit muscle and the as as as. Should I keep writing this rite? Or fade into a fate that is flowers' happening? Just to see and be able to read that's enough tonight. I'm gonna smoke.

Passage and turning. I looked and the Sun was pink I looked again and the moon was a slit bent and now I listen to the valley wave in the form of Lord Franklin and I feel for this mystery. Some things are just that sad. But its Sunday and the week ahead is my burden and I'd give my self to know who I am. I'm Franklin lost at some mercurial sea and the sea is me I look around I'm lost in my self my self lost in me and only a weeping urchin only a frowning clown and only a poor sailor can find me, ah yes, they used to put us out to sea on some Drunken Boat and the Eskimos understood, understand. But lets hope for Franklin tonight, I'm even tempted to say lets pray for him, maybe he's safe? Maybe he's writing this? To Sinead who wonders? And Sinead I'm right here. Then even here is tangential or ethereal or ephemeral or shrouded by thoughts' ghost. The whole fucking world is raising me. I can see that now...token of the loss. Ah but those flutes gently glide in into the in of the inner me, I am fused, tonalities and a cold weary season in the throes dream, and out there their concern concerning. A hundred hunters a hundred seas and me? Where am I but I know I'm writing this I know I'm alive because of this, because of this holy loss, the mysterious widow who gave her song to Connor who gives it to me tonight, among these saint do we dwell?

I could be like Monk tonight punching these keys but there is vacancy, vacancy in my mind and heart and I am writing to fill these spaces.

Listening to Van's Philosopher's Stone and I'm trying to detach my self from the day's minor rebukes. I'm trying to transcend The White Rule which says the witch is a bitch which I say the witch is a which. Many. And man understand like Madame George the mind goeth many ways. Like just now I was trying to find the sliver silver in that

Lucy sky and all I say was all I saw was Buddha's permanent space. Nothing eternal, in both senses and sensing the sense that goes beyond reaction Nell sense beyond man and the streets are thawing and the drums are silent to me but I remember I remember that time I heart heard like Spanish Harlem out there, Nazarene Rican? And Vee simply either a Halloween Woman or white trash? Whatever and there's no future there, that's what I mean about detaching, my seasons with the false white ways or almost over and I'm Satoring to a new way, let the stunted stay stunted and I'll continue running through my own esoteric forest believing in the Dark, believing in the heretics, believing the rose that bleeds all over the purple circles of here and here the heroes contemplate and here the valley is heaven. Harmonica.

I wish Lee Krasner was here to listen to Chris Mars with me and dance, dance, dance. Now that I know she's my sister. And I haven't forgotten The Pretenders too. With a cig dangling from my mouth that's who I lion listenin to at this peasant moment. Stick its your favorite song now, Back On The Chain Gang, I think of you and how you and I share this tune…share a tune with a brother what mo can you ask?

That early star I wrote about earlier in this story well it turns out its Venus, what do you know? Its Saturday night and I'm excited because I'm gonna be in two group shows this summer, one in St. Paul and one in Owatonna at the Art Center. So I've got the canvas I want to show hangin and framed and its that mercury red alcohol picture I did back in the daze of Ant Man. I'm proud of it and I hope the director accepts even though its not stretched. But it's a good night I've drunk two pots of java today one in the morn and one an hour or two ago so I'm rambling with jest and just joy.

The flour aura flowering in the sky we call it MOON

and in another hour that half fish will be insight. Police state nonetheless there is beauty in this world.

Damn its only eight twenty five and I'm thinking of bed.

Listening to Bitches' Brew and reading about Madame Blavatsky wanting to know more about Theosophy. Oh yeah I'm gonna roll a smoke then smoke it man.

Sighing tonight as the fog grows thick and its March first and spring is showing her beautiful face: birds, rain, fog, mud and grass. Pretty soon the ants will be out and there was a spider crawling on the screen all solemn the other day and Vee and I are reasonable friends, we talk but it stays pretty much on the surface. I feel serene now and I'm thinking about listening to all the Innocence Mission CD's chronologically as I stare at my new canvas. I wonder if the moon will cut and cat through the fog's holy breath?

Art, I've got art on my mind. What is it? What's its future? I look around my living room my kitchen at my pictures and I know or feel that what I'm doing is just. I have all of history's many masks to procure through and I want to be "the last man on Earth" or something like that. I want to go beyond my heroes I want to get Karen's attention and show her I know her songs' esoteric meanings, levels, and how we can all be reduced to a final love.

Shimmering.

In the distance is a gold streetlamp not even jealous of the stars.

Heck all the streetlamps look like sulfur in this gypsy Clara dance of the infinite nah.

Perceverating.

It's the act it's the context, Breakdown Café man, I have to take it as it comes with regards to the water on my brain. Ah Book of the Dead…come alive Soldier of Misfortune and enter the entrance unveiling shedding wiping clean. I wish I could write a story like Henry Miller but maybe I just need to read Dostoyevsky? I'll read him one of these daze. For now The Rosy Crucifixion will have to suffice, them books are salved into my very blood.

Pane on my window rain, god damn its fun to be an artist, it all comes, comes together.

Next night and dusk tired spell write about it: weariness. I want to come alive and feel the cosmos vibrate for me but I just pace around with heavy lidded eye.

Amazing, amazing what art can do can pull you through and through and then through. Sitting here reading the Emerald Tablet and listening to Bach and smoking and sipping water I feel the wonder of the released, the sunder of the yeast, and in is in, and in is free. I'm alive now.

Its wild inside the inside. Mind and star. Hall. Unstone the stoned stoning. Feathers in the smoke. This world so fine finer than any word. A circle not perfect but perfectly close. I'll vibrate till the love troops touch my wind. Doin Ti Chi to R.E.M. tonight as the rattle heats.

In sir tan con texts tests eye be Lee Eve. I just sitting havin a smoke listening to Tabletop Joe, singing his stuff, his stuff, what's wrong with having a suicide heart? Oh woe those daze R o'err and now eyes back on the Ba writing with my vibrations my piano brains my delirious crystals of frown. Ah less then greater than...it could glow on four a might E. lawn chime and if the fade you can all ways re wind, oh yeah it was wind de to day and Ann and an. Always with the an and of, my rite tingling. "Those guys got high on nothing?" The bum becomes the Dharma and the fears oh fears are hard in a soft galaxy so water thy plan it ant it the philosophy year Quabala Aquarian harbors a drone. Like in English class.

Thinking, I'd like to read John Fante again, wow.

Thinking, thinking as I listen to Bach the relation of Buk to classical music?

Couple nighs late err listen in to that Franklin song again and gosh golly it's the most beautiful song I've ever heard and my mom said she's Irish and I swear I feel Irish quite most of the time, most of the time I'm in the emerald green of wish and wish four wish is sad sake, but Lord Franklin lost, I'm Franklin, I'll change my name cuz that song is the slowest closest thing to me and my fates that anybody's ever conjured up...listen for your self, Sinead is the truest poet of this age and Venus is bright tonight maybe I'll move dare?

I've rewinded da song and now I'm thinking of Joyce and his daughter Lucia and they went to the valley together to really for sure this time in vent the met a for met a quiz a Klee in that pore valley. Damn. I bet I can understand his and her wakes, his and her feathers of the daring in forlorn Ire Land where the opium is legal where the tongues are bright blue and the pianos sound like violet. Oh lamb of violence who is the spoil who is Victor? Ireland I'll swim to you like Malcolm said make that mental voyage and Lynn is Frank in the ending's zeniths.

Maybe may be born in Man May? My occurrences should I..? I'll wait and water as I listen to Sad Eyed Arthur who is still and Jung in the mercurial night, moonlight and him the among the Emotion Al coming who and where's my drum I heat the solace the plex and Tirus flower and wouldn't no the digested. Child scarred deep by the bullies of bigdick and now I know I could either walk faraway or stalk stark and say a truth windye. Oh woman I'm about to cry tonight cuz the world's worlds wollen and cute and vast and finally fine so fine so beautiful...hoodlums glum and its veneer is harder than leading the lee de Zen sheets of canary one or four un numerable of the theifed fiefed, gate saint, think save. And lo la low! The Arabian Hood am I believable? It's a Moslem guess now. The Blax. Read mean red me an re add ing and hars of mono Ka should I wait still in the still to still the still? But I feel doe justice tonight in my eyes blurred and some Sumerian diamond or Mesa Pa Tame Ion justice and cowpie slowhy drunk on the uncooked Time Cancer and Metal. Am I making too much since? Sensing codes subliminal and dimming the intellect to the match to a counterpart soda Minnie man diver dove holy most hosting ghost. And a triangle in the UFO's sudden mystique and the burritos and the kiss of outer place when I was very jumbled I forgot space and time crunched His come and slammer blow to the crying cries, yeah shitman I'll weigh ta the in the sympathetic in the miss takes farmed and charmed Rimbaud Mozart Bach back in back of the wheel…the truth is…The Truth Is.

Where'd my black eyed Susan dad go? Screen?

Dang that Venus is bright and spiky white in my mostly black window tonight on this heartrise of pacing and listening to my own Ann bro's music waiting for Vee to maybe call.

Reading too much gettin loopy.

With spring oh Venus window comes the thoughts of Egypt.

Pyramid asking the shrine.

I've got a job delivering papers on Saturdays and its going good, sore though.

Awe I'm tired and Beat and but I'm listening to Glow so that's the show…the story is…I don't know. "That was another country." Germany? I'm alright Karen I'm just a little on the forlorn deafeated side tonight a little decks luckless and wan waning wax and I can't see Venus the wind won today and it drizzled. But I imagine the moon will be showing and illuminating my dreamy sleep in a coup la ours.

(I'll go look) No moon yet. Gave the first half a this book to the Chiefs at The Breakdown Café and I hope they dig it. They're the first ones besides me to read it. So I don't know, I don't know if this shits any good or worth the wile.

Long winter blues the wind windy and me stuck stuckling of the interior but I now have in my possession The Secret Doctrine witch I started reading bout an hour ago. Long winter blues I can't wait to get the bike out again or play tennis with Vee. So tomorrow its to The Breakdown Café to talk about the hallucinations I've been having in the last few months but have kept secret. Sunday though and though I'm a lil' restless I feel pretty good listening to Indian music, hey ya hey ho.

Sundog sundog when will you Set?

Geese I'm flying reading the intro to The Secret Doctrine Monday night and may be I'll write a letter to the Theosophical Society in California? This shit is just what the doc ordered. The mysteries man and how I remain unquenched by Christianity and want to know the source of the core of the sources' know. I got to thank Henry again cuz he turned me on to this great find in his The Books In My Life. I'm so high right now I can barely sit down. Its all like like magi magic, sages and seers, the great wheels of the vast mind turning Ann tuning the turn to turn and that hub is arcane though Miles unveiled It in the vast arcana of flux fluctuating into the onto and onto the into. Alive is to not believe in the lie but to search and search, gold in my hand, I the rainbow sake the rain glow snake for to slither come hither come higher in terrain's non-judgment in the trumpets' of Davis and Hubbard the artistry man oh man… and the friend is lamp-like, turn It on and on and on.

Well now I've done it, wrote a letter to em, the Theosophical Society out in bleary California. I hope I hear back! Wow I need a smoke I'm Flying Kate.

I told em about my hallucinations today at The Breakdown Café and they just they just and they roll with the rolls.

I wish Susan or Erica or whatever her currents' name is, Susan, I wish she'd call, I can sitting here now see her beautiful face in my minds' eyes, ah beauty, sister beauty and miles and miles of immaculate glance, chance, will we dance?

Yearning year-ning four her, wow, love? Funk love and the crows' return.

Desire man, desiring a certain woman, me and her, together, want, want, conjunctions depersonalized and brewin that low horn. Desire, that's what we call it, me it, an it, and her soulfully her in a stormy note noting crestfallen mercury kisses unkissed as the gray of the day hides the high in a wind of introspective fish-like bird-like air water to be to be with Susan I'd give away all my ways give away all my secrets to the great invisible and dance like some Buddha Dan on the ground's mounds all sacred all and naked for my spirit is nude now in this throbbing want, god and goddess I swear I love her…

My heart my heart hurts I'm almost crying. Why? Love is pain, pa in, and love is is, Isis or Jesus or whoever in the wan veil of want stripped shedding like a scarlet layer of the very universe. Tuna verse.

God damn I'm sad arrow in the heart, shot through blue.

Seems like most of the illusions have been burned away tonight: god, patriotism, marriage…and I'm left staring at a nothing of the frayed self afraid of the frayed nothing.

But Blavatsky is something, I read her thoughts yellowing to the folds in this pale nation.

The sky is armies of armistices of clouds I have a cold but the coffee has me UP and I'm yearning to talk meta infra universe and religion meta-psychics ah oh I don't know how to spell, I'm reading Helena and Kalpas of thought are entering my egg my noodle and though I'm sickly slept till one thirty my mind feels good.

So I put on Dylan's Love and Theft to glean the thoughts of a mysterious father.

Back with the Coal Train where is the diamond in all that blind?

What Sun blinds ye in the pink and gold glow of springing spring? Ah the sun the sun hath no judgment hath no machinery hath no no cept the hand of fingers of endless rays and the tree crowns of soul banking shafting fating dating fading lone sun lone fiery confessed earlier then than and abandoned shift sift the invisible gold of sulfur the mouths of mercury the valleys of Venus the chaos of adorating Earth and out and out here there generations the Suns of Geb of Gen have seen it all go up but now the sun the desire is rounding away sink and sink faculties breasts illusions rocks translucent and the children shocked out of the shadows like splitting clay the tomb of this room a lie a live and sounds of the comma no time no time unholy legion oh fraternal beautiful war.

Oh pink orange disc egg you The Sun my holy eternal friend unwarring with blankets of black: Space. Space and bibles unfounded, hideously red in the over eight of bop cities in totally millions riverlets civil lie zie shun oh country cunt its gone. To write no story but the history of the sun in this earthly abyss suffered to the fours of brilliance and typing and fasting and visioning and Allen I'll read all of Walt someday rounders of the grift gritty tomato hearts, the see saw the swastika clock the pork chop cock the director the dictator the where the when winds pointing odyssey, and lonely loves unspoken to that hub America, watching the dirt the grass, and flowers' openings now that no one owns beauty, but beauty ownly ons woos winds everyone, every one, every tow every two every privileged book throes of Space to diminish a tied me time in, eternal, and stalks of revelation they three brush the sunset hope man, creating a plane into the circle geometry and my merciful hallucinations my inventions my unconscious my laying it on the line: pale nation explosions. The air the air, bowing trees poems sentient and Thursday bird soaring and how come and come how, rite the mind, indigo, Tropic of Answer, the perfect zones grow crack come egg came out.

Awe I guess its night now and angels are pennies, stars are pennies, and educated by the madhatters of psychics the wrong the wrong the wrong I say. Intuition brought me through to the regretting espousal of sacrifice fiercely wanting a pure nothing, done with the at last before streaked sky skiing clouds gradations you is you is the are, and the new century I am Aquarian schooled virginal writings and too the grieve green evening of emerald leads the dark to a darkening guess dust halo belief only twice and mummies of numeral changed Zend the leaf lion freaks of hidden sorrow alloy. Pained choice naught in the begotten paranoia, ah wake wake up moon I'm waiting and waiting for any Susan to soon the mouth of join ah kiss ah uncross ho the mortal maddened pining Java prophet bliss in the ish psalm day Dzyan Hindus and what not a but a perfect everlasting phantom called calling and we name it what? Clapping? Blow.

With night comes the War Star: con flicked.

Shit I'm tripping digging the distortions the sonic and the youth. And I aint seen Melanie for a wile's while, those breasts...yum.

Do I wanna go into the current? Vee? Dumb fat bitch, made me pay for her coffee yesterday. Catholic. That explains it.

But eyes got the peyote mind tonight rewinding Santana. And the Dawn Coyote.

No dawns for Dawn who sleeps half the day away, High Noon Peyote with the good black strong stuff: coffee.

Journey toll another intense sun afternoon with the Skin Walkers talk to the self. I'll draw the curtains and roll a smoke and listen dig Robbie. I will seeing spots and half blind write the history of this sun on my sacred sigh, I can see the trees howling I can see you and me together listening to the Indians in this horizontal March Chi and the high way the low way speak speckle drink my unborn tears Sioux San and I'll discover the truth of the birds and why the clouds are clowns. Ceremony and police and people and the dance hasn't been forgotten tin in the law and badges for the wicked. The world will fall away and anew we will surf the waves of a wild discipline disciples of the Drum witch heart in this vague wailing outskirts and clouds are countries for the wand and specter, I sing now for all yall I sin fro and for sin I'm in and in is free. The pow wows of uncertainty of cretin of ma of metallic all rise and in the distance of mind fog the powers that are are were because medicine and I have had the Great Rock Indian Dream last night.

Tangled up in blood tracking the shelter for to Sen live. Yellow.

Vee's an idiot.

Mezzy's a Christ Junky.

I have no too to one five undie.

Basically I haven't had a decent relationship, male or female, for years and I rely on myself now for all sorts a things and non-things.

But who is for real? I cannot say. The earth turned into stage instead of Dark Laughter which is what I long for.

So it's a few flu nights flying late err and I'm truly rue Lee digging this World Party CD and man oh man this stuff's It! Music that leans towards enlightenment, I'm not saying I'm enlightened but I'm starring to unerstan. Did and dig.

Okay so I need some juice some inspiration, put in that damn Franklin song I love so. And Sinead, Sinead singing so beautifully and all the lineage of the world and a man's fate in the sea any sea dreaming and deeming the soul loss, solace for me in her wondering where I is? And the sailing oceans of night and procure a cure and into the some of the follower's flower and cruelly cruelly the skin loses to the devil's through. I just want someone to know where I am. I am sitting here listening to this song for the umpteenth time dwelling in mystery dwelling in a swelling brow of tears that are as cold as clay and hard as diamond and soft as coal, its all hid in metaphor, them Irish I tellya, the stories the stories the rhythm the rhythm, gosh the songs already o'er.

My roots? Irish? Indian? Mexican? The holy trinity…the holy song I re ad it Ed and gallantly Don tonight the chiefs reading and the thieves parting and the sailors drowning and Mezzy in that cloud of male know no know and only a tear to save us really. I'm just writing. "The fate of Franklin… and Lord Franklin among these saints do dwell." I just wish Jack or Henry was here to hear this tune and cry with me. Cry with me reader and too the knowing dissolves but the memory is a lotus. I've got my rituals. I like to sob with the Great Unknown and way the sway and swan the wand and span the wan…its like any phenomena its like any rolling jest its like any captain: lost: loss. A woman's heart is oh some gypsy miracle of the sometimes' see and for to traverse the autobiographical in baffling bays off the may off the tongue off the old girl wisdom Sophie something ancient and sleep won't succumb to the logic of Man so and so. And now the weight of universe ten thousand directions and only one road and only the swallowed sacraments of where He is.

Really the next best thing to going to a bar is to open up to Joni's Both Sides Now, especially A Case of You, which is any lovers' lament, ah oh as touching as a wino's red, and Jesus with his body and blood, sketching the demises and roses Rosy Crucifixes purple man and only waiting for her to spring out of spring and the drawn curse and box told the men to pour, told the cat to crouch, told the holy to maim, told the feet to…what? Just another night of clairvoyant and medium and the horns blow to the sad this side sad to the both sad sides of us and now. Now warrior limping home in the city gray dawn of bars and bedrooms closed, limping home with heart forever crushed like shit gold to the hills black and electricity building a below below the below.

Okay cheer up boy the whiskey war is OVER!

Let us dance instead of March.

Is it love we want? Who's love? God's? I just want to dig my life in all its manifestations, idiosyncrasies, spells, I listen to the Candle Gal sing of truth and it stretches to a breathtaking forever, a spellbinding never but, but and but, always maybe in moments touch-n-go are quaking fears and reliving tides in a lasting might. Fade in and the language the language, at peace with the pieces the shards the mirrors the roars, and I can find my feet writing in the sand: stand.

Stand Alice Quixote stand.

Relations and ships and hoods all over, again again, I never know the need till the drop, edges of unknowing and to sing as it ends, I don't want her walls her past, strange as it is now is the only time and before you know it the fell as ghost fallen latent angel and souls together faceless crowding out the in of lies, resurrect any wish all the aquatic Atlases and dream for Pompeii dream for Atlantis formulate

266

postulate before death man, come up with some eye for the quest. Glimpse the fast swift, Cassandra oh she deals the eye deal, I never thought I'd lose my mind, but the wayless weightless bearable lesbians on tomorrow's history will show the keep on waves upon waves of bi justice planks jests and invisible my cane and louder the glory grows like green. We have come to shake the dust off the eternal ebony and mammoths and watch, watch the numbers not changing, vastly Zero. Top man top hat She capitol and the streets man have ye been to the streets? Pure, lovely, dangerous as a piano.

I guess I'm crazy tonight. I'm gonna smoke and I'll probably resist your prayer.

World Party man, what about World Satori?

DEEP.

You look better in the shadows Moses.

Day of poetry and I took the bus downtown and bought former English professor's book, Johanna Floyd and when someone I remember asked her about birth control she said, "Oh, I follow the moon."

Reading my poetry all night, kinda grinds up the mind.

Tonight Venus and the dangling moon next to each other in my window. Like my parents astral in a meek emerald solace. Colors, I got colors in my head after reading Johanna Gray's Van Gogh poems half the day, Because of the Light, and the roses invite me o'er to the vast green porches to beyond despair, hell I cry sometimes, not much of a man anymore, I got Buffalo Tom jamming and I is just writing to find out within, what's within? All that wooden cross does and I stare and sense and change and…

And the Innocence Mission, I think they got through to me.

Still and equal the space is. My tongue I found my

tongue and late Lee I've been drawing stars suns moons planets and thinking it is all profoundly measured by the esoteric by the hey errs and hey awe errs and the wailers and maybe I still like to hide to high but I no longer mutilate my fates by Tom's demon wine and my kites are coffee and tobacco and still yet I don't believe in…in the metaphors of common, woe platitude, search thy mind far and for a fresh explicative and all the seers will find you in a twilight-like destiny, Karen Karen, my aunt my guide my soul singer and were you Calling? Franny? The karma junkies shuddered and shut the shutters melancholy the night the night and glowing don't trade places, don't. Finnegan are you sleeping with brother John? Did you really wake? Ah the lights. Venus and Ireland. Moon and Mexico. I just sigh and cry and now the universe and how she gits to know me or I her.

Ya got to know everything is reloving revolving.

If I could only paint Night Comes In.

Now its Sunday and I'm digging Picasso who Stick said is the funkiest and listening first to World Party but onto then a R.E.M. tape, tried calling Bra Tea and Irene called the other night, think I'll give those two birds some of my art, I got drawings piling up all o'er.

In a artsy mood, digging art, loving art, bangin my eyes my mind on the season's insides March end of and let go and look, look boy look, there he is: Pablo!

The half steps, musical idea originated by the Egyptians, good jazz has it too, but really I learnt it from Paul and Grant and the two Bobs. Still looking through to Picasso and finding him vastly wow, intelligent, the intelligence of a painter and drawer, the content, storyteller supreme and form, its too bad Picasso never went to Asia, that's about the only thing missing from his outputs, he's got Africa down and revealed all of France and Spain and delved into a few of the ancient idea/mysteries, but just think if he had dove into

The Surangama Sutra? Like Jack, to get to that expansiveness and to go pow that guy's funking nearly omnipotent! Okay but the half step…hard to do in drawing and painting, I'm trying to think of a half step painter? Motherwell probably comes closest, or Rothko. Yeah Rothko is a half stepper and a knower of The Void, The Holy Void: space. Matta too. Now I'm in Monad Land with my latest drawing. "And the Blacks crackle and drag," what does that mean? Sylvia quote, have to find the poem.

Upon reading the Diamond Sutra, no longer believing in Matter.

A pawn reading, I'll be leaving matter.

I'm just getting to know The Universes.

Man I wish I had a copy of The Egyptian Book of the Dead tonight and soon I'll read the Pyramid Texts, its coming together, I feel cosmic, fiery, creative, tuned.

So I put in Miles Davis and open up my picture book of Egyptian art, man, Man, MAN!

I'm a little bit like William Blake tonight, battling the elements dancing electric as the smooth sky clears dark blue and I've got Thompson on and he's chanting for forever. Wrote two letters this morning and now I'm looking at art and wondering what's political? I've always considered myself apolitical but looking at my stuff I realize there's been some heavy shit done gone done gone down in heavy Town of metropolises but here I am in Owatonna and Richard says, "One day you'll catch the train…"

Why do I go to Buddhism? I want a religion that has nothing to do with imperialism, colonialism, a religion that has not yet harmed the American Indian.

For I am native.

For I pree for those indigenous ones, like Creole Jean who shows me that a mask is not always a mask.

Looking at a Bosch and wondering.

Looking at Dine and knowing (half).

Take a load off midnight, Annie's Why and Franny saw me fry and drown and now beseech some kinda telepathic forgiveness in the absolute Passion of any question. Read this Franny and know, know something, anything, some flim flam sham we went through and together we burned...ah I remember, I remember your favorite song The Band Put The Load Right On Me and do you recall watching that Dexter Gordon movie? Was that planned or some righteous coincidence? Fin was right in that song, "You've seen me at my worst and it won't be the last time I'm down there." I can't go back and recreate our time together but I'm getting eerie moody glimpses recollections of it, the ash of memory that I hold in my mind's hand, the past of history that like the stars some nights are brighter than name, and standing on the ironic totems of dark you are out there somewhere tonight maybe you're dancing maybe you're crying I don't know but I just want you to know that I survived...barely, nearly, totally, Ann if I had a Chan to do something to make me grow more honest in all this over...the over is over...and for to whom silence is the only way, where eyes tunnel out to blear, and may we you and I make that mental journey in remembrance to the sacred Dark End of the Street, this time I'll probably be able to see you a lil better. Darling tame tumble almost. What do you feel right this moment? Is it you Fran singing to me now in the tambourine sorrow of harlot's street-like gaze graze maze haze or am I just imagining that...ah the songs over, next on the tape is Roxy Music, and they too Brian Ferry sing of love. I guess I don't know now what you think of me and this is disturbing slightly but its not bitter but its close to sweet to me in this burlesque sutra and The Witch of feedback and bi and bio and all I was was a lush, a drunkard. Tonight I could really fuck you good, unlike the past where I pissed every thirty minutes whiskey and wretched up my self enslaved demons of Indian addictions. Lets just say: Sun Dance. And now I ghost write and I play it safe.

What is it? Picasso. What a mystery. I stare and stare and I'm only beginning to see.

What kind of world is it that I should go so far down? Is there justice anywhere? So I take the medicine, little pills, and I feel some relief, but I wonder, wonder when I'll finally completely sober up and come down for real? Wonder when the if-gods will reveal some kind of splendor? I wait and wait and the intervals are filled with body lust tits and cunts at The Breakdown Café burn me up, and in particular Susan lean Susan who I want to desperately join naked with in the moonlights moonights' sojourns. Hey but I got a thrill reading my journal today, I'm not completely gone crazy and the years do make sense. Listening to Toni Childs tonight, my dad likes her music too. And I wonder if one of the tunes is about him, Zimbobway? African solace in her voice and rhythms. The winter is slowly fading sad and wan and the moon in the high East as the sun sat orange in the West. I don't know much. I don't know if the pills are junk? I have to take that Indian leap into unknown and wish for more songs of truth and flower and hurts redeemed.

Patience, patience is what I could do with some more of I reckon. I have to let Susan come to me from out of her own whirl her own chaos, we could share the flowers of low mutual and be. Patience, let her be, she's damn near perfect they way she is even in her crystal sorrow and manic depressive fates. I'll just sway like Africa all of Africa and hope for a soul communion wineless desire and the beat complex.

Venus is shinning like a Miro now as Toni asks the deep soul question Chief and laurel.

I can't fathom the drums the chants but feel I feel em…

I feel like Vincent, addicted to the sun and pastoraly glimpsing seeing and revering each dusk and wanting to tell the world of the sun's awesome beauty, lets go back, go back to Sun Worship and dance to the feathers' true beats of heart radiant. The sun is my lover in these lone six thirties of p.m. and I gather my thoughts of blindness, I gather my doubts of deafness, all my handicaps of the rite secret, and when I watch that bloody sun set on this mysterious reservation I know I'm alive. The sun, at least one undisputable truth in The Tricksters' Paradise. The pure color of light in all its manifestations is no lie, and our atmosphere is the blanket that protects us all.

Blonde on Blonde, I know the meaning of that now. Breakdown Café and she goes off to the Blonde, to the car, to the money. And I know its just my ego that's hurt and not my heart. The last of the…ah fuck it, they'll be someone sometime, patience boy patience.

I'm sad so I put in Naked Songs, Living It Up, We Belong Together, piano and man the man sad…

I think I'll let Vee fade…

I don't know, Vee with her Catholicism. Its too big for me to know, its too small for me to know. And is this Buddhist study just another escape? Just dope? I KNOW television is dope, that's no news to some, but all this searching? When will I find? Intentions, I really have no intentions, I have the desire to fuck Susan, but really I'd do just about half the chicks out there. I'm starting to observe nature: stars, dusk, trees, clouds. I scratch my head.

It's a sad song silence.

Maybe depression means you're seeing the world in all its ridiculous pitiful forms the way it actually is?

My big problem is is that I haven't become a rock star yet.

Okay its been about almost a week since I've writ on this damn story. Now I'm listening to Gabriel cutting the rug a little and with the coming of night comes the coming of me.

I guess I owe Cat Man a thanks, a thanks for submerging me into the music of the great Carlos Santana who I listen to in night's now.

And Miles would dig, does dig, cat's still abreath, and my folks even too, my mom she can dance. Its Carlos' Shaman after the Supernatural. Dang this stuff is too much, I mean wow listen checkout dem horns man blood. The sway the swing the day of wing plays to sing. And Pablo Ruiz on my coffee table and all the memories of the revolution swirling whirling in my skull: getting baked and listening to music for hours, Emily and her Egyptian friend dancing at Ginkos…ah this is the aftermath of the sunworshippers' justice, Shaman, Shaman. The Earth turning green and a ballad for the coming summer.

Looking back I was too Hermetic, no light could penetrate my Book of the Dead. Lost in symbols I was brought forth by the funeral peyote into the mandala sun. And now the matrix of coffee as I gaze like a valley into onto America and I know the revolution is inside me, this very instant, this very walking justice flowing flowering forth and last night I had a vision of water then I saw flames and I think I'll choose, ah I can't choose, I need and love them both.

I like that sad song, "These feelings won't go away, they keep knocking me sideways…" yeah use gots to acknowledge da blues boy. I play it again because Ladies and Gentlemen I

WANT TO CRY. I want to be sad. Sober sad as man alive I know the blues better than any sky.

Rochester Public Library where its at man, I got a buncha CD's like right now I'm listening to the Indigo Girls Ophelia Swamp and its quite beautiful and emotional. Earlier I had on The Black Crowes and was dancing to that, working on a drawing, contemplating my new paintings. I like the harmonies and layers one voice a little angry good angry and earthy but the higher voice almost angelic, earth and heaven: Indigo Girls. My anima sighs in the disbelief of belief.

With the Hermetica on my coffee table and Robinson broze blasting and the sun blazing and the Egyptian quarter-tones of truth wailing us onward, all of this and its only Monday and do the clouds know? Know the licking lions of nowhere?

All my favorite rock bands basically or other employ Hermetic/Egyptian ideas into their senses senses of chords, rhythms, drums, the way in which the universe actually goes up and down simultaneously goes in all sorts of directions at once. Exploding the unseen and imploding the conventional.

God I feel good the sun out and all that plus I got the Goo Goo Dolls on the box and loving Joan Miro's stuff, especially the things he did in the later half of his life. Iris working fine now, like The Doll Guy Anna said to me one high night, "Its bright up here."

A man can go mad playing this game of art.

Only facts can save me.

That Miro is a radical, the proof is my mind tonight, made loopy and aware. Look at me balancing on the high wire haywire and the drop is long and I'm not sure the net can take another? So I listen to the Indigo Women and gaze at and through my window and the black emptiness soothes all the inner fractures, the night is my song.

Art and artists are a succession of revelations, no progress but simply seeing and creating romb for the everything.

I told my mom what I dug/dig the most in art is a mysterious brushstroke.

Day is a door night is the key.

It's amazing how men or women of genius say the same thing. I'm thinking of Krishnamurti to Bacon the painter, and really all the artists are exponents of the cosmos and earth and the greatest of em all go to the Sun and Moon for their answers and questions.

And we think all the shapes have been discovered.

That fiery flower, that endless burning, those curtains of peach and white, those books on the diamond of a coffee table, and Allen on the box inventing new ways of perceiving in a nation mad with industry, my crib and I flip the pages sweet art and the ashtray fills up and the lamp is off…the sun turned orange, orange, doin that ghost dance just to stay alive, doin that sun dance now that the dead control the black.

Atmospheric tangerine the sun gone but the Doppler light filters through to this heaven.

So now the sky black and I go into the bathroom and look in the mirror: I'm not aging. I'm not growing any wrinkles and I'm nearly thirty five. I no longer think of death as a possibility, maybe the smoking will have to go eventually but I'm not worried. I wrote a song a number of years ago called Magic Mirror and it went something like, "I'm here to stay." And I am here to stay as now Black Balloon plays on the stereo, my ideas disseminated, but me I just spent my last three bucks earlier today at the Mexican joint. But that mirror, I know it's a lie…I like the public library water closet with the brown walls and I see how brown I actually am.

Sometimes I think you have to live through things to understand em, like now how I understand Dizzy Up The Girl and have been listening to it all day long, but with understanding comes a certain sense of acceptance, which is nice, peaceful. The bliss of following bliss. That's what its come down to to me, I have heard the callings and ignored the dollar and I'm here to draw and paint and sing and write. I don't know what all those high school cats are doing these days? But I've been through the Hamlet Mill and I can tell you peace is sacred, peace personal peace is the will, Many Rivers To Cross and spiky Venus, the mind velvet yet transparent yet motional.

To be an emotional man in this world? Is it worth it? To wear my heart on my sleeve? Do I even have a heart after all my turmoil? I'm writing to find these things out and however subterranean or abstruse the mind is I know I love light, and night, and Vee at times too. When my mom told me about the troubles of so and so I thought, "The end of maleness." For there is an end to all this bullshit labeled and defined so rigidly as masculinity, the end of looking down on women, they say there's a fool in every wise man and vice versa but more and more I think one needs total enlightenment, vast knowledge, actions of peace.

No one's gonna believe this but I've been blind and deaf all my life. Literally. And nobody told me, but I know its true, rue. Nowadays I seem to have tunnel vision I can see black shadows hovering around as I gaze at my room. And sometimes I'll have music on and three songs will pass and I'll have no memory of hearing em. It was in Minneapolis that I discovered this, I had just walked from downtown to the Wittier neighborhood and suddenly realized I hadn't heard a single damn thing, it was bizarre, frightening. Its my little secret that I'm confessing, my crazy lie, my crazy life. I wanted to ask somebody or tell somebody, I wanted some kind of settlement or justification for all the pain I've been through because of my blindness and deafness and for the first segment of my life I was mute a lot. I wanted credit. And the only person who I talked to about being handicapped was a woman who was or is blind, Kerouin from Ant Man, good ole Kerouin who I saw the other day in Rochester and went up to her in the restaurant to say hi but her eyes were black and blue and it scared me so I let her leave without any recognition. I love her, even told her I loved her once in that coffee shop in Dinkytown. I wish it was blind on blind…

I guess another thing that bothers or intrigues me is being an artist, was I pushed into it? Did they know at an early age and mapped it all out? It haunts me. I love art but there is something missing from my life: love…ah no, I love my folks and brother and cousins and relatives and all that, but what I miss is Calling, I know she's my soulmate, I know there was love with her, but…I don't know? Art? Love? This is supposed to be the modern day story of a Don Quixote, but its just lapsed into thinking on the typer. Its funny, no its sad, the letting go, the letting go.

Open up man, open up Iris. And cry a little.

So here I am a couple nights later…

So here I am pacing listening to Iris.

So I put on some Aretha and ask Mezzy, "Do you believe in nature or the concept of nature?"

"That's hard," he says looking at a Picasso portrait.

"What I'm getting at is there's a difference between nature actual and mental constructs such as god."

"But we must fight for our freedom."

"We? Don't include me in this mess called America,

besides our freedoms are all in the material realm, every day's Christmas for the Wasichus."

"You got that ruddy complexion, but that's why I voted for Bush, for our freedom."

"Ah King of the Wood, religious propaganda in the corporate mare."

"I'm politically prejudiced, you're culturally prejudiced."

"I'm not gonna die for a rich man, on either side."

Aretha singing.

"Franklin's my kind of justice, when I hear her wail I believe," I say, "In most other contexts I want to Ralph."

"You express your ignorance well."

"Yeah…at least we can sit here and talk and talk in peace, not like Tommy with his sexist bullshit of penis envy and Black hysteria."

"Yeah all I did was joke with him and he took it too seriously."

"What'd ya say?" I ask.

Mezzy looks around the room, my drawings all o'er, "I called him a motherfucker."

"Wow. You shoulda known not to go there after hearing about all his problems and bitterness with his ma."

"I fucked up."

"He'll come back around, basically he's a nice guy."

"You want to play some chess?"

"Sure."

We play a few games, trancing on them squares, smoking, sipping cold coffee. After that we continue rapping.

"Here's a book that might make you appreciate poetry," and I pull out Henry's Time of the Assassins. "I have no idea what you'll think of it? But its one of my favorites."

"I'll give it a go."

"Listen to this poem," and I read Rimbaud's Genie out loud, its one of the few poems of his I really seem to understand, and after I finish reading it Mezzy nods and digs it.

So Mezzy splits and I'm left alone again after our session this afternoon at The Breakdown Café. I buy some blank tapes and now I'm taping the Great Aretha Franklin, in particular I love the Atlantic years, those drums, piano, her voice, definite wow. And now its Since You Been Gone, probably my all-time dig.

Haven't been writing this "novel" lately, been writing dozen letters to my cronies, my new kick letter writing.

Yesterday I finished reading Nietzsche's Anti-Christ.

This sky is all Spanish, Spanish blue translucent velvet of the mystery Earth. Tonight.

Venus spiky, petal'd into the black alive alive as Tom sings Hold On and I dance and prance Ti Chi round this room, so I sit down to write something anything, and there's a slight blue, darkly, on the horizon. This song reminds me of Marta and how we let each other go, go into the world without a chance, lovelorn and sheepish and defeated: beat. And space and space…The weather's been pretty good lately and Vee sucking up television, that's about it.

Sad Eyed Lady, was I helping him inside him writing these love songs? I just sway tonight, tonight I just sway, I can't write what I haven't lived, but now I collect recollect and hope for the beast.

That's wild, art should be wild. Looking at a self portrait in watercolors and pen. Sometimes things just click.

With the kitchen window open going through ole sketchbooks, wow, how I love art! There's something about a sketch, loose, unpretentious. Everything's so structured when you attempt to do something big that it loses the spirit.

Mezzy's interest in the Bible is a fad, a passing interest, in ten years he'll look back at it as the supreme bullshit.

Just the same all religion is nothing but a big subjective pile of piles. Many Genesises. Let go and just be. Moment. Ceremony of now. Actuality in strange this.

At the Breakdown Café I recall all sorts a talk. My recovery is the lion of learning and self-education. We all go around the room like serious Indians and reveal or conceal or problems, I in the beginning was very taciturn but but gradually have opened and trusted, nowadays I talk about the great turning of the leaf, the world really whole, "I just now know that since I've been sober my mind is coming back, or maybe not coming back but tranquilizing, that serenity I once thought a crock is true it comes. I could say I'm gonna be sober for the rest of my life but it doesn't work like that, I have to concentrate on just staying sober for today, even this moment. The past was really quite hellish, I never foresaw all the craziness my drug addiction and booze addiction would entail, I never would have thought as a teenager my life would become what actually happened, that is, psychosis, massive confusion...but now I am mesmerized by the fact that I actually feel good and healthy more often than not, I have trust for the folks at this Breakdown Café, the doctors and therapists and case managers. So that's where I'm at, I feel good."

"Thanks Dawn," says Chieftess Breakdown and she goes on to the next person.

So I do that three or four times a week during the day, getting together for classes and discussions, its been really helpful. Breakdown Café man, thanks.

I ride my bike there sometimes, or take the bus, or Mez gives me a ride. Then after the sessions Mezzy might come over to my pad to talk and play chess. Intellectually Mezzy's the only "friend" around here who can talk in abstract manners, politics and religion, art. He's a little weird sometimes but who isn't?

Then now and then I go to the Owatonna Art Center to commune with the great Sylvan who runs the joint. I bring in a picture and sit on the floor and talk. He's got an amazing artistic mind seeing and perceiving things I heretofore had not appended. I've shown Sylvan a variety of things in content and material, and he's always open.

God I feel good listening to Peter Gabriel tonight, smoking and swilling pop, dancing a little, just feelin that ultra-fine of sobriety, health.

Seems like all the great ones connect with and to mighty Africa: In Your Eyes.

Ya read the Bible and feel like god then go out into the world and…nothing.

Whatever I say means opposite and whatever is opposite is what I say.

My spirit is not in me.

The ailing Gnosis.

She hath everything except the thing her parents can't give her: fame.

I guess I have to learn not to open up to whites, they don't want it.

Hide my arms: City.

Dumb Coyote.

"I just called to tell ya thanks for The Church seed," I tell Stick Figure o'er the phone.

"Yeah Set said it might be their best one."

"I think its one of the best albums ever, its fucking fantastic."

We chat a little while more then hang up and get on with our respective lives.

But about The Church CD, it is amazing and like all

coincidental things notions of this awesome universe it falls rite in lie with what I've been studying lately, you know Secret Doctrine and Krishnamurti and A Buddhist Bible.

I just read three hours mostly the Surangama Sutra, I like it.

So now Venus again, are you getting sick of my window observations? I can't help it my window where I write faces the great blackness of black and pierced through are stars interluding the vast smoky fates of mindsmile.

And to think Buddha can see through it, it, her, Nut. A simplistic code for the eyes closed analogous to any Zen of disrepair. The hysterical ideas spit and dissipate: patriotism, god, they just have no bearing on the actual universes. Don't get me wrong, there is no beyond, I am face to face with any of the gods for the gods are black for the gods are space one. I just want to no, no all that whiteness. Respect for blackness. Space, space. A line of disrepute in the form of know. Knowless two too, the very itself-ness carrying me backwards to fours and goes and made believed just fat with animal cum, I turn away, I let my eyes drown. Riders and builders. India and intricate telepaths the songs Forget Yourself and we and we. The forgotten burn. Displayed then destroyed. Only a war only a poor only a man. Escaped the fire by dousing the heart with fatherly functions His bunkosity in now a veritable Nefercity homes. Just to two these ghostly moneys of hellish monads in a crying wish, just two, ah here comes the truth, count up from the paupers' some where here now, savior, ever running clown, spunny, punny, half to half, how come the try just? Why not Ann actual? I hear you Marty, but those drums flesh science and message unfended wear it on your sleaze and proudly flashed. But then the bees the birds happen, oh shit. I can be your lie.

You're a lie.

Wind died down tonight an army like halos and espoused the sun, disappear flush and the coming and but for the paralysis of analysis we git now-here so and so but then the Old Midnight shouts down, "Maya! Maya!" Old Midnight less than, and less than two ours away, so I shant turn on…what? Tube. But I will write like a mountain. I understand five, the first isn't the last in any case, but alphabet and moose. Angelic matters. Though you aren't there in this past in this now Zen and Zen and Zen, and I don't know if you want beauty? What do you want? I got nothing, Buddha give. Shapes of life are purple still the screen out side side out outside slight Ti Chi of wind. The will knows the seas like of, of and like not like, like off man, and the pitiful of emptied battle, Jesus, and how many more dead? The just just aren't that just. But the wicked evil Madonna of disrespect contempt for any pretend thrashing through the symbullshits and the you capitol sleep HEAVE than Heaven and in this future I write for the archetype swimming in the shallow land of. U.S.A…crash!

Read shift.

The tones.

Eventually, but now its actually beautifully intricate, intrinsically insides dance and prance, woe the chance, whoa. Like and like. Reasons come and go and some go and some stay, ah but Egypt I hear You in the pennies and nocturnes and libraries and got no plush. Shoot I just say what I tink. I don't care. I slur my whole fuckin mind. Indian. And the Earth sees me in my prison sister and clown and medium and marijuana and have to and wine and light and paradise and little and shine and naught and drum. Make it to the gay charade. Flesh since dawn. Hip to the show glades spades trains of thought conned by any coal and diamond of easy, coal and diamond, and the fright of Lee flees to the sprees how come how gone man? Go cool away sparkle, spangle, Chan, the bone plays with please and pleas. It'll be death. That's okay, where already on that day I say. Although the Mayans have chocolate too.

Venus about an inch from earth. Somebody revelation. Not folly but actual. Trans and forms and nations. Like that time the mushroom Yoko and I laughed off the militant trash. Oh mem. Or Re? Re yes, re no, all data. That bacteria out there waiting for my brain. That lungless hunger hunting down airfull Jesuses and Henrys. The only way to come off it man, down, DOWN, and the healthy of…end. Endings begat Zendings. To shake off the way. To wake in the frosty needle ridings of the camel in the manly desert in the mirage I see not a. Mo songs four space. The jolly next. But the skin is Huxely's only chance, doors of mescaline and elevators eons the very gonality yelling down the yeah the yea the pi, math equations, nun of em finished, and the conquering goes on and on and on and on, drink some wine, its blood, its good for ya. Out here though I want the breadly moon spent in in and taking in that in I give away steal way bushed to ze core's Ka like a crow with a crown. Old Midnight where are the angels now? Van? No. I went too far ahead in my head a head of disbelief lies its all lies deceit cheaters of the realm. My uncle Polly that peyote grid, I'm laughing now to myself, but the time I tellya went slow and the sadistic Television I had to GO! So we went for a high, a high walk, peyote. Peyote and at night fall the palette, merchant, and the plate was cardboard but this card wasn't bored justly comin dow. Cow. The want the want to eat again. Shit. Not exactly. O' Keefe was is right and Grant just likes to con the fusions all Tomorrow and Sad. Tamara and hands o'er the peyote, the peyote the peyote thep, dep, shep, lep, fep. Here comes Earth. The horizon of night Peyote and Dawn night. Robbie said to hold, "Hold back the night," and He is rite rite rite.

Man I feel too good to even write right now.

Do I believe in God? That quest yawn's Ben in my head all afternoon and now into night. Gee. What do I believe? Ah vagueness. The subjective done gone objective, Chieftess Breakdown Telepath been queening me. God? God. God? God. Dog? Its too fucking simple, its got to be lived, not said. What are my actions? Does it really matter what "I" believe? If you've red this far? If you're red this far. Slide and don't know and no.

Picasso never wore a shirt, it feels good, breeze and curtain dance.

My life is my testimony.

Some of it not even worth going into.

I know this much: don't trust whitey.

But the city is old and the Heroin Crew can't hold out forever. They'll go down in more ways than one.

Alison, Tara, Perko, Shannon, they are all merely junk, junk keys.

I won't be their skeleton key.

The music business merely a junk network, art too.

Now tonight I leave it and pree to the great African Brothers and Sisters to wail down justice in One Verse City. Some kind of justice. Something, anything.

Cuz there's no way out.

There has to be a War goin on going down why else would my life be so tortured?

DON'T BE FRUITFUL DON'T MULTIPLY.

Reading this book, looking back as the bright orange sun hides in the alive trees and I'm listening to The Beatles, I never tire of them nor that mighty ball o' fire…

The Beatles, closest thing to birds, the melodious language ah love. Awe love.

Its rare that I try to write, that is, try. I like it digit when it just flows and pours like a woman aroused and my mind becomes vagina and juicy and the words come from that great blue nowhere. But I'm listening to The Beatles as you know and it makes, they make me want to create something analogous to that which they mustered. Ah brilliance, I want to be as magical and loving and insightful as those four. I want to "save the world from boredom" and redeem those who have an abstract tongue, a clown tongue, a Don Quixote heyoka fate, redeem math four to for and the how. But how? The birds fly close by my window and maybe like Sitting Bull I'll glean the songs of spark and speak?

Roll size of the Rose.

Waiting Tom.

So now I got Peter Gabriel Live in, man. In Our Eyes it should be could be called.

Doesn't have to be either or or neither nor.

Looking at Jackson, he don't hide the suffering. His.

To let people go, to let IT go, to let Stick Figure go to his fates and Vee to her small minded destiny, and not to mingle with the decadence with preconcepters and judgers and all that. I have to stand alone in this world, there's no one who can understand me, no one who can really help, I know this from not from books but from actual experience, that Stick has never been a good understanding brother, he's never been there or here when things got or get rough for me. Bra Tea too is another who should be kicked out of my life, my one life, however banal it appears to her and others of her arrogant ilk. Life is precious and short, I just can't go on this way with half-sided relationships, all theirs and when I try to speak my mind they won't have it. "There is a lot of bastards out there," said Williams and I'm finally realizing that I'm the good one, not them.

Some people are always on the rebound.

To me African music is so beautiful.

Now I'm listening to Midwestern punk music, Du, and I tried to get in touch with Melanie on the phone but nobody answered. So I'm alone as usual wondering what to type? Ah its life, life and now to live it.

And Joni Mitchell gives brings bestows a thoughtful hope in ballad form.

Amazing the greatness of Orientalism and how some certain Americans saw and see this. Spontaneity in the throes of seemingly desolate doves of heartread.

Sunday night with Miles and Nietzsche just wandering and unmasking mentally.

So now its raining and I got my mix tape on which I was gonna give to Lee but now thinking maybe I'll give Melanie the music, she's a great music fan says she's gonna buy a bass. Maybe we'll start a band? I don't know. Her and Mezzy were over here for a bit just talking and digging the tunes, I played The Mats then some Mingus then some more Twin Cities stuff. Melanie knows a lot of obscure bands I've never heard of. We're gonna make tapes and share some music. What more can you ask?

Oh old atmosphere ambiguous and windy and swaying language land.

When will he forgive himself? And dance merely dance without wine?

That the Buddha inspired Jack and Li and Charles is worth looking in to into.

The Dalai Johnny at the Breakdown Café, never have I seen eyes so real.

Finished fished through the Surangama Sutra and I feel a sense...sense of...sense of. Of of. And being and non-being translucently made unabrupt but forlorn folding un of the un and gladly glowing through inside inward and clear as the robin's song. The very newness of it to me, the very oldness of I. I can start now.

And Jackson Henry on the bus spoofing clowning and me smirkling.

I don't believe drugs to be inherently bad but the strictness of society. The ole outlaw plague the ole moral reign of duality.

Eleven and I'm listening to Journey's Infinity, wild stuff, thrilling, all dare albums hit me good.

Nietzsche does to Christianity what Christ did to Judaism, that is, exposion.

Egyptian music very scientific.

I tink its time for me to move out of religion and look at science (again?).

Try and figure what some already know, through one mind into another.

For instance what's my most scientific painting or drawing? Look, look aback.

I don't no.

Young man midnight. Wait I'm middle aged. Sort of red. Pale brown. Who the hell am I? Ah.

I like very physical art. In drawing the act is more strenuous but the final product more refined, the opposite is true of painting.

I could go back and reread my bullshit but I think I'll write something as I sit here listening to Pickle's Saved album. I feel like I'm on peyote tonight, its windy out there and the music salves my mind wounds and yearning for Melanie to call back. "He who loses his life shall find it." I think this is true, hell it worked for Blake, it works for Pickle and his son: me. Justness in the balancing act of thoughts many. Justness in the eye for a yin and a yang for an eye. Its all a garden, Milky Ways and Suns and trees that can't resist naked in the wind the wind which is or could be be spirit spirits. The black night but I'm inside here with my leaning lamp and the harmonica bending my ear. I'm inside after being outdoors all day delivering papers and digging ethnic gospel Jesus the energy the craft, wow, and I close my eyes hard and bob my head and glean the dim you Nin Tiv gamble. The muse is my dad now, really all my life trying to live up to the mystery that he is. We aren't one, we aren't even two or zero, but letting glow the dark eyes of lineage.

Bought Dead Man Shake and I'm just bopping round this crib truly digging, blues, rock-n-roll, where its hat man. Dangerous.

These tunes like Nietzsche with a boner.

Could be the blues is the ultimate foundation of all modernism?

Could be the African Brother is the ultimate father of all expressionism?

In The Garden, I tell you when I heard that song around the time of my first fistly breakdown it scared the hell outta me, I mean I conjured a ruler so powerful and bloodthirsty that I thought it was some kind of Kurtz thing, and me destined hellish Nazi slavery. Now its still reminds me but now it…I don't know? Its existence, that possibility, the Messiah, it's a possibility. I'll say that much, but I only go on my knees for some and not all and I don't broadcast my hopes or prayers or whatever ya wanna call em, I just think and think and sometimes dance. In. But I hope its true, Him, and I hope for a mirror coming.

No writing gonna happen tonight so I just gonna turn off this freakin computer and call it a day, say.

Waiting on Spanish rice, yum.

Friday dusk and I'm feeling it, goodness.

Sunday dusk did the paper route and now the white sun blinding me and the clouds almost nearly electric.

All that matters is the sun the moon and Paul's music.

All that matters doesn't matter in society.

The Doll hath made her homeopathic return the other night, blue mascara and cleavage sets me dreaming dreaming of that great flesh swim, and Melanie and Mez were over too and sat around joking smoking and I did a Charlie Chaplin thing when Melanie asked me something I held my fingers in the cross position and fell off my plastic chair (no couch). It was fun. And she The Doll Two only lives a couple blocks away. Sometimes I think a lotta chicks are hookers and that Mezzy is a pimp and they're setting me up for that ole blue chocolate?

I'm usually wrong, so…

But this I know: I put my love and lust, all of my tendencies into my art and this has saved me. I have keenly read the precepts of all sorts but mostly Marcel who says not to weigh down your life with too much conventionality like kids and cars and all that American pieshit. I stay abstinent because I don't want a creature another being to go through what I've been through, even though I feel pretty good these days. Lingers, the past lingers and eventually it'll all be forgotten even by the dogs and the gods themselves. Melanie reminds me of Calling, that is looking for the quick thrill, afraid of solitude, always complaining about boredom. I'm over that hell I'll be thirty five in a couple months, I got to stay in the realms of sobriety and honesty. If nothing else I can always be honest with myself, I'm not gonna trade that in for some transitory pussy who'll just drive me crazy in the end.

To appreciate the little simple things: hot decaf tea on a sultry summer nocturne and a rolled cig and the Goo Goo Dolls singing with energy and insight and tenderness about life, life man, life is good when its simple and the tea should be ready in a couple a minutes. Like that movie Drugstore

Cowboy, I dig it when he comes down and rents his little room and goes to N.A. and just tries to LIVE. That's all I'm trying to do, but I got to have the music, the rock-n-roll, and I don't care if I'm not hip anymore. All the edges cut.

Looking back with a loving nostalgia when I bought Gutterflower in a paranoid wave then came home and tried to settle back and down. Loading Up The Now Zoo was writ to that great album which I'm still trying to comprehend listening to it now. The Now Zoo is probably my favorite poetry I've conjured, it was a hard time what with those heavy shrill paranoia attacks where I thought the whole unholy world was against me as if I were some Don Quixote in the heroin underworld, so now when I feel that infra-fine I really don't take for granted my sanity. Letting go of some things while holding fast to others. Holding fast to self honesty and the endless research. Letting go of man lust, man pride, becoming hopefully more womanly in my thought while not hating my desires and realizing its all a natural thing: recovery, recovery of a blind alley in a wicked cross crossroads ablaze with deceit.

Well its summer homeboy and what to do? Ninety degrees today and I'm shilling on coffee listening to the blues little beads of sweat on my forehead, its just like Mexico I'm telling ya. I wonder if Melanie will call back? Would be nice I suppose to hear her melodic girly voice all little kid jokes and but. Void, void cuz that sun hath rounded outta ze pix. I'm lone on this here yonder typer typing a thought or two.

So I'm sitting here reading this and that, in the tub it was Holmes' Go, then a lil Charles B. who sends light for the dark and dark for the light. Melanie didn't call back but that's alright, I don't think I'm dramatic enough for that drama queen, not that she is one, but she borders. Wrote a little letter to Irene, she got a lot a my old books that

I'm dying to get back, maybe she'll respond? I got Richard Thompson on the box, its cooled off to eighty and I took my meds and am feeling mellow. I think my sight is getting better, I think. The night is fulla wind and the stars unseen, it might rain. But a calm pervades my inner self and I'm thinking I want to purchase Krishnamurti's Journals as my next endeavor, or Joseph Campbell's? I really enjoy reading journals and letters. Next time I'm in Rochester I'll probably checkout Hank's letters to some chick he dug, could be insightful? The leaves are glossy and seem to reflect the streetlamps as I finish this paragraph...

High noon with the day off and I'm digging Who's Last an old tape from my high school daze. No good mail came today. Expecting a letter from old Skull or my aunt. Nice and juiced on coffee.

I used to feel that what I was into was the best. I only read Bukowski, really and I only listened to The Replacements and Huesker Du. I thought I was really on to something, the geniuses you know? It was more than a hunch it was an obsession. And here I am today the sun a dog a sundog son down sundown and I'm rereading Betting On The Muse and you know maybe I was right to put my chips on the "losers?" Because even after all these years it still rolls thunder into my virgin mind veins, like the veil lifted and it aint nostalgia simply, I don't know what it is, reinforcement? But I been sober nearly five years and Charles isn't a simpleton idiot misogynist who just got lucky, the dude had skills, all the way from haiku to Dostoevsky, man.

Yeah its good, to have a day free of pesky homo sap ions, people, to be alone with whatever thought I happen to be thoughting. Stick's gonna bring a shitload of books and music next time he visits then we'll go on out to Mezzy's pad and play chess. Just some future stuff to look forward to.

So Mez sleeps in the bedroom and I've been up since

four and reading a little of the stupendous Nietzsche and some a my own stuff. Melanie might call and maybe the three of us'll do something, go out for java or come back here and chat and shoot the breeze. I think I'm in love with Melanie, its just that she's so much more alive than the overly moralistic Vee, Vee who sees all things in strict terms of either good or bad, her Catholicism a slow suicide. But last night me and Mezzy talked rapped about religion, the usual pseudo intellectual discourse but hey its fun even if it don't lead nowhere. And we played a lot a chess too. So now its still morn and wondering what my next mood will be? I've had a pot of coffee, that's half my day. Breakdown Café tomorrow then the paper route Saturday. So that's that.

We get out of the car and go into my pad, Melanie has a lot a CD's and sit around the room and listen, most of it white punk off key singing and banal guitar music, but there's a couple songs that hit me and I play her a couple from my own collection hoping she'll dig it. Its really though real that when she puts in Marley No Woman No Cry, I am surprised to hear it and the beauty of it shudders down in me and emotion man, by the middle of the song I can feel the water welling up in my eyes. But she's got a group to go to so her and Mezzy split and I'm left alone, alone in the crib.

Alone in the crib now I just want to know the spirits' true faces, and personages of the East glow and the sky a soft softly silver. The many names of the ones without names, Lao and all the rest restless in the clearing crimson and hovering to the dances of the five hundred nations, "Forget your troubles and dance," sings Marley as I just fill the screen with my own Book of the Dead, my own hieroglyphics and what not before but for and I don't see any birds now just trees and sky, boo cow sky, and subly the mind come forth to the reggae of summer, no bummer here boys just a wail true and just, just the flowers flowering despite injustice for beauty flows to Here in spite of any president's supposed death. Fluttering, my mind is all a-flutter in the coffee almost angel almost night all and most and maybe that beat moon with the flour swim ancient will flood my reckless bed rue? Anyways I'm feeling it, it it it, and therefore shaking spheres can bite me.

Wow the sun broke on through, rays of love as the Aching Baby blows from Ireland. You too?

Attention Baby whoa, but a real funky truth nonetheless.

And after Melanie told her woeful story: love ruined by a male domination, Mezzy asked her to move to Mankato with him having not the slightest comprehension of her rockbottom situation, Mezzy thinking only with and of his prick. He changes when a woman enters the scene, I think he thinks he's some kind a god, demanding his shortsightedness of man quasi power onto a pretty much struggling and down-n-out chick. And me yeah I'd like to get laid too but I realize this much: it, it meaning sex and possible love, it has to be a hundred percent mutual. If that mutuality is not there its simply a game of hide and seek, chide and meek. So maybe I'm in love with Melanie and that love is allowing me to keep a safe certain distance with the hopes that perhaps she'll make a love full move towards my directions, my barely self.

Mezzy like a lotta folk at The Breakdown Café just another whitewashed brainwashed shithead Christ yun. I tell you its no fun listening to them Jesus junkies rant their Kant's and pant their wans and basically they think they know it all, solid. Especially whites. I dig ethnic gospel stuff, Aretha and Pickle's views, but that's cuz its alive. Oh Halloween Cafés and Breakdown pretend, when will we just justly say a simple tooth and eye the invisible the invisible truth?

Man listening to Trudell tonight soft night and deep barely grayly black this is some deep stuff. John Trudell who I saw as a woman at the Black Dog on that Saint Paul vigil. I want Melanie to hear this music I want Melanie to comprehend this music I want Melanie with her hint of Indian blood to recognize the Indian in me…is this pride? Maleness?

I could cry for the Indianess I feel now in this wavering nocturne of midnight almost.

This morning in sleep I'm at my folks' house and there's beer in the fridge I gulp down a couple feeling that good ole booze buzz and I go for a third and then I make a bed on my dad's desk and I'm laying there sipping and my mom comes in and she's worried about the books I've been reading, I tell her, "I've read The Communist Manifesto and it seems to be the only thing that's gonna fix the Earth as a whole." She looks worried and leaves the room then I finish that Old Swill and I'm drunk and I go to the kitchen for another but I can't find any. I start discussing out loud my iconoclastic views and my talk seems to really disturb the folks, we're in the entrance way and my dad says he loves me. "You just say that," I respond, "But your actions aren't love, take me back to Owatonna." Suddenly my Aunt appears and she's worried about my alcoholism, she says, "Don't you remember Dawn what you said? You said that question is on the surface and all you need is a legislator to sweep up one carpet under another." And I say, "I said that? That's pretty good." Then an old former neighbor gal starts chastising me. I go out into the front yard and one of the shoes is bright orange, I find my duffel bag but everyone drives off and I start walking drunkenly down the sidewalk when an unshaven old drinking buddy from my high school days pulls up in a car, its Wiggins and he says or asks, "Donny?" Wondering if its really me? I wake up.

I wake up and take my morning pill then sit in my chair and smoke one and I watch the early sky changing colors and listen to the happy birds, brew up some coffee and listen to The Goo Goo's sip a few sips then turn on the computer and write all this down before I forget. Mission accomplished and now I'm gonna drink more java and roll a choke.

God I swear these songs are for me, Surreal, Clear To You, just feel so much empathy warmth from em in this rare early morning of writing and thinking.

Want Melanie to hear this. This beauty this truth this very shuttering moment captured gently in the form of songs many. Ah shit she probably wrote them?

In this town I don't know which is worse: straights or drunks and druggies?

Woke up from a nap to the sound of the idiots: lawn mower and phone, damn. Put on some Spanish rice and blast the Dylan sounds (Isis). The sun still burning lighting up this one horse town of bitter simpletons. I guess I'm awake now so that's that.

So I draw the peach colored curtains and am happy about the letter I got today from Johanna Floyd my former writing teacher at the art school I somehow made it through. She writes well and funny. But she's gonna be gone most of the summer so we can't start corresponding till August, she said she wants to see my new poetry, that's definitely wow. I used to write at the art school and she was very enthusiastic, naturally so. I got to check on the rice.

Threw away Melanie's phone number, I can take a hint, four days I been trying to get a hold a that luscious one but I should know: she's white.

Logos little spangled sots spots gleaming orange foliage green and tree or tree ease.

Now its morning and the sun in the same spot but the

Earth has moved and I can't see it though the light fills the empty air and I'm drinking coffee and waiting for the bus to take me to The Breakdown Café to learn and glean.

Sky is white with little streaks of pale soft blue and the tree in front of this window swaying like some kind of Ti Chi dance. I'm on my second cup and anxious to go to group and commune with the other crazies, talk and rap and learn.

Its still morning on the sill and for kicks real mind and heart kicks I got my Kerouac CD in and I think to my self wow that guy is really real kicking singing his blues and I think one of the biggest changes in my life, Buddhism, is due to Jack and his views his non-views his sea of swimming angels and it's a Young Demon Morning in the universe. I just listen dig dog glisten hint flog and your name my name the name of Secret Doctrines and all glows in while spreading forth the nameless eternity.

Dusk and I'm wondering, wandering mentally if what if my three major heroes are Indian: Duchamp, Bukowski, Miller? What if they're Indian? That they did not dwell and wallow in their in this plight called America but created and created, juice by juice and mind blood the great the great and the insight. They are so practical, healing. My heroes man and what if I'm Indian? And what if I live to see the fall of the whites? Wouldn't that be something? I'm waiting, reading and waiting and observing and hoping for a Red Sign.

Tonight it's the Blue Feather rules.

Celibated Summer.

I remember riding the bus to a cross country meet and almost crying hearing an acoustic version of Celebrated Summer, Grant and Bob's voices in all that Whitman man love and yearning and actually the expression of it…how?

After a long discussion in my pad with ole Mezzy I lent

him one of my favorite books, an Indian book called Lame Deer Seeker of Visions. I told him that monotheism has had it's day and that why keep alive ideas the same ideas for thousands of years? Its time to expand our religious conceptions to include science and archeology like the great ones of the eighteen hundreds did, just look at Rimbaud for instance his Illuminations. And even furthering that is the blast of and from nowhere Old Angel Midnight. I also told Mezzy that to believe one's truths to be eternal was or is merely an extension of one's ego and he said ego explosion and I said yeah but, and on and on.

Afternoon morning wake up to grayness. Twelve thirty and waiting on the mail. Brewed up some you-know-what (not grass, homes) and maybe I'll write a letter to someone? Who wants to sift through my bullshit though?

What a pleasure what a supreme act of luck it is to have a rainy afternoon to dive into books! First I read a few pages of the abstruse Secret Doctrine then I fish out my all-time hero Henry and his Books of My Life. Henry has the flow man the skill the craft and that delicious combination of I don't give a damn I give a damn, you know? So I'm pacing alive around my pad and the rain a-fallen and the trees shimmying and you know just feeling good. Kind of like in the earlier part of this story when I really read Lorca, I have that feeling again. I just thought you should know.

Last night I looked at family pictures feeling good but turned in and slept and just woke up and now I feel refreshed. Yesterday I was around people almost all day into the night and it kind of wore me out.

White dog white sun white sundog in the amorphous gray of seven thirty p.m. and Miles brewing and me reading reading of Marcel. Pharmacy glean.

Spent a day with Vee who now by some strange glimpse of fate I'm now back in love with, weird how things go?

The emotions my emotions are so unpredictable, its nice to be in love love that feeling that feeling is indescribable and majestic. Just simple conversing and the lips and the eyes coming into a togetherness. I'm just sitting here now after this flowery day listening to Roxy Music and I never imagined life could be so fine so electric so lovely. Vee if you ever read this I'll write what I'm now scared to say: I love you.

One kiss for a thousand nights is enough.

When I was young when I was younger...but now I'm starting to know to glow, now and now, its for real, I feel it, I feel her in my reborn heart, stirring swimming singing.

Maybe she's Marta Martha Jill come back in the shapeshift to renew this tired half man? Maybe she's Aretha or Buddha or maybe she's just she? Who she is? It doesn't matter all that matters is the song of her eyes like moons of...of infinite around and around buzzing in my former diamond crucifix confusions, she is here, that's what matters. Right across the street now. And we are each alone in this moment but not alone, a new anew, Jesus it fell and I fall and man...forgive my wordless search take it slow take it slow, and the strings that snapped a few years back but now the black of night receives me for I am true in my desire simple. Dark.

Dawn big shadow from the building I live in. Bright. The sapphire sky pale-ish in her Egyptian wonder. The formless (Arupa) barely become form (Rupa): clouds. Not much wind but my god the green that hath snuck up and out of the shadow: green. Nobody in the parking lot as the coffee brews and I awoke early because of a middle of the night snack which has my stomach gurgling but I've decided to stay up because I'm supposed to be Dawn, Dawn Peyote? Where does this peyote fit in? Its been years since my grandpa's death that I went on that age-old vision quest without knowing it. Peyote ah its more like Dawn Heyoka blood.

The pale stars of morn lament the loss of white cherries struggling.

Wow here I am here it is: the sun and now the parking lot no longer cast in a heavenly shadow and I'm digging Journey and its nine and what else? Oh the road is quiet and summer is warmly warm in mores ways than one then one.

So me and Vee go for a walk wok and I'd like to get into her wok okay that but really I'm desiring her I don't know if I'll be able to control my glands but were walking nonetheless and then we go into her crib and shoot the breeze. I stand up and move towards her with the kiss itch but I can see she doesn't want it. "You kind of scared me," she says.

"I'm sorry I just feel like kissing you."

"I know you're a man but it'll lead to other things."

"We can just kiss."

"I know what you're thinking: s.e.x. and I am afraid of getting pregnant."

"Okay," I say feeling guilty.

We fall silent but wow I'm attracted to her her eyes green her hair which we discussed and decided its strawberry blond and her fulsome lips, ah, awe woman. Its been for the both of us three years since we've made love and I'm really just feeling an inner urge to get really close, close to her. So she has an arrangement to meet a friend to walk at three and as she checks the ashtrays I run my hand across her back then she turns around and I put my hands into her hair beside her face and smooch a little. "You got me all worked up for my walk," she says after the kiss. One kiss that's all I need once in a while woman. I come back to my pad and in kiss bliss drift off and take a nap.

Wanting to write an honest letter to Vee but I don't know where to start, to begin?

Relationships are weird.

I feel lost.

Waiting for the Moon ah but the sky is soft velvet cloud probably won't be able to see her. Talking on the phone trying to talk my way out of some blues told Sister Pistol I was down and didn't want to burden Vee with my troubles, Sister Pistol was reassuring and sympathetic, great gal. And coincidentally I called The Goy and he too was down in the dumps and we chatted about religo and I told him about my high school preacher who is a sweet and nice and wise man. But I still feel some kind a revulsion about Christianity, like it seems too easy, an easy escape while the wiles go unquestioned. I don't know, I'm running through the wood chased by harlots of fiery lie and when I reach out for a phantom of truth it slips through my mind like water under the red bridge.

Awe ah ha the moon there she is tryin two high be high the trees, I see you moon and I love you.

I wonder about the past sometimes, the holy brothers dark darkly holy but brightly alive. I wonder if I've really had it that rough or if I just feel sorry for myself a lot?

Talking with Vee on the phone last night she was really going and finally she stopped and said, "I know, I'm a chatterbox tonight," I thought that was funny and expressed to her to keep at it, "That's why I called," I told her and we must a talked for an hour and a half. I think she's starting to trust me?

"Are you sure you want to get involved with me?" Vee asked.

I say, "Maybe I should a hung up twenty minutes ago," we laugh. We laugh a lot together these days.

Why this need to shock in art? I sit here trying to formulate some of my own theories about painting...but I'm left with a sort a frustrated nothingness. Duchamp bitched about Matisse but Duchamp has spawned some real crap too, so.

Reading tonight Malcolm X's autobiography, wow, do I say wow too much? What other word would suffice? Dig? Awe? Yeah I think awe will do.

Go pretty interesting book, John Clellon Holmes, I think though that The Horn is a bit better, more exciting.

Morning Sunday morning end of June and I'm really loving the clear sky and the sun still in the East. To get the full import of jazz you have to see Pollock, or, to get the lowdown on swinging mighty Jackson listen to Coltrane's Live In Seattle, I'd be willing to bet they love each other.

To understand Jazz is to understand Pollock and Picasso and vice versa, reciprocality.

Man I feel sorry for Michelangelo all locked up and enslaved. Picasso though, Pablo liberated art from the religions, and his views of reality are not mere caricatures, his "his" women are real, real emotion in the throes throes of sickness and death we do depart, before now and after.

Night Peyote wondering hoping this'll last four eve err. I don't know, is it just coffee this ecstasy? Or have I been slipped something? I've been dancing around the crib truly feeling the music and know its Carlos. Game of Love. Or is it just justly my senses coming alive? But MAN...I feel it tonight the rolling truths and circuses and the mortal candy of the wine done changed back black to water clear. Darkly and brightly I feel, both. And the writing feels strange tonight like I haven't written for a long time. I'm here though, and it's a story of the senses of the desires of the only way of Ching, Chan, zing and Ann. Little bit a widow in the is of the above, the sky royal blue and Vee wore yellow today and the African Brother who communes and the melding unions zooey of Mexico and kind kind kind the breathing heart pumping that god joke that goddess juice by schoolessness. The found is found and even the found is loss, melancholy, holy schizophrenia of nominal liminal reliefs. Just dance prance chance trance and ask the hallowed a million zillion questions: ah, the snake and the dove, I told Vee about the snake and the dove quoting my father (?). I think she digs me? I dig me right now.

Put on Melanie's CD after reading a bit of a book on Dionysus. She goes deep, her music pure color in the gray of America.

I'm overwhelmed beat beautiful by this music Melanie bequeathed to me…released, finally, finally.

I want to write her thank her kiss her love her.

"Stones taught me to fly and love taught me to lie, and life taught me to die…its not hard to fall when you float like a cannonball."

Melanie read this: love I love you with my wounded heart with my stalling mind with my very shuttering singing blood. This music God and I hear I hear I feel I feel and real the reel and love is Allah all its about the meaning. Love revealed NOW. Now courage bravery justice reason empirical all the years make Dionysian sense: music. The very story of this. Like a rose seeing seeking a rose or a tulip. Like a ending shrouded in Genesis, or vice versa, and out here we is now just a tad more than nothingness now now. The callings of the vice found us the seasons in hell found us and Melanie and I didn't know didn't know: deep, deeply, deep blues deeply. Awe. The leaning of the bird on the fence of sensuality and miracles are the years zinging around Ann around and finally we find that Black Elk center. Relationships relating ships and the changing of the mares changing of the guardians and what new secrets now being born in this reborn? What and what? The writing of a story in the night violins cellos acoustic guitars and Lorca resurrected.

I don't need the peyote anymore boys. Love done found me.

End of Chapter Three.

DONNA PEYOTE. CHAPTER FOUR. DAWN THREE.

Ready for womaness. She's got my music, my inner self, I'll give and give and love and love you. Could it be? Could love be? Possible? Ha la Lou you.

Melanie I can't help it I got to communicate to you, to you this music you lent me, lint me. I'm enthralled I'm here in the immaculate karma and the cathartic-ness of song beyond going beyond Dionysus who I've been reading about. Man how I long for your being to be near me. God how I search and search but this music I tell you is a bookend to my life, that is, I'm here thoroughly, and completely ready to love you Melanie. Ah hell I should be writing a letter to you I could be showing you my poetry the psalms of and about recovery and now I'm starting to think that with this Rice crooner that I've recovered? I don't know? But I feel alive, I know that. What could I write to you Melanie? I'm afraid if I spill my tenuous guts to you you'll run. I'll just write and now know the pure dawns crimson pink yellow and the peyote undiluted vision my eyes grow a little stronger every day. Its because of you, its because of us in that diamond potential and me eternally shy or a clown a heyoka in all my megalomania. The why is just. The singing is just. The only future we have that is unknowable is just too.

I can't do anything can't think anything but her...

like Henry this one's for Her. There have been maybe more than a few and each time is new new like like and tropics and comes and returns and well I've been thinking maybe wine? No no. Just a thought just a former Dionysus of the easy score, heel hell fuck, shit, the liquor stores lined up on the damned boulevards like Jokerdads and I don't need nor want want to go back to my former ways. Period. But the wine the wine…water and bread now and cigarettes and Melanie's vast music, what gold lies lies and lies behind her eyes eyes and eyes? The womaness of this. A bright apple for the charity and the snakes dish up the love. The snakes they now they know. Opera and north but summer and tomorrow's July and July's tomorrow and we'll ghetto the heart with slim fishes and exposing my inner voice to you maybe the someday read. The dart hard. Slashing and crying and cry ce senor and you go back up man I tell you…what do I mean? I mean I went way up there and then I went descended even lower than a thousand purgatories but what I mean I mean maybe if you were some Genet of the Time but I say say one goes back up there let Guy Anna know I'm alright and I believe what he said bout the green tea illegal but now I gone done brown black with my coffee dusks and Donna oh Donna pre ma me. Hello goodbye, used to be bye goodbye and Lou knew what I was sayin ba Zen. Will they know now what the choices breed in the sober moment recollect and line? The colors and she said, "Buk in heat," I hope its more than that, this.

Gosh I'm digging this heat July first July fist and the no-justice of justice hoping craving for Melanie to call back.

God is the only genius.

But I'm godless in a secular fire of passed wine and recovered dime in the lonely mind-wheel and whatnot. Whatnot? However the deity unnames herself: Melanie, goddess-like in her hiding and music and I grasp my minds in her heavenly directions the door disappears and like Dante that which is so so so long ago you have offered me a glimmering glimpse of my lost love. My love in the last and found, the sauced and round, the lost and sound, all of this, "Come sit on my wall," you are my heart's song Melanie and brought me back to all the truths and tooths heathen hidden in my chest, my chest, my chest, my growing chest.

Now the Sun is down, now the son is up.

I'm really Jonesing aching to hear her voice in the viceless dusk.

Is Melanie Ricki's daughter?

Are we to meet on this plane of find? Like my father the musician and his muse?

Next day and I'm just sitting here a little after six p.m. and the sun is this pulsing blinding thing white and the trees jigging and like I said I'm just sitting in my lawn chair digging The Black Crowes, we really do talk to angels, us schizophrenics.

Gee I feel like yakking with Melanie Melanie who today smiled like a watermelon and new neighbors are moving in into the crib next door. I'm still listening to Damien it keeps welling up inside me inside the desire of desires: confession and truth, reflection and youth gone gone man but I think I see and feel it she he them us coming coming and coming back, like my songs of old the hopes are slowly focusing: newness and nowness and angels of flesh, so much lust mixed in the wine of love in this hairy chest of want. Thing is she's in and on my mind as my mind for the first time fuses with my tattered heart.

Blue is deep in the above and out the window: night of July night of torn between Vee and her sobriety and straight forwardness and Melanie's voluptuous body. I wish the world wasn't so rigid about love relationships, why can't I long for two women at the same time and be with and have an honest thang with both? Vee is into the oneness of things, she believes in "marriage," whereas I, I told Vee I live in the moment, one day is the only day. I don't want to hurt Vee but...yeah I haven't been completely honest with her, that is if Melanie made a obvious move to me (which I hope she does) I'd fall fall deep with her. If too Vee made a move I'd fall deep with her, so, so, so if? If? I don't know what's gonna happen? That desire though, its wonderful to swim in desire in a night made of infinity.

Its Bee's Wing all o'er again. But am I the singer or the bee? "As long as there's no price on love I'll say," Richard Lana understands, understands me (at least). Maybe? Ah so many stories in and of the universe witch ones are mine and yours? Ours? Ireland spawning the love in this restless nocturne. "Heaven was only half as far away that night." Its even closer tonight. And the Moon will be out too.

"Man," I say to myself, overwhelmed by music and the companions of bard and songstress. Poetess, lass, ordinary? Oh super supernatural, hey we really do belong together Ricki I know I know and are you Melanie? The Nurses, "Man."

Music is myth turned reality.

So its raining here in oh watt nah and its green and probably not as green as my forefathers' land: Ireland, Black Ireland...but I'm writing feeling Irish as all Hell and the next song is that tearjerker Lord Franklin and I know I'll be moved, moved by Sinead who my old bud gal Irene digs. I called and left a message with Irene who I hope'll call back and she spent some time in Ireland actual and I want to hear about it from here (her) wine-like lips of joy of Joyce female.

Ah but here come the flutes the crooning and its Monday and the lamp is on and its grayer than a Subterranean now, unbound now as the song smoothly unfolds, "Concerning Franklin and his gallant crew…" Boy oh boy this song I swear it's the most saddest thing ever. Poor sailors and Eskimos, the lands separated by vast waves waves and whales and goodbye forevers and lords who speak not but leave the unraveling of tears to the unpracticing guides and merchants, hairy tics of mythology burdened by Jean and any pound any price to find to find…the song ends and I get up to rewind the damn thing. Because you see I think I'm the Franklin she's singing about and it's a illimitable metaphor and wow how I swayed sailed away on a ship of whiskey in a ocean of beers, but maybe myth is truth? Okay I'll listen again.

Jesus its like I think I will change my name you know I'm now Franklin and maybe I aint a Lord but what the heck? Change my name and maybe perhaps she'll find me? Almost five years since I stepped off my own Drunken Boat, five years. And what they call euphoric recall I've been getting lately reading of Dionysus and dancing, Bacchanals and whatnot. The Irish too have that madness luck, I pulled Finnegan off the shelf, with a little help from a drunken god maybe I'll comprehend the damn thing the damn book, probably the loosest tongue since you know who? Who? Oh I don't know I don't want Hamlet wallowing in the beat beautiful rainfall like Ozarks of compassion where my pa grew up but I want her to find me find me… "To know Lord Franklin and where he is…" Finnegan and Dubliners I was trotting round this crib trying to talk like an Irishman and its kinda fin fun, then I wondered if the neighbors could hear me and fink and think me mad? So I SHUTUP! And sat down to write this shit. Shat turd. What? Turd's not a word? My god what next? Fucking computers.

Jackson was had that crazed boozed Irish blood thundering through his vein as well.

Melanie there's so much music I want you to hear: Irish. Green and green. The ballad. The dark journey finding a way stealing away to that street Richard and Linda and Aretha sing so well about about my blind passage and how I don't quite recognize people, the stranger always strange always a stranger. Battling not to battle.

Melanie there's so many gardens inside my mind.

Valleys suns too.

Dance baby dance like a Indian dance like and for the nurses and Jim and all the Dionysuses out there in the intolerable wars of distinction.

Buffalo and the moon reeds.

Son Volt on the mix tape I made for Lee Krasner, but she's gone and eyes left with the songs.

Gee z here I is alone aching to share these songs, what brews why like wine turns to water and green gets greener.

High from reading I take a little break, some book on the sacred mushroom and the cross and the origins, oh the origins. Writ by a guy John Allegro, bought it for a dollar at the used bookstore downtown. As I said, I'm high from reading and my mind pulsating alive. Sipping decaf tea and smoking American Spirits, yeah, yea.

Glitter glittering night of rain fell fallen falling, streets all a-glisten like a bluesy in Jean and the electric pecks all this blackness in a wave waves of no matter no matter.

Melanie fades she won't return my calls...so. So Vee has invited me over Friday night and I'm accepting things and dreaming. Accepting myself mostly, and stop trying to impress these two beautiful women and if they want me I'm here.

So its to Vee's tomorrow night to eat and watch a movie. Maybe a little kissing?

Hey Vee that river's holy just like the song the song of Prince who knows the pavements and Minneapolis and whatnot. Hey Vee lets shout the lords' songs from all the antique rooftops and dance and groves of grooves and lies that lead to truth, all this in the relationship of defiance and love, we will defy the platitudes and love without fists. Just because I'm singing and dancing right now doesn't mean I'm an artist but I tell you I try and climb. The sun shines right into my ballad eye as I write this, high high summer in Sumerian trances. Look back and here we are, hook and look ahead and there we are. Further future's tendernesses and oblong fish of Christ seeking any corner to plow the truth through to that all of the any, and really the sky is not blue but blues. Vee I will show the up of heaven revealed and go and go and go, go to the pianos of Aretha and the steps which are there to follow the mighty Star Slaves to Utopian lay. Ah I'm just listening and trying to parallel Prince. Strong eye of the sun the son's god.

Read for a couple hours, Luke and all that Stuff, then the Allegro book in the tub.

I don't know what to think of Ant Man, Colossus of Missouri, pile of piles.

Vee and I made love Friday night.

I think I let Vee down, we tried three times and I could only get it up once, I hope she's happy tonight, I hope she gives me a million chances to make her happy.

But, "Lets go down to the Holy River," and on then on Zen on.

I go o'er to her crib around six thirty and she cooks up spaghetti and has some chips and I drink my usual the mighty coffee. We talk, she says she's nervous, listen to Doctor Vinyl on the local radio station. I rented a movie and after a while we watch that and Vee sits close and reaches over and holds my hand, this surprises the heck outta me. It's a good movie but I can't resist and I ask her, "Can I steal a kiss?" She says sure and kiss a little, then she says to take it slow. So I take it slow and watch the movie, its about a cowboy kinda guy who gets sent to Japan to help form an army against the rebels, its really a good movie but now and then I can't help it and lean into Vee's lush lips and kiss kiss kiss. Then she really verily surprises…. "Lets go in the bedroom," she says, and there we go, first time with Vee, first time since the Doll abandoned my silent way, it feels good, to be naked naked.

After we lay there a while then since we're both smokers we decide to choke one, sit in her kitchen and we didn't see the end of the movie but the radio is back on playing love songs, a good night for love songs, a good night for songs of love we are lovers listening glistening. I down a couple big cups of Coke and smoke some more with just her shirt on and my bean belly sagging over my shorts. We look into each others eyes and its true, I can feel it: LOVE, HER.

After that we try it again and it goes better the second time, she even moans and whatnot. It feels so good and I'm glad she's enjoying herself. After again we gots to have our smoke so its back into the kitchen and light up. The T.V.'s been on with the mute and the radio playing, well I start to nod and get heavy lidded eyes and I crawl into her double bed and try and sleep while she mills around the crib cleaning her kitchen doing the dishes, she doesn't feel like sleeping and I can hear her.

Around three a.m. she lays down next to me. I talk some goofy shit and she tells me to go to sleep, and I don't know when but eventually we both drift off.

I wake at nine in the morn and turn on the radio, radio, got to have it, music. She gets up a bit later and has a smoke, then Vee lays down on the couch and sleeps for another couple hours while I drink coffee, coffee, got to have it, coffee.

She gets off the couch at eleven thirty or so and I've

brewed up another pot, this time strong strong java, four scoops man, and she says my god this is strong coffee and I smile and smirk. We sit at her kitchen table and gaze into each others eyes and talk, then she says, "I feel like you're looking into my soul," when I look into her eyes, "Your eyes are something else." She means it as a compliment and I told her the night before that I love her and now I know I love cuz looking into those great green eyes I feel something deep down in me feel and feel.

So that was Friday and Saturday and now its Sunday night and we talked on the phone and asked her if she wanted to hangout but she needs some alone time. We might meet see each other tomorrow, go for a walk, eat at the Mexican joint, or something like that.

So that's the continuing story of Vee and mee. It really feels great.

Reading David Sylvester's terrific book About Modern Art, I think I talked about reading his Interviews With Francis Bacon earlier and the "profound" impact it had on me and my painting, well it's the same type of experience these last two nights reading. Its like the guts of painting spilling into my Curious George mind and finding new angles and new questions and even answers, ah an inspiration, art Art ART! And to think how I have disliked England and my favorite art writer happens to be an Englishman? Irony strikes again.

I think the musical equivalent of the great Francis Bacon is Bob Mould, you know, real emotion and emotional yet precise, daring. They even kind a look alike. So I'm sitting here at a lil after dusk listening to Bob's Beaster album which I hadn't heard in ten or twelve years and I'm reading Sylvester's awesome thought and I've got Bacon opened up on the coffee table, feeling it, feeling artsy and alive, man.

Artistically I'm in a very lucky place, position, that is

the whole twentieth century there for me to fathom, just that alone is for real and it bends my mind. Tonight I'm so fucking happy to be an artist I just don't know what to say? A rich vein indeed Herbert, and I've got my books and I think what Antonin said about not even begun to think yet, yeah man its just the beginning. And I wonder about "genius?" Am I one? I've done a hell of a lot a painting and drawing and if I ever get a regular studio I wouldn't be opposed to toying around with sculptural ideas. For sculpture I like Giocometti's early surreal stuff the best, also David Smith thrills me. I don't know why I love it when people have animals in their art? Maybe its an Indian thing? Maybe all my heroes are homeopathic and or ethnic, like Jasper sure as fuck looks like an Indian, you know, and Pollock is the first modern painter to assimilate Indian/ Mexican ideas and craft into his thangs. I want to got have the urge to take all this shit further. I don't feel I'm wholly original yet, still researching and re-searching, taking it in, I like the idea of derivation. I miss my old stuff that vanished on me, painting is the most absolute form of journaling cuz it includes all the senses and the really good ones put their body into it as well.

God art.

July morning with the day off the wind nice chilled and not a clown in the sky, and I'm listening again to Melanie's music. Waiting for the coffee to done brew.

Phone rings, I answer, "Hello?"

"Hello. Is Mrs. Peyote there?"

"There is no Mrs. Peyote."

"Oh," says the telemarketer and laughs. Oh yes I don't have a wife, that's such a disgrace, I want to tell her I don't believe in God either but she goes on her sales pitch.

"I had my carpets cleaned about a month ago and I don't

really feel like looking at your machine," she starts laughing again, "I'll be blunt."

"Okay bye."

So the sun nearly almost gone for the day and a hard day of nothing much at all right Paul? Stillness and Melanie's music playing in the room. I hear a child yell in the distance and the cars look so glorious in the parking lot.

Ah a little wired from duskly coffee and waiting blind for anything.

Yeah man I'm lucid vamping coughing up moons with Dylan's Saved album in my box, running rings around my mind.

I know how you feel Jackson, every time you think you've done something original you turn around and Pablo Dylan did it thirty ninety years ago.

I won't even mention my ultimate love…okay I will: ARETHA.

I keep dreaming of my basketball days in high school seeing all those old selfish fools, but I wake in the morning refreshed and have that first smoke then brew up some java and sip and listen to the boom box and read a little or just stare off into space waiting for the bus to take me to group to learn and whatnot.

I tried to read The Greek Passion last night, looks interesting, the used books I've been buying piling up like crazy, so much to read. Other than that been reading the New Testament and Sylvester's book on painting, and halfway through a book on Dionysus the same is true for Will To Power. But mornings I shake the nightly cobwebs and sand from my head my skull and just try to wakan to the day's delights.

Sundry reading at dusk nearly nine and.

Sky's pale almost turquoise with hints of an orange pink and hints of purple in the static wave of cloud of coulds clouds and the trees undulating slight and insects are out there though I don't know what they're thinking? But in the west where the Sun Set is a cloud of white, just a patch. So I have read a while the wily whiles wiling willful to the wild. That's about it.

Sal and Dean, Jackson and Marcel?

Out a nowhere the Blue hits me: sadnesses.

I look in the mirror faintly starting to realize who I am.

Brewing a cup o' Joe to harbor my fugitive coat of daze and bafflement.

So we're hangin together Mezzy and me and rapping and stuff, he does a abstract bizarre drawing and in the corner it says, "Haircut." And I'm discoursing my ideas on art and its Friday July something dusk and now the sun hath disappeared from us Midwesterners and its calm and a cool becoming. The tape just ended and I'm wondering what Mez wants to listen to? I'll axe.

Dire Straits and I haven't heard this shit for ages.

Thinking tinkering around with ideas for the painting I'm gonna do this weekend, "Yeah man get some spray paint," and I'm looking at the watercolors I've done in the last couple/few months thinking of combining all the pages into one painting, its just one idea and I haven't figured it out how I'll do it? But Mezzy's comin to Rochester and my pa is gonna grill out and we'll have gold good ole old time. Hopefully it won't rain and Mezzy's out to purchase The Koran at the mall's giant bookstore. Me I want to go to the pubic library and get art books: Klee, Magritte, Dubuffet. And also I want to checkout two books of letters I've seen previously there writ by the greatest demon of em all, Bukowski. I started one, Screams From The Balcony, back in my art school daze, never finished it, now I'm all jazzed to read em again. Paul Klee…I want to give that cat another chance, people teacher aunt and others have said my art resembles his and it always ticked me off but after reading Sylvester's two articles about Klee I thinking its not so bad after all, could even lead to some new discoveries?

Mezzy reading Pierce's Signs and me not understanding a word of it, Jewel tape plays in the room. Just finished a watercolor and call it Egypt In February and that's that. Mez got his shirt off he's a lean mean philosophy machine. This Jewel sounds good, her Spirit album. I'm not quite as wired on coffee as I was an hour ago so I got that going for me. Maybe call Vee and see what she's up to? Na its ten thirty and the universe of black in my windows open the screens let in an opulent breeze, feels good.

Good flavorful water says Mezzy and I got on my Ticotta album, folksongs written in the Twin Cities in the nineties, wondering what he thinks of them? I recorded it in between drinking and pot smoking relapses so I am unable to judge it, but we're listening anyways and dang its already midnight and Mezzy's started a new ink drawing. Me well I got Jackson opened up and looking looking.

Each painting should have a song and each song should have a painting. Be, be.

Back from Rochester with a Guided By Voices CD and man this is the good stuff. Mezzy and I spent a lot a time together and we didn't bash each others skulls in we actually got along good and I think I had him in ecstasy I was at least in the folks' garage painting and listening to a Kerouac recital. But I bought the Guided By Voices cuz I wanted to recapture re-remember my time in the early to mid-nineties with Lou who really dug these crazy tunes, I want to remember too the…well, my memories are not so good both my memory and the memories because of all the booze and pot, I want to know what that what's gone down what's gone has been real and what hasn't. End of July and the sky is pure and Spanish and I've been banished tonight into the epiphany of absolute now a dancing now and now I know now and believe in so much so many songs to dance to, I bow to the bards to the clouds to the sincere.

I swear Damien's Cannonball is the greatest song I've ever heard.

The holiness of my learning leaning on Bukowski's letters tonight and wondering if he is Mezzy?

GBV its that regular guy rock that I dig so, no personas no props, just a couple guitars and a bass and drums of course, and singing that both fools and redeems.

But all this shit goes back to Buddy Holly and Chuck Berry.

Windows all open to the liquid night.

Morning humid and heavy lidded eyes.

Hot nap slept through dusk and I thought it was raining but it's the infra-mince of the churning fan.

Oh shit almighty its hot I'm cracking and now I know why Vincent went to the birds. End of July man and its sticky and I'm praying for that raw fire that yellow burning phantom to go go down.

Its hotter than a constipated cowboy.

Summertime's for fools and rock.

Soutine's Madwoman geeze she looks just like me. Coincidenceville again and again but this time I dig, dig it, it, Soutine yeah, book open and irony splays my painterly eye like grapes of death and beauty.

Yes breeze, I sit here at this typer and finally a little cool coolness.

Okay now its raining buckets and frogs and I've got Lord Franklin's mystery on the juke again and its greener than an Eden apple out there outside me windows and among the plants and free ones known as animals therein lies my Irish reveries: green now. Sinead sings so smooth so mysterious and now Melancholy is my only glad name.

Gosh tonight as the slivered pale rock robustly shines in my sky (?) I deeply think of Jackson and Lee. Just looking at pictures of them, the beauty of Lee, the vast physical changes Jackson went through, the tragic dirge of drink, and the majesty of their paintings. I got to read this American Saga all the way through, I want in, I want to know Jackson and unshroud this lone mar-tour. The truest genius this land will ever see. And sometimes I think these human creators, Jackson and Dylan, have some blood link to me, I know its probably megalomania (not that word again) but I do feel a brotherly love towards some a these guys and it does go beyond mere affection, ah yes, it is love and fellowship I feel. Being an intensely creative man myself and having been around the block a few times and now with nearly five years sober and this mind clearing I can comprehend. So I'm going back out there and at the same Spanish blue time I can go in as well.

That cat Cat Stevens got it right, it is a Wild World babe.

As wild as the color of the moon tonight.

The ecstasy of the father and his music.

Fuck.

Smoking too much and ma says I eat too much bread.

Listening to the Indigo Girls and god I feel like cutting the rugs.

"Count down count down come to me…"

Man we is goin down to Iowa to see Jackson's Mural. I look at the reproduction I can't imagine, twenty feet of rhythm twenty feet of genius. I compare my own shit and it just looks like dingleberries in a croon's crotch.

Crone?

Shit I'll be thirty five in a few daze, who am I to say?

I listen to Will's Elton John tape and are these the things men or boys can't say to each other? Express? Love?

Okay.

All these things inside, and tonight I don't know how to show the world my love my loves. But these songs suffice and I dance around my apartment and hope the neighbors don't mind but "every breath we draw is Hallelujah." That I will see Jean, Will, all the men that time tried to destroy, we will meet on this very Earth to sing hold hands fly kites and reach for daybreak with that great cactus flower: PEYOTE.

Orange glow horizon.

Jazzed, gonna show some art at the Turf Club in October, jazzed man and I can picture it in my head, drawings and paintings, I can't wait!

"Aint no use in crying stay away from me."

Thinking if anyone describes the schizophrenic experience in art its Klee.

And as well the spiritual aspects of this life come through with Santana.

Trying to come down a little, the usual story: coffee.

I've had a pretty wild life and you probably wouldn't believe me if I told you some a the stuff I've been through.

I've probably learned more about humanity at the halfway houses than any school.

Miller said it should be (creativity) an act devoid of will and I tend to agree with that.

Putting on Damien Rice O to cultivate a moon wave inside.

My dad said once, "Me don't dig that idiot box." I sit here with jazz on looking at my drawings and wondering.

Wow morning at nearly one thirty and I'm refreshed

deeply by some ultimate sleep and the cars roll down the highway and I've decided to quit my job the paper route, I figured it out, two dollars an hour I was getting for all that sweat and struggle and besides I don't...the neighborhood repulses me, flags everywhere and middleclass idiots with their white sub-human childs running around without an ounce of passion for anything.

Ye aint lived till ye hath heard Prince and Miles jam!

As far as I'm concerned its over with Vee.

Hag.

So its another reunion like at the beginning of this book only this time my blood aint full a lithium and I'm in better spirits: we pile in the car the bro the pa and ma and drive and drive then stop in Iowa City to see the modern museum there, Motherwell's Elegy nearly has me tearing and Jackson is the greatest thing ever, "I'll take that over Michelangelo," I point to the Mural and say to Peanut Head.

We eat a lunch on the campus with a beautiful river cutting through and the whole scene reminds me of the U of M but we get back in the car and Stick Figure is driving and a stranger is waving at us, I wave back and then we here a noise a plop, ma left her coke on top of the vehicle, we get a laugh out a it anyways and traverse through Iowa and billions probably of corn stalks.

We reach a town in Illinois a lil before dusk and spend the night dare, we go out to eat and I'm car lagged and it's a Italian joint and the food is good and I tell a couple stories from the Lame Deer book then ma starts on a story and it goes on and on and on and on...I make wisecracks here and there. "We still love you mom, maybe not as much as before that story, but..." After dinner me and pa go to a bookstore, I buy a Corso book, ma and Stick have gone to a clothing joint, we meet up in the parking lot then go back to the motel.

Ma and pa got their own room while me and Stick have a smoking room, smoke we do and I smoke the legal and sip a coke and Stick got the green and does pin che's then I take a bath. We each have a bed and we lay there flipping through the channels on the boob tube, nothing good on, I write a bit in my journal and poetry notebooks, Stick is high and around nine I down my prescription meds. By eleven thirty the damn T.V. starts to grind on me and we turn it off and go to sleep.

Morning arrives, I'm out a cigs so I smoke a few butts and brew up coffee and drink that. We get back in the car and continue south and drive and drive…well we are goin to a campsite in southern Indiana and its lush with trees and the road winds, stop at a little Don Knots store and I purchase some tobacco called Gambler, rollies. We find the beach where the other uncles and aunts and cousins are to meet us but we're the first ones there but eventually they arrive, Polly uncle in his pickup truck, and of course a Minnie van is part of the ole scene. We trot down to the beach and go swimming. Or bobbing? But anyways I go back on shore to smoke.

After a while we drive o'er to the…you see my aunt has rented a floating house boat where several of us will sleep and a three others myself especially cuz I get sailor's legs are sleeping on land at a campsite with a fire in tents.

(Stick's joke, "Did you hear about the fire at the circus? It was in tents.")

Listening to Prince tonight, sing Signs, sing Times, its truth brother.

I sit and listen: Gabriel.

I sit and listen a day later: Dylan.

And I wish I wish Melanie was here, there's so much

music in me of me, my father my father...? Storyteller, his voice is received by his son who digs.

Ah Harry's Love Untold is a sequel to Simple Twist of Fate whether he knows it or not.

Eventually, when that album came out I was down-n-out Jack, but now I play it and jig round this room and know, know the life of introspection and the life of dream projection and any seeing eye really.

Rally.

Abbey Road, how me and my bro dug that record back in the eighties, and now I got it on again, wow man, wow.

Vee you dry up my eyes and mind like a popcorn fart.

Vee all that pale stupidity and mental illness always the excuse.

No I'm not bitter but merely realizing how she lays the guilt trip trap on others (me) then lies about shit then does this then that, go out with some other dude I don't care, just don't expect anything real from me anymore. I tried, its really going nowhere and it never was much to start with so, so that's my side of the argument, take it and leave it.

So now its five in the morning and eyes going to watch the dawn explode, I want to see colors and shadows and trees waking. I got Paul Harry Brother Song Saint on the juke and the urge to read Nietzsche.

(I could get on with the family reunion story but all get back to that later)

Listened to some tunes hey hey ah the sky a kind a grayish blue and sure enough the trees swaying as a Monk album starts up.

Looks as if its gonna be a cloudy day, oh well.

Another chill day for August especially.

Called Mezzy, "Early riser," he says, "I'll pack up some stuff and come over."

Almost eight and I been reading to Monk and now

Miles, Mez gonna bring over a Garcia bootleg and some books, maybe go out to breakfast its been a while since I had pancakes.

So now the sun is just starting to set and me and Mez have been hangin and we read out loud our journals, his like some kind a cubist painting a lot of angular-ness and mine is just about pissing and smoking and coffee, not completely in that order always. I'm wondering if Vee'll call? She was gonna spend the day with The Doll and I can just picture those two putting me down and all that, ah I'm the Paranoia King, they're probably just shopping.

Idea for an art project: get a woman's negligee and silkscreen Freud's face on it, a Freudian slip.

Little red berries on the tree right by this window.

Paul sometimes even when the love is told it goes unheard.

My dad's a good man whoever the hell he is.

Mezzy and I definitely in two different worlds.

He bashing Buddhism, "Tommy thinks the Buddha is a devil," he states, he also says its politics. Now Buddhism politics? Man.

Talked to Sister Pistol and she set things alright, I'm not crazy for wanting out a these sorry relationships, Vee and Mezzy.

Wow the world can be uglier at times than any tattoo.

Its one thing to ask, but Mez just through his shit at me out a the blue, crew cut and all.

I'm just an artist, and barely that at times, so.

"The battle for the soul…"

"I went there and back just to see how far it was, and you you tried to tell me, but I had to learn for myself."

Dylan's Good As I Been makes me feel good, for whatever that's worth.

Starting on Jan's Baby Driver, why not?

August something, middle of…and I dumped Vee and feel free.

I see no hope for Vee, she'll go to her shackjob afterlife.

We're clowns, heyokas.

Nothing attracts a clown like a clown.

So another dawn, five thirty brothers and sisters, I know its not much but I like to watch like the Egyptians the sky change and jangle in fresh new colors, stars disappear and the streetlamps go blind and I've got the Indigo Gals and coffee on and last night Jan had my belly in a uproar with her dancing spider, haven't laughed that hard since "trickster falls in his own excrement." So.

So another dusk.

A day without Vee. I look at it this way: she has something new to complain about.

Nice day of rest.

Early morning once more what with the shadow of the apartment building cast on to the parking lot and I'm listening to Indigo, Indigo Gals, songs of chance and hope in the unholy America.

But the mornings the dawns they are holy, that is the Sun feeding the trees and us with delicious light and the brightness of any Buddha in this tree love moment of writing.

Sunday hopin Melanie'll call.

Can't get my self to read can't get my self to sit still so I look at Gottlieb and study my own shit dangling unframed on my walls and now Damien is singing and I'm waiting, waiting for inspirations of any sort.

So to get back to the family stuff the trip all that, we're all in southern Indiana in relative wilderness and…I don't know, I don't think I can write about it? Okay. But we're there and the sun shines bright of course and we haul most of the shit to the houseboat and my and Stick's and cousin Ja to the campsite, uncle Polly has all his crap in his pickup truck.

We get it together so to speak and the night falls finally… I'm having trouble remembering what we did that night, oh yeah me and Stick and Ja and Polly go back to the campsite and build a fire in the pit and sit in lawn chairs, Stick whips out his guitar and plays for a while and hippy Polly digs, then I play a couple songs. We just sit around no radio and stare into the fire and me I'm wondering if they're gonna dose me again with peyote like at Grandpa Boy's funeral a few years back, I do feel somewhat surreal sitting there gazing at the flames. I got my own tent, around midnight I go into and take off my shirt lay down and sleep.

Wake up to the nexus the next day and I'm thirty five years old, Leo boy, I feel pretty good in the morning and we've rented a boat to go out on the lake. Stick drives Ja and me through the winding campsite and through a country road to the houseboat where ma and pa and aunt and uncle and Charlotte slept. We maneuver the boat off the dock and there we go we're off into the languid waters. We dock then go swimming, the boat has a slide on it which Ja loves. We swim and swim and there's a cooler full a beer and pop, I climb back onto the boat and drink a pop and light up a square and relax in the sun. The day goes on and on like that but then we have to turn back and go to the dock to pick up my other two cousins who had gotten off work for the day and now are going to join us, Eric and…what should I call my twenty year old cousin chick? Soul Number One? Anyways we sail motor out into the lake again, then we slowly slide up on to the shore by the beach, some a us get off the boat to go to the beach, I go in and swim a little then lay on the shoreline water comin up into my shorts and Charlotte says, "You got enough sand in your crotch?"

"Yeah I'm starting to feel very manly," and she goes off in her bikini into the waters.

Man life can be good, sweet, talkin to Melanie on the phone, joking round and so forth.

She wants me to do a painting for her she's going to buy all the supplies and the picture is supposed to be about something that reminds me of her…ah how is one supposed to paint pure love?

Melanie on the phone, "Guess who I heard on the radio?"

"I know Damien Rice I heard it too."

Then she says, "I'm gonna move up to the Cities just for the radio stations."

"Yeah, alright, wow…"

Oh the night don't preconceive any thing, and the women of Moors' regrets now cast the heavenly flow of now onto my teary ear and all the tulips and cauliflowers and all the low lambs singing sinning swinging and then the Arabian gates which equal mercy, justice, intricate and like Jackson's ma lacing her son's mind with the faith in the unreal, I too swim before the nadir of the moon or the gypsy mammy sill is wet forthright in the drum and our wine our wine our wine turned into prayers prees of everyday everyman…but for the wouldn't and who really goes? He that loss and she that boss. Fucking the typer like Old Angel to Pickle's love truly a mystery and then the whereabouts of the should should be here by now and tran the parent into Wovoka leading all the fucking, all the fucking angels into an orgy of dance or is it war? I don't know? I could write about hoods and lums and battlefields but right about how?

How? Guns and whatnot? No. The story is simply riding itself out like Death itself, one world of past that's your show and it's self it it it and thieves will someday and chiefs will someday well Sunday and won't have to, you know? The She. But ladies and germs is about all it amounts to now, men straight you know and the gin bubbles like just like that and ouch the snake the snake don't fight the snake find out that the heart is the skin. Yeah and ghostly Jean said, "To repel…" but I just want compel. Song's over.

So I'll start anew paragraph and Mercury to Melanie, boy oh boy, and silver were cloud ripple desert atmosphere Shakespeare pockets Desires and milky way zenning in fours of disrepute, I almost forget forgot to tell and yell at the drunks, shit, but by the fate is the simpletons of shad and blood to deck out in the silk electric amnesia skull of among them. With the dimming of hell into the Beatrice into the humming hymns lust cum gism ism and catscan and fuck that's in the bat, the blast. Cunt just. Cunt just. I hit the period button like Annie Dolls and ruddy raggedy flame of old: Jill-esque. The curfews one flew under purely now and slow it down Pickle wise as boner, no? The leaves and the berries and the waiting. Farming fanning flagulate yourself elf of mind. Accept this congrats as my phone knee rapping arms city to the we'll come, oh whoa as the this crescent dose doe and fowl man foul canned up like butter asparagus Kennedy and she too came from Canada was were another…dot, tip, slop, sip. Destroying this verse. I need to smoke homes.

(It wasn't till we sat around ate the tuna helper that I realized what that meant)

Bob and Robbie the love I feel.

One wish: for Melanie to hear and feel your music.

Its raining, raining I think cuz a this Peltier song, a mourning rain tis.

(couple days later) And I'm digging wow man Buffalo, it's a Buffalo Tom mid-morning and yeah my nails are long interfere with my typing but I've drank half a pot and smoked a coup pal and I feel good. Call up Melanie and rap talk jive.

As for my own art I discovered LSD and Van Gogh at the same time in hi school.

Where are they? Mezzy and Tommy said they'd stop by after rustling up some grub. Play some chess and drink some pop.

Crusty eyed morning what with the coffee a-brew and The Trane on the sound bleeder.

Man boy a tremendous urge to re-study de Kooning's stuff.

Asparagus and rice on the burner and Bob Marley on the box and it's the middle of the week middle of August and everything's fine man.

Awake to a Black Dawn, four thirty a.m. and the coffee on, three cups, Indigo new one on that ole jokebox and maybe I'll write an artsy letter to someone? Aunt? I don't know.

O dawns of unconceivable beauty, melancholy, the holy only song: dawn. My pa singing to me his most honest confession as I wait for the daystar to cast its precise hymn-like shadows and the light so I can see my friends the trees the tresses and all… "The ghost of our old love…" and out here where the corn grows I don't need to think about the commerce of war, the commerce of Vincent, just the mercy of my own Yahweh or Allah. The rules laid out the puzzles for us fools and suffering entails suffering. Too early to call anybody but I'm thinking I could write my love out with a vast Melanie in my minds' eyes. "Last night I danced with a stranger but she just reminded me you were the one," and every night is the Strangers the Fools, who squarely place their and our lives into the caring touch of Egyptian solace, that Egyptian can make you sleep or make you dance, I happen to be doin both this morning. Awe morning ah.

Cig, cig now and a noggin of Joe, Jean's Joe.

Oh shit I'd even rather be a cowboy out there in the wilderness than stuck in some suburbia but oh well and did they think they could cast me off? Cast out their demons by ignoring me as I chase windmills? The low hum of galaxy's churn, wounded and all.

Okay a touch of darn dark navy blue now as I listen to Mingus.

And read, read David Sylvester's ideas on Willem.

Well the sun's out now and the trees a bright bright green in this sunlit now.

Yeah man fuck yeah a...I'm going to be in three art shows this fall, just got a call from the cat at The Speedboat Gallery and gonna show there in September then the Art Crawl in early October then the same month on the tenth show my shit at the Turf Club! Things are infra-fine I tell you, makes me want to paint up a thousand stormy gardens.

Plus Mezzy and Melanie might be stopping o'er later, Melanie come come with me to this...I don't know, lets just funk all the coffee valleys and roar with the unhunted lions.

Sometimes like now I wonder and feel as if the world is divided between Egyptians and non-Egyptians?

Whatever it is it's a wild mixture at this point.

Buying The Alexandria Quartet by Lawrence Durrell at the used bookshop, "You have good taste."

We talk a bit about Durrell, I tell him and his mom who run the joint, "I've read a little bit by him, the Durrell and Miller letters spanning about forty years, seems like an intelligent dude."

The guy cracks his jaw then I say, "Thanks for the business, four books for seven bucks, can't beat that."

"Thank you, bye."

"See ya."

Then I walk around the corner to see my Greek friend who works at the restaurant downtown, but he's in Greece says the waitress beautiful.

Lore knows I done got a lot a great books there, and my Greek friend even is getting into the arts and has some connections.

Cooling off dusk, zones of orange slice through the trees and blind me.

Sit then pace a lil, now it's the Stones, Only Rock-n-Roll, yeah man I think to some extent the energy of the seventies has been shifted or replaced by rhetoric.

I like what Westerberg said, "We're better than the Stones...ah I maybe shittin ya there."

They came fuckin close though.

Half guitar moon in the south headed west and the instrumental. Tom waits for someone.

Painting as sacrament? The act and the aftermath in the form of image?

Shapeshifting and dematerialization.

Christian bias everywhere America.

Science has proved there is no god or gods, philosophies clearly comport that the morals are merely a mask for social climbers and lunatic politicians, so yeah man fuck Christianity.

And that schizophrenics are essentially a political religious threat to the American way of life is obvious to me, to be locked up without any crime, that is The State's doing, and from all the changes in the system its obvious that the doctors and therapists are puppets.

The whole world's a cemetery, Kafka, you go from

one tomb to another tomb, one cell to another, meanwhile mean wiles, and nature transformed into a square, not even a chessboard, but a massive plot plotted out by plots of plots.

Yeah Walter Kaufman got me thinking.

Life itself is abstruse, Genesis is a laughingstock, and there's nothing more abstruse and obtuse than being labeled mentally ill.

I can't believe it I just talked to myself for an hour.

Cloud formations like the bluffs of Winona.

It's a whacked out Dave Purr Nerd world night.

Just listening to music tonight and worn out but a melancholy gladness for I have survived.

Brewing solace as the black stretches the minute to the farthest be.

Listening to the soundtrack The Rose and dig.

Yeah.

What were Melanie's thoughts while listening to Guided By Voices?

Eleven fifteen morning high highly on my Ja and listening dancing bopping round-n-round to Guided By Voices, and with the wind out there and me in here I feel pretty good but I wish Melanie would call back.

I have all day (Friday) to do what I want everything nothing.

Listening to Run Westy Bum and I'm safe here in Snitchville.

Sun in the tree intricate green patterns mixed with white gold spangling light its better than a cathedral window.

Just just and just finished reading part one of this book, feeling proud of myself and my self's confessions in the vapid nation's tired dead I.

Stick Figure's birthday tomorrow or Sunday, thirty one. Virgo boy, collector of the extraordinary.

Some kind a green rain in my mind, now, tonight.

Now after nocturne's stayed up late it's a morning drizzle as my eyes try to focus.

Dang god man fuck I'm high digging my own shit (art). After noon.

Looking at an old sketchbook I'm fucking out there, how'd I get this way?

Night nig later and I'm listening goin back in the past passed the under and digging Thompson and his tunes, songs that are as deep and plentiful as a novel, dig. Shady Nancy now though I used to be the Shake King what with my Jim Beam tremble, ah now I'm safe as a bud of peyote in the forsaken desert dreaming wishing Melanie was here and how I could turn her on to these musical geniuses of the great seventies, pure, simple, deceptively truthful.

Wrote to Melanie, maybe she'll read it someday? Mac.

She claims to be a punker but she's never heard the Sex Pistols, I could throw that in her face as it rewinds.

Are The Mat's punk? I wonder if I'm one, I don't want to be a hippy I just want to be sane you know.

Am I a square a square for sobering up?

Day hath passed and now its night again. I'm basically just digging and contemplating East and listening to an old Crowded House tape I bought in Minnie and it still works wow. Li Po on my coffee table and last summer I read it now I'm going back into his little movies. Yeah.

I've never felt Christian, even as a kid I didn't buy it, now I bye it in the gentle sober eve of sober morrow, wonder bout my ole Chinese philosophy teacher and how much he resembles the dude guy Tzu, Lao Tzu. Coincidenceville once more into the bitched.

Blitzed.

Its really been amazing, baffling.

Ruined alive like Tibet.

Faded lanterns of heaven.

Miss It in the mourning comes.

I look at this place there is no conception.

Looking back tonight, too in one, and digging my sike warred drawings and then the preceding Breakdown Café pictures which I've been studying in the black and white, black sky and white electricity that is, that is.

Standing on the side, the side of the path the road. It's a pointillisitic verse now.

King Tide on the bleeder and Melanie never done called back, that's okay, I'll just write my unjustness in the justly hundred hungers of not wanting sleep and the ce of rush turns to the howl of relax and deflate. King Tide laying it out Jack, the drums kickin in and starts to come down hi and hell so low you want it...and the world twists turns mists yearns, "I can feel the king tide comin all my senses overflowing," and yea yes I'll paint spheres in the shaky square of any oblivion, I'll play piano with eyes blindfolded and make Mozart look twice, I'll drink all the fucking oceans tonight in the salty sauce of think, I'll ah fuck it I'll just both the chance by distance, King Tide whistling that this and impossibly we flaunt the walls the angles and say its truth but its not brother nod, that cross was used for murder, and murdering still is the geometry tied to bone of violin cat cat and blinking for the attentiveness of any Zen any prajna like Beard Man at the you-know-where, I might have to, ah shit don't know, this nest one's pretty good too because well she is having her way her ways.

Smoke one, okay.

Kant believe my luck.

Afternoon morning and I'm up and buzzing on one and a half cups of Joe.

"I saw the worst minds of this generation destroyed by money."

Its quarter till three a.m. and I'm coming off a potent late-night conversation with Mezzy who always offers an alternative to my chips my shoulders. Well we'll we become buffalo in this early morn? Will we shake our legs Mez and I and get jobs? So much to shake off what with me on my Krishnamurti rants rapping about conditioning and systemizations and schooling and really just now Satori like finding my self in all this. And all this just what is and maybe I am mentally ill delusional the whole nine fucking yards but one has to admit the landscapes are ravaged as ravaged as I and my violin despairs or coming to and by talking with ole Mez gaining insight to my own misguided philosophies, saying this and throwing out that and now R.E.M. singin songs amongst ye Nature and swimming and the watery gentle of voice ah the track I've done gotten off... no tracks on these arms, hopefully never. I don't want to go back to my old ways, mainly alcoholisms, but tonight I'm more than bobbing I'm actually swimming and maybe all my reading is starting to reap and yield something beyond television and those stinky platitudes? "Nick swimming deserves a quiet night," and Stick Figure in the cities, how's he really doing? I love Stick and Mez in the good old now of now, place no bets on forever but grow.

Giving up on Melanie. As lovers that is, but friends we can be.

Put on some Bitches' Brew and start the day at two in the afternoon. Good things happening: art shows and all that. Good friends and good times "aint we lucky we get em?" So that's that for now.

The intelligence of Vincent to paint nature figuratively and man and woman as nature.

Thunder, coffee java is fucking thunder and I can't sit still and its intense.

Turn off the kitchen light and let the single lamp cast its breadly light: somber, solemn. And on my coffee table are my art books and I look and look.

Art is just a fantasy land, histrionics, and I'll probably stay healthy no matter what happens.

Sunday ho hum.

Looking at old art ho hum.

Black Dawn dark six a.m. and the windows shut its September but the trees rustling shivering dancing out there I can see em through my Rembrandt window and the streetlamps are all Starry Night and Coltrane's Love Supreme on. Yesterday I wrote a three page letter to my love my cousin Charlotte and I hope she writes back I hope I don't come across too strong, I have I know a tendency to rant when it comes to art and all that, but I also wrote to some others and it feels good putting the letters into the mailbox and knowing they'll read it and maybe get something out a it.

Guided By Voices by delusions for me, ah vision, read part a Revelations the other night, something. I don't know, I just read whatever and I'm not picky, finicky, with books. Just as long as it doesn't end up like that one Twilight Zone episode, I guess that show used to freak my ma out when she was growing up.

I set two years to write this book but I think it'll probably take a little longer, its been about that now and I'm not even halfway through with this last chapter, so, I'll it'll most likely extend the writing that is into holy October and Halloween, one of my favorite seasons, I dig masks and costumes and candles and pumpkins. Would like to go on down to great Mexico for Day of the Dead and the sugar skulls of some forgotten actress.

Starting to lighten up the sky a kind a gray-blue and wow the wind whipping round those poor struggling trees.

How a tree survives is a mystery to me? Naked through all the changes, naked through all the unpredictable seasons the seasons' gone-like repose or clandestine moments, always transmigrating always all ways.

Thinking about Nietzsche and the folksinger and how I was raised on Dylan and how he would most likely probably dig that. Folk music you know? Its real.

Catchin the bus to go to the library and then to the ole halfway house then walk to day treatment. No use in just festering here without anything to really write about and the sapphire sky and the popcorn clouds the sun starting to cut it all up and break on through.

Last time I was in the library the redhead was checking me out I mean my books and I asked, "Do I have any fines?"

She said, "No, but I could give you some," half smirking.

"Okay," and we laughed.

Now eight in the morn and the trees swaying it kind of sounds like an ocean.

Its one minute past midnight lightning war flashing, maybe it's the angels' coming?

Okay I've been thinking about Hermes tonight and wondering if all my influences could be gathered up under his umbrellas? Con the conner and play the play and mock the mocker and that shit'll dry up eventually. But still the doubts the Arden of my this my mind: hair on? Ah the war, and am I really safe as I believe I am? Is this all unjust Maya? Chris on the tube singing for the crypts and rockin the roll and I wish he'd a danced like that time O.D. Jubilee at Worst Avenue and all the dashed hopes swalling swanning and dawning into oblivion major man. Okay? I don't know.

Blurry bleary morning what with the coffee brew in and me well it's another day say to say day day say.

Blurry bleary dusk what with waking from a nap and the coffee brew in well its another night to un-day the sayfool and gray as gray can be out dare, Skull hasn't writ for a wile and I'm wondering if my last couple letters were too obnoxious for him? Maybe I'll write, ah no I don't have any money for stamps.

And Mezzy might be comin o'er tomorrow and I've got two books checked out from ze librarium: The Faces of Jesus, and a comprehensive one on Vincent. The Jesus book is really something well they both are, and could Jesus be a Semitic Egyptian? A Hermes of Pal a Stein? I bring out my Egyptian sculpture picture book and Thoth and he resemble each other except for the nose...deep.

Black crows of Van and now the modern wows ones who sing and dance and shoo and churn. Sometimes I think Chris is Christ and Christ still around in all his Shamanisms dancing like a heavy rain like now the sky cumming wet wet wet and a flash here and there of mysterious lightning, I guess its like Ricki's song Stewart's Coat where she sings some tin about September and that's when the rain come, and now its true rue and blue and deary I love and dig the rain. I Dig a Tony, huh? The highway silent, the trees drinking, the leaves have not left yet, and fly on the screen unperturbed by me sitting here looking at him.

Medium and large trees shimmy in the unrelenting wind and the sky is a sea of grayness and wondering at this early mornin if the sad sun that momentary fire of the eternal will wake break through and light all this up? As for now its about seven and my eyes pure crust and blur and Paul's singing to me of Plath and her plight into in to great death, the desert no one enters but all re-turn to and hesitant steps but for the cackle and dragstress of song melancholy, Paul said he knew many who went...

(Dang that fly still on the screen)

I'll Chi my. Alchemy. Last night stayed on late and read of it, and beginning to know and Hermes as my truest hero.

Nature and Vincent was right with the rite, there is a lot a yellow out there.

Starting to clear and the horizon white and gradations of that and clouds beginning to form and the gray letting up a bit.

Looking at my painting hanging in the kitchen eyes that leave, leafs that I.

Wow pow brightness coming to day to coming alive and waking.

A river of water running proudly into the ineffable sewer.

(All this viewed from my crib)

Second dawn of the day having taken a nap and the perfect sun the perfect one blinding whiteness and like the rosy hues of any deity that sun BLOWS man the sun I'm telling ya. West, where the dead convey convoy convents and but this light and when I squint I see angles crosses, man. Pointing to Dragon Kid today and the sun shines on him and all ye all.

As beautiful as the sight of the white light is raying out like an impassioned angel pleading with empty space I'd like it if it matched this song of Prince's I'm listening to now and was Purple, a purple sun to make robes of us all.

The clouds a hungry happy un-gloomy El Greco and the music alive. I just sip my coffee and dig, dig it Allah. Yeah and when He sings like a Woman I nearly dive into love…

Crow Dog's book: "I'll jump into the sacred medicine, dive into it. I want to know, experience the knowledge the scared herb can give me. It elevates me into another world."

To see, hey man yeah man, to understand.

Ah man this art business is really something, revel in the revelations now, now, this very night in the crossfire.

Cooking up leftovers corn beans noodles and waiting for the late night talk shows to start up.

Tunkashila morning the light and the gray of yesterday hath passed into a short past, and now after sleeping ten or eleven hours I'm up somewhat and.

Hearing Richard Thompson and looking at Vincent and buzzing on Joe.

Its September something in a couple a days its my first art opening in the fucking city.

This art stuff is really amazing, it'll lead one to a crazy sanity.

The parking lot of yin yang half in the sun half in shadow: morning. Almost nine a.m. and I think the coffee has done brewed? I'll check…

O might E time. The mysterious revealer doused the vales with baptisms and now we are all on fire. The curtains are peach colored and glow in the gnosis of any Zen, for I have woken to the terror of within and overcame, oceans of overcame come in a wave of passions to the compost, compist, common, and where is Hamlet hammy and letting the yellow numbers dissipate amongst thee? O. Z. X. Yoy anew religion partake of my sacramental mind by red-ing this…this where the words deflate to the Sun's brilliance, I done become sol solar so, the sots and spots and interviews with God made through the eyes that reciprocate the shine.

When I woke from my nap I had a chig and thought to myself, "I feel like writing," so I don't know what but what ever what never comes out, its all the same, insame, sane, insane, don't ya know? I'm just waiting with my cigar skin for that holy Moslem drink to finish brewin. I can't hear anything, plus I got to piss a lil.

"Such a antique freak struggling to speak."

Saw the Passion movie earlier today…I don't have anything really to say.

I learned how to type in Junior High, about the time I started drinking beer or wine or whiskey, I gave up the latter but typing has become my saving grace laced with the desert's oldest.

Last time I saw Grant play he had a word abstractly spelled on his amp, I didn't know what it was till Irwin said, "Alchemy."

Melanie where are you? I'm fighting for you.

My belief, my fighting, does it have to? It comes through song, painting, sculpture, words.

Patti Smith for instance.

Listening to Gospel Aretha's music she's my muse has been for a while now.

That Blax dig Jesus…be la X.

Be la Dye Land.

Bob and mold. Easter of beast's decline, music.

Savage, sage, prophet.

Buddha and Moses figurines sit on this table and the night India ink omni.

Last night I stayed up till two or three and now I'm awake and its almost noon and I'm waiting four the mail. A little bit of self discovery last night thinking about the basic shapes of religo, and how much sway they have, and realizing my favorite one is probably the diamond. And when I closed my eyes in bed I saw a black diamond. You know the square turned sideways. Like Mondrian.

End light and meant.

Mezzy's here rode his bike all the way from Waseca. What a Day For a Night.

Gosh I'm excited.

Well its morning and the art show's over and I didn't get laid.

Well its still morning nine thirty and Mezzy is sittin on the floor and I got Harry on the juke and coffee brewed and waiting for me to consume it. Maybe I'll try and write about the art show?

Ma and pa and me and Mez and Sister Pistol pile into the car and off off to the cities…ah shit I can't go into it.

Lets just say: it was interesting.

Let us just say: dead Chan amongst thee tattoo palaces and me pure yellow.

Lets just say: too cool fours in the threes.

Not even three, but consecrated by the almighty two. Duality. Traversing the cool communions of fashion.

Last night after a long rap with Mezzy I lay in bed five in the morning and in my minds' eyes I saw my pathetic pictures hanging there in the box in the romb in the rocks of loom and I see or saw the power of my American calligraphy. The spontaneous image…gleaned by Harts and breast.

Now Mezzy hasn't sat down all morning standing pacing ambiguous and me reading Krishnamurti a lil and now Allen's bio on the coffee table and Howl on the sound bleeder. Finished off a pot o' Joe.

After all the hubbub after the scene I'm back to where I sort a feel best: alone. Alone with my Joni Mitchell tape and coffee and now I an all eyes what happened last night and I think, "Pretty cool over all."

Irwin asking me about the pyramid forms in my art and now I know what I should a said, I'm interested in pre-Columbian art and architecture and in restoring life back to those forms and ways.

Ah morning again once more and what to say? Who is to say? Last nights dreams still reverberating in my blurry skullet and I dream of basketball now and then and it's the

342

same old coach and some familiar high school dudes and I don't fathom the meaning.

Letters of Vincent and A Buddhist Bible, that's all I need.

Fumbling through the Secret Doctrine again, near and nearly dusk and Charlie Parker blowing on a tape.

Open the curtains to silken sundown, gray and white and trees undulate late like fate.

Night of recovery expressionless in the throes of wondering: fate, fates.

My past almost obliterated by the fog and war of time and booze.

Looking at a pix of The Doors, huh?

Kitchen window open wind in the trees I thought it was raining, September step ember.

How to conquer Jesus in this heroin whirl?

Aint seen great Melanie for quite a wile, while, wily now and how to find her find her naked in these virgin arms of forestry.

Notes on the speed of vision? No, just a coffee table with my journal notebook and my littler book of poems called Red Chance and a pen and A Buddhist Bible and photo of my Buddha painting and next to that a black figurine of Him and my smokes rollers and orange lighter and then some Morrison lit, his poems and a bio, and last but not yeast the circular glass ashtray.

I just sit here and trip.

On the southwest horizon the moon MUST be cold, cold waiting for the hollow wean.

Wondering about Shamanism and wondering if I... am one?

Will I be saved by an animal?

Thumb Ling through The Golden Dawn after reading

other bits and pieces of this and that and on the tape player is Neptune by Tony something-or-other.

With a dissolute apple on my head not trusting the middleman.

With a dissolving skull on my apple trusting Thoth.

No stars out tonight just clouds I turn off the computer.

No sun out this morning just clouds as the leaves ah the leaves are changing colors.

Still gray as I've come home from The Breakdown Café not even a sundog.

Gave pa a Shot of Love on the phone, told him, "Love ya," and I could tell it surprised him, then I felt auk word and embarrassed but what the heck its true I do love my pa.

Wow strange orange pinkish dusk as my Van Glow books open on the coffee table.

Not absolutely a Starry Night but a starry face: two stars for eyes and a star for a mouth.

Turned on and studying the numinous of the self-portrait, straight forward, The Logos.

Brewing up tea.

Find a way to combine the vastness of landscape within the face?

Grant Buddy singing pals. Thinking about St. Paul.

One thirty seven in the afternoon and I been reading the introduction to The Golden Dawn last night and today, now I'm thinking of reading this Morrison biography, but I have my art books opened up and am looking at into them too.

Just took a shit, "Where'd ya take it?"

The mystery of life, my life, and life in art or art in life.

Van Gogh was just a misplaced Indian.

Neighbors moving in in the dark parking lot as I look and wonder.

The blue crown on the ground the ghostly bird seer and the eye.

Senior year of hi school and we dropped I think I placed a hit and a half on my silver spidery tongue in the downtown mall, then trotted off west to some punkers' house close by, we sat at a table and I laughed at just about anything everything, then I remember we left there and walked up Pill Hill and sat on some stone steps, I was really fucking out there Jack, man. Then we headed o'er to Bob's on the other side and Iceberg kept looking out the window, he seemed very scared and I wanted to comfort him so I started doodling doing funny wild drawings. We listened to music in Bob's bedroom, a square romb where he had books laying round. We ran out a cigs and went to a grocery store open all night and I remember standing in the parking lot and all that blackness we call space, seemed like a shroud, a mask. Back to Bob's and eventually the sun arose, a fiery rose rising into our fragmented tortured and raw consciousnesses, the come down. And that's one memory.

I thought it was four or five in the morn but I must a got up round six and had a choke and now the Joe is all a brewing. I was just thinking about that acid trip, there was a lot more to it, but that's the best I can do now for now. I'm listening to R.E.M. and thinking and reminiscing in my minds about the eighties, maybe it's the tunes?

Oh yes the sky, a description of the sky is in order, a gray-blue and single armistices of clouds singling themselves out and maybe Christ will appear in one of em?

The farmland looking outside my bedroom window is not too far from what Vincent saw and painted and the sky of gem of soft diamond wonder, Because of the Light right Johanna?

Been reading and getting off on philosophy for the last four hours and now its night, half moon south in my bedromb widow, and Live In Seattle on. Quarter till eight and October about ten or twelve days away, I don't know, a week?

Can't seem to get into my old poetry, I try and read the stuff but most of me just doesn't wanna know, the past, pain.

I look in the mirror, "Am I Jewish? I think I'm Indian."

Is there really any difference? I think now.

How can truth be eternal? It can be cyclical but that's just gravity or inertia, and or the beauty of the sphere.

We live here in America in a very strict society but that strictness sickness may be Maya itself and may possibly be transcended?

On a subtle microscopic basis nature never repeats itself never duplicates herself, see through the mirages of generalizations and know.

I listen to strange music I think weird thoughts I am not me some a the time.

He saw his future, whereas most of us can't even see now.

Going through rapid changes that are foreign to me.

Rustling of the leaves in the parking lot, a kind of dry rain sound, the sound of hammering too.

I am a rock-n-roll child father like a crow is black.

I don't know, but ya got to admit the whole thing is pretty freaky.

Prince's purple boots and its morning and a bag a bed of nails bobbing on that ole juke.

Afternoon after the Breakdown Café sessions and I'm home reading religious junk.

My eyes are curtains.

Mystic of the golden absurdities.
Holy dog cog of the grasses' left.
Infinite one into one into in.
Setup by the (godless?) elders.

Charles wrote about the here and now well but as soon as this society changes mutates his writings will be forgotten, for there is no prophecy either in his words or technique.

Do you want me to believe you? Do you want me to believe nothing?

Mutt of the mute end valley, the words fly about covering the germane hiding of moment's cast.

It doesn't cost anything to be a lone dancer in a field of Ka's.

I run from this empty place till I till the railings of Hades in a mineral thought Tao and Teh and King, but the route en and out of unaware airs heirs the only choice of those of the veil of hidden to the was of of.

Am I hiding love? Am I breeding lust? Am I turning a wheel of lies?

It all makes sense, but not to the senses.

I guess I'm a karma junkie too Emily, feasting on the vibes of others' truths.

Dancing.

I bow to you Minneapolis Hermes: Prince.

Every and each dusk holy, sacred, as the rook crosses the threshold.

I go from the biblical to the Buddhistic to Crow Dog in reading today and tonight all the while music plays.

My dad with me, with me.

My dad my brother my mother my sister, we could find the one, the many.

Cobwebs olden and dust on my computer, U2 plays in this day lit room.

The verse of prose or the slapdash of poetry and jazz,

I dig this verse form of the Tao and likewise Arthur's Illuminations. Its good that we have both.

Slight traces of orange slitting through a swirl of silver, Set on Geb.

Ray Charles in the sonic blue of oncoming night and cooking spaghetti, groove.

So from jacking off too much the left left him, and now the booze sedated and how but the cards turned crimson and yellow and eventually he become perfectly "normal."

In the Egyptian night music of Africa plays in my romb and the chill that ole Halloween chill is setting in.

Last weekend at the folks' home in Rochester I woke up about one in the morning with heartburn from eating too much of the green cheese and decided to stay up, I sat in the reclining easy chair and read Walter Kaufmann"s Faith of a Heretic and really dug it. At round three I brewed up a pot o' Joe and looked at an art book: Chagall. Marc Chagall indeed, and my eyes tripped and gloried across the reproductions and I thought and thought and hummed with joy while sipping black medicine. Then at six or so I went into the family garage, my art studio, and painted danced out a pix.

So this weekend I'm here in Owatonna and I just noticed that the moon is setting directly east where the sun should be in day's time. The moon, feels like I could pluck it out a the sky and shoot buckets with it.

The moon goin north in all that blue baby blue sky and me reading of Nietzsche in my cloth chair with Love Supreme playing and just a glimpse of frightening German history.

Do economics spur wars as much as religious and or ethnic clashes?

There's always those three in the picture, so.

Nice little coffee high and now the crazy love fest moon o' rock is no longer in sight.

Restless as hell now that its afternoon early. Too much java.

Thinking about The Beats, pulled out Holmes' Go, maybe try that again.

Maybe goin back in into Hettie Jones' novel how she became and all that.

Yardbird plays while these investigations take place.

"And I keep waking fully confused," I repeat from Within Your Reach, I wake from a nap to the scorching blinding sun right in my mighty window of season's rite.

Nietzsche fell into the Nazis like Jesus fell into Rome: misunderstood and used.

The last unsightful burst for us, me, here in the Plains of the sun's perfect ardor roundness and amour.

But this whole Nietzsche thing, shit, it could be a con?

Maybe read this damn thing again, I feel like I'm in the throes of fate-ness.

I don't know what's gone down.

Yeah man, fuck, I'm done done done. High. With Freddie Hubbard on, with the candle glowing, with the very dance of caffeine and rice and any war paint upon the star of the horns' lasting last last.

Greatness supersedes.

Ray Charles morning on Sunday and that mystical shadow encompassing the parking lot, the very soul of it man, and sand in my eyes and music in my limbs and heart mind.

The heart ascends to the mind or the mind comes down chakra style to the mighty red blood heart in the piano in the singsong of a man and horn and piano and backup singers solace of African mystery and African justice right here in this awful nation named after syphilis kings spreading blankets of death amongst thee, but Ray, Ray survives with his Indian beak and, "Come on bring back my Bonnie back back to me…"

Old Folker on after listening bits and pieces of others, sipping java and bopping along waiting for my dad to show up. Couple hours anyways away and then we'll go out the mall and browse around.

I used to feel bad that my dad didn't give me any blatant enthusiasm towards my artistic endeavors but now I see that's good for with enthusiasm comes maybe the overly critical, the same coin different sides idea, for he has remained neutral and this is probably for the better.

Sunday and maybe I'll turn on Hour of Cowards?

Noticing the moon again today at eleven a.m. in the northwest.

The mad laugh of the dancer's abstractions.

And Uncle Polly said to me, "You're keeping the beatnik generation alive, it is a good thing, an honest way."

Stick Figure has the Torah at his crib amongst piles of history and beat literature and his records and CD's and tapes, I'm going to visit him next weekend for the bland but exciting Art Crawl.

White disc emitting orange glow and somber light filters through the intricate bare patchwork of trees getting ready for winter's slumber: sundown.

Certainly it's a dying orange Sunday, ah night cometh. Verisimilitude.

Dionysus inventor of wine and the lattice of forest where we all go mad. (Nietzsche)

Husks of pink waves in the cornfield sky.

Okay purple…clouds…man.

They say you can't serve two masters, but with my numerous growing book collection I've got masters all over the place.

The night is horse mare'd in disjunctive turn around, the night is gypsy planets and there are no little fires out there either on land or in space to illumine me like salt, the night is like a piano all the black keys being played at once to sound out the hares the goats the bulls for to float up the dark abode and body of Dionysus, Osiris, Jesus, and Lorca.

Almost three thirty, Bono sings things that could be construed as wisdom and widow and windows to the ask of infinity BLACKNESS man and lips in a ruddy mirror that flower forth silence like all true rue flowers: fear, danger, heaven, desire.

Refound my Damien O Rice tape, it's the ghost of Melanie and her exquisite beauty and all that potential, man, man, woman and man unlinked unfound unconfounded.

Melanie and is she sleeping now? In this dark nocturne all pure coffee in its color? Is she reading this all omni in her ages? Is she in love with crystal and that's it?

I'd have to go back and reread just what I wrote cuz I can't remember, but now beside my shadow soul kitchen and the lamp of lamb on and the we and the us… "Why'd ya fill my sorrows with no words of tomorrows…." Something like that. Like before the Fall were Melanie and I together making such sacred love the gods grew jealous and separated us by drugs by distance by time itself and creeds of blasphemies righteous? It means something to me Melanie, and I don't know why I am suffering suddenly to see you again? But you were the one who gave this music to me and opened my unheld heart in the trembling vortex of possibility, of exploding onto another's flesh, flesh to flesh, and mountains of plead in this early riser's prayer.

Go back go back months become years but least I've got it most of it down on paper.

Its an amazing world though, the Indians decrepit on

Franklin and I thought…but just the fact that Folker exists is enough to change all my suppositions, conceptions.

Why are the artists so self-destructive? Is it this nation's blind materialism?

Saw the shrink for a bit today at The Breakdown Café and I showed him some photos of my recent paintings and he said, "Remember me when you're famous."

"I don't know if I can do that," I responded baffled, "I'm just kidding."